D0212701

The Captive of the Castle of Sennaar
An African Tale
GEORGE CUMBERLAND
Edited by G.E. Bentley, Jr

The Captive of the Castle of Sennaar is a utopian novel in two parts. In this scholarly edition G.E. Bentley, Jr, places George Cumberland's late eighteenth-century work among the earliest historical novels in English and identifies it as a rare example of the "Romantic novel." He shows that while each part of the work adopts a very different form of utopia, the two utopias complement and modify one another. He also shows the work to be unusual for the sexual and political freedom encouraged and the Christian fundamentalism advocated, as well as for its setting in lands never visited by Europeans at the time of writing.

The first part, set on an island in central Africa among descendants of classical Greek civilization, was printed in 1789 but immediately suppressed by Cumberland. A passage describing society everywhere except on the utopian island as oligarchic and unjust was deemed by his lawyer to be potentially seditious; the novel was only published a decade later, and then in revised form. The second part, set in central Africa's Mountains of the Moon among descendants of followers of a fourth-century Christian heretic, is published here for the first time.

Cumberland was a widely cultivated and deeply humane dilettante. A poet, painter, distinguished collector of prints and shells, and scientific inventor, he was passionately concerned with the reform of politics and society. He was also friends with some of the best authors and painters of his time, including William Blake, who encouraged Cumberland's ideals. Bentley describes the similarities between Blake's radical analysis of society and his early ideas on free love, sexuality, slavery, natural religion, and energy and the ideals Cumberland espouses in *The Captive of the Castle of Sennaar*.

Bentley provides historical and geographical appendixes, textual and commentary notes, and a comparison of Cumberland's work to Simon Berington's *The Memoirs of Signor Gaudentino di Lucca*. Bentley's edition of *The Captive of the Castle of Sennaar* will be of interest to Blake scholars and to students and scholars of utopian literature and late eighteenth-century and Romantic literature and culture.

G.E. Bentley, Jr, is a professor in the Department of English, University College, University of Toronto.

Self-portrait (c. 1810) of George Cumberland aged about 56, from his
Sketchbook, f. 18ʳ (Cumberland MSS)

The Captive
of the Castle of Sennaar

An African Tale

IN TWO PARTS

PART 1
THE SOPHIANS (PRINTED IN 1798 AND 1810)

PART 2
THE REFORMED (MANUSCRIPT OF C. 1800)

by
GEORGE CUMBERLAND

Edited by G.E. Bentley, Jr

McGill-Queen's University Press
Montreal & Kingston • London • Buffalo

C969c

© McGill-Queen's University Press 1991
ISBN 0-7735-0742-6
Legal deposit fourth quarter 1991
Bibliothèque nationale du Québec

Printed in Canada on acid-free paper

This book has been published
with the help of a grant from the
Canadian Federation for the Humanities,
using funds provided by the Social Sciences and
Humanities Research Council of Canada.

Canadian Cataloguing in Publication Data

Cumberland, George, 1754–1848
The captive of the Castle of Sennaar
ISBN 0-7735-0742-6
I. Bentley, G.E. (Gerald Eades), 1930–   . II. Title.
PR4519.C85C36 1991   823'.6   C91-090219-4

This book was typeset by
Typo Litho composition inc. in 10/12 Baskerville.

To
Sarah and Julia

for many hours of escape
from my happy captivity with George Cumberland

the editor dedicates this work
with a father's pride and love

University Libraries
Carnegie Mellon University
Pittsburgh, Pennsylvania 15213

Contents

Illustrations

Preface

George Cumberland's short utopian tale *The Captive of the Castle of Sennaar* Part 1 was printed in 1798 but immediately suppressed by its author for fear of prosecution for sedition. It was first published with Cumberland's *Original Tales* in 1810 but was almost totally ignored. This is its third printing and second publication.

The Captive Part 1 is set on the Island of Sophis in a lost lake in Central Africa and deals with the beautiful Greek sun-worshippers who have made the island an earthly paradise. About 1800 Cumberland wrote a sequel to *The Captive* Part 1, subtitled "The Reformed," in which he presented a Christian alternative to the Sophians in the Jovinians, who inhabit a lost valley in the African Mountains of the Moon. This manuscript has only recently been discovered and is here printed for the first time. Though a sequel to Part 1, Part 2 of *The Captive* is almost entirely self-sufficient and can stand by itself. It is a work of considerable interest.

In order to distinguish what I believe to be the discrete characters of the two Parts of *The Captive of the Castle of Sennaar*, I have treated each Part as a separate work, with its own title page and notes. The two Parts can, of course, be read as a single continuous novel. I have placed discussions of the history and geography of *The Captive* in an epilogue, so that modern readers need not be better informed than than author's contemporaries, or than, occasionally, the author himself, until they have read both Parts.

George Cumberland's *Captive of the Castle of Sennaar* has had curious difficulties in reaching print. The first edition of Part 1 was printed in 1798 but suppressed and only achieved publication in 1810. Cumberland had sample proofs of Part 2 made about 1810 and 1835 but did not proceed with them. Parts 1 and 2 in the present edition were printed about 1982 but suppressed by its then-publishers apparently for economic and technical reasons, and only achieved publication in 1991. Part 2, which was written about 1800, has been in proof of one kind or another for over one hundred and eighty years before achieving publication. There cannot be many tales with a similar history.

Acknowledgments

Work on the text of *The Captive* Part 1 was facilitated by a grant in 1973–74 from the University of Toronto for collating the 1798 and 1810 editions. This collation was first done by my friend Dr James T. Wills, and when I repeated the collation I found that his work was a model of detail and efficiency. I owe thanks to Dr Wills and to the University of Toronto for timely assistance.

The Canada Council assisted with the work on the manuscript of Part 2 by grants in the summers of 1972 and 1973, for which I express my hearty thanks.

My wife has worked beside me on *The Captive,* as she has on everything I have written, making the text more nearly accurate, lending me patience, and affectionately distracting me. I am particularly grateful to her for help with the index.

22 June 1988   Dutch Boys Landing
                                                Mears, Michigan

Introduction

GEORGE CUMBERLAND

George Cumberland was little known to readers of 1798, except perhaps as a gentleman of modest means who dabbled in the arts, a dilettante. But he was a dilettante in the best eighteenth-century sense of the word – a poet, a painter, a distinguished collector of prints and shells, a scientific inventor, and a friend and painter of some of the best authors and painters of his time. The friends to whom he gave copies of his long tale *The Captive of the Castle of Sennaar*, such as his distant cousin the very successful dramatist Richard Cumberland and the notorious pagan Thomas Taylor, knew him as an ardent amateur and inventor in a surprising variety of areas. He had engraved his own designs for his book *Thoughts on Outline* (1796), he had published several volumes of poetry and a book about Italian prints, and he had written a number of volumes about his travels in France, Switzerland, and Italy which were – and are – still in manuscript. He sent a stream of essays to the periodical press – on geology, the reform of prostitutes and the navy, the mitigation of poverty, and teaching the blind to read, as well as poems, jokes, caricatures, and inventions. He invented safety rafts, the telegraph, stage coaches, cameras, jet propulsion, ways of constructing railway carriages and increasing safety in coal mines, daguerreotypes, methods of printing, cures for corn blight, and substitutes for sugar – and left it to others to carry out the practical details.[1] He earned the respect of geologists for

---

1 For bibliographical details, see Geoffrey Keynes, "Some Uncollected Authors XLIV: George Cumberland 1754–1848," *Book Collector* XIX (1970): 31–65 (especially for printed books), and G.E. Bentley, Jr., *A Bibliography of George Cumberland (1754–1848)* (1975) (especially for articles and manuscripts).

his contributions to the Royal Society and for his book on fossil shells, and his practice as a water-colourist influenced the young Bristol School of Painters a few years later. He was passionately concerned with the reform of politics and society, a radical deeply sympathetic to society's castaways, the poor, the blind, the slaves. He was a widely cultivated and deeply humane person.

His close friends, such as the popular book-illustrator Thomas Stothard, the journeyman engraver William Blake, and the sensational radical politician John Horne Tooke, would have known that in 1798 he was in his early forties, that from the ages of fifteen to thirty he had worked as a clerk in the Royal Exchange Insurance Office in London, and that in 1784 he had received an inheritance of £300 a year which had enabled him to throw up his job and spend several years in Italy.[2] On his return to England, he lived for several years in the south of England as a gentleman farmer, before he settled, early in the new century, on the outskirts of Bristol, where he lived for the last forty years of his long life.

THE CAPTIVE PART 1: THE SOPHIANS

Cumberland had long been deeply interested in Africa. In 1780 he had printed a short story called "An African Tale," and about 1790 he made notes in his Commonplace Book[3] for a work to be called "Travels of a Philosopher," which may be the origin of The Captive, with its philosophical travellers in Africa. He also recorded there anecdotes about John Stuart (1749–1822), the traveller to Abyssinia, whom Cumberland had met in 1793, as well as details about Stuart's Philosophical Thoughts,[4] published anonymously. More strikingly, he narrated there a story he had heard about the great traveller James Bruce, who went to Abyssinia in 1768–73 to find the source of the Nile.

A Scotch Lady ... had come to Rome with her Mother to meet Mr. Bruce before his Travels in order to be married, but whom he had never met or written to during his long absence – This Lady [who had married a Roman marquis] died in Rome in 1785, and her daughter the only offspring of this match died suddenly

---

2 Biographical details here are summarized from A Bibliography of George Cumberland, ix-xiii. More information may be found in the Keynes article; in The Cumberland Letters [1771–84], ed. Clementina Black (1912); in Blake Records (1969), passim; and especially in Cumberland's voluminous correspondence in the British Library.

3 Cumberland MSS, in the collection of Dr E.B. Bentley and G.E. Bentley, Jr., f. 5ᵛ.

4 Ibid., ff. 50ʳ–51ʳ.

in a Convent in 1787, owing to the Marquis having confined her there and told her at parting that [*she*] would be there for life which threw her into convulsion fits – What occasioned him to take this step was a discovery of a private attachment and a determination to obviate it –[5]

The mother and daughter together unite a number of characteristics of Nazure, who is, we learn from *The Captive* Part 2, the lover of Memmo, the novel's hero. Like them, Nazure was separated from her lover by her parents and confined to a convent, while her lover travelled for years in and near Abyssinia; when he returns it is too late for them to be reunited as lovers. James Bruce may have served as one of the models for Cumberland's hero, and the anonymous Scotch Lady and her daughter may be echoed in one of Cumberland's heroines.

To contemporaries, the title of *The Captive of the Castle of Sennaar* would have suggested that it is a Gothic romance. There were, for example, [Julia Smith], *The Prison of Mantaubon*, or Times of Terror (1809), and Anon., *The Captive of Valence*; or the Last Moments of Lewis (1804), and a whole host of Gothic castles, such as Horace Walpole, *The Castle of Otranto* (1765), Richard Sicklemore, *Edgar*; or The Phantom of the Castle (1798), T.H. White, *Bellgrove Castle*; or, The Horrid Spectre, A Romance (1803), and Mary Pickor, *The Castle of Roviego*; or Retribution, A Romance (1809). However, these Gothic expectations are disappointed. Cumberland's *Captive* is certainly a romance, but it has little of the terror or mystery of the Gothic.

Sennaar, the third element in the title, is likely to have meant little more to Cumberland's contemporaries than it does to ours, for Sennaar was on the very borders of solid geographical knowledge, above the Cataracts of the Nile. The titular site is intriguing, but even more intriguing are the scenes described by Lycas in Part 1 and by Memmo in Part 2. The story of Lycas, the Greek prisoner of Sennaar, is set on an island in an enormous lake in Central Africa where, probably, no European had ever been; and that of Memmo, the Italian prisoner, is set in The Mountains of the Moon in the unexplored lands West of the Nile.[6] This exceedingly ill-known terrain was as little visited in fiction as in fact. Abyssinia figured as something like another Eden in the legends of Prester John of Abyssinia and in Milton's *Paradise Lost* (1667), in Dr. Johnson's *Rambler* essays 204–205 (1752), and in Coleridge's "Kubla Khan" (1798), and the area is traversed in fiction with an airy disregard

5 Ibid., f. 10^r.
6 See the Epilogue, pp. 307–16.

for topographical fact in [John Campbell], *The Travels of Edward Brown,
Esq.* ... Containing ... his Remarks in his Journies through Lower and
Upper Egypt; together with a Brief Description of the Abyssinian Em-
pire ... (1739),[7] in Anon., *Memoirs of the Nutrebian Court* (1747), in John-
son's *Rasselas* (1759), in *Baron Munchausen's Travels* (1786), in [William
Thomson's] *Mammuth*; or, Human Nature Displayed on a Grand Scale:
In a Tour with Tinkers, into the Inland Parts of Africa By the Man in
the Moon (1789), in Adolf Franz Friedrich Freiherr von Knigg, *Benjamin
Noldmanns Geschichte der Aufklärung in Abyssinien* (Goettingen, 1791), and
in Charles Lucas, *The Abyssinian Reformer*, or The Bible and the Sabre
(1808). But there are few other accounts of the area in English fiction
before Cumberland's time. The geographical settings of the two parts
of Cumberland's *Captive*, then, are remarkably original, placed partly
on the frontiers of the known world and partly in areas which had
apparently not been explored by Europeans at all.

Cumberland makes some attempt at local verisimilitude, such as the
kraals of the Caffres, the parrots, hippototomi, and hyenas,[8] but the
book is not remarkable for ethnographical or zoological detail. Even in
the few details he gives, Cumberland was betrayed occasionally by his
inevitable ignorance – an ignorance which no living European could
have enlightened – into putting deserts and camels and pearls on the
borders of Lake Zambre, by finding breadfruit (native to the South
Pacific) and cabbage palms (native to the West Indies) in the forest, and
sheep successfully cultivated for their wool in the tropics under cocoa-
nut palms. However, the interest of the novel depends not on the sites
but on the societies, and it is remarkable how infrequently flora and
fauna are described.

7 On the flyleaf of Vol. II of the 1753 edition of *The Travels of Edward Brown*, Esq., in
   Bodley, C[lara] Reeve wrote in 1775 that she had "a passion for it. Mr Pope was very
   fond of it. ... I do not pretend to decide whether it is a Romance or a true History: –
   I care not which, it amuses, informs & instructs me, and that is sufficient to make me
   value it." "A Relation of the Present State of Ethiopia By a French Surgeon" is in
   Vol. II (1753), 102–33.
      Perhaps the earliest reported fiction about Abyssinia is the Greek *Æthiopica* (?3rd
   Century A.D.) by Heliodorus of Phoenicia (Syria) from a family of priests of the sun.
   It was first printed in 1534, translated into English repeatedly, first by Thomas Un-
   derdown ([?1569]; 1587; 1606; 1895), and later, inter alia, by Nahum Tate and Anon.,
   as *Ætheopian Adventures* (1686; 1753) and by Anon. as *The Adventures of Theagnes and
   Chariclea* (1791). The romance begins and ends in Ethiopia, but its plot seems scarcely
   related to that of Cumberland.
8 Note that there are no encounters with beasts of prey or with monkeys or elephants,
   not to mention dangerous insects and snakes, which are the inhabitants, and often the
   raison d'être, of most later accounts of Central Africa in English fiction.

Perhaps the most interesting aspect of *The Captive* is its utopian char-
acter – or characters. In Part 1, Lycas describes the beautiful Sophians
as representing some of the highest artistic and social ideals of the eigh-
teenth century – a society largely without marriage, priests, or commerce,
finding its highest expression in human love and artistic beauty. In
Part 2, evidently written later, Memmo, the auditor of Lycas' story in
Part 1, discovers an alternative society of primitive Christians, uncor-
rupted and self-isolated, as deeply spiritual as Lycas' Sophians were
materialistic. Each society is interesting as an expression of radical
thought of about 1800, but the two together, constituting coherent al-
ternative utopias, create a very interesting and perhaps unique artistic
tension. The ills of the world are easy to identify, but a cure for them
is difficult to imagine – witness the shortage of utopias at any time. To
imagine two utopias, and to use them to illuminate one another and the
ill-made world we live in, is a remarkable feat.

The technique of Part 1 of *The Captive* is to contrast the stories of two
life-prisoners with profoundly different backgrounds and characters.
Memmo, the narrator,[9] is a rich young Venetian, and Lycas, his cell-
mate, is a poor old Greek-Turk. After hearing briefly the story of
Memmo as told to Lycas, we listen for most of Part 1 to the history of
Lycas as he, and through him Memmo, is gradually introduced and
converted to the ways of the Sophians. The story of Lycas is punctuated
at important points by a return to the prison of Sennaar and the historical
present of the novel, when Lycas has just told about burying the old Jew
(p. 23), or when Lycas is overcome by his memories of Mica (pp. 58).
These interruptions are not merely formal, for important actions occur
in the prison during the pauses in Lycas' story – the saving of the Nile
boat (p. 10) or the rescue of the escaping prisoner (p. 58). As the story
of Lycas progresses, we see his character change, from that of a fairly
conventional young European, greedy for gold, killing game for pleas-
ure, planning erotic exercises, to a temperate, humanitarian, chaste,
selfless Sophian, until he is willing to give his labour and his life, not
merely for the society of Sophis, like any good Sophian, but for mankind
at large – something apparently quite beyond Sophian conceptions, or
at least beyond their actions. Similarly, Memmo progresses from a youth-
ful, selfish despair at the failure of his hopes – even of his hope to die
for love – to an admiration for the intellectual and aesthetic independ-
ence of Lycas and to a deep respect for Sophians and a determination
to imitate and if possible join them. Technically most interesting, per-

---

9 Memmo is not named in Part 1; we learn his name only in Part 2.

haps, is the way in which Lycas blunders selfishly in Sophis, for example with his sexual advances to Mica and his subsequent humiliation and psychological maturing, and the way in which Memmo in prison antiphonally blunders selfishly and from his error learns generosity and selflessness. For example, Memmo suggests that he and Lycas should profit from the generosity of their jailer to escape, until Lycas reminds him that their freedom would be won at the cost of the life of their benefactor (p. 60). Lycas in Sophis and Memmo in Sennaar are learning and growing in parallel. The tale is kept alive and moved forward not only by reciprocity of action between Sophis in the past and Sennaar in the present but by reciprocity of moral growth between Lycas and Memmo. The conception is sophisticated, intriguing, and important, and I do not recall having seen it exhibited elsewhere.

Cumberland's contemporaries would have been shocked by the social, political, and religious freedom plainly fostered by *The Captive*. Indeed, Thomas Taylor lamented that Cumberland seemed to be "defend[ing] lasciviousness publickly ... by the conduct of your Sophians."[10] In some ways, the tale is more radical than "the works of M.rs Woolstoncraft,"[11] and its sexual mores are particularly unusual. "Human love [*is*] the basis of this well-ordered society" (p. 37), and it is frequently a specifically sexual love. The Sophians speak of "hallowed and beneficent [*sexual*] desire" (p. 68), a desire they foster at its first manifestation. "*O*ur children [*are*] not ... unseasonably thwarted" (p. 38), and young people are "studiously taught the art of preserving their lovers" (p. 69).

*H*ere all marriageable people are married. They consider it as a duty imposed on the parent to take care and promote as early connections as are proper,[12] and never fail to observe and encourage the first inclinations that take place; to impede them would be considered as the blackest piece of villainy; for they are fully sensible of the dangers arising from the suppression of the natural fires; and no ones consent is necessary to the connubial union, but those of the parties uniting. [P. 44]

Since the act of consenting union is all that is relevant, the Sophians have "no forms of marriage" (p. 94), and "mutual attachment is the only tie we know of" (p. 68). Polygamy exists among them (p. 68), but ap-

---

10 See pp. xliii–xliv below.
11 See p. xliv below.
12 Early connections are proper when "the organs are ... prepared" (p. 66). Parents must not try "to postpone the great unerring and explicit laws of propagation" (p. 67).

parently not polyandry, and promiscuity rarely occurs. When it does, "we never punish infidelity" (p. 341). The Sophians recognize "that the disorders of the passions deserve our utmost attention; and have people who make a kind of profession of curing them"; indeed "it is no uncommon thing for one of those sages to prescribe a sexual connection, as a remedy for the apparent disorders of the mind. Nor are there wanting instances, where parents have saved their children's lives or senses, by temporary connections ... which have often terminated in the solid settlement of both parties" (pp. 69–70, 342).

The appearance of the Sophians reflects their sexual liberties, for the men are frequently naked, and "the young girls were only covered to the loins".[13] They do not attempt to conceal their sexual parts "and would have spurned at the unnatural depravity that affixed ideas of shame to the most necessary, wonderful, and noble organs of the human superstructure" (p. 335).

In a society in which sexual intercourse for pleasure is virtually sacred, intercourse for profit is an aberration both social and mental. In Sophis, "prostitutes ... are termed the unhappy," and "they are very rare." They are regarded "in the light of [thoughtless][14] women, the disease of whose minds is ... to be pitied." They are "not exclude[d] ... from the rights of society," and, receiving the "best advice and hospitality" from their families, their "errors [or irregularities or deviations] are seldom of very long continuance."[15]

The political liberty of Sophis would have been equally shocking to Cumberland's contemporaries. The Sophians practise a kind of communism, and Lycas is told: "you must consider nothing as your own but

13 P. [171]. In Sennaar, "girls have cloths wrapt round them from the waist to the knee; the men go almost naked," according to J. Seally & I. Lyons, *A Complete Geographical Dictionary* (1787), Vol. II.

14 Within brackets, italic type identifies an addition by the editor, while roman type identifies words by the author which have been transferred from elsewhere to clarify the meaning or grammar.

15 Pp. 68–9. Cumberland later modified the sexual explicitness and liberality of many passages in the 1798 edition of Part 1 (from which most of the quotations above derive). For example, "we [never] rarely punish infidelity" (p. 341); seduction is punished only "when proved to have been [more than once] the practice of any offender" (p. 342); on Lycas' 'wedding' night, "she postponed [the consummation] my happiness" (p. 342); Lycas flew "to the unsophisticated [embraces] society" of Mica (p. 344); and he "inhaled the essential sweetness of her pure [body] person" (p. 348).

Cumberland was much concerned about the plight of prostitutes, and in 1814 he twice wrote to *The Monthly Magazine* XXXVII (1 April): 199–203 and XXXVIII (1 Oct): 210 about homes and methods for reforming them.

what is necessary to your own being, and those whom you preserve"
(p. 87). "General equality ... reigned among them; none being either
remarkably poor, or rich" (pp. 84–5), and the women seem to be the
legal and social peers of the men. Chilo sums up by saying:

> Your sovereign good must be the good of the community; while the laws of
> the community propose only the happiness of individuals, by suffering every
> man and woman to think, speak, and act freely; subject to no restraint while
> they *violate not the innocent will of another*;[16] for the protection of which alone, all
> our customs and all our laws are calculated. ... The first principle of our gov-
> ernment is not to permit any individual to injure himself; the next, that he shall
> not injure any other; and, lastly, that societies shall not exist to the prejudice of
> general society, and the destruction of union and political equality. [P. 41]

The modesty of their wants makes them virtually independent of the
rest of the world; the only want they cannot supply is gold for their art,
which they obtain from "foreigners" like Lycas' old master the Jew
(p. 79).

The greatest lessons which Lycas learns in Sophis are political, and
they govern the rest of his life. He leaves Sophis "to go out a missionary
to mankind, to spread, if possible, the noble customs of this select nation
among my fellow creatures" (p. 90).

The religion of Sophis would probably have seemed a good deal less
alarming to Cumberland's enlightened contemporaries than their sexual
and political liberty, for it was more familiar. Lycas is told that "love ...
forms the chief link of our society, is the root of our morals, and the
object of our silent devotion: – to that divine principle we feel that our
existence is entirely owing" (p. 37). for "universal love pervades the uni-
verse" (p. 82). Lycas is instructed to "*Love ... all things in being*" (p. 83)
and to mingle his "affections with the very elements of existence, [*to*]
respect even a tree as your fellow creature ... not to wound even the
earth for its metals, but for its good, to promote its respiration, by
draining, from the surface, stagnant waters" (p. 41).

"Sophians lived a life according to nature,"[17] which seems often to
mean something very like instinct, and they are worshippers of "nature."

16 "The innocent will" is "That which, if executed, can injure nothing, not even ourselves"
    (p. 211).
17 P. 21. In *The Monthly Magazine* xlv (1 May 1818): 296–9, Cumberland advocated a
    "*return to Nature*," to simplicity, honesty, The Golden Rule, etc., as a cure particularly
    for poverty; his program there sounds very like that advocated in *The Captive* Part 1.

They believe that the sun is metaphorically "the origin and support of all natures here" (p. 82), but they are not merely sun-worshippers. Chilo speaks of "nature, whom we adore under the emblem of love, feeling it unnecessary to frame laws [*governing marriage*] to regulate our instinctive commerce, as pure and as natural as the vital flame" (p. 66). They do not attempt to stretch their reason and understanding beyond nature, for "we know what body is, and not what is spirit ... our business is, by the help of the mind, to attain to the perfection of our material nature; not to lose our time in merely enquiring what mind is" (p. 63).

They have created what they call the "science of humanity" (p. 10), and "humanity [*was*] their religion" (p. 21). God is spoken of as "The good Energy,"[18] but He is never considered as a person or perceived except through His natural attributes such as love and instinct and the sun (see p. 62). "To no other principle than abstract love, can the creation be attributed" (p. 37); "no mortal has hitherto discovered what it [that Power] is", but they know that "it loves all" and that it is "Love which preserves us" (p. 75). The Sophians insist on the uniqueness of their religion – "we alone are acquainted with the sublime truth" (p. 30) – but they guard it carefully in Sophis rather than trying to enlighten the world with it.

This religion is, of course, a form of what the eighteenth century called Deism – it is called "natural religion" on the title page of Part 2, and Lycas is there called "a pure deist" (p. 291). In his second edition of 1810, Cumberland modified the abstract and instinctive Deism of the Sophians. In one place, "The good Energy" is altered to "the good Being" (p. 30), and elsewhere personified "Energy" is reduced to mere human "affection" (p. 44). More significantly, where the 1798 edition says that Love dispenses happiness and longevity "to such as follow temperately their natural instincts," the 1810 edition adds: "and the dictates of con-science" (p. 37). Cumberland seems to have undergone a spiritual crisis remarkably similar to the one Wordsworth experienced in the same years and to have turned, like him, from the worship of nature to Duty, Stern Daughter of the Voice of God. The alteration is most conspicuous on the last page of *The Captive* Part 1, where, in a passage added in the 1810 edition, Memmo says that he hopes to go to Sophis to "engraft ... the noble fruits of [*Christian*] revelation[19] on their wholesome wild stock of natural faith...."

---

18 Lycas demonstrates his predisposition for the Sophian religion when, before his arrival, he feels "true piety to nature," and he prays to "Holy Energy! ... thou art Love!" (p. 26).

19 In the Printer's copy, "Revelation" is capitalized.

The artistic character of Sophian society is as Greek as their language. *The Captive* Part 1 (1798) is apparently one way in which, as Blake wrote in 1799, "my friend Cumberland [*is attempting*] to recreate the lost Art of the Greeks." The emphasis in Sophis upon the arts is very notable, with dancing at every meal, songs, instrumental music, plays, fine jewelry, splendid architecture, sculpture, and painting. The arts are important even in the dungeons of the Castle of Sennaar, for Lycas has created such visible luxury and beauty in his bare cell that Memmo is left dumbfounded. With his music, Lycas even soothes the savage jailer, so that he comes to them for help (p. 58) and returns from their cell singing – they measure the distance to the next locked door by the receding sound of his song (p. 33). For Sophians, the arts are the fullest expression of an harmonious society and the manifestation of its existence. They are not simply singing peasants; some of the arts of Sophis are sophisticated and communal, with their fountains and Greek public buildings and their formidable theatre.

There are a number of minor aspects of *The Captive* which are also rewarding. It is noteworthy for the toleration, indeed the admiration, it exhibits for other races and religions,[20] for idolatrous Negroes such as Lycas' guide Yahomy, for Muslim Turks (particularly in Part 2), and for commercial Jews such as Lycas' master; in these respects it may remind us of Blake's "The Divine Image" (1789):

And all must love the human form
In heathen, turk or jew.
Where Mercy, Love & Pity dwell
There God is dwelling too.

The ingenuity of some novelties of Sophis are most enterprising, with all houses built beside running water, the theatre with its machinery for exhibiting "an almost endless variety of buildings" (p. 84), and the long, single-stringed T-shaped musical instrument without frets (p. 52). Medically, the emphasis upon daily bathing and upon virus as a cause or carrier of communicable disease (p. 86) seems advanced.

Though the tale seems beyond Cumberland's time in some respects, its two heroes are very much of his time in their extreme sensibility. They swoon and weep with surprising frequency, and their lives are governed by extraordinarily idealistic love, for each is driven by thwarted passion to become a missionary. Further, while both Lycas and Memmo

20 "We must make no distinction of [religious] faith among noble minds" (Part 2, p. 257).

are extraordinarily adventurous, they are both essentially passive in the new environments – Sophis and Jovinia – in which we see them. The knowledge they bring from the outside world is comparatively insignificant in their new situations, and they become men of action once more only when they return from Utopia to the outside world.

THE CAPTIVE PART 2: THE JOVINIANS

The Jovinians in *The Captive* Part 2 were clearly conceived of to complement or correct the Sophians in Part 1. Where the Sophians were art-loving deists, the Jovinians are art-less fundamentalist Christians of a Protestant kind who practise "primitive Christianity" (p. 217), "pure Christianity" (p. 183). The Jovinians were "guided by the hand of God" (p. 165), and many of their religious reforms are directed specifically against "the lamentable errors of the Roman church" (p. 164). The Jovinians oppose celibacy of the clergy and the worship of images (p. 164), and they liken monasteries to prisons (p. 215).[21] They have a "Propaganda-College" (p. 165), and the highest goal of their society is to send "missionaries ... among the heathen" (p. 185). Indeed, they think of themselves as a community of missionaries dedicated to bringing Christianity to Africa.

Politically they are a federal theocracy, or, more accurately, "a Christian republic" (p. 174), "a Christian commonwealth" (p. 183). The Bible "forms the body of all our laws, and is the basis of ... [our] constitution" (p. 217), for Jovinius their "founder thought the Bible was the best law-book for a Christian people" (p. 211). They have a "free constitution" (p. 165), and "every man among us has an equal vote" (p. 191). The form of government is a pedantocracy, for "the people elect the schoolmasters, the schoolmasters [choose] from their body the elders, the elders the deacons ... and from them ... [is] annually selected" the President or Jovinus (p. 180). They hold annual councils to revise the laws, for they do not believe in infallibility (p. 236), and even the Founder's laws may need to be altered, but their laws are so simple that they have no lawyers (p. 211).

In social terms, they are in some ways surprisingly like the Sophians. They speak of the "sacred [sexual] dictates of nature" (p. 216), and, though they have marriage in a formal sense, it is neither a sacrament

---

21 Note that Memmo shares this belief at first because Veronica, whom he loves, has been put into a convent, but that he changes his mind about monasteries by the end of the story.

nor a church ceremony (p. 234). "Temperance and frugality I saw were the pillars of their commonwealth" (p. 233), and "temperance ... was the main spring of the happiness they enjoyed" (p. 236). All social benefits are for the good of the community, and though "goods were not quite in common" (p. 174), they have many aspects of social communism. They have no "trade but barter" (p. 168), and their only contact with the world beyond the Mountains of the Moon is the annual exchange of cattle for salt with the Negro tribe on their border. They produce little in the way of manufactured goods and speak without chagrin of the "low ... state of our mechanic arts" (p. 167).

The most striking difference between the Jovinians and the Sophians is in the fine arts, which are eschewed by the Jovinians and cultivated, embraced, by the Sophians. The Jovinians "cultivate no arts that are not absolutely useful," for they think that "Painting and sculpture ... had corrupted and led mankind into idolatry" (p. 184). They seem to have no sculpture or painting and not much poetry, and most of their buildings are simple and functional, though some of their public buildings are "founded on Greek and Egyptian grandeur" (p. 186). The chief exception is music, for the Jovinians are a singing people: wherever he goes, Memmo hears songs at work and at worship. They sing "very scientifically" (p. 186), and though they have "no rules for [*musical*] composition ... they sang in parts as it were by a certain sympathy or affinity, such as one musical string receives from another in its octave" (p. 236). But almost all their songs seem to be religious. Memmo is less persuaded by the Jovinian artlessness than he is by other aspects of their culture, and we hear little of it when he leaves Jovinia; there is no sign that he took down the pictures in his grandfather's picture-gallery, for example.

With all their theological conviction, the Jovinians do not believe that their society is perfect or that man is perfectible; "Man is still a mystery to himself" (p. 177). As they conclude from the suicide of the desolate lover, "with all our attention to moral government, there will always be circumstances over which they have no influence" (p. 177), and "no human precaution can exterminate evil" (p. 218).

Despite the stress upon "pure Christianity," most of the emphasis of *The Captive* Part 2 is upon society and social reforms, upon "practical religion" of "elevated benevolence" (p. 150). Some of their social institutions, such as the Gloria for Elders (pp. 220–4) and the Riposo for the insane (pp. 206–8), are truly impressive. The essential precondition for converting the idolatrous Negroes to Christianity is converting them first to agriculture, and when Memmo tries to establish his own Christian community we hear more about distributing land and teaching the people to read than we do about perfecting their souls. This muscular Christianity is clearly related to the Victorian energy which carried the flag and the Church of England around the world.

The greatest emphasis of *The Captive* Part 2 is upon the utopia of Jovinia, and when he is describing the ideal political and social qualities of the state Cumberland does not much illustrate his principles "by palpable images, by proverbs, and by tales suited to the moment" as Memmo's friend the teacher in Jovinia did (p. 229). Too often the story is abandoned to concentrate upon its message. but there are passages in which individual actions and emotions are effectively and impressively displayed. The renegade hermit Antonio speaks with genuine spiritual passion; when Memmo and the Jovinus seek him out in his mountain fastness and offer him refreshment, he replies: "Who shall refresh my soul? I have suffered an agony this night, *Jovinus*, that was terrific – not more than I deserved but nearly as much as I could bear. All my sins came, and stood before me, accusing me, some with rage, some with bitter scoffs. I saw no angel near – no help! This whole rock was covered with fire – When I would pray, my lips became parched – and had not you awakened me, I had died!" (p. 194). The sympathy shown for the hermit is the more impressive because Memmo, the Jovinus, and Cumberland think him perverse and wrong.

Memmo's irrepressible impulsiveness is one of the mainsprings of the story, as he enthusiastically embraces ideas and individuals before he understands them. His return to his home, shedding hope as he goes, is one of the most consistently well-represented parts of the book, and the portrait of his mistress, Nazure, become the nun Veronica, is, I think, remarkably skilful. Most of Cumberland's characters, however, are somewhat faceless, and it is striking that the few who are named were given names as afterthoughts – blanks were left in the manuscript, and the narrator of Part 1 is not named at all until Part 2. Many of the individuals in the story are allegorical puppets representing utopian ideals, but at the end we have vivid pictures of Giovanni Gerson, the clerical reformer, Veronica, the monastic reformer, and Memmo, the secular reformer, and the conclusion seems justified:

We shall probably never again meet in this world of probation, ... but we have both calmly and without undue enthusiasm pursued our assigned employments in our several paths; he by his writings and exhortations; she by her reformed monastic discipline and prayers; and I by my secular exertions to amalgamate the interests and affections of those around me into an aggregate of human society, free from absolute want, alive to universal charity, pledged to their

religious duties as the bond of their union to God and to each other, and humbly
prepared to receive with humility that sentence which infinite wisdom, goodness
and justice shall, in mercy, award hereafter. [P. 295]

And in the last words of the story, Memmo gives thanks to providence
for his trials: "I have been taught humility in the school of adversity, to
know myself, and value my fellow men – to despise riches, except as
applicable to useful purpose by benefiting others, and finally after sub-
duing the passions by the aid of our holy religion to bow myself humbly
at the foot of the cross" (p. 296).

   Some aspects of the story are clearly Romantic, and it is well to re-
member that Cumberland was both a painter in the Romantic period
and that he knew Romantic painters and poets such as William Blake,
S.T. Coleridege, John Constable, Thomas Stothard, and John Linnell.
Many scenes in the tale call for graphic and poetic delineation, and the
Castle of Aronzo is "picturesque, the haunts of painters and poets"
(p. 276). Memmo exhibits a Romantic fascination with scenery, and there
are frequent descriptions of sunsets and sunrises, clear pools of water,
leafy recesses, strange flowers, and splendid trees. Such sights expand
Memmo's being in a characteristically Romantic way; he becomes a
larger, more generous person, participating in nature through all his
senses. In the sunset, "The rocks were like gold from the furnace, the
woods like emeralds, the sky a blaze of glory ... We seemed to inhale the
breath of roses, and imbibe life at every pore" (pp. 275–6).

   The exotic settings, the stress upon the arts, the insistence upon social
reform, the love-sick heroes pursuing supernaturally exalted ideals, the
enthusiastic reponses to nature, all mark *The Captive of the Castle of Sennaar*
as that very rare phenomenon, a Romantic novel. It has more in common
with the poetry of Shelley and Byron and Wordsworth than any other
novel I know of the time. It is not a great novel, but it seems to me to
be unquestionably Romantic. And some of its defects may suggest why
the form was attempted so rarely – and succeeded in never.

   We must be careful not to claim too much for Cumberland's *Captive
of the Castle of Sennaar*. It is not very successful as a novel – indeed, strictly
speaking it is not a novel but a romance – and many of its flaws are
obvious. Cumberland had ingenuity but little genius for expressing char-
acter, he was far more concerned with principles than with people or
places, the work has no formal division into chapters, even the grammar
is sometimes uncertain, and he forgot in Part 1 to tell us the name of
his narrator. The work is valuable primarily as an Utopian romance,
with its remarkably original settings, its advanced social and political
ideas, and its somewhat stereotyped heroes acting in extremely unusual

situations. The work provides not an Utopian escape from the world but a practical cure for it. Very few of Cumberland's contemporaries would have been at ease with the ideals and reforms he advocates. And the contemporary likely to have been most sympathetic may never have read it.

THE CAPTIVE OF THE CASTLE OF SENNAAR AND THE MEMOIRS OF SIGNOR GAUDENTIO DI LUCCA

Perhaps the most remarkable parallel to Cumberland's *Captive of the Castle of Sennaar* is to be found in *The Memoirs of Signor Gaudentio di Lucca*, an exceedingly popular novel[22] purporting to be "Translated from the Italian" but in fact written in English, apparently by a Catholic priest named Simon Berington[23] and first published in England in 1737. It is strikingly similar to Cumberland's *Castle of Sennaar* Part 1 in its setting among the mythical Mountains of the Moon (though they are not so called by Berington), in its depiction of an ancient race of admirable sun-worshippers isolated in innocence for thousands of years from contamination by the degenerate world, and even in some details of the framing story of the modern Italian who discovers this wonderful race. The parallels are sufficiently striking to make it worth rehearsing *The Memoirs of Signor Gaudentio di Lucca* in some detail.

The History of Gaudentio di Lucca

The story of Signor di Lucca is wonderfully varied, adventurous, and amorous, quite enough to catch the attention of the reader. The original

22 There were eighteenth century editions *in English* published in London, 1737 (the Garland facsimile of it, ed. Josephine Grieder, appeared in 1973); Dublin, 1738; London, 1748; Dublin, 1752; London, 1761; Glasgow, 1765; Edinburgh, 1773; London, 1774; London, 1776; London, 1786 (*Novelist's Magazine*, Vol. XXI); London, 1793 (ibid); Norwich, Connecticut, 1796; Dublin, 1798; Philadelphia, 1799; Baltimore, 1800; Wilmington, Delaware, 1800; *in French* in n.p., 1746; Amsterdam and Paris, 1746; Amsterdam [i.e., Paris], 1753; Amsterdam [i.e., Paris], 1754; Amsterdam and Liege, 1777; Amsterdam and Paris, 1787; Paris, 1797; *in German* in Frankfurt and Leipzig, 1751; Frankfurt and Leipzig, 1758; Leipzig and Altona, 1792; and *in Dutch* in 's Gravenhage, 1775. Notice that there is no edition in Italian.

23 The novel was published anonymously, but it was attributed to Berington by W.H. in *The Gentleman's Magazine* LV (1785), 757, on "very good [*but unstated*] authority", and this attribution is reported and uncritically accepted by Leo. M. Ellison, "*Gaudientio di Lucca*: A Forgotten Utopia", *PMLA*, L (1935), 494–509. It had been attributed to Bishop Berkeley, but this was denied emphatically by Berkeley's son George (*Gentleman's Magazine* LV [1785], 723, and Ellison, p. 497).

title of the book is *The Memoirs of Sig^r Gaudentio di Lucca; Taken from his Confession before the Fathers of the Inquisition at Bologna in Italy. Making a Discovery of an unknown Country in the Midst of the vast Deserts of Africa, as Ancient, Populous, and Civilized, as the Chinese. With an Account of their Antiquity, Original Religion, Customs, Polity, &c: and the Manner how they got over those vast Deserts. Interspers'd with several most surprizing and curious Incidents. Copied from the original Manuscript kept in St. Mark's Library at Venice. With Critical Notes of the Learned Signor Rhedi, late Library-Keeper of the said Library. To which is prefix'd a Letter from the Secretary of the Inquisition, to the same Signor Rhedi, giving an Account of the Manner and Causes of his being seized. Faithfully Translated from the Italian, by E.G. Gent.*[24] Signor di Lucca is Italian, like Cumberland's hero; he was born in 1669, the son of a merchant to the Levant. He takes up his father's trade, but on his first voyage in 1688 he is captured by Algerine pirates and sold as a slave to a mysterious merchant in Grand Cairo (pp. 17–18). This amiable merchant, "of what country no body knew," adopted him as his son and "took him along with him, through the vast deserts of Africa" (p. xii). Their journey is apparently commercial in motive, but its purpose is really to return to the merchant's native land in what Cumberland and others call The Mountains of the Moon.

On their arrival in the fertile land of Mezzorainea (middle earth?) beyond the barren wastes, Gaudentio discovers gradually that his adopted father is the hereditary ruler or Pophar of the people and that his (Gaudentio's) mother, Isiphena, was the Pophar's long-lost sister, who had been sold as a child in Grand Cairo by a perfidious Turkish woman and adopted by "a noble merchant of Corsica" (p. 41). Gaudentio falls in love with the Pophar's daughter, also named Isyphena, who is only ten years old when he arrives (p. 85). He marries her and has a son by her, and then, after "near five and twenty years" in the country

---

24 This is the title of the 1737 edition. The quotations in the text are taken from the
    edition in *The Novelist's Magazine*, XXI (1786), with an altered and abbreviated title:
    *The Adventures of Signor Gaudentio di Lucca, Being the Substance of His Examination before
    the Fathers of the Inquisition, at Bologna, in Italy, Giving an Account of an Unknown Country
    in the Midst of the vast Deserts of Africa, Copied from the Original Manuscript in St. Mark's
    Library, at Venice. With Critical Notes by the Learned Signor Rhedi, Translated from the Italian.*
    (In the same volume of *The Novelist's Magazine*, appeared *Peruvian Tales*, [Smollett] *The
    Adventures of an Atom, The Sincere Huron*, and *The English Hermit*.) I chose the *Novelist's
    Magazine* edition of *Gaudentio di Lucca* because it is apparently the last London edition
    before Cumberland's *Captive* (1798), because it was published in large numbers and
    was easily accessible, and because Cumberland is likely to have known it through his
    good friends Thomas Stothard, who designed many *Novelist's Magazine* plates, and
    William Blake, who engraved some of them.

(p. xii), he loses both his wife and son.[25] Desolated by his loss, he returns home with his father-in-law via Grand Cairo (p. xii) and Candy (in Crete), where the Pophar dies (p. 48), leaving Gaudentio immensely rich (p. 95). After being captured by pirates again and taken to Constantinople, he is freed and arrives via Marseilles in Venice on 10 December 1712 (p. 101). There at a masquerade he meets a modest Bolognese woman of great beauty, and on her account he moves to "a neat house" in Bologna (p. xii), "and having some knowledge in nature and physick, I took on me that character [*of a doctor*] to be the oftener in her company without scandal. We were neither of us inclined to marry" (p. 103).

After he had been about three years in Bologna, in "talking one day with some of our spies [*of the Inquisition*] about the customs of foreign countries, he said, he had met with a nation in one of the remotest parts of the world, who, though they were Heathens, had more knowledge of the law of nature and common morality, than the most civilized Christians. This was immediately carried to us, and explained as a reflection on the Christian religion ..." (p. viii–ix). In such overheard conversations, he "had dropped some words of several strange secrets he was master of, with mutterings of an unknown nation, religion, and customs, quite new to the Italian ears; for which reason the Inquisition thought fit to seize him, and, by ways and means made use of in that tribunal, obliged him to give an account of his whole life [*i.e., to write a confession*], which is the most surprising I ever read ... the man stands to the truth of it with stedfastness that is surprising" (p. iv).

As the story ends, in 1721, after two years of questioning him about his story (p. vii), "The Inquisitors are so far persuaded of the truth of it, that they have promised him his liberty, if he will undertake to conduct some missionaries the same way, to preach the gospel to a numerous people ..." (p. iv).

25 P. 63. There are several gaps in the story, including the accounts of his love affairs, the death of his wife and son, and the description of loose women among the Mezzoraineans (p. 89), gaps caused by "the loss of some sheets belonging to the middle part of the history," which may have disappeared when "the custom-house officers at Marseilles ... tumbled over his effects at a very rude rate" (p. v).

Gaudentio is "so very engaging in his aspect" (p. vii) that women fall in love with him on sight and cause him difficulty. He and the Pophar have to flee up the Nile from Cairo when the daughter of a great noble falls in love with him on sight (p. 31), and on his return to Venice a beautiful courtezan named Favilla falls in love with him at a masquerade, offers to marry him, and, on his refusal, hires bravos to attack him (pp. 102–3). His Cairo suitor later becomes Regent of Turkey and frees him when he is enslaved there (p. 100), and Favilla repents and becomes a nun at Gaudentio's instigation (p. 103).

The Land and People of Mezzorainea

The chief interest of his *Memoirs* lies in the strange land and people discovered by Gaudentio. The location of the land is somewhat mysterious. After journeying up the left (west) bank of the Nile (p. 31), Gaudentio and the Pophar reach "the middle coast of the vast desart of Barca," where they turn abruptly west and "cross the vast desart of Barca, as fast as his dromedary could well go" at first (p. 31), to avoid pursuit. The subsequent journey takes ten to twelve days, but it can only be made in the rainy season (p. 52). The land is "in the heart of the vast desarts of Africa" (p. iv), thirty-five to forty-five days' journey northwest from the [Indian] Ocean (pp. 90–91).

The land itself is "something mountainous" (p. 58) and is "past the tropick of Cancer" (p. 35), "almost on the ridge of Africa" (p. 36), apparently among those "vast ridges of [*mythickal*] mountains, which run several hundred miles, either under or parallel to the equator" (p. 62), and which in other books are called the Mountains of the Moon. When the Mezzoraineans first discovered it, they found "an immense and delicious country every way," with "no inhabitants" (pp. 52, 53). It is "a perpetual paradise" for fertility and happiness (p. 62), "the most opulent country in the world" (p. 23), with "two summers and two springs" (p. 69); "no country in the known world can parallel it" "for riches, plenty of all delicacies of life, manufactories, inventions of arts, and every thing that conduces to make this mortal state as happy as is possible" (p. 63). In agriculture, "they have little more trouble than to gather" fruit and vegetables (p. 69). Their most common metal is gold, and "One would think the curse of Adam had scarce reached that part of the world; or that Providence had proportioned the fertility of the country to the innocence of the inhabitants" (p. 62). Their only horned beasts [save elk] are goats, they have dromedaries and small, swift horses, their carriages are drawn by elk, and the only exotic or non-European mammal encountered is "a wild ass ... of all the colours of the rainbow, very strong and profitable for burdens and drudgery" (p. 63). They hunt boar, elk, and goat (p. 82), and they fish for "crocodiles [*of Africa*] and alligators [*of the Americas*]" (p. 84). Clearly it is a land fit for heroes.

And the people themselves are heroic. They are "the handsomest race of people ... nature ever produced " (pp. 55, 61), with black, curly hair and brown complexions, though "fairer than our Italians" (p. 61), and they live an heroic length of time – the Pophar is almost two hundred years old (p. 48). They are also dressed not only like heroes but like princes, for both "men and women, wore those fillet-crowns with a tuft of gold" (p. 60).

The History of Mezzorainea

According to their legends, the founder of their race was Mezzoraim, one of six persons who appeared when the "earth first rose out of the water" (p. 42). He settled in Egypt with his sixty children and grand-children and invented the arts of grace and government (p. 42). After a time of prosperity in Egypt, "the wicked descendants of the other man, called Hicksoes, envying their happiness, and the richness of their coun-try, broke in upon them like a torrent, destroying all before them, and taking possession of that happy place our ancestors, had rendered so flourishing. ... these impious Hicksoes [the first authors of all impiety and idolatry] forced them to adore men and beasts, and even insects for gods" (p. 44).

Some of the children of Mezzoraim escaped to the Euxine, some to China, and Gaudentio's ancestors fled south up the Nile, first to a valley they call No-Om (the House of the Sun) (p. 47), which seems to be Thebes, and then yet further southwest into the desert to their present happy valley (p. 52), where they have lived unknown for over three thousand years (p. iv).

Incidentally, this part of the story bears a curious resemblance to the myths of Cumberland's friend William Blake, who has a wild man in Egypt called Heuxos in his *Tiriel* (1789) whose name is apparently de-rived through unknown intermediaries from the historical nomadic ene-mies of the Egyptians called Hyxoes or Hicksoes. Further, in Blake's *First Book of Urizen* (1794), corresponding mythologically to the first book of Moses, the sons of Urizen led by Fuzon settled for a time in Africa but are then driven from their homeland:

> They called it Egyp*t*, & left it.
> And the salt ocean rolled englob'd.

We are not told where they went – can it have been to the Mountains of the Moon?

Mezzorainean Religion and Morality

The Mezzoraineans seem to be "the most moral men in the world, [*but at first*] I could observe no signs of religion in them" (p. 25). In fact they seem to be deists, though the term is of course not used of them.[26] Their religion is largely sun-worship, a benevolent form of "natural religion" (p. iv), tinged with ancestor-worship (p. 34), with a strong emphasis upon morality. Gaudentio explains, "The religion of these people is really idolatry in the main; though as simple and natural as possible for Heathens ... worshipping the material Sun, and paying those superstitious rites to their deceased ancestors.... These people however acknowledge one supreme God, maker of all things, whom they call El, or the most high of all. This they say natural reason teaches them.... Though they make a god of the sun, they don't say he is independent as to his own being, but that he received it from El" (p. 63). They call themselves "children of the Sun" (p. 23), and they swear by it – "Great Sun"! (p. 40) The young men all wear "a bright gold medal ... with the figure of the sun engraved on it" (p. 40), and it is by his wearing of such a medal given him by his mother that Gaudentio is discovered to be a Mezzorainean (p. 40). They believe that they will be rewarded or punished in an afterlife when their souls transmigrate into appropriate creatures, and indeed "the souls of brutes enter into the bodies of men in this life ... they believe the body of a voluptuous man is possessed by the soul of a hog, of a lustful man by that of a goat," women by chameleons, peacocks, tigresses, etc., and consequently they are "addicted to the study of Physiognomy" to learn what sort of beast possesses a man (p. 66). Though their religion is depicted as admirable, or at least as on the whole harmless, the emphasis of the book is primarily upon their morality and civilization, for they were "the most civilized [*people*] I ever saw in my life" (p. 23).

All the emphasis falls upon the *naturalness* of their morality. "Their laws ... are nothing but the first principals of natural justice, explained and applied by the elders" (p. 67). "In a word, the whole country is only one great family governed by the laws of nature" (p. 70). The very rare murderer or adulterer is merely imprisoned for life (p. 68), not executed, and their sexual customs are particularly generous. "Whoredom is only punished, in the man, by chaining him to a *he-goat*, and the woman to a *salt-bitch*, and leading them round the Nome. ... [*They*] encourage a generous and honorable love, and make it their care to fix them [*young people*] in the strictest bonds they can, as soon as they judge, by their age

---

26 Indeed, the only person called a "Deist" is an English cast-away they rescue; he is a moral monster, utterly selfish and wanton, who eventually commits suicide (pp. 92–3). Somewhat perversely, the only plate in the *Novelist's Magazine* edition (at p. 95, by C.J. Burney) depicts this English hermit.

and constitution, of their inclinations" (pp. 68, 74). The initiative in the choice of partners seems to be entirely the woman's: "Where this is approved of by the governors or elders, if the woman insists on her demands, it is an inviolable law that the man must be her husband. ... I believe the world cannot furnish such examples of conjugal chastity as are preserved between them by these means" (p. 74).

The head of state is the Pophar, and the title is inherited by his eldest direct male heir when he is fifty. The state is divided into five tribes or Nomes, and if the Pophar has no direct male heir, the eldest male in the next Nome becomes Pophar if he is of age (p. 70).

There is comparatively little emphasis upon the arts, though the Mezzoraineans are capable of being excellent performers. They enjoy music but are not as good musicians as Italians (p. 76), and when Gaudentio teaches them painting, they succeed at it prodigiously well and erect a statue of him in gratitude.[27]

Berington's story establishes a tension when it opens, with the hero under examination by the Inquisition, and he manages skilfully to extend and vary this tension throughout the work. It is easy to see why the book was so popular in Britain, France, Germany, and Holland, in the progressive, enquiring West, in the eighteenth century.

Cumberland's Captive of the Castle of Sennaar *and Berington's* Gaudentio di Lucca

The similarities between Cumberland's *Captive of the Castle of Sennaar* and Berington's *Memoirs of Signor Gaudentio di Lucca* are significant and pervasive, both in the framing narrative and in the accounts of the utopias in Central Africa which are the foci of the stories. A curious feature of the parallels between Berington's utopia and Cumberland's is that some apply to the deist Greeks in Cumberland's Part 1 and some to the primitive Christians in his Part 2. The effect of Cumberland's novel is very different from that of Berington, but many of the settings, incidents, and plots are strikingly similar – so similar as to point strongly towards Cumberland's acquaintance with *Gaudentio di Lucca* and even to his presumption that the reader may recognize the similarities and understand the ways in which Cumberland is modifying and extending Berington's utopia.

27 P. 77. They had erected a pyramid to honour Mezzoraim, the founder of their line (p. 36). In this context, it is worth remarking that the eponymous founder of his race in Blake's *Tiriel* (?1789) is shown in the designs to the poem with pyramids.

The first similarity is in the utopian setting in a delicious, fruitful refuge south and west of the vast deserts of Upper Egypt in an area never visited by Europeans, called by Cumberland (in Part 2) and others the Mountains of the Moon. There is even a large lake in Berington's novel which may be related to the huge lake in Cumberland's Part 1 where the utopians live on their islands.

The terms in which this fertile paradise are described by Berington and by Cumberland in his Part 2 have much in common, and the means by which the inhabitants maintain the purity of their isolation are also similar. (The "Happy Valley" of Johnson's *Rasselas* [1749] has significant features in common with both Berington's *Gaudentio di Lucca* and Cumberland's *Captive*, and it seems possible that Johnson derived significant elements from Berington's book.[28]) To a twentieth century eye, the flora and fauna of Central Africa in each novel seem surprisingly familiar and European, with scarcely an attempt to depict the giraffes, hippopotomi, and great serpents known even in the eighteenth century to be peculiar to Africa. In Berington the only very remarkable beast is the wild ass "all the colours of the rainbow" (p. 63), a creature which, fortunately, does not reappear in Cumberland's Africa. Neither author is very interested in the *Africanness* of his setting.

The people of each work have lived for ages in deliberate isolation from all other society, both African and European: Berington's for some three thousand years, Cumberland's for about two thousand – a little more in Part 1, rather less in Part 2. In each, the people are protected both by physical isolation beyond formidable natural barriers and by the psychology and deliberate policy of the founders and elders of the race.

The people, too, are similar. In Berington and in Cumberland's Part 1, they are perhaps the handsomest people in the world, virile, active, athletic, with features which are European, not black African. The religion of each is deism, in the form of sun-worship, deriving from Natural Religion rather than from revelation or supernatural intervention of the deity. But the most important aspect of their culture is their moral code, based upon natural justice, particularly as it relates to sexual customs. Each values sexuality and femininity far more than their eighteenth century contemporaries did, each treats sexual irregularity as social abberation rather than as a psychological or moral crime, and each fosters early and affectionate sexual relations among the young. The sexual

---

28 See "*Rasselas* and *Gaudentio di Lucca* in the Mountains of the Moon," *Revista Canaria de Estudios Ingleses* VIII (Noviembre 1984): 1–11, in which the summary above is adapted and the connections with Johnson explored.

liberality of these utopias must have seemed titillating or shocking to many of their first readers. The two utopias in Berington and in Cumberland's Part 1 have, then, a great deal in common.

The adventures of the narrator also have much in common. The narrator of each is an Italian, and in each a character travels with a merchant from Cairo up the Nile, though in Berington it is his narrator who does so and in Cumberland's Part 1 it is the old prisoner of Sennaar who had done so. Each of these discovers a wonderful Good Land, marries the daughter of one of the chief citizens, has a son, and, after many years, loses both wife and son and returns in sorrow from the happy valley. When the two narrators return to their native lands, they travel by way of Cairo and touch at Candy in Crete, and each is threatened by the interests of the Inquistion. Each finds a lover in Italy who enters a convent, and each story concludes with the narrator preparing to spread the Gospel, Gaudentio perhaps somewhat reluctantly. The similarities are surprisingly extensive.

This is not say that Cumberland was merely imitating Berington's story, though it is hard to believe that he did not know it. Cumberland's moral and philosophical purposes are much more important and profound than Berington's, and they differ in important respects. The basis of the society in Cumberland's Part 1 is aesthetic, with marvellous Greek accomplishments in architecture, music, dance, theatre, and painting, while Berington's people are skillful in the arts but only incidentally so. Berington's novel is set in the historical present, only a few years before it was published, whereas Cumberland's is an historical novel, set in a carefully defined, remote past. And, most significantly, though both Parts of Cumberland's novel seem to echo Berington's in important ways, the crux of the combined work is that it offers complementary utopias, the second and dominant of which is as emphatically Christian as the first Part was deist and Greek. The design of Cumberland's complementary utopias is much more sophisticated than anything attempted in Berington's *Gaudentio di Lucca*.

Some of the similarities between Berington's novel and Cumberland's may be mere coincidence – the European character of the utopians, for instance, is natural in the work of an European author, and the inhabitants of Berington's Happy Valley may not be literally Europeans in race, but clearly they are not black Africans either. The deism, too, is natural to Eighteenth century idealists. But the similarities are so many, and some of them are so particular, as in the site among the Mountains of the Moon or touching at Candy on the way home, that it is tempting to think that Cumberland intended his reader to recognize the similar-

ities – though the effect of the book does not depend upon such rec-
ognition. He may even have intended the reader to compare the works
in order to focus upon the differences between them, in effect to improve
and correct Berington's concept of utopia, the Good Land.

Ultimately, however, I think such comparisons are intriguing but dis-
tracting from the most important effects of Cumberland's novels. Had
he wished to direct our attention explicitly to *Gaudentio di Lucca*, he could
have referred to it directly, quoted from it, named it. Cumberland does
not depend upon Berington's book, and indeed he *may* even have been
ignorant of it. But the parallels are intriguing, whether deliberate or
coincidental. Berington's tale and the two Parts of Cumberland's novel
are each valuable in themselves and insufficiently known today. Bering-
ton achieved a wide audience in his time and clearly hit the public taste
with the variousness of his story and his skill in narrating it. Berington's
work may have a wider appeal, but Cumberland's two utopias, I think,
have a deeper significance and deserve a longer life.

WILLIAM BLAKE AND CUMBERLAND'S *CAPTIVE* PART 1

William Blake and George Cumberland were good friends for many
years, probably from 1780 to 1827 when Blake died. Blake etched some
of Cumberland's designs for Cumberland's *Thoughts on Outline* (1796),
which Cumberland took as "a compliment, from a man of his extraor-
dinary genius and abilities, the highest, I believe, I shall ever receive:
– and I am indebted to his generous partiality for the instruction which
encouraged me to execute a great part of the plates myself."[29] When
Cumberland was living in and near London, he probably saw Blake fairly
often, especially when Blake was teaching him etching,[31] and after he
moved to Bristol he used to call on Blake when he came to London to
collect his quarterly dividends. For years Cumberland tried "to purchase
everything Mr. Blake engraved,"[32] and on a number of occasions he

29 George Cumberland, *Thoughts on Outline* (1796), 47–8.
30 See Blake's letter to Cumberland of 6 Dec. 1795, Cumberland's Commonplace Book
    note about "Blakes Instructions to Print Copper Plates," and Cumberland's note written
    on Blake's "Enoch" lithograph (collection of the late Mr Croft Murray) about how to
    make lithographs according to Blake.
31 See Blake's letter to Cumberland of 6 Dec. 1795.
32 Though, as he told Blake's widow in 1827, he could not do so "latterly," apparently
    because he could not afford to – see *Blake Records* (1969), 359. He told his son of his
    "former purchases of nearly all his singular works" (p. 361), and these included *Poetical
    Sketches* (D), *Thel* (A), *For Children* (C), *Visions* (B), *America* (F), *Songs* (F), *Europe* (D),
    Song of Los (D), *Descriptive Catalogue*, and *Job*. In addition, he made extensive annotations
    in *Europe* (D), and perhaps in *Visions* (B) and *Marriage* (A).

helped sell Blake's works and recommended him to patrons as a designer or engraver.

Just as the time Cumberland was concerned with his *Captive*, about 1795–99, Blake felt peculiarly in tune with Cumberland's ideas. On 6 December 1795 he urged him to "shew all the family of Antique Borers, that Peace & Plenty & Domestic Happiness is the Source of Sublime Art, & prove to the Abstract Philosophers that Enjoyment & not Abstinence is the food of Intellect", which seems a fair enough summary of the first Part of Cumberland's tale. A year later, on 23 December 1796, Blake wrote to Cumberland to thank him for the gift of a copy of his *Thoughts on Outline* and urged most eloquently: "Go on Go on. Such works as yours Nature & Providence the Eternal Parents demand from their children[:] how few produce them in such perfection[:] how Nature smiles on them[:] how Providence rewards them. How all your Brethren say, The sound of his harp & his flute heard from his secret forest chears us to the labours of life, & we plow & reap forgetting our labour."

Three years later, on 26 August 1799, Blake repeated the same theme: "Your Inventions of Intellectual Visions are the Stamina of every thing you value. Go on[,] if not for your own sake yet for ours who love & admire your works but above all for The Sake of the Arts. Do not throw aside for any long time the honour intended you by Nature to revive the Greek workmanship."

And on 16 August 1799 he wrote to Dr Trusler, to whom Cumberland had recommended Blake as a painter, that he was "compelled by my Genius or Angel to ... fulfill the purpose for which alone I live, which is in conjunction with such men as my friend Cumberland to recreate the lost Art of the Greeks."

Even allowing that most of the interest Blake shared with Cumberland was in the art of design, that the "Art of the Greeks" above is probably painting, and that the letters between the two men never explicitly discuss literary subjects, still it is likely that they shared profound literary sympathies.[33] And "recreat[ing] the lost Art of the Greeks" is very much the subject of Cumberland's *Captive of the Castle of Sennaar* Part 1. We cannot be sure that Blake ever saw a copy of *The Captive*, for they were always scarce, and only five copies of the 1798 edition are known to have survived today; we do not even know that Cumberland talked about his tale with Blake. We can observe, however, that many of the ideas in *The Captive* Part 1 are strikingly Blakean and guess that Blake would have heartily subscribed to many of them – at least in 1798. We may also say

---

33 After all, Cumberland did acquire Blake's *Poetical Sketches* (1783) presumably for its poetry, for it has no designs.

that he would have approved of Cumberland's major alteration in the
1810 edition and most of Part 2, for Cumberland's ideas about Chris-
tianity seem to have changed in ways remarkably like those of Blake.
We cannot prove that some of the more strikingly independent ideas in
The Captive came from Blake – but they well may have.

One of the more curious ideas in *The Captive* concerns the depiction
of nudity. Lycas describes a picture of a beautiful nude girl which "was
much applauded – but to my then weak judgment it seemed, though
pleasing in one respect, preposterous; – every fleshy protuberance being
so warm and rosy that I called it a red woman. 'You wonder (said Chilo),
at the artist's having given so much carnation; – have you never observed,
that all the prominent parts of muscles blush, like the cheeks, when
exposed to fine air? The fleshy parts of muscles are red, porous, and
consequently are the warm points of the body, like the ears, heels, &c'"
(p. 85). This ruddy nudity is, I believe, an idea very uncommon in Cum-
berland's time, or at any other, and indeed I have only encountered it
once again. Several critics of Blake's 1809 exhibition commented on the
sanguine appearance of the flesh in the paintings. Robert Hunt com-
plained that "the colouring of the flesh is exactly like hung beef,"[34] and
Seymour Kirkup said that "The Ancient Britons" which he saw exhibited
there " was too red."[35] Blake had anticipated such complaints, and in
the *Descriptive Catalogue* (1809) of his exhibition (para. 87) he drew at-
tention to the way he had represented "The flush of health in flesh
exposed to the open air." He contrasted his practice with "the sickly
daubs of Titian or Rubens" or Correggio, whose "men are like leather,
and their woman like chalk ... in Mr. B's Britons the blood is seen to
circulate in their limbs; he defies competition in colouring."

This rosy or carnation colour of nudity, "The flush of health in flesh
exposed to the open air," is both striking and unusual in Cumberland
and Blake. It seems very likely that they had talked about it together in
the 1790s. Cumberland wrote about it in 1798 and Blake in 1809, but
Blake, as the more original mind, may have been the inventor of the
idea. At the very least, the striking coincidence of thought demonstrates
remarkable artistic sympathy between the two men.

Many of the most interesting and unusual ideas in the *The Captive*
Part 1 concern the free expression of energy, particularly sexual energy,
in a way strongly reminiscent of Blake's *Marriage of Heaven and Hell*

34 *The Examiner*, 17 Sept. 1809, 606 – see *Blake Records* (1969), 217.
35 *Blake Records*, 222; see also 399. "The Ancient Britons" has disappeared.

(?1790–93).[36] For the Sophians, instinctive energy is the source of life,
is virtually the principle of life; they speak of God as "the good Energy"
(p. 333), and they pray to, and exclaim by, "Holy Energy!," which is
"Love!" (p. 42). God for them is a principle rather than a person, and
the principle is largely instinctive bodily energy.

This is wonderfully similar to the Devilish, Blakean truths of the *Marriage* (pl. 4):

1. Man has no body distinct from his Soul; for that calld Body is a portion of
   Soul discern'd by the five Senses, the chief inlets of Soul in this age.
2. Energy is the only life, and is from the Body; and Reason is the bound or
   outward circumference of Energy.
3. Energy is Eternal Delight.

In the *Marriage* (pl. 24), the Devil argues logically that Jesus broke all
"these ten commandments" and "acted from impulse, not from rules."
It seems to be Blake himself who says (pl. 17) that the Messiah "was
formerly [*and truly*] thought to be one of the Antediluvians who are our
Energies." The Gospel of Energy is very similar in Blake's *Marriage* and
in Cumberland's *Captive*.

In both works, this Energy is most memorably manifested in sexual
form, and Blake's emphasis upon the beauty of sexual energy in the
Marriage and elsewhere is as marked as Cumberland's. In the *Marriage*,
the Devil teaches that "Those who restrain desire, do so because theirs
is weak enough to be restrained" (pl. 5), and among his Proverbs are
"He who desires but acts not, breeds pestilence" (pl. 7) and "Sooner
murder an infant in its cradle than nurse unacted desires" (pl. 10). At
the revolutionary last judgment in *America* (1793), "The doors of marriage are open ... Leaving the females naked and glowing with the lusts
of youth" (pl. 17). Blake writes often of the beauty of "The human form
divine" and "naked beauty displayed," and the Devil's Proverb in the
Marriage (pl. 10) speaks of "the genitals Beauty." In *Visions of the Daughters
of Albion* (1793), Oothoon passionately evokes "The moment of desire!"
and cries out to "Love! Love! Love! happy happy love! free as the
mountain wind!" (pl. 10). She glories "In lovely copulation bliss on
bliss ... Red as the rosy morning, lustful as the first born beam." And in
his *Notebook* (p. 105) about 1793, Blake wrote:

36 Cumberland may have written annotations to a copy of the *Marriage* (A) which have
   since been lost.

Abstinence sows sand all over
The ruddy limbs & flaming hair
But Desire Gratified
Plants fruits of life & beauty there

and

He who bends to himself a joy
Does the winged life destroy
But he who kisses the joy as it flies
Lives in eternity's sun rise.

Blake clearly felt as Cumberland did that prostitution is an aberration fostered by a corrupt society, by religious distortion of our sexual natures, and in the *Marriage* he wrote that "Brothels [*are built*] with bricks of Religion" (pl. 8) and condemned "pale religious letchery" (pl. 27).

Both men exalted the role of Innocence, Blake most conspicuously in his *Songs of Innocence* (1789). One of the maxims of Sophis is "respect the innocent will in all things" (p. 38), and indeed "all our customs and laws are calculated" to protect "the innocent will." This respect for the integrity of others is extended by Cumberland to all living things, and Lycas is exhorted to "respect even a tree as your fellow creature" (p. 41) and to "kill nothing that breathes and lives" (p. 41). This is surely very close to the feeling for the sanctity of all life which Blake expresses repeatedly, particularly in a favourite phrase, "everything that lives is holy."[37]

A few more isolated points may be noted. Lycas' decision to become "a missionary to mankind" (p. 90) preaching a political rather than a religious gospel illustrates Blake's aphorism in *Jerusalem* (1804–?20), pl. 26: "Jerusalem is named Liberty Among the Sons of Albion." The need of Sophis the philosopher to establish his own unique "system" (e.g., p. 75) may remind us of what Blake wrote for Los in *Jerusalem* (1804–?20), pl. 10: "I must Create a System, or by enslav'd by another Mans." And a peculiarly Blakean phrase, "the current of Creation," (*Jerusalem*, pl. 77) is used by Cumberland in his *Captive* (p. 67) as a synonym for "tender [*sexual*] desire."

In sum, Cumberland's *Captive of the Castle of Sennaar* of 1798 exhibits many of the ideas which seem so unusual, original, and profound in the

---

37 Annotations to Lavater's *Aphorisms* (1788), 309, *Marriage* (?1790–93), pl. 27, *Visions* (1793), pl. 11, *America* (1793), pl. 10, *Vala* (?1796-1807), 34.

writings of his intimate friend Blake in the 1790s and later, particularly in Blake's *Marriage of Heaven and Hell*. We know that Cumberland bought most of the works Blake published in the 1790s and that he not only admired the designs but studied the text sufficiently closely to make very illuminating annotations in several of them. We know that Blake and Cumberland talked and corresponded extensively about artistic matters, and it is virtually certain that they discussed literary, political, and social matters as well, on which each had similar and profoundly heterodox views. The surviving evidence does not amount to proof, but we may be virtually certain that Blake's ideas helped to shape, and in turn were at least partly shaped by, those of George Cumberland. In particular, several of the more striking ideas in Cumberland's *Captive of the Castle of Sennaar* must have powerfully reinforced, if they were not derived from, those of Blake. Cumberland's *Captive* Part 1 expresses some of Blake's poetic ideas in prosaic form and it seems in these respects to be the first printed Blakean tale.

Later, of course, Blake's attitude toward such social reforms altered – as did Cumberland's. Blake's new Christian spiritualism is expressed in his great epics *Milton* (1807–?8) and *Jerusalem* (1804–?20), and two lines from the former seem almost to be addressed to Cumberland:

Come bring with thee Jerusalem with songs on the Grecian Lyre!
In Natural Religion: in experiments on Men. ...
Where is the Lamb of God? where is the promise of his coming?
[pl. 17, ll. 46–7]

Cumberland might have replied, look in my new testament, in *The Captive* Part 2.

The History of The Captive
Parts *1* and *2* and the Bases
of the Present Text

The Captive Part 1 was probably written in 1797, and when it was finished Cumberland asked his friend Horne Tooke "to look [*it*] over before it went to Press". Tooke agreed to do so on 22 January 1798,[1] and "he sat up till 2 oclock in the Morning to hear me read it in manuscript without suffering any one to interrupt us, or allowing me to leave off a moment."[2] Tooke liked the tale, "advising me to Print it directly,"[3] and Cumberland evidently did so.

However, he did not see proofs, and he later complained that the printer W. Wilson "not understanding my hand as he said, filled it with errors, so that it was not fit for the Public eye."[4] Some of these errors are certainly striking, such as "soil" for "soul" (p. 339) and "darling" for "daring" (p. 348), but the work does not seem to be as "full of Press Errors"[5] as Cumberland implies.

The printing was completed by the early autumn of 1798, and probably Cumberland immediately sent copies to a few friends. One of these, the devoted Platonist Thomas Taylor, replied on 16 October 1798:

I think it more entertaining than instructive, more ingenious than moral. I will not, indeed, I cannot suppose that you would undertake to defend

---

1 According to Cumberland's manuscript "Anecdotes of ... John Horne Tooke" (?1823) (see G.E. Bentley, Jr., *A Bibliography of George Cumberland (1975)*, 85–92). This *Bibliography* (pp. 20–6, 105–10) is the source for much of the bibliographical information given here about *The Captive*.
2 This MS note by Cumberland is in the Bodley copy of *The Captive* (1798).
3 Cumberland, "Anecdotes of ... John Horne Tooke."
4 Cumberland's MS note is in the John Rylands Library copy of *The Captive* (1798).
5 MS note, Bodley copy of *The Captive* (1798).

lasciviousness publickly; & yet it appears that it is as much patronized by the conduct of your Sophians as by the works of Mrs Woolstoncraft.[6] You will doubtless excuse the freedom of this opinion, when you consider that as I am a professed Platonist, love is with me true only in proportion as it is pure; or in other words in proportion as it rises above the gratification of our brutal part. Hence, I consider the delight which lovers experience, when in poetic language they drink large draughts of love thro' the eyes, as far superior to that arising from copulation, because the union is more incorporeal.[7]

Another copy of *The Captive* went to the lawyer Henry Erskine, and his reply was even more damping than Taylor's. Though "he liked it he said," "Mr Erskine, deemed it [*the passage at page 175 (p. 78)*] dangerous, under Mr Pitts, maladministration, to publish it."[8] The offending passage concerns the badness of human society everywhere but in Sophis, with "single tyrants framing arbitrary laws ... or ten or a dozen men, under pretext of guardianship, dividing among themselves, the property of millions; supported by ... armed ruffians." Cumberland concluded that this squeaking baby trumpet of sedition was likely to be subject to the penalties of Pitt's new gag laws, and he therefore "Cancelled [*the*] Edition ... it was never published or a single copy sold to any one".[9] Indeed today only five copies are known.[10]

Cumberland did not give up hope that the political climate would become more tolerant. In the summer of 1808 he recorded in his Notebook that he had "Trusted Captive to Mr. Cromac [*R.H. Cromek*] to Dispose [*of*] for £25 or 28 to [*the London publishers Thomas*]

---

6 Mary Wollstonecraft (1759–97) had lived in Taylor's house for a time.

7 British Library Additional Manuscripts 36,498, f. 246. In 1829, Taylor told W.G. Meredith: "'When my first wife had home 6 children, she proposed & recommended to me, as we had now as many as we could possibly support & educate, to abstain from all sexual intercourse, that I answered if she would agree to it, I would willingly, & we acted acc[*ording*]ly; for, for the last ten years of her life altho we still slept in the same bed, we never cohabited.' [*Meredith comments:*] This is pretty good from the mouth of a man who after[*ar*]ds married his cook & had another child by her, when he was about 60 yrs of age." (J. King, "The Meredith Family, Thomas Taylor, and William Blake," *Studies in Romanticism*, XI [1971], 156).

8 MS note, Bodley copy of *The Captive* (1798).

9 Ibid.

10 A few years earlier, Blake or his publisher had suppressed Blake's *French Revolution* (1791), presumably for similar reasons.

Cade[*l*] & [*William Davies or John*] Murray"[11] but this too was un-
successful. Cromek was more interested in working as an entre-
preneur in his own interests than on behalf of others, as William
Blake discovered about this time.

When Cromek failed him, Cumberland evidently turned for help
with publishing *The Captive* to his friend Charles Henry Bellenden
Ker.[12] The London publishers William Miller and William Pople
were persuaded to undertake the work, and Cumberland corrected
a copy of the 1798 edition for the printer.[13] These changes are
almost entirely substantive, affecting meaning and not merely form,
and they are very extensive, almost six hundred alterations on about

11 British Library Add. MSS 36,519, f. 362.
12 Ker (?1785–1871) corresponded with Cumberland in 1810 – see *Blake Records*
(1969), 227–8. The name in Cumberland's manuscript which I have transcribed
as "Ker" is, however, hard to read and could be, say, "Thin."
13 This copy is now in the John Rylands Library. Cumberland's responsibility for
the changes in it may be established on the basis of his handwriting and of the
MS note which he prefixed to this copy and signed with his initials. Most of the
changes are in ink in the text, but a few are in pencil in the margin (pp. 8, 10–
12, 26, 95 ["their" to "there"], 196). Only one of these marginal pencil corrections
– an obvious misspelling on p. 95 – is incorporated in the 1810 text; perhaps
Cumberland made them in anticipation of the "third edition corrected" of which
he wrote in the Bristol Central Library copy (1798).
      In another copy (now in Bristol Central Library), Cumberland made a few
of the same changes on pp. 26–7 (as in the 1798 Errata list), p. 89, l. 21, p. 173,
l. 25, and p. 208, l. 5.
      In a third copy (now in Bodley), he made slightly more extensive duplicate
changes: p. 6, 8, 25–7 (as in the 1798 Errata list); on p. 95, p. 125, l. 8, p. 173,
l. 25 (as in the Printer's [Rylands] Copy); corrections of typographical errors on
pp. 16, 59, 152; and
p. 89: "living, just as" altered to "living, just so"
p. 126: "[which *del*] you can only judge [of *del*] from"
p. 175: The paragraph beginning "For, here excepted" is bracketed to indicate
            that an alteration is necessary – this is the passage which Erskine told
            Cumberland might be actionable as seditious
p. 208: "[there *del*] forth"
      A fourth copy, now in the Australian National University, has MS changes in
what appears to be Cumberland's hand in old brown ink or in pencil (pp. 92,
95) as in the Errata, pp. 6, 8, 25 (l. 5), 26 ("money exchangers"), 27, and in the
Printer's Copy, pp. 89, l. 21 ["Just so"]; 125, l. 8; 126, l. 15; 173, l. 25; 208, l. 1
["forth" substituted for "there"], plus:
p. 5, l. 14: parentheses added round "to my afflicted soul"
p. 6, l. 9: "he" added before "held out his arms"
p. 92, l. 21: "no water" altered to "any water"
p. 95:   "there" altered to "their."

five pages in six.[14] In particular, he made a change on p. 208 anticipating the Christian tenor of Part 2. Since almost all these changes appear in the 1810 edition, it is plain that this copy in effect served as Printer's Copy, though Cumberland may have abstracted the changes and sent them to the printer in a separate list.

Since Cumberland by this time lived in Bristol, he "left [*The second edition*] to the care of Mr Ker who chose to alter [*probably in proof*] several passages without my knowing what he and the Printer was about".[15] Indeed, "I never saw [*The second edition*] till I got it sadly mutilated."[16] These alterations by Ker may be identified by comparing the copy of the 1798 edition which Cumberland corrected for the printer with the version printed in 1810; they appear on about two pages in three, and the vast majority are merely stylistic: altering prepositions, making subject and verb agree, and the like. Frequently the changes are manifest improvements.

A few of the unauthorized changes may introduce new corruptions. For instance, in the 1798 sentence "I ... fell into a repose as sound, and uninterrupted, as my earliest infancy had enjoyed" (p. 8), the word "infancy" was altered to "fancy." A very few substantive changes were plainly made by Ker from prudish motives, and these must rightly have roused Cumberland's indignation. The chief of these are:

1798	1810
misusing it [*the cloak*], so as to throw an odium on one part [*of the body, i.e., the genitals*] more than another [p. 335]	using it otherwise than as conveniency dictates
would have spurned at the unnatural depravity that affixed ideas of shame to the most necessary, wonderful, and noble organs of the human superstructure [p. 335]	in their active and athletic images, a Phidias would have found an endless number of the finest models of the human structure

14 See Appendix 1. MS text for the 1810 titlepage, advertisement, and motto does not survive.
15 MS note, Rylands copy of *The Captive* (1798).
16 MS note, Bodley copy of *The Captive* (1798).

we esteem chastity [p. 341]   we esteem female chastity

The artist had painted her   The artist had painted her
quite naked [p. 346]

The second edition of *The Captive* and the first to be published
was in ORIGINAL TALES, / BY / GEORGE CUMBERLAND. / IN / TWO
VOLUMES. / = / VOL. I. / = / LONDON: / PRINTED AND PUBLISHED
BY MILLER AND POPLE, / 72, CHANCERY-LANE. / — / 1810. (The
second volume of *Original Tales* consisted of eleven short tales in
prose and verse.) The work was announced as "in the press" in the
issue of the *Journal of Natural Philosophy, Chemistry, and the Arts* for
June 1810 (III, 378), and there were five advertisements in the
[London] *Chronicle*, two in the [London] *Courier*, two "at Bath," four
in "Bristol" where Cumberland lived, and others in Bent's *Advertiser*
and in "British Press".[17] A thousand copies were printed in 1810
at a total cost of £147.18.9,[18] but two years later the publisher Pople
complained to Cumberland that "the Reviews have never taken
notice of the work,"[19] and the only review known to me appeared
tardily in *The British Critic* for June 1813 (XLI, 643). The poet
Samuel Rogers had written on 29th May 1810 asking for a copy
as soon as it was published,[20] and Cumberland's friend Joseph
Lancaster, the school reformer, wrote on 18 September 1810 to
say that "thy excellent little volume of tales ... is one of the best
things of the Kind I have met with in my life,"[21] but few copies
were sold. By August 1812 only 226 copies had been disposed of,
including those Cumberland presumably gave away with his usual
generosity to his friends, and on 18 March 1814 William Pople,[22]
who had taken over the remaining 774 copies, offered to return
them to Cumberland.[23] As late as July 1816 Pople was still com-
plaining that the work had not cleared its expenses.

17 According to Cumberland's accounts for the book dated 13 Aug. 1812 (British
Library Add. MSS 36,503, ff. 240–1).
18 Ibid.
19 Ibid.
20 British Library Add. MSS 36,502, f. 217.
21 MS in Bristol Central Library
22 Pople remarked seductively, "should you determine on taking the book into
your own hands you can have fresh titles printed and call it a second edition."
23 According to Cumberland's accounts for the book dated 13 Aug. 1812 (British
Library Add. MSS 36,503, ff. 240–1).

In sum, *The Captive* Part 1 was printed, badly, in 1798 but immediately suppressed by Cumberland; only a few copies were preserved for his friends, and only five are known to survive today. It was first published in 1810 with Cumberland's *Original Tales*, but that edition was a disappointment, with only two hundred some copies sold and only one review three years later. The work was scarcely visible to Cumberland's contemporaries.

THE HISTORY OF PART 2

Undaunted, Cumberland wrote a second Part to his *Captive*. The date of this sequel is obscure, but it may well have been about 1800.

The 1798 text of Part 1 ends firmly with "FINIS", and it seems a fair conclusion that Cumberland then intended his uncorrupted primitive Greek Sophians to represent an ideal. There is no indication in Part 1 that he planned a sequel.

"The Captive of the Castle of Sennaar ... Part 2" was written, as he said, "to shew how much revealed religion, surpasses natural."[24] It may have been drafted any time before 1810, but the revision of the conclusion of the 1798 edition for printing in 1810 clearly anticipates the Christian tenor of Part 2; by 1810 Cumberland had at least the idea, if not the draft, of Part 2 "Exhibiting the fruits of ... revelation." After the second edition of Part 1 was printed, he wrote: "If I live I shall give a third edition corrected & add another volume to shew clearer my object."[25]

If Part 2 was drafted as early as 1800, this draft has been lost, presumably abandoned when the present clean copy was made. The surviving MS is written on sheets watermarked 1830 and 1831, with corrections on interleaved sheets watermarked 1834. Part 2 in its present state can be no earlier than 1834 – and it could have been written at any time up to Cumberland's death in 1848. But the chronology which seems most plausible to me is: a draft c. 1800 – at least by 1810; a new transcription c. 1830–31, with revisions in 1834–35.

There are with the manuscript two specimens proofs on unwatermarked paper with passages from Part 2, indicating that Cumberland looked into the feasibility of printing it. One bears text

24 MS note, Rylands copy of *The Captive* (1798).
25 MS in *The Captive* (1798) in Bristol Central Library.

from f.23 of the manuscript;[26] it is heavily printed on only one side of the leaf, there are a number of uncorrected typographical errors such as "neecessary" and "likety," and there are manuscript notes calculating the number of sheets required for the whole volume: "13 [*sheets*] − 10 [*leaves, i.e.*] − 14 sheets Demy 12°/ 29 lines [per page] 17 In[?] Pica then leaded 18 ems wide", with calculations of the effects of having "27" lines-per-page ("658" lines per sheet) as in the specimen (and in the 1798 *Captive* Part 1), or "2 lines more," "29" lines-per-page ("696" per sheet).[27] The type-face appears to me from about 1810, when *The Captive* Part 1 was reprinted with Cumberland's *Original Tales*. But there is no reference in *Original Tales* to a sequel.

The second proof specimen[28] is printed on only one side of the leaf with 14 lines from *The Captive* Part 1 second edition (1810), Vol. I, p. 85 (corresponding to 1798 pp. 69–70 corrected). This is followed by a space equivalent to 15 lines and a passage of 25 lines from the manuscript of Part 2, f. 61^{r-v}. The leaf bears no annotation save "10". Though the two proof specimens are the same page-size, this second one has the equivalent of 54 lines to a page and about 2.6 times as much text as the earlier proof. The type-face appears to my untutored eye to be of about 1835. The evidence of the specimens suggests, very tentatively, that Cumberland was getting information about printing *The Captive* Part 2 in 1810, when Part 1 was reprinted, and again about 1835, when the present draft of Part 2 was evidently completed.

The draft of Part 2 has remained with a group of Cumberland manuscripts. It was included with them in a printed "List of Works ... by the Late George Cumberland ... Now in the possession of his family." The Cumberland MSS evidently passed about 1873 from George Cumberland [Jr] to the dealer T. Kerslake, disappeared for half a century, were found about 1926 in the basement of the Manchester bookseller J.E. Cornish, and were then acquired by the firm of E.M. Lawson (of Birmingham), which sold them in June 1971 to E.B. Bentley & G.E. Bentley, Jr.[29]

---

26 Reproduced in Bentley, *A Bibliography of George Cumberland.*
27 There are 22 lines per page in *Original Tales* (1810).
28 Reproduced in Bentley, *A Bibliography of George Cumberland.*
29 Ibid.

THE TEXT OF PART 1

Five copies of *The Captive* (1798) have been discovered, all except
the one in the British Library corrected by George Cumberland.

1 Australian National University Library (pressmark: BRN
  736400), inscribed by John Deakin Heaton "Purchased at the
  sale of the Lib^y of [*Isaac*] D'Israeli Senr," presumably that at
  Sotheby's, 16–19 March 1849 (though *The Captive* is not listed
  there); it bears corrections on pp. 5–6, 8, 25–7, 89, 92, 95, 125–
  6, 173, 208;
2 Bodleian Library, Oxford University, with corrections on pp. 5–
  6, 8, 16, 25–7, 59, 89, 95, 125–6, 152, 173, 175, 208;
3 Bristol Central Library (B16855), with corrections on pp. 1, 26–
  7, 89, 173, 208;
4 British Library (12613.i.9);
5 John Rylands Library, University of Manchester (R98755), the
  Printer's Copy, with corrections on pp. 2–32, 34–52, 56–62, 64–
  89, 91–6, 98, 100–6, 109, 112–14, 117, 119, 122–39, 142–7,
  149–60, 163–5, 167–9, 173, 176–188, 190–8, 200–8.

The text of *The Captive* Part 1 presented here consists of the first
edition of 1798 (copy in Bodley) revised regularly as to substantives
and occasionally as to accidentals according to the second edition
of 1810. Most of the substantive changes in the 1810 edition were
authorized by Cumberland in the Printer's Copy (now in the John
Rylands Library). Most of the merely stylistic changes were made
by Cumberland's London agent C.H.B. Ker. (I have drawn atten-
tion in notes to substantive changes made by Ker in the 1810 edition
of which I think it likely that Cumberland would have disapproved.)
    Since the substantive changes not authorized by Cumberland in
the Printer's Copy rarely alter the meaning significantly, often
sharpen the point and improve the grammar markedly, and a few
of them may have Cumberland's authority or at least approval, I
have incorporated them all in the text printed here. At worst, these
changes can be identified in the "List of Substantive Emendations"
(Appendix I), and the original reading may be restored.
    I have also incorporated the marginal pencil changes in the Ry-
lands copy which were apparently made by Cumberland after the
1810 edition was printed.

The "accidental" changes to the 1798 text found in the 1810 edition are of three kinds:

1 Changes in house style, chiefly reduction of long "f" in 1798 to short "s" in 1810, omission in 1810 of parentheses around page numbers and of ligatures, and the addition in 1810 of generous leading between paragraphs;
2 Normalization of spelling, e.g., irregular changes of
   1798:   shew   gaoler   principle
   1810:   show   jailer   principal
3 Alteration of the very heavy punctuation, chiefly elimination and simplification in 1810.

The first kind of change is never found in the Printer's Copy, and the last two kinds are rare there. Evidently most were made solely on the authority of the compositor or of Cumberland's agent Mr. Ker. In respect of accidentals, therefore, the 1798 text is probably closest to Cumberland's intentions.

The text of Part 1 given here generally follows the 1798 text for accidentals. However, long "ff" has been reduced to short "f", ligatures are omitted, typographical and orthographical errors have been silently corrected when the 1810 text does so, and the punctuation of the 1810 text has occasionally been silently followed when the improvement is manifest. In a very few cases, chiefly relating to quotations, even the 1810 punctuation has been silently altered.

The sub-title of Part 1 ("The Sophians") is provided by the editor to match that for Part 2 ("The Reformed").

THE TEXT OF PART 2

The manuscript of *The Captive* Part 2 is, on the whole, clear, legible, and coherent; it is a clean but not a fair copy. There are a few manuscript additions, incorporated in the text here, and some deleted words, which are here ignored. The paucity of alterations suggests that Cumberland corrected as he transcribed the novel. In the few cases where there are alternative readings (e.g., "who whom") or self-contradictions (e.g., a redundant "not"), the irregularity is normally reported in the notes.

As a gentleman author, rather than a professional writer, Cumberland would certainly have expected his printer to make many

changes in translating his handwritten tale into type. His manu-
script is not fit for literal translation into print by the standards
either of Cumberland's time or of ours. I have tried to make such
changes as a printer of his time might have made, as follows:

1 I have *expanded* abbreviated terminations (e.g. "offerd" to "of-
fered"), written out "&" as "and," and given Arabic numerals
(e.g., "10") as words ("ten").

2 I have *regularized the spelling*. George Cumberland was an un-
certain orthographer, as may be seen in his vain gropings after
"hippopotamus" ("hippupotamis," "hypopotamos," "hypopota-
mii") and "hieroglyphic" ("hierogliphicks," "hierglyhic," "hiro-
gliphicks," "hiergliphical"). None of Cumberland's spelling habits
is consistent, but he tended to omit a silent "e," particularly in
the past tense (e.g., "tatood"), as well as virtually silent ones ("ad-
ministring"). He often omitted the "u" in words ending in "our"
like "vigour," and he doubled terminal consonants unnecessarily,
as in "shrubb" and "matt." I have regularized his spelling by the
standards of his time, though leaving a few characteristic eight-
eenth century forms such as "hieroglyphick" (but not "cloa-
thing").

3 I have added some *punctuation*, chiefly commas, periods, apos-
trophes for possessives, and quotation-marks – most quotation-
marks in the text are mine. I have deleted a few marks of punc-
tuation, mostly commas, mid-sentence periods, and dashes; and
I have altered some punctuation, primarily dashes to periods.

4 I have indented Cumberland's *paragraphs* – his are mostly flush
with the left margin. I have also created a large number of new
paragraphs, chiefly in dialogue, for both his paragraphs and his
sentences tend to run on at inordinate length.

5 I have *capitalized* Cumberland's lower-case letters at the begin-
ning of sentences and for proper nouns ("arab"), for "negro,"
and for "god." I have reduced to *lower-case* a number of capitals
which Cumberland seems to have made at random, particularly
with the letter "J" ("Joy," "Journey").

6 I have occasionally *altered the number of a verb*, for Cumberland,
like William Blake, was not scrupulous in making subjects and
verbs agree (e.g., "nature and religion has taught us" [p. 195] or
"one of the inmates are coming" [p. 200].

In all these respects, Cumberland was merely careless, and I have regularized his eccentricities as he would have expected his compositor to do.

Cumberland was addicted to connectives, such as "and," "for," and "but," which I have reluctantly allowed to stand. However, I have sometimes separated his very long sentences into two or three sentences by altering the punctuation.

Neither the printed Part 1 nor the manuscript Part 2 is subdivided into chapters. I have tried to mitigate this awkwardness by giving descriptive running-heads to the pages and adding chapter-divisions in Part 2.

The Captive
of the Castle of Sennaar

PART 1
THE SOPHIANS

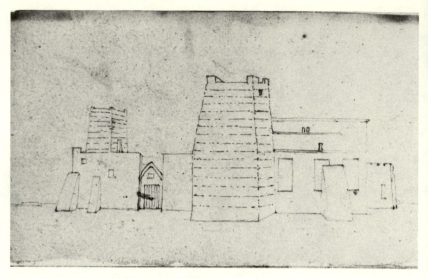

Sketch of "The Castle of Sennaar, as seen by Major Felix in 1828" inserted in the printer's copy of *The Captive* (John Rylands Library of the University of Manchester)

The Captive
of the Castle of Sennaar

An African Tale

CONTAINING VARIOUS ANECDOTES
OF THE SOPHIANS HITHERTO UNKNOWN
TO MANKIND IN GENERAL

by

GEORGE CUMBERLAND

London: Printed for the author; and sold
by Messrs. Egerton, opposite the Admiralty.
M DCC XCVIII

IN times so remarkable for political duplicity, religious hypocrisy, and barbarous ambition, to publish such mild correctives as moral tales seems at first sight a folly; yet to write gravely against the utter corruptions of this age of Gold, might, perhaps, be deemed a greater weakness, when in war, government, and even law, men seem to have made up their minds to be guided only by their pecuniary interests, their pride, and their passions. All, therefore, that can be advanced in the way of apology for these sportive wanderings after Truth and Nature, is, that there are always some readers who approve of independent thinking, and are happy occasionally to take up an author who is not guided by the fashions of the day; and that the professional Critics must be glad sometimes, by way of change, to relax a little with one of those disinterested writers, who, as I once saw a child do at a Carnival, run up to the crowd, and gently lift here and there, some ugly masks from better faces under them; faces, that if it were not for an idea that they must go with the stream of society, would blush to assume any mask whatever.

IMMURED WITHIN THE WALLS OF A CHAMBER constructed of
Egyptian granite, high suspended above the earth, and too strong
to nourish any hope of escape, even if I were inclined to make the
unpromising experiment; how can a man, habituated to confine-
ment, better pass away some of his vacant hours, than by recording
the singular relations of a departed friend, who could have no
motive to deceive him; who partook, while life remained, of the
same restraints; and kindly taught the companion of his fate to
mitigate its extreme severity?

It is, moreover, pleasing to indulge the idea, that these detached
Memoirs may one day be read in a clearer light than that, which,
arrested by the bars of a rude grating, chequers the paper on which
I inscribe them; that they may perhaps even fall into the hands of
some being of refined feelings, and convey to him the pleasing
consolation, that no events are capable of totally overwhelming a
mind enriched with useful knowledge, the love of the arts, sim-
plicity, and truth: — for such with opulent resources, the soul, at
certains moments, feeding on her gathered fancies, realises the
features of imagination.

That merciful first Cause, who frequently strengthens the mental
faculties of the blind, and secretly consoles the oppressed, has
cheered me also in my confinement with a venerable companion,
whose sweet and composed mind influenced my impatient sensa-
tions; and the silent remembrance of whose calm conversation, now
that he is taken from me, is dearer to my senses, than even liberty,
in a bad world, could possibly have been.

Holy shade of my departed friend! Shed thy complacent influ-
ence on thy solitary pupil, disciple, and admirer; who, while prac-
tising thy lessons of serenity, and philosophic resignation, consoles
himself, in his cell, with recording the pleasant pictures of thy
almost unknown country, and the agreeable communications of a
liberal-minded man!

Eyes exhausted with study, a constitution weakened by fatigue,
and a heart lacerated by disappointments, were the early fruits of
my too sanguine expectations. I had, before I was thirty, seen too
much to find any thing very interesting; and knew, alas! too well,
what was excellent in most things, to be likely often to meet with
that which I could approve.

---

* An ✒ in the left-hand margin beside a line of text indicates that an editorial note
  on material within the line is found in the Notes on the Text.

At this period, a train of long and melancholy events conducted me to the gloomy gates of a prison, of which, although for many years my sad abode, I know not to this day the secrets of the dark interiour. Too much afflicted to lift my eyes from the ground, I was rudely thrust forward into a cell, that I chose not to behold; and when the heavy door closed upon me, the sound of whose jarring hinges seemed to take away my breath, I fell senseless on the marble pavement that supported it. On recovering from this swoon, I found myself seated on a sopha, and supported by a venerable old man, who, with a pleasant smiling countenance, bade me be cheerful.

"Is this (said I, pressing his hand, which in a friendly manner had taken hold of mine), – is this the abode of cheerfulness? Have confinement and chains any thing to offer me in exchange for freedom, probably for ever lost? – No, (said I, the tears pouring down my cheeks, while I threw myself at his feet, in the extremest agony), if you talk to me of cheerfulness, restore me to light and liberty. – O Sir! if ever compassion touched your heart, let it now plead in behalf of an innocent man, who has been barbarously betrayed!" – Without attempting to speak or raise me, he suffered me to weep for some moments on his knees; when, surprised at his silence, I, at length, lifted up my head, to seek in his face for a reply; and perceiving his eyes swimming in tears, exclaimed, "Yes, yes, I behold my deliverer!"

The generous man, who guessed at my erroneous idea of his situation, by what had before escaped me, would not suffer my mistake to mislead me any longer. – "Companion of my confinement (said he), look for no other relief from me, than what my councils can afford: like you, I once experienced nearly all the bitterness of your present feelings, yet without such a friend as you have found to share them. – I, alas! am also here a prisoner! – But the invisible hand that bruised me, has bound up my wounds, and sent philosophy to teach me that resignation, which I despair not of making you partake of, when nature has done lamenting within you."

Though his words deprived me of my first hopes, yet, to my afflicted soul, as they were spoken they conveyed an unexpected ray of hope; and I rose up, to look at the man, or rather angel, as I then thought him, more distinctly.

He was tall, well proportioned, and seemed to be about sixty years of age, with fine silver locks, and a strong beard, that descended in waving lines to his girdle; his face was regularly proportioned, and his features were full of intelligence. – He had a small yellow turban on his head; and a fine white woollen garment reached to his feet, in many folds, fastened beneath the chest by a narrow black girdle and clasps of gold. – His feet were bare, but beneath them were light wooden sandals. He had a small oval gold ring in one ear, and the cuffs of his sleeves extended to the backs of his hands. Such was the interesting figure that then stood before me, and, with an air of benignity, held out his arms to embrace my emaciated form: taking me by the hand, "Come (said he, with a gracious smile), the sight of these bare walls contributes to depress your spirits, come into the apartment which I occupy; had I expected ever to behold again another human face as my guest, even this should have been adorned in a better manner."

But judge of my astonishment, when, on lifting up a piece of matting that covered a small door-way, he introduced me into a spacious oblong apartment, that seemed to be elegantly furnished, though not very well lighted; the walls of which were ornamented with about a dozen fine drawings, regularly arranged, and highly finished.

Above a flat cenotaph of white marble, of the justest proportions, and with the most beautiful ornaments, hung the portrait of a female of a divine countenance and figure, reposing on a sopha, and embracing a child as lovely as a cupid, while another lay sleeping at her feet. On the cenotaph were two bronze figures; and, in the middle, a vase of the same materials, which, for the richness of its workmanship, seemed inestimable; near it lay two rolls, richly bound, whose title I could not decipher; on each side were high bronze candalabra, with each its lamp of an antique form; and all round the chamber ran a low seat, which appeared underneath to be furnished with manuscripts in rolls, mathematical and musical instruments, and many things of forms to me unknown. But what most of all surprised me was, that, on one of the pictures nearest to me, I saw several figures employed, whose dress was altogether as singular as that of my new acquaintance: in a word, if before I was struck with horror on approaching my prison from its dismal outside, I was now equally confounded with astonishment, at the elegance of its interiour; a circumstance, which, considering the motives that had sent me thither, I was altogether at a loss to account for.

I had remained motionless some time, contemplating this incomprehensible scene, when the old man went up to the wall, extending his arms and looking back at me with a smile – "It is time (said he) to undeceive you; whatever you behold is only the effect of an agreeable art, and nothing is solid in this chamber but the four smooth walls, the bars of its windows, and the seats that surround it. "– So saying, he withdrew two pins that extended a sort of embroidered curtain at the upper end of the room, disclosing behind it a recess, with a small grated window, in which was placed his mattress, elegantly neat, and the sides and top of the recess were adorned with rich inventions in bas-relief.

"After what you have told me (said I), I am apt to distrust my sight; is that a real bed or not?" "It is (said he), assuredly, but the sculpture is not what it seems; you find all these ornaments agreeable, and I am happy in the opportunity of shewing you, that the appearance of even a dungeon may be considerably improved. – When you know how many of my leisure hours this operation has beguiled, your wonder will be diminished. – Sixteen years it has agreeably amused corroding thoughts; the materials are only charcoal and my finger; and you are the first stranger that has as yet inspected the effects of the operation.

"But we shall have time enough, I fear, to explain it all at our leisure. At present, take some refreshment, and retire to rest; compose your spirits a little; to-morrow we will talk of our situation, when, if you chuse it, you shall relate to me your story, and I in return will acquaint you with mine; which, I can assure you beforehand, is of a nature very uncommon; and such, as I hope, added to my precepts, is able to suspend at least your present chagrin, if not altogether to banish it from your mind."

The gay air with which he uttered all this, joined to the extraordinary scene before me, and his kind assurances, diffused a sort of calm over my before-agitated frame, and I not only ate heartily of the frugal meal he offered, but that night fell into a repose as sound, and uninterrupted, as my earliest fancy had ever enjoyed.

When I awoke, and the memory of the last evening's adventure returned, it appeared so like a dream, that, although the sun's rays shone on the gratings of my prison, I was at a loss to believe it real; but the quick sensation of poignant regret too faithfully confirmed the certainty of my immurement, and a strong suspicion of the duration of this captivity, smote so rudely at my heart, that I could not help breaking forth into loud lamentations. – "Cruel, accursed tyrant! (I exclaimed) may you yet feel *what I feel!*" A shower of tears followed, and I lay extended on my mattress like a man in despair. When, at length, looking up, I perceived the old man sitting in the window, the very image of patience and resignation; his action seemed to reprove me; but, till first spoken to, he uttered not a word; – when, without rising from his seat, he observed that the day was far advanced; and asked me in kind accents if I would partake with him of some slight repast; observing, that nature required repairs, especially after such immoderate grief.

The word *immoderate*, though expressed with a softened tone, recalled me to reflection; and I replied – "Good old man, whoever you are, your conduct, so much the reverse of mine, makes me blush." – "No, (said he) but you ought to consider, as you will soon, that complaint only weakens our powers of suffering, and that no situation is without consolation on this side the grave. Let me assure you, that I came hither only because I loved truth and liberty above all other earthly blessings, and was severed from all that makes existence desirable in the prime of life. – Yet am I now tranquil, easy, nay almost content, after a long and solitary confinement; deprived till now of all connection with rational society; let me repeat this to you, young man, and let it kindle in you a hope that you may also be one day composed and resigned if not happy".

I listened as to the voice of a parent, took some food from his honoured hands, and he continued his discourse.

"That you are destined to this abode for life perhaps, I can scarcely entertain a doubt, because my own confinement has so long continued, and I know so well the temper of the tyrant to whom this place belongs. – What has been the cause of your misfortune, if not too painful to recite, you will oblige me by confessing; that you may have been sent here without having done any thing criminal, I can readily conceive, both from a knowledge of my own innocence, and the ingenuous air of your countenance; – yet still, my child, whatever may have been your faults, or even crimes, do not hesitate in disclosing them to a man, now almost without passions (at saying which, he cast a tender look at the portrait of the female) "there is no situation that precludes amendment, if the heart be softened by repentance; no affliction for which the understanding has not an antidote; no suffering without its alleviation; except the satiety which springs from habitual unrestrained viciousness, and a totally corrupted heart."

"What! (said I, rising up, and clasping my hands together) will my good intentions soften the rigour of my confinement? will my virtues, for they brought me here, give light even to this sombre dungeon? – yes, venerable sage, when, like you, I am divested of my passions, they may perhaps, help me to be resigned; but now they only aggravate my misery, like a splendid but useless possession: for what active bent can they now take? whom can they serve? whom protect?"

"*Yourself* (said the venerable man, with ineffable sweetness), and the repose of your immortal mind: when cut off from society, the care of ourselves becomes doubly a duty. Perhaps I also may receive your benevolent services, and possibly I may convince you, that even this vast massy tower does not exclude us from assisting our fellow creatures."

"I blush (replied I), at my own selfishness and impatience; but bear with the petulance of a child. I hope to learn much from your example; yet own I cannot comprehend what you mean by our *here* serving mankind."

"Many things have I to relate to you (said he), that will shake your confidence, but this is easily explained; scarce a week passes in which I do not save many lives: I am now at the station of humanity, 'tis that which keeps me so close at this little window. – Come hither, and behold that dark spot in the stream, which so rapidly encircles the rocky promontory on which this castle is constructed. It is a sunken rock, on which, at my first imprisonment, while I was bewailing myself as the most unfortunate of the human race, I beheld a merchant-boat, filled with several families, strike and go down, while my ears and eyes were shocked with the cries and struggles of the unhappy sufferers. The event produced its full effect; and from that day I have considered it as my most pleasing duty, when the Nile is at a certain height, to give notice to all boats approaching by the stream of this invisible danger. Many have I preserved since that time; they hear my voice, but they see me not; and I observe, by their actions, that I pass for the good demon of the tower. Is not this some compensation for perpetual confinement? does it not give some importance to my irksome solitude? some scope to my virtuous powers? could I, if I had continued in the world, have hoped, in the same space of time, to have done so much good? You too may, perhaps, be indulged by me in a participation of this benevolent office, if you do not disdain these consolations: your voice is stronger, and you are young enough, if you pass your probationary studies in this science of humanity, to succeed, when I die, to the honours of my exalted post."

"Your words are life and light (said I). O, excellent philosopher! I am abashed before you: your commands shall in future be my laws; prepare to hear the abridged relation of my sufferings.

"I am a native of Europe, and was born in the city of Venice: my family is noble, and I am an only son – heir to considerable estates. – It was the wish of all my relations, that my education should further their prospects; the best masters were procured for me, my exercises were becoming my rank – my proficiency was corresponding; and, before twenty years of age, I was flattered, caressed, and ruined, by the partiality of all around me.

"A considerable match of interest was now contracted for me; but my heart disclaiming the connection, I made no scruple of refusing the alliance, and should probably, from the great influence I possessed, have escaped the censure of my parents, had it not been discovered, that my refusal arose from some previous engagements, contracted, during my studies at Padua, with the niece of my tutor, whose affections I had gained, unknown even to her uncle; and whom, in the boiling effervescence of my youthful passions, I had sworn to espouse, when time should make me master of my estate.

"The disclosure of this connection was instantly followed by her arrest; and when, with all the ardour of an enraptured youth, I flew to communicate to her our triumphs, I grew almost frantic at finding she was gone.

"After two years fruitless search, in which I exercised all the ingenuity and finesse of my countrymen, united to the zeal and impatience of a disappointed lover, I discovered the convent where she was concealed, and, by a bold, well executed manoeuvre, had the glory and the happiness to receive her in my longing arms – but this exquisite satisfaction was of short duration; for we were scarcely out of *Venice* when we were both arrested, owing to the superior vigilance of the government; and, after being torn from all that I valued in life, I found myself, almost the next instant, in the bottom of an accursed state-dungeon.

"Here I passed four whole years, pursuing the most intense studies, as an alleviation of despair; and refusing all compromise with our family, determined to prefer the honour of keeping an oath, to obtaining my liberty; till at length my parents, weary of this firmness, and unwilling to lose their only hope, set me free, on the condition of accepting a knighthood of Malta: – terms, which my vehement passion made me prefer to a perfidious alliance – and I embarked for the island, determined, by the severest service, to obliterate, if possible, the warmth of an enthusiastic passion; or, by perishing in an honourable manner, to extinguish my existence and my love together.

"It would be tedious to relate the adventures of a life so irregular as mine now became: debts, duels, and gaming, occasioned me many moments of remorse and chagrin; but, by this dissipation, my attachment only became stronger; and it was in vain I tried to suppress the calls of an affection, which had taken root in my very frame. Overcome by its force, I flew to the Grand Master, threw myself at his feet, resigned my honours, and returned almost distracted to my native country. – Then it was I arrived only to receive a dying father's embraces and fruitless repentance, to find myself in possession of a large estate, and to hear that my mistress had taken her vows of celibacy, and was lost to me for ever!

"Disgusted with every species of arbitrary power, weary of myself, and of mankind, my first resolution was to reform the abuses of the state, or to quit for ever the Venetian soil: but I was much too warm, and too sanguine, to prevail; and the idle attempt had nearly cost me all the honours and fortune to which I had just succeeded.

"Stung with this fresh disappointment, I meditated a voluntary exile; and having passed much time in the Mediterranean, I determined to make a voyage up the *Nile*, fondly flattering myself, that a new scene would afford an oblivion to my sorrows, or that time might conduct me to some spot, where freedom and happiness were united under the protecting shade of obscurity. – In this journey, taking a circuitous route I saw the miseries under which France groaned, the despicable state of the Spaniards, and the horrors of African tyranny; the brutal stupidity of the Turks, and the stupid brutality of the Egyptians: and, sick of civil absurdities, I determined to seek for men in a savage state. After a year's residence at Cairo, I laid my plan to penetrate, by the deserts, up the Nile; and, by the advice of some Turkish merchants, found my way into this detestable country.

"My retinue was splendid, my air was military: finding the king engaged in a war, I offered my services, from an idea that he was oppressed. My sword sustained his cause with effect: I returned to his capital to demand a passport and a convoy; but, conceive my astonishment, when he ordered me to be arrested, disarmed, and brought before him like a criminal.

"'You have fought well (said he), and I am obliged by your services; but you are a stranger, an adventurer, and, if I let you go, your valour may be one day as dangerous to me, as it has now been useful. We live here in continual suspicion; with us power is all and you must not hope to be exempt from the policy of my court. – If you had been a merchant, or a physician, I might have been prevailed on to permit your departure: as a foreign soldier, it cannot be allowed. Adieu, my friend – my officers will take care of your property; and you will be maintained, till your enlargement, at my sole expense.'

"From his presence I was instantly hurried to this place; but how I came here, I scarcely know, nor how long I was in coming; as rage and indignation from that moment almost deprived me of my mental faculties.

"You see, therefore, a lost man, whom love and virtue have undone. From the Bastiles of Europe, an escape might have been meditated with some prospect of success; but here, where the whole country is a prison, and its sovereign the jailor, what hope is left me, what consolation, but, in the goodness of your heart, to find what I have long sought in vain, and die in the arms of a real friend.

"Born to an exalted station, which promised much happiness, seeking it only by pursuits the most laudable, it has still eluded my grasp: Can it be, that where I least of all expected repose I should find it? Am I to receive my first lights within the walls of a state-prison on the Upper Nile, poor, a captive, and wronged? And shall a heart torn with disappointed passion find balm for its wounds in the forced retirement of a space like this?"

I here paused, and shed, in abundance, a warm shower of tears, that relieved my agitated breast with a medicinal virtue; – we both remained silent some minutes, and looking at each other with eyes of compassion; when finding I had no more to add, the patient man, calmly uniting his hands, and letting them fall upon his vest, began as follows:

"I embrace you, my child, and give full credit to all you have related; for your voice, your physiognomy, and your gestures, were it in the least your interest to deceive me, contribute to confirm the relation: for my own part, I hope I shall be able somewhat to soften your afflictions; when the mind is in a proper state, all places are alike; there is no dungeon can confine thought; and wishes, properly directed, tend only to the desire of that repose, which noble sentiments can confer, even within the bowels of the earth. – The passions are violent in mixed society, but, after a certain period, lose their force in confinement, or only agitate like distant rumours, and the sound of subsiding thunders; this I have learned from experience; for, although now aged, I came here in the prime of life, and left behind me not only all the delights that youth's happiest state can afford, but a country where, of all others, man seems to me to be blessed with the enjoyment of that mode of life for which he probably was created."

The latter part of his speech having excited in my features an air of satirical doubt, he quickly observed it, and added, "If your incredulity has already commenced, as I told you it would, prepare yourself to be still more staggered as I advance in the relation of those adventures, which I have promised to relate to you; yet if you find nothing in them that the state of mankind, and the construction of our organs, render impossible, nothing in them related but what your virtuous feelings would wish to exist; be patient to the end, and I engage you shall be a wiser man at the conclusion of my narration.

"But, as the hour of noon is fast approaching, it is time to repose; already has the sun arrested the travellers; the birds of prey are silent; and nature, in this climate, closes the eyes even of the crocodiles of the river: the Hippopotamos has descended to his cooling weeds, and the hyena to her lonely den; let us conform to the universal example, and when, refreshed by sleep, we are awakened by the notes of the reed sparrow, and the mild breezes of the evening, then let us commence my singular history."

I followed his advice, retired to my pallet by the window, and, on returning to the conference, was agreeably surprised to find the sage sitting again at his post, with a filtering jar of pure water beside him, some of which he was holding up in a glass to examine its brightness against the light, with all the gay ardour of a *bon-vivant*, mixed with the enthusiastic rapture of a devotional pietist: having quaffed it off, he presented me with another, "take it speedily (said he), and enjoy the innocent luxury, which my policy has procured for us both. Our jailor has been here whilst you slept, or you would have learned, by observation, the whole magic that I employ to render his uncouth manners subservient to my purposes. The tyrant, who sent us here, has not such good water; yet he would kill a subject to obtain it; whilst I, like Orpheus of old, bring it hither by virtue only of a few sounds of my guitar. – But you shall lose nothing by your nap (said he), an air may enliven you, and make your water more palatable." – He then took up a kind of Indian Mandolin, that lay at his feet, and began an *adagio*, which ran through my very soul: a native of Italy, bred in the bosom of harmony, was enraptured with finer sounds than he had ever heard; my ears were astonished, and my musical enthusiasm inflamed; I forgot for a moment our situation, and soon after he had concluded his dying strains, – "Where! Where! (exlaimed I) did you acquire this talent? Whence derive those melodies so new to my ear, yet so full of just proportion, and fine sentiment? – Every hour you astonish me; virtuous, humane, a painter, musician, all things seem to your accomplished mind alike easy to perform: in your society, confinement is no longer irksome. Proceed, my friendly guide, relate your adventures; after such a beginning, nothing will surprise me; he who possesses talents like yours will always procure confidence."

"Your eulogium (he replied) would have better pleased me at the end, than at the beginning, of our narrative; but when I reflect, that you have never resided in the Island of *Sophis*, I the rather excuse your wonder.

"My name is Lycas; my mode of life was, in its commencement, less rational than yours. I was born among the Greek subjects of the Grand Seignior, slightly instructed in a few ornamental arts, the child of an uncertain origin, perhaps the fruit of an illegitimate amour; – some personal accomplishments, and, what the world calls, ready talents, recommended me to the attendants of that court: I was first made a page to some ladies belonging to the Haram of Greek extraction, and afterwards got a more lucrative post; but the following accident in an instant entirely changed the tenor of my life.

"A Turk of some eminence, who presided in an office, from which the janizaries' pay was issued, and who had extensive dealings with money-changers, and people who trafficked much in the precious metals; had an attachment for one of the ladies of the haram: this man, whose passions were violent in the extreme, used every means to carry on an illicit correspondence, and selected me, as one of the most adroit young men of the palace, to further his views. To this end he began by distant flattery, agreeable presents, and sometimes by open praise before my superiors, to ingratiate himself in my esteem. On a sensible mind, just beginning to expand, this species of conduct operates as an irresistible charm; I fell into the snare prepared for me, with pleasure, and without hestitation, after a very short period, would have scaled the walls of the palace, at the risk of my life, to promote his wishes. The event, as might, by a more experienced mind, have been expected, was the momentary gratification of his unbridled passion, the death of his unhappy mistress, and my total disgrace.

"Dismissed from the seat of ease and luxury; ignorant of the world, and suddenly plunged into the streets of Constantinople, well dressed, but poor, and without a friend, my senses were confounded like a man's after falling from a precipice; I looked around me, and all was strange, – but the first thought that occurred to me was to enquire after the residence of a merchant who dealt in trinkets, and whose presents had been employed to seduce me from my duty. The man was a Jew, well known, and easily discovered. He received me with cordiality; but soon shewed an anxiety to be detached from me, on learning, from my own lips, the story of my dismissal and its motive.

"'You are a lost child (said he), you must fly this city, if you would be safe; disgrace is here soon followed by ruin; let me persuade you to your good. I have a correspondent, a merchant, who travels into Upper Egypt annually, to barter commodities in exchange for gold dust; he wants an assistant; Egypt is the country where Turks thrive best; you may yourself become a merchant in time; a fine figure like yours is always a passport; your good sense, your good heart, which here has undone you, may there contribute to your fortune.'

"There was no need of so many fine arguments to induce a curious youth, who had forfeited all his friends, to travel: the thoughts alone of a voyage would have been to me sufficient; I readily embraced his offer, and, in a very short time, discovered, that nothing makes travelling agreeable but independence.

"We landed at Alexandria, and sailed through the Delta to Cairo, without meeting with a single adventure worth relating: My master was a Jew, and perhaps the most taciturne of his tribe; a reserved habit, which the perils of his trade had brought on him, seemed to characterise his nature: yet I found nothing unkind in him; on the contrary, many instances of his humanity marked the progress of our voyage. – Severe to himself, scrupulous, and timid in outward appearance, yet continually exposed to the greatest dangers, I knew not how to reconcile these appearances to his choice of life; but an accident disclosed his soul to me, and, from that moment, my contempt of his character changed to the most settled esteem. I had often angered him, often offended him by my volatility of temper; my careless loquacity seemed to prepare an irreparable breach; but, in taking me out of Constantinople, I thought he had saved my life, and my nature was corrected by a lively principle of gratitude. At *Yambo* he fell ill, and would have died, or been murdered, but for my care, and youthful courage – the impression it made on him, seemed to have entirely changed his reserved conduct; and, from that moment, I experienced a very different treatment. You are worthy of my whole confidence (said he, after his recovery); whether it arises from your principles or your heart, I owe to you my life: though the ties that united us were slight indeed, yet I have experienced from your care, attentions that my own children have denied me: your gentleness has healed the wounds, inflicted, many years past, by their unkindness: *be my son, and I will be a father to you.*

"You may readily conceive how gladly I accepted so disinterested an offer: he communicated his whole plan of life to me, shewed me the perilous voyages he had undertaken from mere disappointment of happiness at home, and laid before me, with a fatherly kindness, all the risks we had to encounter before we arrived at the end of our dreary journey. In passing the kingdom of Sennaar (said he), we shall be hemmed in with troubles: Abyssinia will afford us some pleasant scenes, but when we have crossed those vast regions of mountains that are the sources of the Nile, and the south of Africa opens to our view; though wealth approaches us, danger is ever at hand; – we shall have to deal with the inhabitants of the river Zebee, whose tribes are wandering, and the country ill calculated for commerce; and, when our traffic is happily completed, the return offers a picture of disasters very difficult to avoid; but, should we get safely back, we will travel no more; I have found a being worthy of my confidence – and you alone shall be my heir while we enjoy, in repose, the reward of my long-procrastinated labours.

"We passed up the Red Sea to a considerable port; and travelled, with few accidents, through this accursed kingdom of *Sennaar* (under whose intolerable tyranny we now groan), meeting with every accommodation we could wish for in the Abyssinian dominions: we passed above the fountains of the Nile, and descended the river Zebee, where we had the good fortune to complete our objects of commerce very profitably, having made a large purchase of gold dust: my conductor was elated with his uncommon success, and attributed all his good fortune to my resolute assistance.

"We then prepared to return, but the hospitable Africans, with whom he had dealt honourably, would not let us go till we had partaken of a festival; and, the whole tribe being assembled, the day was passed in jollity and dances. – The honest Israelite for once unbent intirely, he became another man, and we communicated our ideas with the rapidity of those who are exhilarated with wine: – 'Why (said I), should we leave this happy climate, where peace seems to reign in comparison to the country we have quitted, to return through the nations of villains we have seen? The farther I go from Constantinople, the happier I feel.' – 'Son (said he), your observations are just, yet habit and the love of wealth lead us back: the first voyage I made, I felt the same sentiments; but what would you say, if you knew, that a few weeks farther journey to the south-west, there exists a people, who so much surpass these in all the enjoyments of life, that those few, who know them, speak of their country with rapture. They inhabit peaceably an island in the upper end of the lake of Zambree; and, without gold, or scarcely clothing, seem, if one may judge from accounts of them, to be *the very happiest, the most beautiful, and the best people on earth.* – But, as they have no wants beyond their own island, and no commerce whatever with the rest of mankind, it is difficult to learn many particulars of their habits of life.'

"His assertions excited my curiosity exceedingly; 'naked, without gold, without commerce, without war, and happy, said I, you astonish me; – what then are we doing? wherefore do we risk life, when happiness is so near at hand? I am as a leaf before the wind; you own you have no connexions in Europe that you esteem, why should we not then, now we are so near this blessed spot, attempt to visit it? Come, my father, let us go, who is there can hinder us?'

"By such discourses as these I strove to persuade him, and we continued long in conversation on the subject; but, when he found I was heated by the descriptions of an old African, a native of Caffraria, whom he called on to vouch for the facts he had related, and seemed resolved on the adventure, he endeavoured to dissuade me, by a contrasted account of the difficulties we should have to encounter, on our way, to get among, what he now called, these naked savages. The more he objected, the more I was inflamed by opposition: we drank, we reasoned, we disputed; and in the end, the old Caffre having offered to become our guide, my ascendancy prevailed over all his scruples, and, overcome by a real affection, he embraced me with warmth, swearing, by the God of his fathers, that, whatever it might cost us, my honest curiosity should be gratified. The next morning, however, he seemed to repent of his oath, and came to me, with a string of apprehensions, that nothing but my unshaken resolves could have overcome: we accordingly, after partaking of all that African hospitality could produce, accompanied by the old Caffre, commenced our uncommon journey.

"He was armed with the weapons of his nation, two spears and a shield; I had an European double-barrelled gun, and my master was not without instruments of defence. For the first week, our path lay through the most fertile country imaginable; vast forests of shady trees, thronged with birds and antelopes; healthful springs, and beautiful lakes surrounded us, but we afterwards found the road less agreeable, sandy desarts, brackish waters, and scanty provisions, succeeded; some scattered hordes occasionally alarmed us, more with their looks than their hostility; for we always found them harmless, and at last even I began to abate of my enthusiasm for the island in the lake of Zambree. As to my master, he said little, but I could see he deeply repented his condescension, and began to entertain fears for our success, although he had no suspicion of our guide: we, however, pursued our journey, among hordes of Caffres, whose generous hospitality surpassed our expectation. In this manner we continued journeying onwards, our difficulties encreasing, as we advanced into a mountainous country; and, two months having been already expended, came to the swampy margin of a mighty river.

"Here, our guide told us, it would be necessary to pursue our way upwards, till we could find some means of crossing the rapid stream; and afterwards to ascend some very high mountains, beyond which we should see the commencement of the lake of Zambree, whose vast extent must be traversed, until we could throw ourselves among a nation on its borders, to pass the winter; there, before the dry season, we might get proper animals to conduct us to the head of the lake; and, being well supplied with provisions, a fortnight's journey on the desert part of its coasts, would conduct us to a marshy neck of land, that, during one month alone, at that time of the year, opened a communication with the island in question.

"We were both appalled at the description of the difficulties yet
to be subdued; but to return was now too late, although we all
found, we had somehow miscalculated the distance. The worthy
Israelite, however, notwithstanding our united care, and the sa-
lubrity of the climate, sank at least under the continual anxiety and
fatigue we were obliged to undergo; and, before we could even
approach the quarters where we designed to repose, a fever seized
upon his spirits, that no efforts could remove.

"Thus situated, we formed for him a verdant hut, by a spring,
under the shade of some spreading trees, on the borders of a
mountain, and near the edge of the lake, which now had all the
appearance of an unbounded ocean. Here we rested some days,
while our guide, hoping to cheer his employer's spirits, en-
deavoured to persuade him, that the island we sought, was indi-
cated by a long cloud that seemed to reclined on the bosom of the
water; but the distance was too great, to afford much consolation
to the worn-out and weather-beaten traveller. – 'I shall never reach
it (said he); you perhaps will, who have youth, strength, and cur-
iosity, to conduct you: may the event answer your expectations! In
which case, I counsel you, never, if you can avoid it, to return: and
although the wealth I resign to you may probably be of no great
use among the people whom you are going to visit; yet preserve
it, lest, as I suspect, your stay not being permitted there, on your
return to the contaminated part of the world, you should perish
for want of resources.'

"With such-like discourses, many of which made me conjecture,
that he knew much more of this country than he chose to com-
municate, were we entertained during our stay; but his fever en-
creased daily; and finding, at length, that his life approached to
its close, he joined my youthful hand to that of the old Caffre,
recommending me to his care, in the most earnest manner; and,
taking his solemn oath of fidelity, embraced us both, adding, with
almost his expiring breath – 'My son, confide in this man – he is
virtuous, though poor; in our dealings he has never deceived me;
and he alone, of all his tribe, has visited the island of Sophis, at the
head of the lake Zambree; where, during the short stay permitted
him, he learned good and generous habits by example: your in-
clinations are right, though you come from a bad seminary; may
the sight of these people of virtue inspire you with a lasting affection
for its practice! When I am dead, bury me in this tranquil spot;
raise a pile of twelve stones over my body; and, should you ever

return, you will pause to shed a pathetic tear to the memory of your departed friend.'

"I could only answer him by my affectionate looks and tender embraces; he died, and, after piously fulfilling his last request, I resolved to pass here the season of the summer rains, being encouraged thereto, by my desire of preserving his honoured ashes from the inroads of wild animals, and by the advice of the old Caffre, who assured me that we should be able to maintain ourselves very well with our arms; and, that early on the closing of the wet season, our cattle being refreshed would be able to conduct us, with ease, in two months, to the borders of the desert, from whence we must gain the desired island.

"With the aid of my African friend, I soon raised a kraal, circular, lofty, and with a small aperture at the top, to let out the vapour: a circumstance to which he very unwillingly consented, alledging, that we should lose all *the benefit of the smoke* in the winter, when it would be most conducive to health; and I was obliged to contrive a moveable cover, in order that, during the night at least, we might be medicated with this fine fumigation.

"Nor could I, without smiling, reflect on the contrast of my present and former situation: nursed in the elegance of a Turkish seraglio, accustomed to artificial baths, splendid clothing, ostentatious festivals – to live in crowds without reflection, and perform the ceremonies of religion, without piety. – Here I found myself in a situation that no European had ever before reached: among men nearly in their natural state; my covering, untanned hides; my lodging, the ground; my food, such as my arms could procure on the side of a mountain, not unfrequented by beasts of prey; and with a companion, whose language I could but little comprehend: a circumstance which proved the most vexatious of all, as it prevented me from forming any idea of that of the nation I was going to visit, and of whose customs and manners, I was particularly solicitous to gain some information. My old master spoke the Caffre tongue fluently, but I had only acquired enough to supply the wants of life: however, by means of interrogations, varied infinitely, and the aid of intelligent signs, he made me comprehend, that these Sophians lived a life according to nature, in a fertile country; that gaiety was their characteristic; humanity their religion; and equality among them is as nearly general: while want and disease were almost unknown. But what most of all surprised and delighted me was, that in the words he pronounced, as appertaining to their tongue, I discovered a great similarity to the sounds and accent of the modern Greek. This unaccountable similarity, which, I some-times began to think, was only a conceit raised by my fancy, re-doubled my before-heated curiosity to go amongst them; and I thought the rainy months of summer would never end, although very agreeably situated, full of health and strength, enjoying free-dom, a real friend, and possessed of wealth enough (if wealth could have done me any great service here) to maintain a large family. – On that head, he explained to me, that the gold I carried was in high esteem among the Sophians, who possessed none of it in their own country; but why they valued it, or how they made use of it, he could never succeed in making me comprehend.

"In such enquiries as these, or rather attempts at enquiries, we passed all our leisure hours; when often, in pursuit of antelopes, being carried to the borders of the lake, we retired into a spacious refreshing cave; near to which, I was, one day, very much surprised to find, on the surface of a rock, the sculptured figure of a man, with a venerable beard: a work much worn by time, but indicating the traces of great skill; and near him a naked youth, of a most beautiful countenance, whom he seemed in the act of caressing. The place was surrounded with a magnificent grove, overhung with climbers, and many flowering shrubs grew spontaneously around; while the waves of the lake came, on a fine shallow, up to the very roots of the trees, forming a circular bay, after washing over a yellow, and almost transparent sand. – The youthful figure, which resembled a winged Cupid, was seated on an elevated rock; its action was, I thought, very majestic; and was aided, in a great measure, by the skill of the artist, who had contrived to make him above twice the size of the old man; and to add another figure, of the same noble character, but without wings, reposing in his bosom; and, oddly enough, inserted, as in a cell, by which, having been preserved from the injuries of time, it was left in fine pre-servation.

"To this remarkable place, the old Caffre had conducted me, as it should appear, rather with a view of enjoying a fresh spring that trickled down the side of the rock, than from any other motive of curiosity: for he seemed to take no notice of the figures; and to all my enquiries, on that head, only answered by pointing towards that part of the horizon where the island was supposed to lie, and pronouncing the word *Sophis*, while he placed his hand on the body of the marble: and, hence, I began to conjecture that they were a nation of idolaters, who had wandered from the Nile.

"We found on this spot many fruit trees, plantains, and cocoa nuts; also a tree, whose fruit resembled bread, and, when dressed, was to me a delicious repast: wild vines also grew here, but as their fruit was unripe, I could form no idea of the quality of the grape.

"All these circumstances served only to sharpen my impatient ardour to terminate this voyage; but no eagerness on my part could persuade my companion to stir till, according to his judgment, the proper season arrived; and his observations on the sky seemed to be his guide, united with the remarks he made on a particular plant, which put forth monthly shoots.

"At length, the so much wished – for day happily dawned: our two camels having quite recovered their flesh seemed as alert as ourselves; and having completed their lading, I dropped the tear of affection over the grave of my foster-father, and set forward, on my journey, with the Caffre, and his three dogs, not one of which perhaps would he have parted with, for half my gold; an article, about which he seemed always very indifferent; for once, when a valuable packet fell from one of the beasts, he smiled and by signs, expressed that we had better leave that mischievous yellow sand where it was, than take the trouble to put it up again."

Here the companion of my confinement made a long pause, and then added, "I feel myself rather exhausted; you are probably in the same condition; night approaches, and as I have brought my history to its first period, we will, if agreeable to you, postpone its continuance till to-morrow afternoon. When the heat of the day begins to decline, then conversation is doubly agreeable, as a pleasing relaxation after the labours of the morning, and the refection of noon: the pleasure of your society, perhaps, makes me too talkative; but, to-morrow, if I do not mistake, you will have your share."

He then rose up to depart, received my warm thanks with a benevolent inclination of his head, and I returned to my pallet, so full of his history, that my dreams were mixed with affecting and confused imagery. I fancied myself with him near the grove, saw the cave, the flowering shrubs; and then, on a sudden, dreamt that my first, and only love, loving and lovely, came gliding towards me with inimitable gracefulness, and a countenance glowing with the noblest sensibility; that she embraced me with tenderness, dried my tears with her flowing hair, and entreated me, with a soft suffocating voice, to be calm; and we should never never more be parted!

The agitation of this seraphic vision awoke me just as day had begun to dawn; the night-dews hung in great drops on the bars of my window; I started up, received them on my feverish lips, and exclaimed – "unsullied messengers of the regions of air, ye cannot be more pure than were our mutual affections! why then were we forsaken?"

Scarcely had this impatient exclamation escaped me, when I was recalled to myself by the enchanting sounds of the old captive's melodious airs, the notes of which were, at that moment, a balm to my burning imagination; and, at the same time, they pictured to my mind my present fate, and reminded me of the courage of him, who was the companion of my miseries.

Ashamed of this weakness, I presently rejoined my friend, with a countenance of as much serenity as I could assume; and being seated on the sopha of marble by the window, after his usual attentive enquiries, he thus continued his entertaining narrative.

"I left off, my son, on our journey to the island rather abruptly, but not without design: I perceived, that your curiosity had been excited by the adventures on the road, and I wished to keep it alive.

"We continued travelling during the space of three weeks along the banks of the great lake, whose waters are slightly brackish, but not salt; always resting at night, either in caves, or under a temporary kraal; and living on such game as the ancient forest, which skirts it, supplied in abundance: but when we arrived at the head of the lake, which made our road take to the east, it became necessary to seek the negro colony, of which my guide had spoken, in order not only to lay in a provision of grain, but also of water: for the remainder of the way, he assured me, would be both barren, and void of wells and shelter; that we should have no other guides but the stars, the waves of the lake, and his feeble experience. Among his worthy countrymen, we found the most hospitable reception; our wants were supplied, our very wishes anticipated, and our property remained in the most perfect security. They seemed rather a timid and gentle race, yet strong, tall, and finely formed; their women, even to me, who had from my youth been accustomed to the sight of Asiatic beauty, appeared very noble creatures; and their simple manners not a little endeared them to my heart.

"After a short stay we took our leave, parting with mutual cordiality, but we carefully concealed from their enquiries, the destination of our voyage; as their countryman knew had they suspected such to be our intention they would never have permitted us to take to the desert, for they entertained such a perfect horror of the waste at the upper end of the lake, that if they had thought we meant to attempt to travel into it, they would have confined us, out of pity, as madmen.

"For my own part, I will not conceal from you, that, however strongly my curiosity had been excited, I began at this period of our journey to tremble at the undertaking. A thousand anxious thoughts crowded on my heated fancy; noxious winds, burning sands, venemous reptiles, and the night-wandering animals of a wild waste, were united with famine, disease, and drought. My guide also seemed to have lost his accustomed gaiety; and the first night that we lay down between our camels on those burning sands, without a prospect of shrub, water, or hill, all my feelings were so affected, by the expanse around us, that I enjoyed but very little repose.

"The next day's lonely journey brought us very near the margin of the lake, from whose surface a refreshing breeze sprang up, that considerably cooled the air; and thus we went forward, always sleeping within view of its borders, which were covered with birds to me unknown; when, on the fourteenth day, at sun-rise, I beheld, to my inexpressible satisfaction, the boundaries of the ridges of that island to which all my wishes extended themselves.

"Hitherto we had encountered no animals of prey; but, at this spot, we saw, on the sands, distinct traces of the feet of hyenas, and of course became doubly vigilant.

"The country before us had no forests, or even underwoods; but the whole borders of the lake were, to a considerable distance, green, with large juncs and reeds: the seat, as my Caffre told me, of multitudes of ostriches and bustards: the truth of which was the next day confirmed by our seeing a drove of these before us in the distance, and lighting on a nest, from whence we took fresh eggs; all which circumstances were signs that seemed not a little to cheer my good guide, who now assured me we had nearly conquered all the difficulties of our perilous undertaking.

"That night we supped in uncommonly good spirits; I was even gay, and slept soundly; but towards morning was suddenly awakened by the loudest clap of thunder I had ever heard, and on opening my eyes saw the whole hemisphere darkened around, with dusky and sulphureous clouds, among whose bellying curtains lucid flashes of forked lightening darted with inconceivable fury.

"The awful peals, which continually pursued each other, the solemn stillness of the air, and the fiery meteors that burst exuberantly around us, petrified with astonishment even the old African, although early accustomed to such tremendous exhibitions: and, for my own part, I must confess, that my whole frame seemed to contract with terror; expecting no less than total annihilation, when the camels lay down and moaned, while the dogs crept near to us, crouching to the earth; both of them strong symptoms of some fearful approaching crisis. All this while not a drop of rain fell; but the air seemed scorching hot, and infected with a burning vapour; insomuch, that our respiration was sensibly impeded by its pressure.

"At length, after a violent and sudden gust of wind that involved us in a cloud of sand, there followed such a shower of heavy drops, that, had we not made the beasts rise, and stood under them and their packs, we must, by its force, have been nearly swept away. In an instant, the thirsty sands were converted into a shallow lake as far as the eye could explore; and, shortly after, lay smooth and humid as the shores of the sea recently abandoned by the tide. The clouds passed speedily over us, opening and shewing, at intervals, the brightest patches of ether; and, at length, scudding away entirely, exhibited a serene and delightful canopy, whose contrast with the yellow sands, blue tops of the island, and deep green waters of the lake, made one of the noblest and simplest landscapes, my eyes had ever beheld.

"Joy at our escape, the thoughts of our journey being near its close, the fineness of the day, and success of our uncommon voyage, expanded my bosom with the most unfeigned benevolence; while, from the overflowings of gratitude, my heart swelled, and beat against my breast; – I felt the animating glow of true piety to nature, and went on in a sort of enthusiastic exultation, that felt like a divine phrensy.

"Inspired by perceiving the precious link of the chain that bound and united my existence with the universe – *O Holy Energy!* (I exclaimed), *that imaginedst me, where art thou? thou answerest my sighs, yet I cannot shadow thee forth; I feel thy universal influence; thou pervadest me throughout; impalpable essence, I shall see thee; I shall know thee; thou art* Love!

"During these sublime reveries, I seemed to tread the air, and had advanced so hastily, that my guide, who was almost out of sight, gave a shrill whistle to recall my steps: – When he joined me, we were at the very edge of the lake, into whose cool and refreshing water all instantly plunged, with the eagerness of aquatic fowls after a long flight; abundance of which were then making airy circles over our heads, and displaying their gay plummage to the sun.

"We took up our lodging at this place, in full view of the island so long the object of my desires; but how we were to arrive there without a canoe was still to me an inexplicable mystery: it was soon, however, explained, for at peep of day, the African, to my great alarm and astonishment, led our camels right into the wave; and I then found that we were advancing upon broad shoals, covering a bottom, smooth, and every where visible to the eye: it was chiefly composed of little white shells, solid like cowries, but considerably smaller, and interspersed with others, of such beautiful colours, that the whole seemed a natural Mosaic, full of exquisite but irregular ornaments, rich as the carpets of the country I was born in, but infinitely more brilliant: and, to complete the enchanting picture, shoals of gold and silver fish frequently darted across our way, making regular pauses, as if they were plying their transparent fins to music.

"A long day, spent in travelling in this manner, seated quietly on our cattle, seemed to have passed in an instant. I was giddy with sensations of delight, and felt elated to extravagant admiration. The old man also seemed to partake of the intoxication, singing to the camel's splashing steps almost all the way, a monotonous, but plaintive strain, that pierced my very entrails; for it recalled to my remembrance too much of my lost country, and those still evenings, when, on the Bosphorus, our sailors, returning home, chaunt, to the sober stroke of their steady oars, a thousand heartfelt strains, under the walls of the seraglio.

"Tear after tear of the sweetest water rolled over my youthful cheeks; I panted to communicate my thoughts; and, for the first time in my life, now began to comprehend that there was a value in the other sex, which I had not hitherto sufficiently appreciated.

"At night we lodged on a little rocky island, covered with a shelly beach, but destitute of large trees; and it was here my guide contrived to explain to me, the reason why we were obliged to select our season with so much precision: for it was only during one month in the year, when a certain wind prevailed, that these shoals were fordable, as its effect was to drive the waters from the higher to the lower end of the lake; and, by this means, to render, once in the year, the island of Sophis accessible. The storms also, that usually accompanied this wind, contributed not a little to this purpose, as, by flooding the sands suddenly, they forced the beasts of prey to retire to another quarter, and thence also preserved the island from their invasions.

"Every new trait contributed to exalt my ideas of this happy place: and it encreased my satisfaction considerably, to hear it was also exempt from noxious reptiles; or, at least, that it was inhabited by none whose venom was of a deadly and cankerous corrosiveness, such as I had beheld the effects of in Egypt, stealing, with a bitter malignity, through the crimson stream of life, and, with subtle poignancy, boring towards the heart.

"Mine beat high, when he told me that, the next day, we should probably see some of the *Sophians*; for that, at this season, it was not uncommon to find them on the bank on which we were to repose, come to collect those beautiful shells, or diverting themselves with observing the motion of the glittering fishes.

"The near approach to these people made my bosom flutter with impatience, and filled my imagination with a million of images; at one time, I fancied they would, as to person, be much like the nation I had left; for I doubted all my information concerning them; then again, I pictured them as magnificently dressed, and profusely decked with gold and jewels; sometimes I thought they would be warlike and rude, then soft and effeminate; but my great regret was, that I should not understand their language; still I could not forget the remarkable words of my old master – '*That they were the happiest, the most beautiful, and the best people on earth.*'

"Nor will I conceal from you, what my selfishness and pride at that time kept me ignorant of, that among the motives which then influenced my conjectures, some there were which did no credit to my heart. – Who knows, thought I, but these people may possess the precious gems, so much valued in Europe, which their simplicity may induce them to part with for a trifling consideration? Shall I not also, at my return, be accounted a great traveller, and be thence honoured by my countrymen? Who can tell but my gold may purchase for me some of their most beautiful females, whose charms might make my fortune at Constantinople? – These, and other unworthy thoughts, the fruits of an European education, passed slightly over the mind, as unwilling to disclose, even to myself, the secret baseness of my soul: nay concupiscence, as it were unknown to me, had contributed to provoke my curiosity; and I almost openly ventured to think of forcibly revelling in the arms of some of their women of the most accomplished forms. Ah! little indeed did I know them, as you will see by the sequel; little also did *I know myself.*

Among a less virtuous race, probably my nature might have been soon entirely corrupted; but he who has visited the Sophians, must be made of the grossest material, if their example does not, in some degree, purify his heart.

"I will not any longer exercise your patience, as mine was exercised by the rest of the journey: two more days brought us to a small island, covered with lofty trees, we plainly saw both men and habitations at a distance. The instant we reached the so-much-desired shore, my conductor fell prostrate on the earth, and kissed it fervently; and, as it were by instinct, I followed his example. We found ourselves in a meadow covered with flowers of every dye, a rich pasture for our cattle, and under the shade of a lofty clump of cocoa and cabbage trees, we sat down to repose. Some very fine cows were near, walking slowly into a cave under a little ridge, which seemed the first stage of an irregular and pensile country, whose mountains were all graceful verdant swells, crowned with majestic groves to the topmost hill of the little island.

"This is not Sophis (said my guide), but is closely connected with it, and is famous for its pasture for cattle; it also abounds in eggs of various birds, and has many warm springs, whose waters encrease the milk of cows." – While he was explaining, with difficulty, all those particulars, a flock of birds of the parrot kind flying by, I shot amongst them, and brought three or four to the ground; but, on preparing to repeat my shot with the other barrel, the old man snatched my gun with as much agony as if I had committed murder, and running to gather up the birds, was attempting to hide it in a bush along with them, when suddenly there came forth, from the cave, above a dozen of the stoutest and best made men I ever beheld, of dark complexions, with short curling hair, and nearly as adorned by nature.

They ran up to him, seized my guide, the camels, and the dogs, in an instant; and two of them approaching me, payed me the same compliment, but without any menacing air. Indeed that would have been quite unnecessary; for, beside that, it was not my intention to make any resistance, having been assured by my guide that we should be arrested by the first people we met, on account of our strange appearance; all opposition would have been useless, as their Herculean strength was nearly sufficient to lift me into the air.

We were now conducted to the cave, whose front was an oblong entrance of three enormous masses of white marble, rudely laid together on two uprights, the ends being rocks, with a threshold

of the same materials, and two long squared pieces at its entrance,
forming a kind of benches in a rustic porch, near the centre of
which was a bason of the purest water. The men seated themselves
with us on the square benches, our camels were brought into the
area, and the first thing they did, was to bring out large earthen
bowls of milk, which they offered without any ceremony, both to
us, to our camels, and to our dogs. All this while not a word was
spoken; but presently there came from the interior of the cave,
with a slow but unaffected pace, an aged man, whose beard was
full, folded up in a woollen garment as white as snow, the broad
edges of which were of the brightest scarlet; he had a long ebony
stick in his hand, with a crutch handle on the top of it, on which,
when he stopped, he leaned, by placing it under his arm.

We rose on seeing him, for his noble presence seemed to com-
mand respect, and with us rose several of the young men; but on
his coming nearer to us, as if with an intention of speaking, a little
boy ran up, and pulled his robe violently, from a seeming motive
of fear of us. He turned back, took the infant in his arms, kissed
him, covered him with his drapery; and, looking at one of the
youths, to my unutterable astonishment, in a language that was so
nearly modern Greek, that I perfectly understood him, asked where
they had encountered the intruders, and if there were others of
our nation on the island?

"'I hope not (said the youth to whom he addressed himself), for
they are evidently of a bad race, as we found them in the exercise
of cruelty; killing the birds of the air who do them no harm; and,
after having passed the dangers of the shoals, they are come hither
to disturb our peaceful tranquillity with noisy instruments of death.'

"'My child (replied the old man), they do wrong only from
ignorance of a better life, and are to be pitied more on that account
than any other. By chance, or want of guides, they have, probably,
been driven here from the main land, where you know I have often
told you the worst habits of life prevail: all other nations but our
own live by the destruction of the works of the good Being, whose
office is to create: we alone are acquainted with the sublime truth,
that to preserve is better than to destroy; let their instruments of
death be broken, but let the men be taken care of, and debarred
from mischief; while they are treated with humanity, kindness will
soften them, or fear keep them in order, till the time comes for
transporting our superfluities to the main land; and then they may
be banished along with our supernumerary bulls and rams, and

will be useful to drive and disperse them in the wilderness. In the mean time, let their strange beasts be looked after, with whatever they carry, so as to be scrupulously restored to them at their departure: nor let any one, out of foolish and unjust curiosity, look into their contents; things of no apparent utility to us, may, to these men, be of infinite value, in their way of barter; and never let it be said, that the genuine adherents to human rights infringed the prerogatives of others.'

"Having thus concluded his orders, he was about to return into the cave, when the old African ran towards him, caught him by the garment, and then, falling almost prostrate, crossed his arms on his bosom, and, with a look of admiration and fear, uttered the word, *Yahomy*.

"'*Yahomy!*' (said the old man, turning round quickly, and lifting him from he ground), is it possible, can it be you? Why do you again invade us, and with such barbarous manners, and a companion so wild and savage? Has all our kindness to you, when in distress, been thrown away? This is rather ungrateful from a man who seemed to be penetrated with a love of our manners, and amended by our society.'

"'I own my crime (replied the innocent *Yahomy*), or rather my stupidity, in not attempting to warn this good young man of your customs, before I ventured to conduct him here; but what could I do? He understands neither your language nor mine; and I was carried away by my selfishness, united with that tenderness, which you taught me, towards the prayers of others; I longed to come here and end my life among you; I wanted an excuse; I feared to come alone, and this youth offered me the means which I also wanted, and the security which my cowardice demanded: he seemed to love truth, and good people; was in company with a just man; and the love of virtue, as it appeared to me, was his sole motive for persisting in his demands, that I should lead him here. I know I have done a wrong thing, but the lenity of your laws has been partly the occasion of my doing it; he brings gold dust in abundance, a commodity valued by your artists; may not this, if no other consideration can, excuse my intrusion, and pave the way to peace and pardon?'

"At the conclusion of my guide's speech, the whole of which I did not comprehend, I could observe a complacent smile circulate through the crowd that surrounded us; and the old chief said, 'Go, go, you are a little of a flatterer, yet honest, I believe, in the main,

Yahomy; but as to your companion, we know nothing of him, and therefore, as is my duty, I must send you both together up to the seat of justice in *Sophis*. My post here, you know, is to guard the coast and examine new comers; you are the only one that ever returned a second time, for no one ever carried any worldly gain from us; and I must be inclined to believe that you are half a convert to our habits; try therefore to explain them to this good looking youth who is in your company, in order to induce him to conduct himself with modesty and decorum, while he remains among us.'

"I now thought it time to break silence: 'Behold (said I), the son of a Greek among Greeks! for such you must be, if I am not all this time in a dream; what you say, I, without much difficulty, understand, to my inconceivable surprise and admiration. A governing Providence must have conducted me here, to unite with my countrymen; wonderful are the ways of Alla!'

"The old patriarch drew back at my speech, examined me from head to foot, with the most penetrating eye I ever beheld, assuming a look of scrutinizing sagacity, while the youths all came nearer to me, and some put their arms around me, with a sort of brotherly affection.

"'Who Alla is (said the old man), I know not; or who are the Greeks of whom you speak; but that you have our tongue is incontestible; you should therefore have been taught it here, and be a *Sophian*; it is to me a strange thing, but at any rate it entitles you to our confidence and friendship beyond the ties of a stranger: come therefore into my abode, and repose to-night; you, your friend, and what belongs to you, both are sacred; we will converse more with you to-morrow.' On saying which, he took me, very cordially by the hand, and we all retired into the interior part of the cave."

Lycas, at this period, was interrupted by the noise which our gaoler made on unbolting the prison door; the clanking of his massy iron keys, the drawing of two long bolts, or rather bars, and the fall of a heavy drawbridge, which connected the high turret we inhabited with an outer wall, were a complete contrast to the scenes the good man had just been describing; and soon recalled me to a recollection of where we were, which I had nearly forgotten, owing to the eagerness with which my ears imbibed his singular narration. – The gaoler was a middle aged man, a soldier in the castle, and as miserable and brutish a looking creature as I had ever beheld in the deserts of Egypt; almost black, lean, haggard,

and ill-apparalled; but his temper had been softened by the mild
ingenuity of my companion, who, finding he liked music, had in-
vented certain airs to his taste of a lively nature; and the instant
he entered, the guitar was taken in hand, as by this means he made
sure of his punctual attendance. After dancing till he was weary,
during the short time he was permitted to attend us with our daily
provisions, he usually retired, singing as he descended; and, by the
length of time I could trace his declining voice, it was easy to judge,
that we were an immense distance from the guard-chamber; a
circumstance that I instantly communicated to *Lycas*, and asked
him, if, on that account, he had never meditated his escape?

"Never (said he); have you forgot the country where we are? It
is not the castle only that confines us: we are at the mercy of a
lawless tyrant, and in a country impassable without money or
friends; but after all, lay aside the thought, for I can assure you
the obstacles are too many in the prison alone; for, besides being
strong, it is seated on the peninsula of an island; so that if you
could pass all the gates and guards, there would still be the barrier
of a deep and rapid stream to overcome, which no one, in his senses,
would venture to cross at night; and which cannot be crossed unob-
served in the day-time: and after all, have you forgot, in your
eagerness to escape, what you yesterday remarked, that the whole
of this dire country is one continued prison?"

Again I blushed at my want of reflection, and that my impatience
had so violent a power over me: "I bow (said I), to your superior
understanding; but I fear it will be long before I shall possess
sufficient resignation to keep me from admitting, into my mind,
flattering dreams of escape, even under the fullest conviction of
its impossibility."

When we met the next day, he continued his narrative as follows:

"I was not a little surprised to find, on entering the cave, that it
led, through a long aperture, lined on both sides with healthy cattle,
who were reposing on dry litter, to the arched entrance of a very
large apartment, with a high roof, and whose front commanded a
magnificent prospect of the country through a shady grove. The
floor was earth, strewed with dry rushes; and the end opposite to
the opening was one continued raised platform, covered with long
mattresses of pale yellow, whose texture seemed to be of tufts of
wool, but shining as the brightest silk: between every mattress there
ran a low partition, smooth as glass, and dark as ebony; and at the
head of each lay a hollow wooden box, with a pillow on it of the

same material as the mattresses; over the pillow was suspended a small shelf, and at the foot of all the mattresses was placed a low stool of the same black and polished material: the walls of the apartment were of a pale green, ornamented above with pannels, in the centre of which some flower, fruit, or animal, was represented.

"These mattresses were evidently their beds; beyond the apertures in front, there extended a long and broad portico, sustained by rustic pillars, whose pavement was composed, with much art, of the little shells I had observed in the shoals; it was furnished with abundance of low stools, ranged against the wall with great order; each pillar was covered with some creeping flowering plant; and to many of them were brackets affixed to carry little earthen vases, containing each a single flower: but what most of all pleased me was, to find the building bounded by a shallow and perfectly transparent stream, of about twenty feet wide, and to see flocks grazing beyond it, beneath lofty groves of healthy and graceful trees. We were followed into this rural hall by the male part of the family, and our cattle left behind in the cave, which was only separated from it by a low partition, over which we stepped with ease; on passing on to the covered way, we perceived, on the lawn, through the grove, a number of females very busy, some milking the sheep, who were all yellow like pale gold; and others, under a rural shed, preparing food: nor was it long before they served it up to us, accompanied with a ceremony, to me, very agreeable, both from its propriety and novelty.

"For now, as if by a signal, the men leaped into the stream, and began washing their bodies; playing, laughing, and rolling in the water, out of which all came in less than a minute; and skipping and running in the portico to dry themselves, each took a stool to sit on, and another for a table, and thus arranged, a song, or hymn, was begun by the old man, in which the whole company joined; at the close of which, a boy got up and blew a rustic air on a small pipe, when instantly the women entered the portico, each carrying a tray very much like a japan tea-board, on which were some vessels of the like materials, but rose-coloured, containing boiled rice and milk, with some fruits and nuts to me unknown; these with smiles they placed before each man, and retired, singing, as they went away, in general chorus.

"They were of all ages, and more or less cloathed, but none seemed to have more than a single garment, which varied in length according to their ages; the elder women being cloathed to the chin, while the young girls were only covered to the loins; all the dresses were white, and none were long at the feet but those of the aged, who likewise wore sandals of basket work; some had one, some two, and others three platted girdles, made, to appearance, of the yellow wool of their flocks; their arms were bare, and their hair had no other ornaments than a few flowers, or little fillets of the same materials as the girdles: most of them were what we should call clear brunettes, with large dark and piercing eyes, abundance of black hair, rather inclined to curl, separated in front, and tied behind; their stature was low, but exquisitely well proportioned, and they were in general what the French call *en-bon-point;* a fascinating gaiety accompanied their whole deportment, and every one said something arch as they passed in with the supper-trays, to create harmless mirth.

"For my own part, I must confess, I should have liked it better had they staid to partake with us of what they brought; and so I expressed myself to the chief, who laughed heartily at the remark, and repeated it to all in his hearing as a proof of my good taste; but, added he, have a little patience, young man, and you will have enough of their company; I would also advise you to eat heartily, or the exercise they will presently give you, may cause you as speedily to wish them away. – I blush even now to think how unjust a conclusion my intemperance formed from this speech; but I was soon undeceived for supper being ended, the trays were removed by ourselves into a shed beyond the building, from whence the woman first came, and the boys assisted the men in throwing vessels of water over the pavement, which, as it was formed of a gentle declivity, soon trickled away with the fragments into the river. The women now again entered, old and young, accompanied with girls, and several who played on a kind of harp, or lyre, others on small drums, and immediately a general dance began, in which I was invited to join, both by the chief, and a lovely maiden of about fourteen. I would willingly have excused myself, but they told me there was no difficulty in their dances, if I could but keep time, and use agility; 'this lass (said one of them), will soon make you a good dancer, I promise you, if you have strength to hold out.' Charmed with her figure, I made no further objection, but soon had reason to be ashamed of my performance; for their steps, though simple, were inimitably regular, and the gracefulness of their motions not only took off all my attention from my own part, but made me quite ashamed of my awkwardness. – No one, however, seemed to take any particular notice of it, and they made even the old Caffre take his share, which he did with the best good temper in the world.

"Finding I made so poor a figure, my pride induced me to decline proceeding any further; and I told the chief I would, with his permission, be a spectator for the rest of the evening.

"'Do as you please (said he), but as you must be warm, you had better walk about.' My partner now took me by the hand into the great chamber; and, after shewing me the pictures over the couches, and explaining to me that each served to distinguish the couch of its particular owner, she led me by the hand to see our camels feeding; where, finding ourselves alone, and seated on a soft pile of fodder, in the recess of the cave, forgetful of decorum, throwing my arms around her, I, to my eternal disgrace, endeavoured, without any further ceremony, to take improper liberties; but how keen were my feelings, when, disengaging herself like lightning, she flew along the cave toward the dancers, exclaiming as she ran – 'Infamous, base stranger! you are no true Sophian!'

"A moment after, I saw the chief approaching me, and would gladly have parted with all my wealth to have avoided the interview; my soul sunk with contrition at the idea of my ingratitude; and, not knowing how to look him in the face, I pretended to be busily employed about the cattle.

"Looking at me with stern composure – 'How, young man (said he), are you preparing so soon to quit *Sophis?* I fear you think rather contemptuously of us, and that you have made a long journey on very unworthy principles; if you really came here to indulge vicious propensities indiscriminately, you are to be pitied, not only on account of the little consolation they ultimately afford; but because you have chosen a country, of all others, the least calculated to gratify them; perhaps, however, the girl has mistaken you, and your proposals were not injurious; perhaps, –'

"'Hold, hospitable man (said I), my motives were worse than my actions; and my actions have been unworthy of myself; the charms of beauty and innocence, instead of exciting respect, inflamed my desires; and I am compelled to confess, that I had formed conjectures very discreditable to the purity of your females, merely because they had treated me with the most cordial familiarity; yet remember, I beseech you, that I came from a corrupted continent; inflict whatever punishment you please on me, except that of banishment; and, for the sake of that tie you have found in my language, take pity on a friendless youth, who, whatever may be his faults, is not naturally a despiser of modesty.'

"'It is not in my power (said he), were it really my inclination, to banish you, for my duty compels me to send you up to *Sophis!* but I am really grieved, that equally imperious motives will prevent me from reporting that fair character of you, which I could wish, or of detaining you any longer here; yet, for the sake of your companion, and your language, which somehow persuades me that you are one of our children, I will, if you condescend to listen to it, now give you such advice, as may enable you to procure the goodwill of those on whom your future destiny depends.' So saying, he took me by the hand with much complacency, and leading me back to the portico, bade me sit down by him.

"The sun was just sinking behind the tops of the hills, and gilding the branches of the grove with an exquisite lustre; the youths had ceased to dance, the women were all gone, and each man was retiring to his polished pallet in the chamber. As soon as all was still, 'My son (said he), your candid confession has quite disarmed my anger, and encreased the agreeable suspicion that you are one of us; yet the fault you committed demanded the utmost severity of reproof; for the maid you offended was a stranger to my family; and therefore it became doubly my duty to protect her honour: but now let that pass, and let me acquaint you with somewhat of the way of thinking of our country in that particular.

"'We are no enemies to love; on the contrary, it forms the chief link of our society, is the root of our morals, and the object of our silent devotion: – to that divine principle we feel that our existence is entirely owing; without its continuance we should have been only to be miserable; if it ceased to exist, but for a moment, we should be lost.

"'Sensible, therefore, as we all are, that to no other principle than abstract love can the creation be attributed; since all things are supported by an invisible and generous agency, that not only dispenses to all their proper nourishment, but adds munificently to such as follow temperately their natural instincts, and the dictates of conscience, the ornament of happiness, and the blessing of longevity; our ancestors made the principle of human love the basis of this well-ordered society: – Love first links us, as well as other animals, to our females; love compels us to support our offspring; our kindness procures us their love; and hence that which originally springs from self-esteem becomes the reward of its pure principle: we have no other criterion, by which to judge of right and wrong, but that of the action procuring to others either good or evil; whatever is painful or unpleasant to be done to others is unlawful for us to do; and we *respect the innocent will in all things.* Hence our children, not being unseasonably thwarted, are seldom capricious, for their natural timidity preserves them from dangerous attempts; and we content ourselves with watching over their safety, without hindering them from gathering the fruits of salutary experience. Hence the complacency of our young people; for as nothing is to be gained in this country but by persuasion and affection; and since force is even prohibited to be used to our cattle unnecessarily, we are continually employed in inventing new, innocent, and affectionate methods of enticements.

"'If, by means of kindness and sympathetic allurements, we have won the heart of a virgin, who was unattached, we must, by the same proceedings, bring her to a closer union; and by the like measures alone can we lawfully retain her in it: so that, at all times, she is at liberty to break or continue this tie, if it be not found to procure mutual happiness: – hence, as the bond of union is vigorous at first, and lighter afterwards, it seldom happens that it is suddenly dissolved, after having continued any length of time: the fibres of the butterfly's wing are not of bone, yet they resist the winds as well as the bat's – for it is the very essence of love and liberty to preserve what they mutually generate. You see, therefore, how necessary it will be for you to put no rash construction on the innocent freedom which our females enjoy; but to treat them, as we do, with the same respect, justice, and sincerity, as the men. No embraces may be forcibly taken here, or any other thing; the most powerful among us are the politest, and the most persuasive; but none are considered as understanding truly the art of persuasion, who are not sincere. To say one thing and to act another, with us, constitute what we call insanity of reason, or want of human sense; and we have people employed, and places appointed, for the sole purpose of curing such diseases of the mind; which, however, are not very common among us.

"'Let me, therefore, hope, that what I have now said will not be despised; since I really feel something interests my bosom in your behalf, and shall be afficted if you condemn the simple honest manners of my countrymen.'

"Here he took my hand, and placing the palm of his upon it,

squeezed it with a parental warmth and kindness, and, looking affectionately in my face, seemed anxiously to expect my reply.

"For my part, I was so overcome with the generosity and gentleness of his reproof and advice, that I found myself only able to answer him by a sudden tear, which trickled on our joined hands.

"But, as soon as my recollection was recovered, I threw myself at his feet, embraced his knees ardently, and, with an involuntary exclamation, cried aloud, 'My friend! my father!'

"Endowed with pure sensibility, he felt the force of my apostrophe; 'I will be both (said he), to the utmost of my power; and to-morrow I will take care to give you an abler guide than *Yahomy!* you shall be accompanied by my eldest son; place confidence in him, and he will take a pleasure in instructing you in all the manners of our separated nation.'

"He then led me into the hall, which we trod softly, most of the company being composed in tranquil sleep; and having placed me on a couch adjoining that where the inoffensive *Yahomy* lay, he retired to his own; when, calmed by that peaceful joy which reconciliation ever inspires, and lulled by the soft murmurs of the gliding brook, I soon dropped into a sweet and profound repose.

The next morn we were awakened by the voices of abundance of singing birds, and others whose cries much resemble the paroquet. On opening my eyes, my senses were revived by a gale of odours, which I soon perceived issued from the pots of flowers with which the portico was embellished: the little boys lay on their pallets sounding mellow-pipes, which seemed a kind of flagelets; others began to beat little drums, and soon the whole hall was filled with groups of naked figures, very few of which might not have formed a model for the heroes of former times. After taking a few turns, leaping or racing, they indiscriminately plunged into the waters of the stream, where I saw incredible feats of swimming and diving performed; afterwards, running again in the portico, till their bodies were perfectly dry, each man then took a long piece of woollen stuff, the only kind of garment they wore, and wound it variously around his chest, or threw it carelessly in folds over the shoulder. It seemed, indeed, to serve them for an infinite number of purposes; for sometimes it was used to shade their heads like a turban, sometimes to gird up their loins, occasionally as a veil, when they were stooping in the sun, or as a screen from the quarter whence the wind blew cold, often as a pillow, and generally as a coverlet. The old men gave it the form of a long cloak, covering them behind from head to foot, but the young and robust affected to roll it up very small; and I remarked, that no one seemed to have any idea of using it otherwise than as convenience dictated: like the statues of the ancients which still remain, they appeared to glory in the form the Creator had assigned them; and in their active and athletic images, a Phidias would have found an endless number of the finest models of the human structure.

"After our morning-meal, which was conducted just like the supper, and only differed in its consisting of boiled milk and fruit, with lemons to refresh our water; my worthy host introduced me, in the presence of the whole company, to his eldest son, and consigned me to his care, with all the tenderness of a real parent. On this occasion, the young maiden, who had been the cause to me of so much blame, and so much kindness, rushed in among us, like a bird on the wing; and, taking my hand, struck the palm of it twice, saying, '*Stranger, I freely forgive you your mistake;*' when she instantly disappeared among the surrounding crowd.

"'That was voluntarily and handsomely done (said the old man), and I congratulate you on her generosity; for now the whole affair is buried in oblivion, and I am no longer obliged to communicate it in my report, when I write to my superior officer, on the subject of your arrival and conduct here. She is a strange, but a sweet tempered, good, and sensible girl; and very likely led you to the grotto, to know if your manners corresponded with your person.'

"We now departed with a small company of men, and some women; the women sitting upon their cows, on the yellow mattresses before mentioned; the men wading through the shallows, for some miles after we left the island, to cross a shoal that separated it from *Sophis!* in which I took care to imitate them, knowing they would have smiled to see me riding effeminately on my camel: when, having marched silently about an hour, my companion and guide, whose name was *Chilo*, placing his hand familiarly on my shoulder, said, 'Are you thinking of that maiden still, the little firefly! has she stung you?'

"Conscious that he was right, I made no scruple of confessing he had divined my thoughts; and indeed, I had all along wished for an opportunity of turning my first enquiries to that subject.

"'And who is this fire-fly, *Chilo* (said I), that so artfully misled me? for I own there is more of liking than resentment in my remembrance of her?'

"'She is (replied he), an orphan, the fruit of a very passionate attachment between two young people, who both perished by a stroke of lightning, while she lay in their arms, and received no injury. One of my father's wives, with great care, brought her up; her name is *Mica*, — we look upon her as a sister; she is very gay and very lively, but has as yet formed no attachment among the men; and had you been a native, it is not unlikely, from her conduct towards you, that you might, had you liked her, have soon gained her confidence and affection. But let me persuade you, if possible, to avoid any engagements of that sort: by the customs of *Sophis*, strangers are not allowed to stay long here, but on terms that few have ever complied with; and none, who are once incorporated among us, are willingly permitted to depart, lest they should make the road too common, as has been the case with your guide *Yahomy*.'

"'Will you tell me (said I, sighing), what are the terms so difficult to comply with?' 'You must live strictly as we do (said he), on the most simple food; forego all the thoughts of excessive gain; kill nothing that breathes and lives; use no violence towards any thing; and employ all your spare strength and time in public services, and in attention to the wants of individuals, without any consideration of former acquaintance: in a word, you must consider nothing as your own but what is necessary to your being, and those whom you preserve; and, mingling your affections with the very elements of existence, respect even a tree as your fellow-creature, so as to aid and not destroy it; not to wound even the earth for its metals, but for its good, to promote its respiration, by draining, from the surface, stagnant waters, or conducting toward its pastures refreshing and invigorating streams.

"'Your sovereign good must be the good of the community; while the laws of the community propose only the happiness of individuals, by suffering every man and woman to think, speak, and act freely; subject to no restraint while they *violate not the innocent will of another;* for the protection of which alone all our customs and all our laws are calculated.'

"'What do you mean by the innocent will? (said I).' – 'That which, if executed, can injure nothing, not even ourselves. Thus, no species of intemperance may be lawfully practised; nor are men allowed to live solitary to follow sequestered vices; for the first principle of our government is not to permit any individual to injure himself; the next, that he shall not injure any other; and, lastly, that societies shall not exist to the prejudice of general society, and the destruction of union and political equality.'

"After a moment's pause, I replied, 'all you have described appears to me very beautiful both in theory and practice; why then should you doubt of my power, if I have the inclination, to comply with them? Know then, that I came here only because I had heard that you were better than the generality of mankind: you see, therefore, that I am no admirer of the vices of the continent; and if, on my first arrival, I slew your birds, it was only because I did not conceive, that there was a nation who could live without animal food.' – 'What (cried he, with a fixed expression of horror), did you mean, after murdering them, to eat them! and make a *grave* of your bowels – Holy Energy! is it possible that men can coolly commit such abominable crimes merely to live! Have you no roots, no grain, no fruits on the continent? I would live on the grass of the earth sooner than commit such cruel and filthy actions.' The tears stood in his eyes as he uttered these words, and he seemed so violently affected, that I regretted the subject had been introduced; but assured him he need not be under any apprehensions of my continuing the practice, as I had resolved, in all things, to comply with their customs. Still he was very anxious to hear all the particulars of this detestable practice, as he emphatically called it; and I gratified his curiosity, not without many blushes, which, in a certain degree, served to convince me of the justice of his objection; but at length, I could not help asking how they avoided the vast increase of their animals, if they killed none? 'Do you kill your children then (said he), when they become too numerous for you?' I replied – 'no, we send them out into the world to get their living.' 'Just so (he said) we dispose of our superfluous cattle, by sending them to the continent, if there are more than can be well kept, but that rarely happens; for, as we consume much milk, many cows and sheep are wanted; and, as to other animals, they have never been found troublesome: they seem to multiply only in proportion to their proper food: – doubtless, the good Energy encourages or restrains them; for, as all things are conducted by the principle of *Love*, no disorders, from its influence, can arise; and the brutes, our fellow creatures, are true to their instincts.'

"Here he ended, and I was glad that his enquiries did not lead to the horrid subject of war, lest it should give him a still worse opinion of us.

"By this time we were ascending a mountain in the island, and seemed to be approaching a kind of village, whose buildings were low but regular, and of a delicate pale tone of colour: they seemed of an oblong form, without chimneys, and, externally, without windows, though each had a handsome, well-proportioned, projecting doorway or porch: every house was surrounded by pleasant groves, and stood on a small eminence, but I found that there was no want of light in them; and that, in general, they consisted of a square court, composed of four long, distinct, and detached buildings, each of which had its broad open portico, sustained by small double columns, at large intervals, behind which was a range of chambers open to the view of those who walked in the portico, and separated only by a low wall. In a word, except the solidity and exquisite finish of the workmanship, they seemed on the model of the country-house I had first seen: but I was told there were no absolute rules of architecture, and that every one might build as he pleased, provided only, that they constructed no chambers that were not open to the air, and accessible to every inhabitant of the mansion. Doors were solemnly prohibited, and no coffers allowed to be made with fastenings of any kind, which extended even to baskets; insomuch, that most of them were constructed with open work, and their chests looked like elegant cages; in making which, as well as seats, they were wonderfully skilful, comimg nearer to the fine works of the Japanese, than any thing I had ever seen. The taste of every thing around, indeed, much surprised me, for all seemed beautiful though quite plain; and I could not help expressing my astonishment, and asking my friend to account for it.

"'If our houses strike your senses agreeably, (he observed), it must arise from their being competent judges of order and proportion; for order, proportionate dimensions, and simple utility, are the only rules in art we acknowledge – and there are certainly those among us who know how to carry their effects to surprising lengths, as you will witness, I trust, when you see the public halls in *Sophis*, our seat of justice.'

"The court of the building we had now entered was an ample square, in the centre of which stood a tank of white marble, about four feet deep, full of the purest water; the sides of which were shelving for about eight feet from the border. This, *Chilo* informed me, was the family-bath and that it was served from a spring, and emptied and cleaned every day; for, by their customs, no house was permitted to be built but in a situation that could be served with water in abundance, yet whose position was such that any water could lie near its foundations. The consequence was, that every house was detached, and always placed on a declivity, or close to the margin of a river or brook.

"Neither age nor sex were exempted from the necessity of washing or bathing twice a day; which habit seemed to have rendered necessary to all, insomuch that many were really almost amphibious, and seemed as naturally to take to the water as spaniels; to this practice, I think, in a great measure, may be attributed both the clearness of their skins, the robustness and firmness of their bodies, their excellent digestion, liveliness of spirits, and general good state of health.

"Our dinner consisted of raw eggs, the bread – fruit, and milk in abundance – my friend, the Caffre, *Chilo*, and myself, were seated round a low table in a shady porch; where we were not only served by some charming young women, but were entertained during our whole meal with agreeable songs, sung by a party of girls and boys, who seemed to take a pleasure in varying our entertainment.

"Our meal was scarcely finished, when *Chilo* rose up and left us abruptly. Finding he did not return for some time, I enquired where he was gone; and the Caffre, who now had discovered, to his great surprise, that I understood their language, informed me, that it was a custom for all the married men to retire, after dinner, to the society of their wives, and to remain together, if agreeable, till near the hour of supper; when the females went to prepare it, supped, and returned to the men to dance; after which, each bathed separately, retired to separate dormitories, and never met again, in private, till the next day at the same time.

"At that hour, all laborious occupations were suspended, and the generality reposed in sleep, as the still silence which prevailed was very favourable to that indulgence. For at the hour of noon, all kinds of noise were as strictly forbidden as with us during night, no one being permitted to walk in the porticoes. – 'And, what do the young people do (said I), who have no wives?'

"'Those who have no wives (replied he), are too young to require any; for here all marriageable people are married. They consider it as a duty imposed on the parent to take care and promote as early connections as are proper, and never fail to observe and encourage the first inclinations that take place; to impede them would be considered as the blackest piece of villainy; for they are fully sensible of the dangers arising from the suppression of the natural fires, and no one's consent is necessary to the connubial union, but those of the parties uniting.'

"When *Chilo* returned, I asked him what were their marriage ceremonies? At which he burst into a loud laugh, – 'How (said he), do you, who are not a boy, ask such a question? – The lovers retire to some grove, or fountain, and affection instructs them in the rest.'

"By which I perceived, with regret that they seemed to have no forms of marriage; but that, with them, cohabitation constituted matrimony; and this induced me to think, that there wanted nothing but *Mica's* consent, when we retired to the cave, to have made *me* a married man.

"Without knowing exactly why, I found myself every hour more and more inclined to adopt most of the manners of this singular nation; and grew actually impatient to arrive before the chief magistrate, in order to urge my wishes. There seemed so much calmness in all I had witnessed, so much order and tranquillity, that I became determined, by adoption, to become a Sophian, if it were possible to gain such an indulgence. Thus meditating the measures I should take on my arrival, we passed on in silence till evening: and although we travelled through a most delightful country, highly diversified with natural charms, yet my mind was so rapt that I took but little notice of it, but passed on musing, and soothed with the melody of the birds; nor did any one attempt to interrupt me, for all were equally engaged, most of them in conversation, others in small parties, chaunting low but sweet and popular harmonies.

"In this manner we arrived at the foot of a hill, when we were suddenly alarmed by the loudest outcries, and saw a number of people running towards us, who seemed frantic with despair. The forest with which this hill was surrounded echoed with their lamentation; nor was it long before we met two young women, followed by an aged man, and these again by a group of boys and girls, who were all violently agitated, and seemed wandering they knew not whither; from the women it was impossible to learn any thing, except that some miserable misfortune had happened to their children; but the old man, who seemed sinking under fatigue and distress of mind, sat down among us quite overcome, and soon explained the sad calamity.

"A public building of an amphi-theatric form, which was erected on the side of the hill, surrounded by trees, and solely applied to the purposes of educating very young children, had been undermined by a small spring which encircled it; and the whole, at once, aided by a very slight shock of an earthquake, had sunk down, accompanied by the fall of its trees and stones, so as to precipitate, in a mass of ruin, numbers of infants, with all the masters and mistresses of this useful establishment.

"On hearing this report, we took the old man's directions and redoubled our speed to arrive at the spot where the accident had happened, which we found a complete scene of distress and confusion; the men all actively employed in removing the branches and stones, the women encouraging them by their praises. We all joined ardently in the labour, and, by this acquisition of new strength, it was not long before numbers were extricated from very dangerous situations. On calculating their loss we had the pleasure to find that these good people had been more fortunate than they at first imagined; for out of above two hundred children one only was actually killed, though several had limbs broken; and none among the teachers had suffered but a very aged man, who sat under a kind of arch-way, and whose sole office was the superintendence of the other masters. Him we took up dead, with the young child near him, whom, it was supposed, at the time the accident happened, he had been holding in his arms. I was assisting at disengaging his body from the ruins. – It was of an uncommon size and bone, with a countenance impressed with the most venerable marks of sense and gravity.

"We carried him and the child into the village, where a bed of sweet-scented herbs had been prepared for their reception; and after numbers had, by tears and embraces, testified their respect for his remains, they were covered with dry branches of pine-trees, and other combustible woods; after which the whole was set on fire, and in a very few minutes there was left nothing but a heap of ashes, which were instantly interred on the spot: – each man bringing a stone from the ruined building, by order of a person who seemed to be a magistrate; in the space of a few hours a noble square platform was raised, which they told me would, when converted into a handsome tomb, be dedicated to the memory of the aged tutor, and the child who accompanied him to the grave.

"The greatest part of the night, which was moon-light, was employed in these amiable offices; and the morning was ushered in with the most affecting dirges, in which all the inhabitants of the village seemed to unite as if accustomed to the pious exercise.

"Having exerted myself exceedingly, and having been seconded stoutly by old *Yahomy*, we were both complimented in a handsome speech from the magistrate, and requested to repose during the day, and take some necessary refreshment previously to continuing our journey.

"To this proposal we readily consented, with the approbation of our conductor; and, after retiring to rest at a lodging appointed for us, rose up and went to his house. It consisted of a semi-circular area, embracing the sides of the hill, and down the descent of which, many small alleys were contrived through a species of beautiful blooming heath, with occasional openings and seats of turf for repose, over which aromatic flowering shrubs and orange trees were artfully conducted, so as to afford a light and pleasant shade at all times, while small but clear streams ran bubbling by the sides of the paths, occasionally flowing into little stone basins, of a pale red colour, whose edges were always ornamented with small flowers, or the most beautiful mosses and lichens.

"I was commending the elegance of his taste, when he interrupted me, by remarking, that I should rather admire the rustic cheapness and ease with which these walks were accomplished. 'I have done nothing (said he), but make declining paths, in conformity with the plans of my neighbours, who have pitched their habitations on this side of our mountain; and many of whom have, to my shame, outdone me in industry and neatness: for you will observe, the whole is nearly in the same style; and we lose nothing by it, as these winding tracts serve the flocks as well as ourselves, and these fountains slake their thirst, while the shrubs afford them shade: as to the seats, they serve for resting places for the aged, schools for our peripatetic tutors, and couches for the shepherds to recline upon during the heat of the day.'

"'What then (said I), are not those grounds your exclusive property?' – He stared at me, with fixed astonishment; and, turning to *Chilo*, exclaimed, 'Does your companion take us for tyrants? Could all this be mine, who am an old man, and not a tyger of the desert? Thanks to the laws of *Sophis*, such inequality is among us unknown: – Did you think, (turning to me), because I directed the people yesterday, that they were all my slaves, or my cattle? No, young man, I only supplied an office which my age, and long residence here, imposed on me in my turn, and which at the end of the year will belong to another.'

"I blushed at my mistake, and acknowledged the justice of his reproof; but inwardly resolved to be more cautious for the future in guessing at the system of these primitive people, whose every action I felt myself compelled to approve and admire. – But the next day, as we were preparing for our departure, I was entirely thrown off my guard, by finding that neither of our camels was to be found, and at the cool indifference with which my friend announced this disaster.

"Hitherto I could have no suspicion of being robbed, for I had seen no gold ornaments whatever on any of the inhabitants, whether men or women, except a single ring in the left ear; and concluded, that whatever use they might have for it, no attempts would be made to deprive me of my merchandize by fraud or force; much less, that in company with such just people, I should be plundered of what they seemed to consider as highly valuable property, though not even *Chilo* could inform me what return I was to receive for it, if I chose to leave the yellow dirt among them. But being thus, at once, divested of my whole wealth, I began, inadvertently, to give way to the most unjust and imprudent suspicions; and, after declaring openly, that if the camels were not speedily restored, I should lay the loss to the charge of those in my company; I ran, followed by the afflicted Caffre, all over the village, looking into every house, overturning all that came in my way, and, after two hours of vain search, came back covered with sweat and dust, quite exhausted, enraged, and almost beside myself.

"Here I found only *Chilo*, engaged in close conversation with the venerable magistrate: they looked at me with countenances of pity and compassion, which revived my former confusion; but I leave you to judge what were my feelings, when the latter gravely addressed me as follows: –

"Stranger, your conduct wrongs us all; but most of all my friend's son, who is your generous and affectionate companion: as for myself, I am too well known here, to suffer in the least from those hasty conclusions, that have wounded his inmost breast: whatever your animals carried, he is void, as we all are, of the knowledge of it; and, if they were lost, would be innocent of any designed wrong; although, in the hurry of yesterday, he did not take that care of them which is customary. The cause of their disappearance is unknown to us; but I do not believe they are stolen, because, we trust, there are few men among us capable of such an unprovoked atrocity, the which would be sure to be punished with perpetual banishment from Sophis: when, therefore, they come to light, I leave you to reflect on the effects of your impatience, which will be long recorded here; for already are you abandoned by all but my friend and myself; the rest having resolved to go no further with you, lest your intemperate passions should lead you to commit some acts of violence, or their own contempt of such unmanly conduct induce them to forget the sacred laws of hospitality.'

"All this he said with a most serene countenance, as I perceived in the beginning, for towards the latter end of his speech, my eyes were intuitively riveted to the ground, when shame and confusion took entire possession of me – my very soul seemed to be abashed within me.

"Tears now poured from my eyes in abundance, and relieved, while they degraded me, (as I then thought), but they made a very different impression on my Mentor; — him they softened: '*Lycas* (said he), your heart I see is uncorrupted. Base people shed tears when they receive personal and painful injuries, or when they are deprived of sensual enjoyments; you weep at the just reproof of my worthy friend, and thereby acknowledge that you are erroneous, but incapable of injustice: — Let us go on together to *Sophis*, we have somewhat tarnished our fame here, my friend; but we will shew them, in other places, that we are become wiser men from experience.'

"While he was speaking, we heard a great shout, and soon saw a crowd of people coming up with our camels, exclaiming, 'they are found! they are found!' and, to my accumulating distress, it soon appeared that the animals had only been conducted to a rich pasture on our road by a kind villager, who thought thereby to do us a grateful service.

"I was soon surrounded by a host of witnesses to my disgraceful conduct, and could have almost wished the earth to open and swallow me up; but *Chilo*, relieved me, with a kind and sanguine act of friendship, by speaking for me, and saying, "We own we have been wrong to suspect you, O valuable neighbours! we hope for your pardon, and solicit you to forget and forgive the errors of humanity.'

"So saying, he took me by the hand, and conducted me on our road to *Sophis*: we went on in silence — nor did I dare to look around me, till we had travelled an hour in the valley which surrounded the village; when, lifting up my eyes, I was not a little surprised to see in our rear all the company, but far behind.

"*Chilo* observed my astonishment, 'Come, come (said he), our faults are forgiven, let them be forgot: *Yahomy* is near you; I am the son of your first acquaintance; and know my countrymen well enough to assure you that they will never more think of this adventure.'

"These cordial assurances dissipated the clouds from my mind, and a serene composure took place, something like the clearing up of the sky, after a sudden storm of thunder in the middle of summer. At that instant, in passing round a winding path in a thick forest, we were agreeably surprised with the sight of a party of noble looking youths, accompanied by two middle-aged men and an older one: all of them were sitting nearly in a row, on a sloping bank of flowery verdure, the foot of which was washed by a cool, unruffled, and transparent stream.

"My friend told me they were a peripatetic school going to the place we came from; that as the object of education with them consisted in acquiring a thorough acquaintance with the first principles of morality, their laws, arts, and general habits of life; it had been a custom, from times past, to remove from place to place, with the youths, as soon as they had acquired strength enough for the exercise of walking; beginning first with conducting them to the environs of their own village, and terminating their education during a tour of all the islands: 'By this means (said he), many useful effects are produced: agriculture is studied by an actual view of all our improvements; all the branches of art traced to their sources; each citizen becomes acquainted with the whole state; health is promoted; good manners taught by practice and observation; and, while the mind is maturing, all the useful exercises of the body are learned, as it were, by way of amusement. – They swim, run, leap, wrestle, and, by intervals, carry burthens; music is practiced when they repose; painting, and modelling, from the face of nature, and the observation of their own bodies: arithmetic they practice walking, by the aid of their fingers, or a small tablet, divided into four parts; for we have four figures, which, when added together, make ten, and the thumb is the multiplier, serving for one, two, three, four, ten, or any other number.' – I desired him to explain this, not without feeling some degree of compassion for their ignorance of our mode of arithmetic.

"'It is very simple (said he); the little finger stands for one, the second for two, the third for three, the fourth for four, and the thumb for the number ten, or any number composed of these, acts as a multiplier. Thus, by touching the fore finger with the thumb, we express forty; by uniting all the fingers with the thumb, one hundred; two, three, four, and any number to ten hundred, is described by using the fingers and thumb of the other hand as second multipliers.' – I was obliged to confess it was simple and useful, lest he should demand an explanation of our method, which it would not have been quite so easy to detail; but never suspecting that there could be any other mode in the world, he did not enter into the enquiry.

"Observing that we stopt, and seemed to be talking about them, they all rose up, and, in so doing, saluted us; at the same time, extending their arms towards us, with gracious and complacent smiles: we returned the compliment, and requested them to partake of the refreshments which were brought up by our party, that had by this time joined us; none of whom, I was pleased to remark, directed their looks particularly to me. We feasted on eggs, with which the place abounded, sipt the pure wave, finished with a wild fruit like a strawberry, danced, had a chorus-song, and separated well pleased with each other. – But I must not forget to tell you, that before we parted, the old tutor informed me his chief duty was instruction in morals; that neither of them were brought up expressly for the purpose of educating others, but that he had pursued it voluntarily all his life; the others, at the express desire of the community they belonged to, having been always remarkable for their good conduct and solidity of parts; that the excursion would last only during six months, when they returned to their homes, at the commencement of the wet season; and that each of them had relations among the troop of scholars. Most people of talents, he told me, accepted this office once or twice in their lives, considering it as a high distinction to be selected for it. Many perform the duty oftener, as it is always accompanied with the reward of the esteem and friendship of our fellow citizens, the praises of the magistrates, and that important self-approbation arising from the consciousness of having coincided with the object of our creation, the promotion of love and happiness, which puts all apprehension of personal danger, as it were, afar off, and makes the man seem invulnerable.

"While he was speaking, I forgot how the time passed, and could have listened to him all day with pleasure; but finding our troop were almost out of sight, and that I was left alone, I found myself under the necessity of taking leave. 'Stranger, we shall meet again at *Sophis* (were his last words), and then I will take that opportunity of making some enquiries in my turn; in the mean time, may your journey be agreeable, and your reception such as you may reasonably desire.'

"I was in no haste to join my company. Every thing I encountered humbled me in my own opinion; and I, who before thought myself a giant, from my personal and mental strength, travels, and resolution, seemed, among these Sophians, to be shrinking, into a pigmy.

"We slept that evening, on the side of a hill, at a kind of caravansera for the accommodation of travellers. Near it fell a prodigious torrent, that raised a refreshing mist, and gave to the woods in the neighbourhood a remarkable verdure; innumerable singing birds inhabited the boughs; monkies played their gambols about us on the branches of the lofty trees; and herds of antelopes fed around us, as calmly as a flock of sheep, with whom they were occasionally mixed. We lay scattered in various groups, glowing with the reflection of a finely setting sun; while some were employed in preparing supper, others, in forming mattresses of leaves and moss, and the young men in enclosing some of the wild animals in thickets, in order to procure their milk; with some drops of which the aged made a libation on the ground, placing also thereon a small portion of every thing we partook of, as a testimony of gratitude to the great giver of life, and the means of preserving it, 'Which, (said *Chilo*, as he deposited the offering with reverence), is of itself a continual bestowing of the blessings of vitality.'

"While all this was transacting, I strolled up to the shade of an old tree, where I found a young woman playing to some others who surrounded her and listened with great attention, on an instrument to me totally unknown, but which, as she recited a sort of hymn, made an agreeable accompaniment to her voice. The instrument consisted of a long, hollow, and very large cane, with a foot placed at a right angle, which gave the whole the form of the letter T: the broad part rested on the ground, and the other had a crooked head, which, bending over her shoulder, served to keep it steady. It had a string of one gut that passed over a bridge near the cross of the T; instead of fretts there was a roller of ivory, which she managed, with one hand, to conduct, by a handle below, up and down the cane, so as not only to stop, but actually swell a note; and with the other she struck the string, louder or softer as the tune required. The air was elegant, and much affected me: to this day I remember it in part, it began –

*'Give me a lover, with the sturdy roots of whose heartstrings, the small branches of mine may so entangle themselves, that no wind may ever be able to tear them asunder.'

"Of the refinement of music I then knew little; but the air, the instrument, the song, and the singer, satisfied my heart.

"There were also, not far from them, some children dancing to a kind of dulcimer, whose strings were struck with a plectrum, the bridge of which instrument was two horns moving on fixed points, whose approach on the board was adjusted by screws; the whole

---

* An Indian song perhaps.

of the strings being passed round pullies, fixed to these horns, and consisting of one catgut of a great length. The accompanying instrument was a broad drum, which a boy beat with his fingers, and clappers, with which the principal dancers kept time.

"I now returned to the building, or rather long portico, for it was nearly open, and its marble having, by the effects of weather, acquired a fine orange colour, the contrast was remarkably agreeable, when opposed to the azure of the firmament.

"*Yahomy* was there, sitting in a pensive attitude in the shade, as if buried in deep reflection; and I could not, under our present circumstances, help thinking, that his looks on my arrival conveyed a secret air of reproach; so active a censor is the consciousness of unworthy conduct, on a mind endowed with any degree of sensibility.

"Placing myself by him, I immediately communicated those reflections that tormented me. He laughed during my relation; 'You are entirely mistaken (said he), slight faults are not so severely punished in *Sophis*, where there reigns so much goodness of heart, and so much happiness. Error acknowledged, is error forgotten; but I was, like you, bending under the weight of self-reproach, which was occasioned by the enjoyment this delightfully-shady place confers: behold that bust, with a name under it, in a corner of this portico; it is that of a man who, during his life-time, caused it to be erected as his monument: for it is the custom here, to raise none over the dead; since they think, that he who shall neglect the performance of some such useful act towards society, while living, is unworthy of his country's remembrance when no more: but I, what monument have I raised? what benefit have I conferred on mankind? a childless wanderer, my mother-earth maintains me, an unworthy son!' – It was no difficult matter to prove to him that I stood there a living monument of his kindness; and, as to external offices, I promised that, after my arrival at the capital, we would not long delay to strengthen this noble custom, by consecrating a part of my wealth to some purpose useful to society; on which occasion his kindness to me should be recorded, and our friendship perpetuated in sculptured marble. – 'So far as it is done (said he), with modesty, and gives employment to ingenious artists, such an act would please the Sophians, especially if we inscribe on it only,

BY THE TRAVELLERS,

OR,

BY THE STRANGERS.'

"'Or suppose we were to repair some fountain fallen into decay (replied I,) would not that be more decent in our situation, without adding any inscription at all?' – 'It would (said he), if any such decayed buildings were to be found; but you know not, as yet, the country, any more than the way of thinking, of its citizens. All useful monuments of this kind are repaired by the community; while frivolous ones, after the death of their founder, are destroyed: and this law operates with good effect on those who are desirous of fame; for, every time they are repaired, the original founder's name is carefully restored, together with the date of the monument; and, as the views of the man who first erected it are sacredly adhered to, whether he intended it for shade, refreshment, as a bridge over a brook, or a habitation for the aged, he whose generous mind first projected the most useful service to his fellow men, is sure of a lasting record of his name to the end of society.'

"In this conversation we passed the rest of the evening, anticipating the end of our long journey, and our reception among the heads of the nation.

"The next day we pursued our road, at the dawn of light; myself, *Chilo*, and *Yahomy* leading on foot; for such I found was the manner of travelling, when approaching the capital, at all times where ceremony was used: which served at once to ascertain who were the leading people of the troop, and prevented many mistakes on the road; our departure being always a signal to those, who accompanied us, to prepare to follow with expedition.

"We now ascended a steep hill, cut with care into a winding and easy slope; at the summit of which, it was an agreeable surprise, to find a resting-place, surrounded by trees, and a fine gushing spring pouring into a white marble shell, whose brim perpetually overflowed, and trickled, in chrystal drops, on the flowers that surrounded it.

"The rising sun, which had dispersed the mists, presented to our view a large town, lying on a swelling knoll, at the foot of the mountain. The buildings were all low, their lines, from that circumstance, long and picturesque; but frequently broken by fine groups of graceful trees, or separated by the meanders of a silver stream, on whose surface, glowing with the sun's early rays, I could easily distinguish abundance of aquatic birds in playful motion. – Beyond the town rose a lofty country of great extent, well wooded, and diversified with innumerable pastoral residences: the back ground was composed of rocks shaded with aged forests, and broken with some capacious lakes – while the whole expanse presented to us a scene as sublime, rich, and interesting, as any I had ever seen on the face of the earth; but I can scarcely describe my surprise when they both told me, that the place we then beheld was *Sophis*.

"I had expected to be longer on the journey before we arrived; imagined it could not but be a vast city; looked for innumerable houses, and magnificent public buildings; and so hastily explained these ideas to *Chilo*, that what I said had almost an air of contempt united with disappointment. Of this he took no other notice than by observing, that the city was formed on their ideas of what a capital ought to be; for, with them, its smallness constituted its greatest eulogium; as many people huddled together, must, necessarily, be prejudicial to health, and industry; and the arts might be more beneficially followed where the artist's family enjoyed the breezes of the country, and the advantages of horticulture, both of which were indispensably necessary to a nation that subsisted on natural productions. – 'Nor indeed (said he), should we have had any capital at all, were it not necessary to have a place where our archives might be recurred to with certainty, and secured from decay; where our first magistrate should reside to do justice; and the delegates of the people assemble to execute the general will. – Yet small as our capital appears to you, it is chiefly composed of public buildings; the capaciousness and utility of which I am persuaded will meet with your approbation when you have considered them, and are better acquainted with our laws and customs: for the basis of them is an attempt to preserve to man in society all the advantages of the natural state, and to prevent him from falling into those corruptions which crowds are too likely to engender.'

"An hour on the summit of this agreeable eminence thus engaged soon passed away. When the company joined us, a messenger was sent to *Sophis* to announce our approach, and the motives which had occasioned our journey.

"The whole of the descent was very easy; the path winding through groves of tall trees, whose underwoods were chiefly of sweet-scented and flowering shrubs, watered by many trickling streams, the freshness of which invited and detained a numerous tribe of beautiful song-birds. Herds of goats also with long and silvery hair were frequently seen browsing on the banks. Many shady alcoves, the monuments of departed citizens, graced the road, whose walls were covered with vines, and overshadowed by date-trees, and pomegranates. Little farms filled the open spots;

and, when approaching the city, the whole way seemed to pass through a prolific garden of fruits, esculent plants, and gaudy flowers.

"On each side the gates, or, more properly, entrance, for gates there were none, were two immense fountains, whose waters were received into circular marble basins, and never overflowed, but were carried silently away through subterranean channels: the entrance itself was a noble arch, which formed only the segment of a large circle, whose roof was parallel with the earth, and beneath whose shade, at each extremity, were two long marble sophas, on which the magistrates and officers were constantly seated in rotation. Two we found there, accompanied by several citizens, – whose only distinction consisted in the marks of age, and the ebony rods which they held in their hands.

"*Chilo* delivered one of them a paper, containing an account of all his father knew of us, which he read with an audible voice; and, after an agreeable conference of a few minutes, we were informed that we might proceed to the mansion appointed for strangers.

"Before we left the place, however, I stopped to examine more minutely this singular entrance to a city without walls; and found that it was not a mere work of ostentation: for, besides that it composed a justice-seat, the whole served as a grand sun-dial, the roof being grooved, and furnished with two flights of steps; and, in the front, instead of any other ornaments, were two small alcoves, from whence, on certain occasions, the laws were promulgated to the people.

"The whole was constructed, with much solidity, of green, yellow, and white marble; and, although nearly without embellishments, finished with a degree of accuracy that I have never yet seen surpassed. The pavement, both under and about it, was of porphyry and presented a platform of considerable extent, bounded by an irregular grove of shady trees, through which an avenue was conducted, that led up to the great square.

"On our arrival there, every thing was so new and agreeable to me, that my mind was quite overpowered with amazement – the crowd, the buildings, a magnificent tank in the middle of the purest water, parties dancing to the sound of various instruments, others exchanging refreshments, flowers, or fruit; some offering seats made of cane, others umbrellas of papyrus leaves; the groups of elegant men and women, who rose at each step to survey us, all contributed to encrease my confusion; and I whispered *Chilo* to take me away, before my head was turned with pleasure and admiration. Nor did I conceal from him the principal cause of my agitation. I saw, or thought I saw, among the crowd, the image of *Mica*, on whose account I had suffered so much reproach and internal shame.

"The pleasantry of my conductor, however, tended not a little to recover my senses from the disorder into which they had been thrown. Putting his right hand on my shoulder, he placed the other over my eyes, 'Let me secure you (said he), from again seeing this dangerous vision; the girl may have deep designs; it is proper we should keep you from her sight: love is sometimes malicious.'

"No, (replied I, feeling then the full force of my happy situation), I will not be protected from her just resentment; it may be salutary to me to receive correction from that quarter; take away your hand.' – 'Alas! (said he, with a sarcastic smile), the bird is flown, and mocks us from the clouds.'

"By this time we were come to the place appointed for our accommodation, – a noble building, occupying nearly one side of the great square; it was elevated, spacious, and had two extensive porticoes, one above the other, continuing all round; the lowermost for the accommodation of male travellers, the uppermost for females – much resembling the saloons of the Asiatic princes, but more simple in the general effect; the lower order being grave, the upper light and exquisitely elegant, suitable to the purposes for which each part was destined. Nor were the materials less appropriate; the first story being composed of a marble or stone of a dark amethyst colour, ornamented by lines of a pale yellow; the upper of an olive-green, with similar ornaments of white. But the most singular thing was the roof, which was entirely converted into a tank or basin for water, and supplied from a neighbouring mountain by marble pipes, in the centre of which was a pillar of the same material, which, while it served to support an immense covering, was perforated, so as to convey the water of the basin through the centre of the building. From this pillar, as from a conduit, all the apartments were amply supplied; while below, as well as above, it served an abundance of small baths, with which the whole building was surrounded; and lastly, watered a great number of large orange-trees, two of which were planted at the foot of each bath, so as to form a noble alley in the front of the whole building; which composed one entire side of this extensive square.

"The opposite side consisted of halls for the dispatch of public business, all of one ground floor, shady, spacious, refreshed with fountains, airy, having large porticoes, and ample accommodations for repose; the symmetry of whose architecture, you can only judge from the imperfect specimens here depicted on the prison-walls, rather from memory than actual measurement. A tender remembrance, it is true, warmly agitated me when designing them; but I warn you against giving me credit for accuracy – they are mere sketches; for who can pretend to rival the sublime and chaste ideas of the Sophian architects; whose public edifices, although nearly unornamented, and wholly depending on geometrical correctness, and nicely balanced proportions, inspire the soul with dignified and virtuous pride – such as noble minds exult in on contemplating vast productions gradually created by human industry, with fitness and simplicity."

Here we both remained silent a few moments; but while I examined one side of the chamber, on which the steady hand of *Lycas* had finely delineated these lofty halls, I saw, by a side-glance, his manly breast heave like a swelling sea, his colour fade and return; when, covering his face with his shrivelled hands, he uttered a long-drawn sigh, that seemed to describe the flutter of his departing soul. "These, these, (he exclaimed), can affect you but feebly, as efforts of taste; but to me they speak too audibly – they remind me that *there* I first was reconciled to *Mica*; *there* wedded a woman who, under an apparently frivolous outside, concealed a soul of prodigious fortitude, unparalleled affection, and whose frame alone rivalled in symmetry the immortal works of her countrymen!" – When recovering himself suddenly, "Pardon me (rejoined he), this burst of passion – no other subject can now agitate my icy veins; judge then what must have been her merits, who, although now long lost, still retains the power to controul this aged bosom, which sacredly enshrines her beloved image; and the memory of whose virtues has been my almost sole relief during this long solitary confinement."

While thus giving vent to his griefs, which, by my silence and gestures, I religiously respected, a sudden and piercing cry was distinctly heard near the door of our prison; and, an instant after, the poor fellow, who had the care of us, hastily unbarring the ponderous valves, rushed into the chamber, and fainted at my feet.

By our joint efforts we presently recovered him; and, the cries still continuing at intervals, demanded of him the cause of his alarm.

"The spirit of the Nile (said he, his teeth chattering in his head), has, taken entire possession of this accursed tower! now, more then ever, infested with howling demons, who daily play their pranks up and down its gloomy galleries. – Neither Alla, nor Mahomet do they respect, although his holy name is scored with charcoal on the door of each chamber; nor have you, O, *Lycas!* with your good heart, or your music-box, been able to drive them to their habitations in hell – do you not now hear the yells they utter? Not content with rushing before me at every corner, to make me break my water jars (whose pure element they abhor), and extinguishing my torch with infernal vapours, I am now to be scared with terrific blasphemies, and the howlings of the damned; let me beg of you, therefore, to take the koran, and come down to the sally-port watch-tower, for, undoubtedly, all the devils of Egypt are now clawing each other in that lonely angle."

"I have no koran" (said *Lycas*) – "Come then (said the affrighted keeper), with your own sweet voice, that so charms me, and *charm* them." The apostrophe was too civil to be resisted; we descended, therefore, rapidly following the fellow, who went on puffing with impatience, and getting two hearty falls by the way, all of which he attributed to the spiteful goblins of the castle. At length, after winding towards the gloomy spot where we distinctly heard the direct lamentations, and finding no human form from which they could proceed, we were all at a loss to account for the strange phenomenon, till looking out of a narrow and deep loop-hole, the jailor drew back, with the countenance of a man that had beheld a ghost – he could not articulate, but pointed to the place; and my companion being much too feeble to get up to it, I mounted on the keeper's shaking shoulders, and thrusting out my neck, for which the aperture scarcely allowed room, I beheld a sight that might have petrified any one – it was no spirit, but a poor fellow-prisoner, who, in a desperate attempt to escape, had miscalculated the depth he had to descend into a gloomy fosse overgrown with reeds, where he hoped to lie concealed; and having, by accident, slid below a projecting stone, from whence he probably intended to make a second sally, hung suspended from a cord by his hands, blown backwards and forwards by the wind, and now nearly exhausted, and ready to drop into a deep and watery hole, merely to look down to which, produced in me a sensation of indescrible aversion.

Fortunately for the poor man, we found a place from whence we could seize his cord; and he was soon, by our united efforts, restored, more dead than alive, to his forsaken cell.

The poor gaoler now laughed heartily at his own folly; while we returned to our confinement, and found our frugal evening's repast much sweetened by the benevolence we had been enabled to practise, and the proof we had acquired, that imprudence may augment even the miseries of captivity for life.

Next morning, the old man met me with his cheerful countenance more than usually enlivened. The gaoler, from gratitude for our assistance, or perhaps from a desire to make us forget his ridiculous fears, had brought a basket of limes, some coffee, and a jar of palm-wine. We knew he would conceal, for his own sake, the attempted escape of the poor prisoner; and, to ingratiate ourselves still farther with a man, on whose good offices many of our common comforts depended, we invited him to partake of some sherbet; while my philosophical companion in confinement, touched the vina for our mutual entertainment. The strain was enchanting; for my own part, I forgot I was a prisoner; and the citizen of *Sennaar*, quite transported, remembered no longer his occupation: – "Go, (said he), begone! escape! – let me die, let me perish for such a friend!" For my own part, I confess, I was almost ready to take him at his word; but the noble sufferer made the blushes come into my cheeks, when, throwing down the instrument, he arrested my purpose: "How (said he), have I, in imagination, conveyed you to *Sophis* only to see you return to this ignoble selfishness? – Freedom is, doubtless, inestimably, *immeasurably sweet*, but, in base society, there is no no true liberty. We should both forfeit our good opinions, were we to accept of the offer this man's transport of gratitude has laid before us – could we *ever* be happy under a freedom procured by an artifice that must cost the life of our deluded benefactor? – No, it is undoubtedly lawful to interest him in our behalf, so as to humanize his guardianship, but not for the purpose of teaching his unguarded heart to betray his trust." – When, turning to the keeper, "My good friend, (said he), take your keys and begone; your offer will not easily be forgotten. When we can procure the blessing you propose, without causing the ruin of others, you may then repeat it. You have been too kind to me hitherto ever to find in me your mortal enemy."

The astonished keeper looked first at one, then at the other, and retired without speaking a word. The speech of *Lycas* excited in me fresh admiration, and I felt sorry for the part I had acted in the scene; for the magnanimous sentiment exalted my soul, and seemed thereby to have softened my captivity; but just as I was going to apologize, he cut me short, and, with much complacency, thus resumed the narration of his history. –

"We were now in the great caravansary of *Sophis*, and the ensuing day was fixed for our audience with the ruling men of that country;

the intervening time was passed in admiring the interior of the building, the whole of which was finished in a manner more splendid than I had ever before witnessed; black, red, and gold japanned wood, highly wrought and polished, made every apartment look like a curious cabinet: nor was ivory and ebony spared in the construction of the sophas. We ate out of bowls of fine porcelain; reposed on exquisitely soft yellow mattresses; and, in a word, partook of much innocent luxury, amid such magnificence as is even unknown at Constantinople.

"*Chilo* was gratified with the notice I took of every thing, telling me, that the reason why this splendour was banished from other habitations, was in order to preserve general equality, and that it might be the more noticed here. Some attractions, he observed, were necessary to bring the citizens to attend to their public duties at this place; some grandeur, to give them an idea of their own public importance, and that of the tasks they came there to fulfil; some comforts, to compensate the lover of domestic felicity, and rural employment (which was the reigning passion of the nation) for that temporary loss which this journey annually occasioned: for, he explained to me, that once in every year the heads of families of each tribe, of a certain age, were by law required to appear in rotation, in order to maintain a perpetual representative senate which sat daily all the year round, for the purpose of dispatching public business; their guide in which was a constitutional code, long ago brought nearly to perfection; so that the assembly, by a continual influx and efflux, like a sea gently agitated by regular tides, was secured form corruption, and that undue influence which long habits of governing are but too apt to produce in the minds of even good men. This period, however, did not commence with them till the prime of life, about thirty years of age, nor continue beyond sixty. From this duty none were exempt but those who were naturally incapacitated, or had forfeited their character by some highly criminal action against society; and all, in attending to it, were equally maintained at the public charge, both the rich, and those less wealthy, for the law allowed none to be positively poor.

"Every male, by being born in the island, had a title to a certain portion of land; not to cultivate which constituted a very high national crime, and was, if proved, punished by compulsive labour. His title also to a rotationary seat in the assembly was equally simple, as it consisted in his having children born to him by his wife.

"I felt my eyes obscured by a watery humour when he came to this part of his description; and involuntarily demanded, if I also

might not have children born to me in this country, and become
at once, a father, a citizen, and a senator?

"'Undoubtedly (said he), you shall, if *Mica* consents; *if* she love
you, *she* can make you a Sophian; for, being the heiress of a worthy
family, she can in her own right depute you as her representative,
after cohabitation, and the fruits of it appear: *on no other terms* could
you possibly become one of us, notwithstanding the apparent title
your language gives you; and I verily believe my father threw her
in your way, from some motive; for you see plainly, either that, or
her own inclinations, have conducted her after us.' – I siezed his
hand, and kissed it, as he uttered these words, which seemed like
soft music to my attentive ears; and retired soon after to those
delicious slumbers, which, like waking dreams, fill the whole mind
with transporting images, too confused to be recovered, too en-
chanting ever to be described.

"Day had scarcely broke forth, when we rose, took a slight repast,
and, accompanied by *Chilo*, and the good old *Yahomy*, went straight
to view this original city.

"That stupendous orb, the sun, was just risen, and observing the
respectful attention which *Chilo* paid to the first emissions of its
rays, I could not help asking him what he thought of that wonderful
ball of fire, of which so many ages had not been able to diminish
the lustre?

"'Do you really then take it for a ball of fire? (said he), the idea
is new to me – we always considered it as one of the eyes of the
universe, through which the eternal Energy emits what light it is
pleased to bestow on us; and that light is itself both heat and life.'
– I smiled, but could not help asking again what he meant by the
eternal Energy, – did he mean a first cause? which I felt *must be*,
but wondered that I could not reach it. 'I will shew you (said he),
why you cannot reach it.' We were then near the gate, to ascend to
the pointed summit of which, were steps on both sides. Instead of
replying to my question, he bade me go up before him; and when
I arrived at the top, told me to go on; of course I descended –
'How! (said he), are you descending? You should still ascend!'
– 'Nay (said I), that is impossible, there is no higher foundation for
my feet; should I attempt it I shall break my neck; I had better,
therefore, remain where I am.'

"'Just so (said he) is the path of man's reason circumscribed.
We may ascend to a certain height on the steps of our reason, but
we have our highest point where we totter, or, attempting to ad-

vance, decline; we must either stop there, *or descend and know ourselves.'*

"'What (said I), are we not immortal, is not the spirit of man a god-like thing?'

"'Most probably (replied he with great calmness), but we know what body is, and not what is spirit: we should go out of our sphere to make mind the chief object, as much as we should do were we to neglect the intimation of so noble and sincere a monitor. If our soul be immortal, it will be so; if it be not, *it will be where it ought to be*. During its mortal connections, it will be employed, probably, as it is with us, in guiding matter, as far as its powers extend. For our part, what I humbly conceive to be our business, is, by the help of the mind, to attain to the perfection of our material nature; not to lose our time in merely enquiring what mind is. Our first duty, I conceive, is to preserve and prolong our own existence, which can only be done by leading simple and innocent lives; our next, to multiply and provide for our offspring; and lastly, by the help of the experience we have acquired, to enable them still to improve their modes of life, and still to augment the sum of their happiness and virtue.'

"Here he paused, and I was silent; but I felt my whole frame calmed like the sea after a storm, when, bounded by an unruffled mirror, the sandy beach lies cool and unblemished, to receive the soft access of the evening breeze.

"Discoursing thus, we came to the senate-house, on the opposite side of the square: our business being extra-judicial, an early hour had been appointed – my heart palpitated, yet I knew not wherefore, as no guilt dwelt within it; notwithstanding which, I felt like a criminal preparing for execution, – Should they banish me (said I, inwardly), I am lost! Can I support the thoughts of leaving this country? Can I live without – the name of *Mica* was on my lips, but I suppressed its utterance.

"The entrance was of that sublime proportion, which is rather felt than seen. The vestibule spacious and solemn, yet I noticed its particulars but little; but, on approaching the theatre, where, with becoming gravity, the assembly were all seated on polished benches, gently ascending, and so contrived, by passages, as to give convenient access to each, I was recalled to myself by its imposing awfulness; not on account of any peculiar habit, for all were in their common dresses; the more aged in one much like this I now wear, the younger were without either turbans or robes; but, for the most part, possessing large dark eyes, graceful beards, and hair in abundance, overshadowing features full of generous expression.

"*Chilo* did not keep me long in suspense, but, advancing to a sort of tribune in the centre, ascended it, unfolded his father's letter, and, having received a signal that he might proceed, read, to the representatives assembled, a short narrative, which related the manner of my coming into the island, my conduct since, my professed motives, those of my companion, the commodity I had brought, the singularity of my being acquainted with much of the language, and our desire, if not inconsistent with the principles of their constitution, to remain incorporated among them.

"Having finished, he descended with as little ceremony as he had before used in ascending, and joining us, conducted us to a sort of platform, where we stood in sight of, and within hearing of our judges, who instantly proceeded to the business in hand, by simply putting the question of our stay or departure; which, after about a quarter of an hour's silent reflection, was decided, by a ballot of black shells, in the negative as to my stay, but in the affirmative with respect to *Yahomy*.

"On receiving the report, which *Chilo* gave me with great reluctance, I fell senseless on the earth; nor do I remember any thing that followed, till I found myself, some days afterwards, languid and faint, on a sopha at the caravansary, in the arms of the kind *Yahomy*, while *Chilo* was feeling my pulse with a look of despair; and, – O! unutterable happiness! the lovely and compassionate *Mica*, with dishevelled locks, affectionately embracing my feet.

"Having been some time in the strong delirium of a fever, owing to the shock which disappointed hopes had produced on my frame, every thing appeared to me like a dream. I would have arisen in order to throw myself before her, but my frame was too much weakened for the effort. All I could do was to stretch out my arms, extend my eyes towards the desired object, utter a deep sigh, and burst into a violent flood of scalding tears.

"These, by relieving my over-heated brain, at last gave me utterance; but what I said was too incoherent to be understood, in any other light, than as an expression of the violence of my grief, and unbounded passion for the object before me.

"She approached, clasped my hand, and sat down by my side; *Chilo* took the other, but I insensibly withdrew it, to press her's with both of mine. Her languid head reclined on my shoulder. We remained, for some of the most delicious moments of my life, quite silent; during all which time, a seraphic fire, a healing balm seemed to steal through my very essence. How long it lasted I cannot recollect; but I shall ever remember, that when the sensation was reduced to the sober idea of common existence, I found that we were left together, heard the music of her voice, inhaled the balsam of her breath, and often repeated, as well as words could convey them, the tender ardours of my unlimited, enthusiastic love.

"But I beg your pardon (said the old captive), I see I have affected you too sensibly; for time has not yet dissolved the sharp impression, nor age undermined the pleasing fabrick of former enjoyments. *We cannot, it is not possible, to eradicate an early and true affection!*' — "I feel it (I replied, smothering a sigh), but in opening my deep festering wounds you relieve accumulated pain."

"To shorten the narrative, I must inform you (he rejoined), that the fever, after this interview, took a sudden favourable turn; and that my recovery was not a little advanced by the assurances of my friend, in addition to the happiness which I felt in the unreserved communication of *Mica*'s attachment — that the decrees of their assemblies were not, in such a case as this, irreversible. On the contrary, it was the boast of this reflecting people, that their senate was always open to appeals, guided by reason: intending only public good, they knew of no rule without an exception, so that they could never be ensnared into a decision by artful men, or studied eloquence. The chief motive for the ballot which banished me (he told me), was the strict letter of the law, united with its spirit, as far as related to my being an importer of merchandize. An uninvited guest, they thought, should come with clean hands. This they found manifest in the case of *Yahomy*, who entered poor, and seemed captivated by the irresistible attraction of their manners: 'But when (said he), I pleaded your cause the next day, explained to them, and offered to be bound, that you were not arrived a mean trafficker for profit; declared that you were in possession of the affections of a female citizen, and were ready to undergo any probationary trial — they reconsidered you a singular case, and, at length, consented to permit your limited residence of two years; but, on the express condition, that you should, in all things, conform to the manners of the island; and, in proof of your sincerity, part with none of your gold but to those employed in constructing public works, or in the preparation of rewards to be disposed of by the public assembly.'

"And here it was, for the first time, I learned, that every male, and every female, received, on arriving at a state of puberty, golden ornaments of an equal value, though not similar construction: the males, a plain ring for the middle finger; the females, a small single ear-ring: that, on the decease of those of either sex, they were returned to the national treasury: by which means these singular people kept a simple register of all their active population, the date of the year being engraven on each, on the day of assuming them, which constituted, in every family, a species of festival annually observed.

"The business of our journey being now completed, we prepared for our return to the habitation of *Chilo*'s father, with *Mica* and *Yahomy* in our company. Their dress I adopted immediately; and their manners being perfectly unaffected and natural, it would have been mortifying not to follow them; for, while they relieved me from the fatigueing ceremonials of affected politeness, they instilled the most disinterested sentiments relative to social and mutual services; and perhaps a great deal of that urbanity, so remarkable amongst them, arose from their high ideas of natural freedom, mutual dependance, and reasonable equality.

"The laws alone were paramount over all; but, in private families, the father preserved his natural authority, merely from habit, and the effects which the practice of humane actions always produce; for there existed no law to enforce, *in all cases*, obedience to the will of parents, as it is by no means a matter of certainty that the parent is always a proper judge of what may constitute the welfare of his child: yet I never witnessed more domestic happiness in any country than this; and nothing seemed to be wanting to compleat my felicity, but an indissoluble union with the generous and accomplished object of my choice.

"This earnest wish I took an early opportunity to suggest both to herself and to the father of *Chilo*. – She listened to me with much complacency, but never returned me any answer; and, on these occasions, seemed always, though tender and gently affectionate, to be under some embarrassment: but the old man quickly set all to rights, by explaining to me that, in *Sophis*, this sort of engagement admitted of no ceremonial rites, whatever others might demand; 'It is a compact (said he), which concerns alone the parties to it, and is so certain of taking place some time or other, between the sexes, that it neither demands encouragement to promote it, at its proper time, nor dissuasion to prevent it, where the organs are unprepared. – We leave all this to nature, whom we adore under the emblem of love, feeling it unnecessary to frame laws to regulate an instinctive commerce; as pure and as natural as the vital flame.

– You are therefore (said he), the possessor of *Mica* exclusively, while your mutual attachment lasts; and I am much surprised, that you have not already accomplished that, which must have been, long ago, the wish of both parties.'

"I wanted words to express my astonishment at this speech. Instead of being charmed with this unlimited licence, I began to think I had been mistaken in the favourable opinion I had entertained of these extraordinary people; and, in the rashness of my judgment, took upon me to suspect, that, with regard to women at least, they had no notions of delicacy. I flew to my friend, *Chilo*, unburthened my whole bosom to him, and, before I would suffer him to utter a word, recounted all *our* hymeneal system, ceremonies, and laws.

"My account appeared to astonish him little less than his father's discourse had alarmed *me*. He told me, that he was not, after all, so much surprised at what I had related of foreign nations, whose customs, he had often been told, were the reason of the *Sophians* separating themselves from the world, as he was at my approbation of such ridiculous errors, who had hitherto professed myself to be a man guided by nature and reason. – 'What! (said he), at the first genuine irresistible impulse of tender desire, do you check the current of creation, and, forgetting your duty to the Maker of all, delay its exigent service at the command of those who are past feeling the divine impetus? Or, still worse, are there among you, men, who dare to interpose their feeble wills to postpone the great unerring and explicit laws of propagation? – Can youth be so tinctured with sordid passions, as to seek in wealth a compensation for the finer feelings of their frame? Or, so corrupt as to demand, in the presence of witnssses, oaths, in proof of that which the eyes have declared, and a continued pursuit of tenderness ought to have established past dispute? But, above all, are there with you, men so wickedly cruel, as to insist on continuing a brutal commerce between what you call married people, after the affections are dead and cold? Or tyrants, who can think deliberately of engendering the children of hate and animosity? A thought so profligate sickens my very soul! – As to your women, I am pained to make unpleasant reflections; but surely it must be a strange effect of custom that can reconcile them to such habits as you describe, when you say (if I mistake not), that, in most countries of Europe, they fix a day to consummate the espousals of young virgins, who retire from the presence of all their family, friends, and acquaintance, to ascend the marriage couch; and the next day appear without blushes, though ruffled with the inordinate first rites of impetuous love: and, still more strangely indelicate, instead of fanning the mysterious flame, by soft denials, and secret conjunctions, they occupy the same pallet openly, and nightly; as if they either hastened to extinguish the lamp of hallowed and beneficent desire, or even, after all their bonds and sacred engagements, entertained doubts of each other's fidelity!

"'No wonder (added he, with a shrug of inexpressible disgust), that faithlessness often follows such ill-contrived connections; or that the men who are capable of forging those chains for the feebler sex, should, with cruelty, revenge on their helpless victims the slightest deviation from their mandates.'

"Here he paused; and, while his just remarks penetrated my understanding, and threw a bright light over the former prejudices of my mind, I could not but rejoice to find they admired so enthusiastically the virtues of fidelity and modesty.

"'You admit then (said I), O, my friend! of pure connubial ties, and hold sacred the flame of love? *Mica* may become mine exclusively; and I ought to demand no other security of her fidelity than the stability of my affection. – I see, I feel now the delicacy of your customs; but have the goodness to explain those which relate to this delightful union that sits so near my heart?'

"'There is little to explain (said he); mutual attachment is the only tie we know of. *All others must be weak*, and we rarely punish infidelity: if caused by wantonness and intemperance, it must at last prove its own punishment, by diminishing confidence in such a character; but we esteem female chastity, as being in itself a proof of an honourable mind, not light, but solid, strictly keeping its first engagements: nay, we crown with green leaves those pairs who can boast of long continued connections, and, the usual result of them, a numerous progeny. – We do not object, nevertheless, to polygamy, as you call the having more than one wife, when all the parties agree; because there may be many reasons which may make such an arrangement in some cases prudent; but it is very uncommon, on account of the necessity of that agreement. As to the females whom you call prostitutes; but who, with us, are termed the unhappy, they are very rare; since such connections are totally inconvenient to men who live by agriculture, and whose strength often consists in the number of their children. – But we do not exclude them from the rights of society, for having adopted those disgusting irregularities; neither are they spurned by their own family. On the contrary, viewing them in the light of women, the disease of whose minds is equally to be pitied with those maladies that affect the body, they consider it as an incumbent duty to afford them their best advice and hospitality. And hence these errors are seldom of very long continuance; for the repeated neglect of their lovers either drives them back to that family asylum which is always in mercy open to them; or perceiving how much their character suffers by inconstancy, while health is injured, and beauty decayed, by those relaxing gratifications, they learn, from experience, the necessity of adopting a more prudent conduct. And it often happens that one of these, at first thoughtless women, becomes at last the best guardian of her rising relations. – As to those who could be capable of reproaching them with their former deviations, they would be regarded with as much abhorrence and contempt, as the person who should consider it as criminal to have had an access of a frenzy fever, or a stroke of the palsy.'

"'All this (said I), is very humane, and, even according to my ideas, most just: but pray tell me, when an alliance has been formed, from mutual attachment, and one of the parties, attracted by superior accomplishments, or guided by an inconstant spirit, quits their first connection, and the offspring that has arisen from it; in what manner is the offending party punished, and on whom devolves the care of the children; what also is done to the seducer?'

"'I cannot help smiling at so strange a question (said he): nevertheless, as you appear to be serious, I shall answer it with gravity. Did I not just now tell you that inconstancy was followed with the loss of our esteem: and, as to the other case, we say, that he, or she, who cannot preserve the affections they have gained, must attribute the loss to their own negligence or fault. For whatever men value, it is generally observed that they enjoy without ostentation, and never neglect the care of. With us, beauty and merit, when acquired, cannot be locked up (as you say it is with you in Turkey), but it is seldom paraded about, or brought unnecessarily forward; and as we give both sexes the same education, both are studiously taught the art of preserving their lovers. We know that the disorders occasioned by passions deserve our utmost attention; and have people who make a kind of profession of curing them, tracing them generally to physical causes, and whose prescriptions are bounded by no limits that are not contrary to nature; so that it is no uncommon thing for one of these sages to prescribe a sexual

connection, as a remedy for the apparent disorders of the mind.
Nor are there wanting instances, where parents have saved their
children's lives or senses, by means that have often terminated in
the solid settlement of both parties; for it constitutes a part of the
skill of these intelligent practitioners, so to pair their patients, that
a double cure may be effected by the same regimen.

"'But these are cases which occur but very seldom. The general
freedom of our manners gives, to almost every one, an opportunity
of forming as early an alliance as they find necessary. That equality
which prevails among us, as to fortune, and the labours of life, also
contributes not a little to make parents less opposite to the attach-
ment of their children, and occasions mixed society to be by no
means dangerous. Equal citizens of our free country, we can con-
ceive no distinctions, but those of superior beauty, virtue, talents,
or experience: and hence, although I have hitherto had no reason
to doubt your veracity, I can scarcely bring myself to believe that,
in the part of the world you came from, there are men so meanly
foolish as to pay a personal respect to hereditary titles; and others
infected with the madness of actually receiving the homage due to
a superior race, when they do not find themselves exempted from
the disorders of their fellow-creatures, or surpassing them in un-
derstanding.

"'But, I beg your pardon for this disgression (said *Chilo*). I should
have told you, in answer to your question, that the children, in case
of separation, are always left to the care of the father, when the
separation arises from the determination of the mother; and the
reverse in the opposite case. And this law was made, in order to
encrease the difficulty of the step on both sides; and, that nothing,
short of a confirmed destruction of esteem, should operate to bring
about an event so unpleasant. As for seduction, or a deliberate plan
to invade the mutual happiness of others, when proved to have
been the practice of any offender, either male or female, from the
prevalence of vicious propensities, our laws banish them to one of
the islands on the lake, where labour for life, accompanied with
wholesome instruction, is the lot of all. But, when it appears, that
the attractions of youth and merit unworthily treated, improper
opportunities allowed by those whose interest and duty it was to
prevent them, warm passions, and sincerity of love, have drawn a
gentle pair into this vortex; we lament the consequences, which
generally are the disruption of the first union, and the loss of one

of the parents to the children; and, by all the means in our power, we foster the new engagements, by way of encouraging them, by a closer affection to each other, to repair the breach they have made in society, and to avoid themselves the errors of that man or woman, whose first neglect of his or her duties led them to the situation in which they stand.'

"Here he paused – my questions were all fully answered; I had no longer any fears. My violent and enthusiastic regard for *Mica* whispered me that she would always be mine, if constant attention, tender regard, and ever-lasting love, could bind her.

"Full of these ideas, I rushed impatiently into her presence, seized her hand, and consuming her, as it were, with my ardent gaze, renewed and repeated all my former professions, acting and saying also a thousand extravagant things.

"The scene was enchanting around us. The deepest shade of a venerable wood, on the margin of an irregular winding ravine, at the bottom of which the purest wave tumbled over rocks into shallow transparent basins; brakes of odoriferous shrubs, and graceful plantains, mixed with cotton, cocoa, and palm trees, surrounded us on every side. The dark grove, the sweet melody, the solemn hour of evening all contributed, with the presence of one of the finest proportioned women on earth, to make me think this world a paradise. But when I wildly thought to press a willing victim to my throbbing breast, and riot in delights – I gazed, and found her cold and drowned in tears. The scene that followed was too touching to be described; it soon checked all my impatience, and turned it to a momentary confusion. She charged me with possessing only a brutal passion for her; wept, and acknowledged my influence, but complained bitterly of the use I was about to make of it: 'This is only I fear, (said she), a second access of your feverish passion; when gratified, perhaps, *Mica* will be forgotten! – Yes, *Lycas*, I feel I am to be yours; but I had hoped you would also first promise to be mine; that you would give me your honourable word, never to be the lover of any other but me; that you would *break the pebble with me*, and wear it ever in your bosom?'

"Joy now succeeded in its turn. – Her delicate simplicity charmed me. I kissed her ivory feet; a lambent fire spread through my veins, and I made my vows *just as she dictated them*. The altar was the flowery margin of the stream – we divided one of its pebbles. By artful repetitions she postponed my happiness till the moon rose;

but, when her brilliant horns mercifully dipped behind a flying cloud, then was it that we reached the perihelium of those soul-delighting ecstasies that the warmest fancy could imagine or desire.

"It would be madness to attempt a description of the weeks that followed. The transporting hours we enjoyed were greatly enhanced by the imagined secrecy of our appointments; and, although there is no doubt that the good family in which we resided, saw, and rejoiced at our union, they had the generosity to conceal from us the discovery; so that it was not till *Mica* was far advanced in the capacity of making me a father, that she was prevailed on to shew any *open* partiality for me. In due time, she brought me that son, whose portrait you there behold, traced by this unfortunate hand. I took possession of her portion of territory. *Yahomy* had a small lot given him, and became our assistant. The next year she gave me a daughter. The waters of the brook, which first witnessed our union, ran before our habitation; and to its ever flowing stream we often compared our increasing affections.

"To embellish the spot became my delight, and one of their best artists taught me, for that purpose, the rudiments of painting and sculpture – fostered by the smiles of *Mica*, I soon became a proficient. How little did I then think, that, in a few short years, it would be my sole amusement in this solitary castle in the kingdom of *Sennaar!*

"My time now passed only too rapidly. The tender offices of love, the study of my new duties, the practice of my new profession, which, however, had no reward in view but fame, fully employed me; insomuch, that, in a very little time, I had nearly forgotton that I was by birth a European. To be adopted by the senate became now the height of my ambition; and I eagerly sought, by every act of conformity to the delightful customs of *Sophis*, to render myself worthy of their entire approbation.

"*Chilo* and his father were among those we saw most frequently – those who are happy, as we were, are little solicitous of a numerous acquaintance. *Innocence and the gentle passions, ever unobtrusive, are content with silent peace.* When, with a calm splendour, the sun was declining to the west, we generally saw one or other of those friends approach our humble habitation, which was composed of no other materials than thick clay walls, coloured, and covered with a deep projecting thatch. The rooms were lofty, though few in number; the doors low, and shaded with mats exquisitely wrought by the hands of *Mica*; the floors embellished with the same; the windows, which were oblong openings, had each, below them, a niche containing a mattress of yellow wool to sleep on, with a platform on the outside, to be used in hot weather; mats rolled up closed the inner aperture, and the roof sheltered the outer platform. In the rainy season, our couches were removed to warm alcoves constructed in the mass of the walls. Attached to the larger building was a little cottage of two rooms, which solely belonged to *Mica*; and, at the opposite end, forming a sort of wing, was another for our friend, *Yahomy*: and our implements of agriculture, clean and carefully preserved, constituted the principal ornaments of the hall.

"A well-shaded and capacious rustic porch was the scene where we always met, whose rude pillars were clasped with odoriferous climbers, and whose pavement consisted of a tessellated figure of shells of all colours. Here we sat, talking with chearful seriousness, while our children played before us; enjoying a wholesome and simple refection, and forming a tranquil group worthy of the contemplation of the eternal powers, when they deign, in complacency, to survey the scale of their vast universe.

"One evening, when our conversation naturally turned on the subject of the children, I entreated the old man, if not too fatiguing, to teach me how I ought to conduct the education of my son.

"'My idea (he replied), of the education which you ought to give your son, *in preference to all others*, is this: That, attending carefully to instruct him in natural habits, as well with regard to diet, as exercise, and cloathing, you should burthen his memory as little as possible; yet so continue, in the way of amusement, as daily to add to his stock of information relative to the construction of the most common of useful instruments and conveniencies; particularly such as are constantly necessary to his existence with decency and comfort. You should also daily, yet not so as to interfere, by any means, with his healthful exercises, teach him the rudiments of his own language, the art of numbers, and that of writing, which includes painting; by all means taking especial care, from the moment you perceive the first dawnings of reason, to suggest to him, with energetic solemnity, the real necessity of practising *truth*, even on the most trifling occasions; the rules of justice next; and, as fast as he is able to comprehend them, the generous principles of universal benevolence, humanity, and condescension: prudence also, or the restraining art, must be inculcated early.

"'When, under this gentle discipline, you find the body well grown, and the health permanently established, accompanied with

habits of regularity, and the love of order grafted and striking into
the vigorous stock; then, when the desire of information strength-
ens, you must feed the mind less sparingly with instruction in most
of the useful arts. The nature of the earth in all its parts must then
be investigated; but the leading feature of all education should, I
think, decidedly, be its tendency to confirm him in the valuable
opinion, that *his native spot ought to be the seat of all his useful actions,
while he lives, and that he should reject, at the outset, every kind of knowl-
edge, which does not promise to be useful to his existence there.*

"'His first object must be, to learn to live on little, to acquire that
little by his own industry, and with as small a quantity of labour as
possible; for you are bound to teach him, *that health, strength, probity,
and liberty, are the handmaids of peace, and the land marks of happiness
and longevity.'*

"After a short pause, he then continued –

"'A peripatetic tour of our island will of course follow: the chief
object of which will be his improvement in the theory of agriculture,
in all its branches, together with an intimate knowledge of the
virtues of our healing plants. Moderate exercise will preserve his
health; moderate wealth insure his temperance; and limited knowl-
edge secure him from the assaults of vanity: thus will he learn to
economise the most valuable part of that which nature has bestowed
on him, *his time, his talents, and his life.'*

"Finding he had done speaking for the present, and that he did
not touch on the subject of religion, a subject I was myself but ill
acquainted with, even in my own country, and had almost lost sight
of during my travels, I eagerly requested him to give me his opinion
on that head; explaining to him, first, as well as I was able, my
ideas of the creative power, its purity, &c. and was not a little
surprised to hear him express himself as follows:

"'When our ancestor, accompanied by his numerous family, came
first into this island, having descended from the springs of a river
called the Indus, on the other side of the world; after crossing a
great water, suffering inconceivable hardships, losing many of his
people in passing large spaces of sand, others by the jaws of wild
animals; when he came at last to the borders of this lake of *Zambre*
(which so happily encircles our islands), and found himself free
from the persecutions of mankind, in a solitude where nothing was
wanting for the support of life, he then began to put in practice
the solid reflections of his penetrating mind.

"'For having spoken with manly freedom on the subject – his

own countrymen had banished him. To discover a spot, where he might establish his system, had been the object of frequent emigrations; for he had long perceived that it could only flourish, free from interruption, in a perfect solitude. At the springs, on the borders of the lake, where you first discovered a monument of his opinions, did he at leisure form our religious code; and that colossal juvenile figure, with the infant deep planted in its bosom, the work of his own hands, was the emblematic idea of his belief. By that statue he meant to represent *Love* the universal cause of all; by the little figure so carefully lodged in his breast, its providential care of the creation; and the old man embracing it was designed for himself.

"'On a tablet near it, he inscribed the final result of his enquiries, we weak mortals have never been able to extend them.

"'Before time had obliterated them, they were as follows:

"'"*The cause of all things is that Power which always is: and no mortal has hitherto discovered what it is.*

"'"*All things being, for a period, preserved by it, we thence conclude that it loves all.*

"'"*To bodies originated, it has united life, instinct, and limited mind.*

"'"*Life confers the power of action; instinct prolongs and propagates life; mind governs, comprehending whatever is necessary for conduct.*

"'"*Experience, and the result of mental reflection, discover it to be Love which preserves us, and is given us to preserve ourselves.*

"'"*Here, therefore, we must pause — silently reverence the vast impenetrable first cause, and practise love to ourselves, to each other, and to all things, in obedience to the manifest will of that which made them all.*"

"'When he discovered this island, at that time totally uninhabited, and some smaller ones nearly adjoining, he speedily conducted his followers hither, making them solemnly promise, never, but in cases of extreme necessity, to construct any vessel for navigation, or to destroy any thing that had life. The few beasts of prey which we found here were carefully driven from the soil, and a guard placed at the only part which, during a short period, is accessible, to prevent their return. The sheep, with their fine yellow fleece, which he had conducted from the country called Upper Indus, were carefully propagated; and they now form a considerable part of that wealth, which, almost without labour, clothes and subsists us: for while, in a climate so genial to man as this, where the sweet cane, the vine, and trees, bearing food, abound, what have we to wish, or to fear, while our manners are virtuous and simple?'

"'Nothing (said I, enthusiastically, taking both him and *Mica* by the hand), but that our numbers should encrease beyond the ability of the island to sustain them.'

"'That (said he), at present gives us no uneasiness in perspective; for experience shews us, that great numbers may subsist on a small spot, by means of careful cultivation; and we do not see that the laws of nature permit either our animals, or birds, or even the fish of our lake to multiply beyond what is fitting.'

"'Because (I replied), beside what are diminished by natural decay and accidents, I suppose they destroy each other.' 'Not those of the same species (said he), as I have heard you say men do in other countries; and, since we are upon this disagreeable subject, tell us, is it really true, that there are whole nations of men who are continually at variance with the good Principle, and who take a delight in each other's destruction?'

"'It is not only true (I replied), but there are many beings who devote their whole lives to the practice of those arts which tend to this end; who glory in their bloody calling; and, without any bodily infirmities, are content to earn their daily bread by indiscriminately turning their arms against whatever part of mankind has unfortunately offended their inhuman employers.

"'And now, in return (said I), for your communication to me, if agreeable to you all, I will, as nearly as I can, describe the nature of this sect, such as I have found them in *Turkey*, and what I take to have been their origin; since it will not a little tend to confirm you in your mild customs and happy resolution to keep apart from the rest of your fellow-creatures.

"'It is my idea, that the use of arms first became general from men's taking them up to defend themselves from others, who, preferring a life of violence to a life of industry, attacked their folds and fields.

"'Victory probably made them insolent, and induced some of them to continue the hazardous employment; flattered by the praises of the wealthy, who now paid those for their protection, that might otherwise become powerful enemies.

"'And here, perhaps, began a military life, the most unnatural of any; the chief inducements to which are power, show, pay, plunder, and licentious indulgences: a profession once restrained by some false principles of honour, but now, become a dishonourable, mercenary occupation; always of a homicidal cast, now deliberately founded on suicide and murder: a profession which no virtuous reflecting man, can, as it is now conducted, deliberately adopt; to which parents consign their children from either want of means, or want of feeling; in which many remain through false shame, idleness, vanity, or vice; others continue, because they consider all things that men practice in numbers as lawful; whose rewards are bloody laurels, the applauses of the artful, the unthinking, or the timid; whose art is to diminish mankind, and to bring themselves to set at stake thoughtlessly blessings which other men study continually to prolong, such as health, life, and all its true enjoyments. – An art that not only militates against the peace of society, but also undermines the quiet of its own professors; since it operates to blast the early blossoms of tender attachment; – affords scarcely any means of accumulation for the benefit of relatives, or for retirement in old age – degrades the person by its near resemblance to absolute slavery; may be made the instrument of the most arbitrary power; and denies to its votaries the liberty of choice in action; thereby undermining the most valuable privilege of our nature, free-will – in a word, whose principal consolations must arise from the gratification of the lowest vanity, that of personal appearance decked with the gaudy badges of dependence; from the meanest applause, that of the great and little vulgar; and whose profits are only to be augmented by the death or disgrace of their brethren and companions.

"'Such are the men I left, such the predatory troops of the man who ridiculously styles himself our Grand Seignior! – Do you think, then, I can ever resolve to return to them?' A mixed sentiment of contempt and aversion, seen in all their expressive countenances, told me that they had no suspicion of it. – 'But (continued I) there are other occupations, though less apparently criminal, which yet have no baits to allure me; since I have long been convinced, that, of all arts and habits, nature seems to have encouraged man most to adhere to that of cultivating the earth, both by the peaceful advantages it procures, and by the frequent disappointments that attend almost all other modes of life.

"'The hunter, the fisher, the fowler, the robber, find no certain provision; it is with them alternate profusion and want; but the cultivator of the soil seldom finds the earth deny her increase.

"'The hunter, the fisher, the fowler, and robber, all risk life, expose themselves to the inclemency of the seasons, travel to live, and consequently find rivals and enemies; but the stationary cultivator of the soil, if he once get settled, finds his security encrease

with the number of his off-spring, augments his property as life
extends, and prolongs existence by the means of both.

"'On the other hand, the hunter's family declines, because it does
not possess that tranquillity necessary to the rearing of children.

"'It is remarkable also, that the arts of hunting, fishing, fowling,
and robbing, all require more strength, more talents, and more
industry, to render them productive of the means of existence than
that of agriculture; for to stir the soil, to sow, to weed, to reap, and
to clear the grain, are pointed out to the dullest eye in succession:
of all arts, indeed, agriculture is by far the simplest.

"'Nor is it less true, that even the shepherd's art demands more
skill, and produces fewer advantages; for disease ruins him at one
blow – he cannot be stationary, but wanders, is robbed, and, in the
general bad state of human society, must watch by night as well as
by day.

"'For, except in this island, *bad*, I can assure you, I have found
that state almost every where; either single tyrants framing arbi-
trary laws, and, by hereditary force, over-awing the multitude; or
ten or a dozen men, under pretext of guardianship, dividing,
among themselves, the property of millions; supported on the one
hand by servile agents, who, for a portion of the plunder, undertake
to persuade the majority to submission; and, on the other, by armed
ruffians, threatening every species of resistance with the edge of
the sword.'

"From all these reflections, I concluded that man was formed to
till the earth. 'You have taught me that he wants no animal food,
and may safely be delivered from the hazard and labour of pro-
curing it, with all the dire diseases it engenders. I have now, there-
fore, reached the haven of my desires – may no sinister accident,
or perverse will of mine, rob me again of the reward of my long
travels!'

"At this instant they all rose up, cordially assenting to my prayer;
and, when my guests were departed out of sight, I flew with ardour
to the unsophisticated society of her, whose bosom I had selected,
of all her sex, as the repository of all my virtuous thoughts and
everlasting affections.

"Thus was I seated in the very lap of contentment, all my pros-
pects smiling around me. I cultivated, for mere amusement, the
polished arts of a nation that practised them only as the ornaments
of life; who were unacquainted with commerce, but by way of

immediate barter, and never carried that beyond the necessaries of existence; whose taxes were a mere contribution of their superfluities, and where none thought of occupying more land than was necessary for his subsistence. Nothing was now left me to aspire to, but the high honour of being received among them as a fellow-citizen; and, as I unfortunately could contribute no useful arts by way of recommendation, I resolved to exemplify the truth of my conversion to their principles, by disinterestedly dedicating the whole of my property to the exigencies of the state; especially, as I had learned, that the procuring, from their neighbours, the richer metals, had, at times, been attended with no small uneasiness to the whole body, as it had led to an introduction of the knowledge of the island; it having been the custom, on former occasions, when gold was greatly wanted, to invite some foreigner to procure it. This had brought my old master there, whose profit arose from an exchange for pearls of a considerable size, that were occasionally found, on one particular spot, on the borders of the lake.

"These pearls, although of little value among their immediate neighbours, might have purchased, in Europe, almost any thing; but beside that, they knew little or nothing of Europe or Asia: their being nearly without any wants rendered jewels of scarce any use to the *Sophians*; so that, upon all occasions, those who possessed them as curiosities were proud to give them up when useful to the community.

"Having decided on my plan, by the advice of *Yahomy*, the good old African, I prepared, at the end of two years of probation, to put my scheme in practice; and, with no other companion but this faithful friend, proceeded immediately to the city of *Sophis*.

"What I felt at parting, for the first time, from my beloved *Mica*, whose mind I had now found to be not less beautiful than her person, I shall not attempt to describe. – She accompanied me the first day; the dear pledges of our affection were also present; and, at separating, which was not without heartfelt sighs on both sides, we exchanged two garlands of amaranthus buds, in token of unalterable amity.

"Elegant as I found the capital on my second arrival, and pure as were its ornaments; sweet as seemed the artless strains of their simple and touching airs; noble as appeared their manners; I still found, when absent from my adored home, with all its rustic simplicity, a void place in my *heart*; and the chief pleasure that played around it, consisted in recollecting, that, on my return, *Mica* would exultingly behold, on my finger, the badge and honourable distinction of a *Sophian*.

"With the senate our business was speedily dispatched. I produced too many respectable testimonies to be refused the privilege we courted; and my disinterested offer occasioned it to be conferred on us with peculiar expressions of approbation.

"As these people as carefully avoided parade and obstentatious festivals, as other nations affect them, this remarkable event occasioned no further loss of time than was necessary to read the documents, and inscribe the fact on a large papyrus-leaf, according to their manner, in columns downwards. But, although scrupulously avoiding the ceremonials of religion, as well as the tediousness of long orations, esteeming brevity in business, as in wit, with which many of their short comic narratives, and refined pieces of poetry abounded (for they had neither matter nor taste for tragedies); notwithstanding, however, this indifference to external shew; – yet, as if all others were purposely avoided to enhance one grand display of magnificent festivity, they, once every year, on the same day, as well as on each supernumerary day (for they calculated their years with great exactness), held a national festival; which happening at this season, as I could not with any propriety refuse to attend it, I shall, for your amusement, as briefly as possible describe.

"It was called the Feast of Love – and commenced at the western end of the great square, with the dawn of the day, by uncovering the plain cubical tomb of *Sophis*, the founder of the nation, and *Zambre*, the mother of his children.

"The plain shrine, when thus uncovered, becomes double in height; for its sides, composed of bronze pannels, when lifted up, form another cube, on the inside of each pannel of which is written, in an inlay of gold, the testament to which I before alluded. The shrine itself is of the yellow marble of the island, three sides of which are adorned with bas reliefs, exquisitely finished, representing almost all the humane offices of life; but the front space contains a singular curiosity – it is an antique table of metal, on which, not in bas reliefs, but inlay of silver and gold, is represented, as before described, the beautiful winged image of universal love, with the smaller figure enclosed in the pit of the breast.

"The attitude of the figure is formal and dry, but inconceivably grand. The wings extended are of silver; the body of gold, with

exception of the hair and nails, which are enamelled, as well as the
little figure in the shrine of the bosom. The figure erect, and the
soles of the feet resting on a circlet of silver. The back ground of
the whole is a kind of dark sardonix; and on it, under the wings
of the principal figure, were three small metallic circles, one of
gold, and two of silver, which every body knew to represent the
sun, moon, and earth; five other small dots were also there.

"This table, once kept as a relic in his family, *Sophis* had brought
with him into the island. – It had been the prototype of the statue
he had made on the borders of the lake. But wisely reflecting that
these representations might lead to established idolatry and error,
the combating of which had driven him from his country, he en-
joined his descendants never to repeat it: and although all sorts of
representations, by way of ornament, were modelled or cut in the
island, sculpture being in high esteem as a creative art; yet no
temple, or idol, being permitted by the laws, such a thing was never
thought of. And to secure this ancient monument from being con-
sidered as sacred, an inscription was placed over it, signifying that
it was a work of art of one of his remote ancestors (all having
followed the arts), intended poetically to personify his ideas of our
present state in the universe. But to return to the festival:

"No sooner did day appear, than the square began to fill with
crowds of both sexes, each bearing a flower-pot with some choice
flower in it, or shrub in bloom, placed in a woven basket; and a
circle on the pavement being marked round the tomb as a guide,
every one, as they arrived, placed on the ground their flower-pots,
which, to preserve their freshness, were covered with wet moss; so
that in a few minutes a gay parterre was formed, that, as a ring,
kept off the crowd, and gave to each an opportunity to see the
tomb and its ornaments; and between the cavity of the exalted
pannels was inserted some select plant of exquisite beauty. The
rest, as they arrived, placed their baskets all round the square; and
presently the whole was converted into a flower garden, by which
the eye and nostrils were agreeably refreshed: for most of these
plants had been carefully chosen for this occasion from amongst
the great variety with which these polished people adorn their little
gardens and houses.

"With the scarlet, white, purple, and yellow, amaranthus, and
fillets of fine wool, variously intertwined among their shining black
hair, was each interesting head adorned. Nor did the maidens
neglect the pardonable piece of natural coquetry, of partially con-

cealing, in this manner, the firmest, and most finely proportioned bosoms, that the eye of youth could desire, or maturity contemplate with instinctive admiration. – Indeed, had not the perfect symmetry of *Mica's* form been indelibly imprinted, and, with delicious infatuation, wrought into every fibre of my brain, while the elegance and delicacy of all her habits, like a fine frame, supported the bewitching picture, I should, certainly, on that occasion, have filled up the void in my heart, as did, I doubt not, multitudes of others, since the festival had long become, from the circumstance of its having contributed to the first meeting of lovers, the commemoration of the lasting alliances of innumerable individuals.

"After about an hour passed in congratulations and playful conversation, a signal was given by a sort of Herald, who appeared in a gallery over the entrance of the magistrates' portico, and chaunted a melodious stave to inform us that the representatives of the *Sophians* were prepared to open the festival. – On his retiring, there came forward a well-made youth, who had been elected speaker to the people, on account of his remarkable powers of delivery. What he had to say was taken from an ancient code, two copies of which were unrolled by two old men, who steadily kept their eyes on the manuscripts, as bearing testimony to the fidelity of his repetition.

"The most profound silence reigned – when, after solemnly reciting the inscription on the tomb, he added, after a pause:

"'SOPHIANS,

"'The good *Sophis*, whose wisdom lay in limiting his enquiries within the bounds of his duty; who beheld in that glorious body of fire now above us, the origin and support of all natures here; learnt from the constant effect of its systematic benevolence, that reciprocal, and regulated, acts of kindness must be pleasing to the generous first Cause, whose image we see is light, warmth, and uniformity.

"'Hence he drew the idea, that universal love pervades the universe; pouring its essence into our souls, like the rays of that light which promotes universal animation.

"'Of death he knew nothing, save its certainty. Why all things are as they are, he thought, it would be folly in him to enquire, who neither made, nor had power to alter, any thing.

"'He saw, that existence, for a limited period, was lent him, accompanied with the desire of happiness – in preserving and prolonging life, he found man's true interests; and self-love taught him, that it was his duty to extend this just sentiment to others.

"'Experience confirmed his discoveries – and following up this true principle, he endeavoured to overthrow the dark superstitions and idolatries of the times in which he lived; but men, calling themselves priests of the Gods, drove him from his country with his family and followers, here to establish a select nation, who, by restraining themselves to the proper enjoyment of their mundane natures, and following up the system of universal benevolence, have attained to that peace, health, and longevity, which is denied to the cruel, rapacious, and unjust part of mankind.

"'*Love therefore each other, and all things in being – and leave the rest to the inscrutable original Nature.*'

"With this short harangue he dismissed the assembly; all of whom, at that instant, united in a kind of vocal shout, accompanied with the notes of a thousand stringed instruments; formed together the most awful diapason that ever my delighted ears received; whose tones still vibrate sympathetically within the cells of my memory; and whose sentiment will ever, while lasts the lamp of life, be rooted in my heart!

"The rest of this charming day was passed in the pleasing contentions of singing, dancing, leaping, running, in which much graceful skill was displayed; making mutual presents among little parties of friends and relations; but all in the great square, or its neighbourhood – not a few retiring under the lofty trees, to enjoy the pleasures of music, or to attend to the compositions of some of their best poets, who generally attracted, into their vortex, the fair, the tender, and the betrothed.

"The evening closed with an illumination of innumerable lanthorns, whose sides exhibited transparent paintings – the light of which, being composed of bundles of aromatic woods, afforded a grateful perfume in every quarter.

"Thus, at an early hour, finished the first day's festival. The second was introduced in the same manner; but it was distinguished by a report of the number of criminals, whom solitude and retirement had completely reclaimed from such evil practices, as were prejudicial to the peaceful order of society. For on the lake they had several small and exposed islands, to which criminals were banished, being conducted thither on rafts, and from which they were removed gradually to better situations, on shewing signs of amendment; many *Sophians*, among whom were chiefly reckoned the aged and the childless, making in their sole employment to restore, by good councils, these members to the community. Nor, on this occasion, did the successful tutors fail to be present, accompanied by these renegerated children of the country, who went by the name of *the band of reconciliation*; receiving with modesty the reward of praise from the citizens, and carrying garlands, on which were inscribed, *'by experience we are purified.'*

"The whole closed (for there were two supernumerary days this year) with a splendid supper, consisting of an infinite variety of farinaceous cakes and puddings; with soups of vegetables, vegetables raw and dressed, eggs, honey, cheese, butter, milk, sweetmeats, and sweet potations from the sugar-cane; candied fruits, sugar in various forms, with nuts, ripe fruit, as well as dried; and, to crown all, a small quantity of wine, which had generally been hoarded for this long-wished for occasion. In fact, wine was a commodity in which they but little indulged; as the general consumption of grapes at meals allowed it to be made only in extraordinary years of plenty. As to the immoderate use of it, it constituted one of those crimes, which never failed to be punished by banishment to the islands; and indeed their laws were very vigilant, to check all those vices which tended to debase and weaken the species.

"On these occasions, they sometimes indulged in theatrical entertainments, in which there was nothing very remarkable but the form of the theatre, which consisted of a semicircular cavity scooped out of the sides of a hill, with benches of sun-dried clay, covered with soft moss – the stage was confined by beautiful groups of trees, beneath which there played two superb fountains. But the most singular thing was the scene, which was composed of three immensely large hollow prisms, perpendicularly erected, turning each on a centre, the inside of which served for the apartments of the mechanicians; and which, by the simple operation of being moved on the fixed point, afforded an almost endless variety of buildings, illustrative of the drama, while even those who moved them were concealed from the spectators.

"They had also another ingenious contrivance to afford modest merit an opportunity of displaying its talents, and receiving just criticism, without exposure. It was a hollow passage, covered with a thin substance, which, from a concealed chamber, obtruded itself into one of the corners of the square. Here the votaries to music, or poetry, made their first essay; and, under the shade of concealment, received the praises or blame of the impartial multitude.

"Thus did these people occasionally indulge in all kinds of innocent mirth; but what distinguished them from all the nations I had ever seen, was that general equality which reigned among them; none being either remarkably poor, or rich, although the possession of extraordinary talents might be said to confer an indisputable distinction and evidently obtained respect.

"Of the state of their arts, the following anecdote may give you an idea:

"I went one day to see a celebrated picture of a female, just arrived at the age of puberty. The artist had painted her, examining her own exquisite form in a fountain. She stooped a little over its margin, holding her hair, to prevent its interrupting her view, with one hand, while she rested on the other. The picture was much applauded – but to my then weak judgement it seemed, though pleasing in one respect, preposterous; – every fleshy protuberance being so warm that I called it a red woman. 'You wonder (said *Chilo*), at the artist's having given so much carnation; have you never observed, that all prominent parts of muscles blush, like the cheeks, when exposed to fine air? The fleshy parts of muscles are red, porous, and consequently are the warm points of the body, like the ears, heels, &c.' I was satisfied with the remark, as it shewed reflection. – *Chilo* once talking of order, I asked him what it was? 'Order (said he), is only the reverse of disorder.' 'What then (said I), is not all the surface of nature without order?' 'No (replied he, not at all dismayed at my question); but you judge of her by parts, not by the whole. Hill, mountain, sea, and river, answer to hill, mountain, sea, and river; but she does not put them close together, as you say they ignorantly do in Europe, when they would imitate her. When you wish to imitate her, study convenience and propriety, and you will not be very far from her footsteps.' – I felt all he said; for I remembered the vast difference between the humble entrances to the inns on the Levant, and the porticos to the few ancient temples I had visited.

"They allowed of no retrospective laws; no imprisonment for debt; never dreamed, as to nobility, of titles of distinction; held slavery of all kinds in abhorrence; put no criminals to death; and seized the persons of bad men, in order only either to amend them, or to prevent them from further injuring society. Weapons constructed for offence were not permitted by the laws to be made in the country; and, as to civil wars, their principles must have been all reversed, before such a thing could be even known.

"It one day gave me no small pleasure to meet with one of the very few people among them who made medicine their study. Their mode of proceeding was singular, as, indeed, were most of their customs. It consisted in going about giving a sort of lecture on the conduct of life as far as related to diet, bathing, and animal indulgences, inscribing the apartments with aphorisms of health; and endeavouring to shew that nature, in her operations, is always beneficent and simple.

"Wounds were dressed with green herbs macerated; cathartics and emetics, with the lavement of warm water, all sorts of exercise, and chiefly abstinence from food, were their grand specifics; but diet, bathing, and air, constituted the great arcana: and to this it was he attributed the almost universal health they enjoyed. Man, he told me, *was merely a tube, with a continuity of surface*, both the inside and outside of which must be kept free from irritation, and clear of obstructions. Water (said he), is equally good for both purposes: by drinking it, we sustain the heat of the stomach; by injecting it, we neutralize acridities in the viscera; externally it has the same uses. In removing excrescences, they applied the caustic rather than the knife; knew nothing of bleeding a vein; and, except by scarifying, or slight puncture, never drew blood at all in any disease.

"Pregnant women entertained no idea of danger from childbirth: whatever was so natural they were taught to expect to succeed as a thing of course; and, like most of the inhabitants of warm climates, they had easy labours. Absolute quiet and perfect cleanliness were strictly enjoined in this and all cases of a critical nature – and the word silence was inscribed over every sick person's chamber. The healthy were also strictly separated from the unsound; and, after attending the sick, to visit another without previous purification, was punished as a crime of a base nature. To carry, in this manner, to a fellow creature, a fever, or any other disease, was considered among them in the same light as inflicting a wound in the dark; but voluntarily to administer to the cure of others, placed a man in the highest rank of virtue. According to their opinions, *water cleansed from infectious taint by destroying virus*; and the patient, as well as all those about him, with the garments they wore, must be as often as convenient passed through that element. And thus much for a general idea of their medical practice.

"Justice and liberty might indeed be said to reign among them: and to prevent temptations to amass wealth, so common in other countries, *the law* disposed of all acquired property; with a careful attention to what ought to have been the will of the deceased; never in reasonable things opposing his testmentary recommendation.

"Thus situated, you will not wonder that I gloried in my naturalization, and the discovery I had so fortunately made. It had, in some degree, been the reward of upright wishes, generated by disgust at the vices of the Ottoman Imperial Court. Yet here, alas! you behold me, reduced to a forlorn old age, hurled at once from the summit of human bliss, and dashed on the sharp rocks of inconsolable privation.

"Had guilt conducted me hither, I had indeed been deeply wretched! By what sad reverse my misfortunes were ushered in, must be the subject of our next conversation; for I am now too much exhausted to continue the melancholy recital: and even, if I were not so, I should be sorry, immediately, to rob your mind of the pleasing images I have had the happiness of exciting, since they may serve to lull your pains – adieu then, and may the recital of my future misfortunes urge you to try to bear up under those afflications, to which you are subject, in common with all the other sons of men."

I could make him no answer, for both our souls were full of deep reflection and we parted – but, as his venerable shadow passed along the wall, I saw, by the action of his head, that he had retired from the conference only because he could not suppress the involuntary emotions raised by intruding remembrances.

I was kept awake, through the night, by a variety of disquieting recollections, and the elements seemed to sympathize with my perturbed state; for a storm, more tremendous than that which now arose, I had never witnessed in Africa. The prison was struck with lightning, and part of one of the bastions rent away. When day broke, the atmosphere was still gloomy and obscured, nor had the yelling winds subsided – yet I found my respectable friend at the post of honour, exerting his tremulous voice to warn a boat full of people of the danger of the sunken rock in the river, which the agitation of the stream, now, more than ever, concealed.

The moment he saw me, he called to me to aid his pious purposes; but our united efforts were of no avail. The noise of the tempest, and the cries of the distressed mariners and passengers, effectually drowned our voices – the vessel was suddenly struck on the rock, and was wrecked before our eyes; the screams of the women, which we heard at intervals, between the peals of thunder, were now followed by a gloomy silence, more dreadful, if possible, than their cries – all went down to oblivious repose; and the next moment, the transitory glare of lightning exhibited fragments of the wreck, and convulsed carcases rising and falling with the ebullition of the vortex. – No creature could be saved, and the ungovernable stream soon hurried from our sight every image of the fatal accident.

The distant hills now began to appear; the dusky clouds to depart in broad volumes; and the glorious Sun (to whose image I observed my companion always paid particular veneration, whenever it could be viewed from the cell in which he slept) came forth from under an aqueous curtain, adorned with all the lustre and true majesty that belongs to his superior frame.

Already the birds of the river had returned to the dripping reeds; the sands wore a purer tint from the effects of the rain which had fallen; and our frames partook of the natural calm which the refreshed atmosphere communicated to all things within its influence.

Being both seated, *Lycas*, viewing in my impatient looks, a demand for the performance of his promise, began as follows:

"That the catastrophe we have just witnessed has affected and afflicted me to the degree you must have noticed, and thrown me into an unusual state of agitation, you will be the less surprised when I tell you, that a close resemblance of the greatest misfortune of my life was then before my eyes.

"But to proceed, I departed from *Sophis* after the grand festival, travelling with all the alacrity of a passionate lover; and, in less time than could have been expected, considering the age of *Yahomy*, arrived within one station of my house. It was late when I got there; and I expected not only to see *Mica* and my children, but the friend of our family, *Chilo*, and indeed nearly all our connections. My speed encreased as I approached, except that I stopped, at intervals, to listen for the sounds of their expected songs of rejoicing; and looked forward anxiously to see some generous torch, the signal of my beloved society.

"I carried one in my hand – I called aloud occasionally, but no cheering reply was made – my impatience redoubled – I left all my company behind, and felt alarmed at arriving alone at the spot where I had made sure of kindly and jestingly reproaching the dear group for letting me be before-hand with them in friendly impatience. As to *my Mica!* my glowing imagination had already fancied her clasped in my arms; already did I feel her breath glowing on my cheek, and inhaled the essential sweetness of her pure person. I pictured my head nested in her flowing tresses, our lips united, our senses confused, our tears of pleasure intermingled

*– No, no, the die was cast – we were never more to behold each other – I
was never again to embrace either of my children!*

"All around me was suspicious silence – an ominous presage came
like a cloud over my heart – my breath grew short, my countenance
fell. I stood still a moment, and contemplated the spot where she
had promised to meet me – unwilling to give entrance to the serious
apprehensions that pressed on my mind, I tried to bear up, but
soon found it impossible; when, to my unutterable satisfaction, I
saw a female figure rush from a thicket, and flee from me. The
first idea was, that they were sporting with my feelings; it hurt me;
but joy quenched my anger, and I sprang forward more like a lion
than a man – '*Mica!* (I cried), you flee but to be taken;' and at the
same instant I held in my disappointed arms, not, alas! my love,
but one of her female friends! 'What is the meaning of all this?'
(said I, as soon as I could recover my surprise). 'Ask me not (she
replied, embracing my knees, and shedding a shower of tears), but
let me go. Be patient, *Lycas*. *Chilo* will tell you – *I dare not!*'

"'By the great Cause! but you shall (I exclaimed), I will not lose
all that my soul adores, and be patient – something dreadful has
happened in my absence – say, is she unfaithful? Am I already
hated? Is she sick, and I absent? *Is she dead?*'

"'You have said the word (she answered) – for pity's sake let me
now go.'

"At that instant I felt a strong revulsion of my whole frame. Kind
nature unbraced the tension of the brain; and when I awoke from
my swoon, I found the whole of my company around me, and each
weeping bitterly.

"I sprang from them, and ran, or rather flew to my habitation
– *Chilo* was in the porch – I rushed by him rudely, calling aloud
to my dead partner, as if she could hear me; and, after searching
every corner of the house, returned to him, exclaiming, with a
voice of exalted misery, '*Where is my Mica? – Where is my love? –
Give me back, at least, my children!*'

"He clasped me in his friendly arms, and looking at me with a
countenance of unutterable anguish, 'Can (said he) the things that
are passed be recalled? When the light of the sun is withdrawn,
can we follow it? *Mica* is mixed with the dust, your infants are no
more. – She was good, and we all enjoyed her society; such a woman
must be forgotten, if you would ever again be happy! – The nest
and the tender bird are annihilated; the fresh buds of the water-

lilly are snapped and fallen off; but the root is still left to renew the stock.'

"'Never (said I, with emphasis), shall it be again renewed! But sit down, I am calm, tell me all the manner of it – you shall see I am a very *Sophian* – the ring, the ring, look! I have got that instead of a family!' – 'Your words are wild (said he) – but, perhaps, so to talk relieves you instead of tears.' I frowned at him, and sternly bade him go on.

"He then proceeded to relate to me very circumstantially that the whole had happened in an instant: that *Mica* had been engaged in constructing a little arbour on the borders of the river which washed our walls, when one of the children, having fallen into deep water – by an involuntary motion she, with the other in her arms, darted forward to save it; and that in consequence of that incumbrance they all perished together, in the presence of a very aged woman, who could not afford them the smallest assistance.

"It would be dreadful to describe, if I were able, what followed. In an instant like this, all my assumed firmness forsook me. On the fresh earth which enclosed the *dear* remains, I lay stretched, without sleep, and without food, for many days. They had interred her ashes under the arbour which, sweet spirit! for my pleasure at my return, she had been constructing. – There I remained extended, calling on her night and day; and, but for the careful attention of my friend, and *Yahomy*, who never quitted me, my grave also had haply swelled the sod.

"At length, time, and this burst of uninterrupted grief, produced some calmer sensations. I then wandered throughout the whole island, accompanied by the good old African, visiting all their institutions, examining all their habits, practising all their arts; among which, painting afforded me the greatest delight, as it enabled me to re-create the family I had for ever lost; but nothing could fill up the void which this loss had occasioned. Not even music could alleviate reflection – it, perhaps, only encreased the pains of remembrance, for she still lives in my veins.

"Become at last an object of pity to the whole nation, it seemed to be by all agreed, that I had better return to my original country, since every thing in *Sophis* seemed only to cherish my mind's disease. – I therefore came to a resolution to go out a missionary to mankind, to spread, if possible, the noble customs of this select nation among my fellow creatures; nor was it till I had resolved on thus transferring my affections from particular to general society that

I found my reason comparatively calm, and my bosom less disturbed.

"Then, filled with the sublimest philanthropy, I braved every danger for the accomplishing of this benignant purpose; and, without any companion (for *Yahomy* was too feeble to follow me), entered once more the vast desert; and, conducted by enthusiastic zeal, escaped every danger, preaching and teaching every where humanity and love to all creatures whether men or beasts. – Numerous tribes of wandering blacks entertained me with kindness and hospitality. I found, indeed, these simple Africans always received favourably those who wished to instruct them; but when I came into the kingdom of *Sennaar*, in proportion as I succeeded with the people, I excited the jealousy of their cruel rulers. Liberty, justice and even humanity were here almost unknown. Craft, and that coarse and crooked policy, which ignorance engrafts on power, were alone practised by a Court, barbarous, indeed, as to manners, but refined in the arts of extortion, nearly equal to some of the governments of Europe. No sooner were my principles understood, than my liberty was in danger. Setting, however, all false policy at defiance, I persisted in the most zealous efforts to sow the first seeds of rational freedom in the bosoms of the *Sennaarites*; till merciless and unfeeling tyranny seized me, as I expected, in her fangs, and destined me, as a punishment, here to end my days, a willing martyr to the noble cause.

"A man must put himself in my situation to see the propriety of my conduct. Had *Mica* lived, perhaps, this daring virtue would never have possessed me. That gust, which extinguished the lamp of my life, gave to these poor deluded people a new star – the dawn of civil freedom has appeared in their horizon – may the piercing rays of independence dissipate the mists created by treacherous policy! Man is by nature a rational creature – and shall he be always a prey to rulers who make him the dupe of artificial systems? No: many of the first legislators have been well-intentioned men; but, instead of forming a code founded on truth, they have fancied, because they were better informed than the generality, that the multitude could never be brought to the like degree of knowledge. In place of establishing simple institutions, suitable to the nature of mankind, and all living things, they have commenced, by putting man first over the creation, and then extending the power of a few over the whole; setting up some fantastical leader of their own contrivance, as their inspirer, and making his pretended communications the criterion of right and wrong: whereas, had they owned their ignorance, with the candour of the good *Sophis*, and taught the doctrine of just equality, and humility – to seek natural nutriment, and to follow natural habits – their disciples, I am persuaded, must have superseded in time every other sect, and the whole earth been beautified with its inhabitants."

Here the liberal-minded *Lycas* concluded his narrative, and left my mind impressed with a determined resolution, should I ever escape from this fortress (a thing very improbable under such an arbitrary government), to attempt, at all hazards, to gain the sacred asylum on the lake of Zambre, where I trust I may succeed in engrafting the noble fruits of revelation on their wholesome wild stock of natural faith, thereby adding all that is wanting to make them the best and the happiest nation on earth (first however depositing this manuscript in the hands of some European trader). And may the lesson have its proper effect, if, happily, it should ever come forth: *for freedom and virtue, although depressed, are not extinct; deep rooted in the heart of man, I feel that they will survive all the injuries they have received, and at length (triumphant over the crooked policy of Machiavelian statesmen) behold the emancipation of reason, and the return of universal justice!*

FINIS.

———————

I. The Maid of Snowdon, a Tale. Quarto.

II. A Poem on the Landscapes of Great Britain. Quarto.

III. Some Anecdotes of the Life of Julio Bonasoni, a Bolognese Artist, who followed the Styles of the best Schools in the Sixteenth Century; accompanied by a Catalogue of the Engravings, with their Measures, of the Works of that tasteful Composer; and Remarks on the general Character of his rare and exquisite Performances. To which is prefixed a Plan for the Improvement of the Arts in England. Octavo.

IV. An Attempt to describe Hafod, and the neighbouring Scenes about the Bridge over the Funack, commonly called the Devil's Bridge, in the County of Cardigan; an ancient Seat belonging to Thomas Johnes, Esquire, Member for the County of Radnor. Octavo.

V. Thoughts on Outline, Sculpture, and the System that guided the ancient Artists in composing their Figures and Groupes:

Accompanied with free Remarks on the Practice of the Moderns, and liberal Hints cordially intended for their Advantage.

To which are annexed twenty-four Designs of Classical Subjects invented on the Principles recommended in the Essay. Quarto.

———————

Speedily will be published, by the same Author,
IN ONE VOLUME, DUODECIMO,
SIX MORAL TALES.

Also preparing for the Press,
LETTERS from ITALY, with Seventy Views of the most remarkable Scenes beyond the Alps, and Habits of that Country, &c.

The Captive
of the Castle of Sennaar

PART 2
THE REFORMED

The Reformed
or
The Captive of the Castle of Sennaar.
a Salutary &c.

by
George Cumberland.

Part 1. Exhibiting the fruits of natural religion.
Part 2. Those derived from revelation.

He that travels the beaten road may chance
indeed to have company; but he that takes his
liberty, and manages with judgement, is the man that
makes useful discoveries, and most beneficial to
those that follow him.

Molyneux Letter XCV.

Manuscript titlepage of *The Captive* Part 2 (Cumberland MSS)

The Reformed

OR

THE CAPTIVE OF THE CASTLE OF SENNAAR
A SALUTARY TALE

by

GEORGE CUMBERLAND

Part 1. Exihibiting the fruits of natural religion

❧ Part 2. Those derived from revelation

    He that travels the beaten road may chance indeed to have company; but he that takes his liberty, and manages with judgement, is the Man that makes useful discoveries, and most beneficial to those that follow him.

Molyneux Letters xcv.

❧

Contents

In completing this philosophical Romance of the Captives of the Castle of Sennaar my object has been to exhibit Man in a state of nature, as well as under a divine *revelation*; also the knowledge to be obtained by the exercise of his reasoning faculties, and the happiness which both states afford, and to shew that the miseries of mankind arise from the indulgence of the passions and that God alone is able to deliver us from evil. If the reader will follow this tale without prejudice I trust it will not fail to make him a better and a wiser man; for although he may differ from the writer in many inferior points, in the general principle here laid down, I cannot doubt of his acquiescence in the advantages of pious humility and the true happiness its practice ensures; that the customary miseries of life are the fruits of our own perverse nature; and that pride and selfishness can only be overcome by a communion with the precepts of our holy religion; not of the prevailing dogmas of its venal professors, but of its essential character, the love of God and the love of our neighbour, and if I have embellished my narrative with agreeable episodes, it has been done to allure young minds, and lead them, by amusing pictures, to the discovery of wholesome truths.

CHAPTER I

Lycas had been loosely instructed, and had no fixed religious prin-
ciples; a Musselman at Constantinople, a Jew in the desert, and
among the Sophians a deistical admirer of pure natural theology
– I had the mere forms of the Catholic faith, deeply instilled indeed
in my youth under the discipline of my father confesser, but not
sufficiently grounded, on examination, to enable me to set about
the conversion of my aged friend, and although my mechanical
credence made me conceive a hope of becoming an apostle to the
Sophians, should I ever reach that delightful spot, yet I had not
the courage to attempt to disturb the belief of one who on all
occasions seemed so decided in his moral opinions, which become
visible only by their effects – and thus we lived amicably until the
unhappy hour that took him from me, during which period he
assiduously employed himself in giving me instruction in the art
he knew how to practice so well, so that between us we ultimately
converted all the walls and galleries that were accessible to us, into
scenes of well proportioned architecture, and agreable deceptions.

In this manner two whole years passed away to us not unfruit-
fully, as our occupation never interrupted our philosophical con-
versations, and I learned, at least, to be patient under an almost
hopeless condition – but I preserved my health and strength by
continual exercise, temperance, and moderate repose; in short, by
attending to the councils of *Lycas*, I grew athletic, whilst age di-
minished his powers; and sitting one day on his pallet, from whence
he had risen unusually late, he beckonned me to approach him
and in a more than usual placid manner thus addressed me. "You

have probably observed that since your arrival my strength has been almost daily decreasing, the result of age and long confinement united, but you are not perhaps aware that the period is nearly arrived, when the end of my sufferings will be the augmenting of your own. I flatter myself however that I have taught you, the advantage of submitting calmly to the dispensations of that Being who governs the universe, and into whose motives not even philosophy will enable us to penetrate. That he holds communion with his creatures I know and feel, or *Mica*, in a dream this night, has assured me that the end of my troubles is come, and that we shall speedily be united, never more to part.

"I dreamed that after having purified my person, as is my daily custom, by every ablution in my power, I had reposed myself in the recess of the grated window, and after consigning my Spirit to the all protecting Being, whose we are, and whom it is our duty to obey, I lay contemplating the sweet crescent moon, lulled by the soft notes of the evening birds, and the rushing of the stream incessantly gliding, without abrasion, along our prison walls – and that thus I remained musing, in harmony with all things around me, until gentle sleep drew her veil over my eyelids; when a pleasing change gradually took place, and I found myself in an arbour composed of sweet smelling flowers, and before me was a garden abundant in fruits, and fountains of the clearest water, which issued from a brook, whose bottom was paved with fragments of gems of all colours, and the margin, of the finest turf, enamelled by daisies and the blue forget me not with its inviting eyes. Methought I traversed this lovely garden formed in the recess of a well wooded valley, and at last came to a cottage that exactly resembled my former habitation in *Sophis*, where in the porch, in the full bloom of her resplendent beauty, accompanied by my children, sat *Mica* composing a garland from some rich flowers in an elegant basket, with the active aid of my little ones. Methought she arose gracefully, and came with open arms to embrace me, saying, in a voice that went to my soul, 'Where have you been so long, my *Lycas*? The children and I have had few tranquil moments since you left us to gain the honourable distinction of the King. But I see you have succeeded, and we will part no more, but live in bliss together from this happy hour that reunites us. Tomorrow we shall feel as if no interruption had intervened and all our sorrows will be forgotton forever!' Now I believe all this", said he, "will really happen, and my joy is perfect, I shall depart in peace."

And having concluded, his countenance seemed irradiated, self complacent, and happy – he paused for my reply.

"Yes, my dear, *Lycas*", I said, "you have indeed taught me much in teaching me to subdue my passions, but you have scarcely prepared me to bear your loss; in you I have found a tender father, and sad will be my state of existence when you are gone! I shall indeed have occasion for all my fortitude where every object will remind me of my solitude, deprived of all human society, and that after such a feast of reason as yours has afforded me, even the records of your pictorial talents will be no longer interesting. And how shall I continue my necessary labours with no one to witness or approve?"

"You will have *Hope* always with you," he said, "and in me a witness that human misery is not endless, where human intellect is properly exerted."

"True," I rejoined, "but when the buttress is decayed and gone what is to sustain the edifice?"

"The solidity of the internal structure," replied he; "your opinions and practices are grounded on firm principles, despair will never enter such an habitation, and events revolve with time. Your deliverance may therefore occur when you least expect it, for governments, like this we suffer under, are seldom lasting. Something indeed seems to whisper me that a commotion is breeding here; the gaoler tells me there have lately been stormy conflicts in the guard room among the officers of the governor, and several arrests and executions, and should a rebellion break out your freedom would assuredly be the result, from your known former services. I prophecy your liberation, for I know you now too well not to know that you will never again serve in arms or in war; and that your first object will be to escape from this polluted soil, and take shelter among the *Sophians* where, when death has gathered my ripened days, I may probably become your good Daemon, for my spirit I think will ever hover there."

Overcome by his kindness I could only silently assent to his aspirations – when the heavy doors of the passages were heard to open with much clamour, and the bolts of our chambers were hastily withdrawn, the heavy keys thrust into the massive locks, and before us stood the cordial keeper in whose heart we had acquired so much interest. "Joy! Joy!" he exclaimed, "Allah be praised! I can now with safety open the road to your escape. The Tyrant is slain, by his confidants, and I am no longer his slave! I have now a better post, and can not only insure you a convoy out of the territory but will accompany you to its utmost boundaries with pleasure."

We regarded each other with silent astonishment. *Lycas* could not speak, but he fell back on his seat, letting fall his arms, and seemed expiring or in a swoon. The keeper and myself lifted him forward to the window in which was his couch and mattress, applying all the usual remedies for a long time in vain. At length his colour returned, he feebly opened his eyelids, turned his head to look at me with earnestness – and closing them again forever said, in a faint whisper, "*I am happy!*"

He was gone; the brilliant lamp of his intellect expired, the fruits of his talents surrounded him, but their exercise was terminated. A body of clay was all that remained, and what lay before me was no longer *Lycas*. I had long known his wishes to be interred in the floor of the chamber he had so often trod, beneath the picture of his beloved *Mica*; we dug a grave on the spot, and I watered the earth as I turned it out with my affectionate tears, in which mournful office the honest keeper joined me, and laying his usual pallet at the bottom of his grave, we deposited him in his ultimate bed of repose, without removing his garments, and on his talented remains I deposited his Vina and instruments of art, covering the spot with a massive piece of granite, his favourite seat, which long use had polished, and on which he had with his own hands inscribed the names of *Lycas and Mica*.

In these offices, and in preparing for my escape, we employed the greater part of this eventful day, and during a week of extreme anxiety, I filled up the time of sad suspense in terminating the first part of this extraordinary narrative, little thinking of the salutary adventures reserved for my own purification, or of the almost hopeless escape from such a dungeon in such a country – for the keeper soon began to discover unforeseen difficulties, which induced me to enclose the manuscript within my garments, as a thing destined to be interred with my remains; for my spirits were so depressed from hopes made sick by disappointment, that a species of apathy had overwhelmed me. But providence had reserved for me a better fate, for when I least expected it, the humane keeper came at midnight and awoke me, stating that the hour had arrived when with safety to us both he could effect my escape, and was of opinion, that if I were resolved to quit this country altogether, there was no course positively safe but to cross the Bar-el-abaid, and throw myself on the mercy of the savage inhabitants who herd on the banks of that extensive stream, for if it was known to the present rulers among the Sennaarites that I refused to abet the new powers, I should find it very difficult indeed to quit the City. The Bar-el-abaid, he informed me, came southerly from the Mountains of the Moon, and passed through a very fertile country of great extent, no one knowing its sources with any certainty, that it was called the white-river by many, and the roving savages who frequent its borders resist and generally exterminate foreign intruders – but that many periods of the year they retreat upwards, towards the sources, and that at this time there were parts bounding on Sennaar which were open, and to these he would see me conducted. "But," he added, "there is now no time to deliberate; whatever you decide on must be executed this night, as in the morning I must deliver up the keys of the Castle and my remaining prisoners." Thus situated and determined on quitting the territory, I readily accepted his assistance and taking only such things as were absolutely necessary from our mutual property, and sufficient to load myself and a young Negro whom he entrusted to my care, we closed the doors by torch light, and descended together, through many intricate windings in this ancient building, of whose heavy walls no one knew the origin; a mixture of all styles of construction, a union of the earliest Egyptian with the bronze embellished windows of the upper India.

But how shall I express my feelings on emerging to outer day; they were a mixed sensation of grief for the loss of *Lycas*, of joy for my deliverance, and of fear lest I should again be detained; so that it appeared like one of those feverish visions when the object we seek seems to forever retreat from us, and doubt and obscurity accumulate as we advance toward the end of our wishes. We passed out of the city in silence, by intricate avenues, and taking a circuit which to me seemed very extended, but the object was to avoid all observation, and thus we journeyed on the greater part of night, and at dawn of day entered a thick forest of noble trees with but little underwood, in a path evidently but rarely trodden, in turning from which for a short space we arrived at a clear spring near the ruins of an ancient tomb or rather a monolithic temple, built in the style of those of upper Egypt. It was of red granite and had the globe and wings above the gate in the cornice, with two small but well executed Sphinxes in good preservation on each side the entrances. Some large acacias almost covered it, and the cell, for it had only one, served us for a place of repose and shelter. After a hearty meal and a sound and refreshing sleep we awoke about noon, and enjoyed the shade, and the pure beverage of the fountain, secure from the piercing beams of a burning sun, and safe, as the honest Senaarite assured me, from pursuit or molestation. "You are now in the track," said he, "that leads directly to the borders of the Bar-el-abaid, and at that period of the year when it is least of all frequented by the savages, who retire to the mountains towards its sources during the great heats which we are now to expect. This forest is very extensive and leads quite to the broad arm of the river, beyond which I have never passed, but it is said a more settled and better nation of Africans are found beyond its forks to the West – among whom caravans occasionally pass towards Suez with slaves. I therefore counsel you to keep quiet in these forests during the heats of summer as near the river as you can with safety, and seek an occasion to cross it by a raft which my slave will assist you to construct, if you can find settlers on the other side who probably will conduct you to where you can intercept a Kofila on their road. I must now leave you, you have a good camel and an active, honest and brave servant, and do not want money, or skill to travel. May Allah take you under his protection! Adieu! When you are safe at Cairo or Suez communicate with your friend – I shall probably never see you more." So saying with a stifled voice, he mounted his camel and was speedily out of sight.

A tolerable good map of Africa, a legacy from *Lycas*, shewed me where-abouts I was as to latitude, but all to the south was mystery, and to the west we only knew, by report, that this great River had numerous branches intersecting countries entirely unknown as to their inhabitants. My Negro knew only that they were reputed to be a mild and industrious race of Mahometans, and were continually plundered by the *Sangalli* in their incursions on the banks of the Bar-el-abaid, a river to which they claimed the exclusive possession, with a savage ferocity, so as to become an object of apprehension to the Kingdom of Sennaar; which however they seldom invaded, on account of its maintaining a regular army. On this river, especially on the left or Eastern bank, when they came down, at the time it was swollen, in heavy canoes in great numbers, they drove every one from the banks of the river and made many slaves, entrapping them and living by fishing and the chase, which was at that time abundant in every species of deer, hippopotamus, and wild hogs. They were of a Negro race, tall, muscular, and cruel to their enemies, even reported to be cannibals, and pagans of the lowest grade – yet speaking a bastard Arabic mixed with a language resembling that of Sennaar.

Such being the account from both my deliverer and his slave, it became necessary well to weigh what, under existing circumstances, was to be done. To return to Europe, even if I could accomplish it, I had an aversion; the society of her for whom I had made so many sacrifices was denied me by unjust laws, and barbarous prejudices; my family I had no doubt would force me into legal proceedings to recover my estate, and drive me to misanthropy, or madness. I had almost pledged myself, if possible to seek the Sophians in the ardour of my first impression of their virtues, and I even thought, on such a pure morality, I should have little trouble to engraft Christianity. To make the attempt therefore seemed to my mind to be reasonable, and even if I should fail my discoveries in Africa would amply repay me the time dedicated to the enquiry, whilst if I succeeded my mind would recover its composure, and my days terminate in tranquility and peace.

Such were the impressions which agitated me for several days whilst I continued on this retired spot, where all my wants were supplied by the Negro, who was a good hunter, and cook, without any exertion of my own, except taking long walks among the forest trees which were truly magnificent, and many overhung with flowering climbers, full of small birds, and lovely butterflies, whilst lizards, unknown to me before, ran like living gems upon the boles of the trees, and sweet odours arose from the impression of my feet on the sward. At length I decided to advance to the River and cross it on a raft, proceeding towards the south in that direction Lycas had recommended to me, and one fine morning, before day break, having made up our packages over night, I bid adieu to my solitary cell after inscribing our names on the wall – his was *Musumba*; and I called myself – a Citizen of the World.

CHAPTER II

The grey dawn saw us depart, and, under the shade of the lofty trees, we were enabled to make a long day's journey, so that by evening I could see, through the boughs, from any eminence, the sparkling waters of the *Bar* in rapid motion. We had shot that day some game, and on a sloping hillock shrouded by evergreens, we sat down to supper like kings and lords of the soil, for nothing interrupted our sway, but the native inhabitants of these wilds, the monkeys, who alone seemed to envy our repast. Some were very beautiful, and others very agile and strong, who advanced rather boldly with a view to purloin our feast, but *Musumba* knew how to scare them, no less than to kill, and assured me that, in want of other food, they were incomparable eating; a luxury which I convinced him I had no inclination to indulge in, and which I recommended him to abstain from, as well as all animal food, when roots, grain, vegetables, and fruits could be procured. Here we bivouaced and slept soundly on our nap sacks, having first made a fire to guard us from the approach of hyenas, the only night prowlers with the jackal and fox we had as yet encountered.

At day break we descended to the banks, which were but little encumbered by trees, and were rocky at the margin, from whence commenced shoals of pebbles and sand, that extended to the flood which was low, shallow, and rapid in the middle, the waters being more than half absent, whilst the margin, and some pools left at intervals, were crowded by flocks of water birds in uninterrupted motion, wading or skimming, or running against the wind, so as to display their ruffled plumage to the sun, and splendid colours, changing with every motion – sometimes escaping in flocks as we advanced towards them, or plunging into the waters with a velocity that almost escaped observation. We also were not long in following their example, on a brilliant sand bank, and drinking the pure wave as if we had never tasted water before – but I had scarce enjoyed this pleasure, when a cry from *Musumba* put an end to it. He had launched into the deeper part of the stream, and seeing a crocodile rise at no great distance before him, set up a loud shout, and began splashing the water with his feet, warning me to make for the shore for security. Here we found plenty of impressions of the feet of the hippopotamus, and animals of prey of the fox tribe, and our fright over, feasted on the eggs of aquatic birds left on the sands in exposed cavities ready for hatching.

It now became necessary to muster up all the strength of my mind so as to form some plan for my future proceedings. We knew we were not likely to be interrupted among these extensive and solitary forests, whilst the river continued to fall, neither could we want provisions or shelter, for with his bow *Musumba* brought down every thing he aimed at, and my habits of temperance demanded little but eggs, fruits or the wild grain or roots, every where indicated by the operations of the monkey tribe. To gain the opposite coast was not difficult, but a short way from its banks it was evident to view that it became arid and shelterless; probably a great extent of sands uninhabited. To follow the current downwards as it expanded, as far at least as the forest extended, was next a consideration, so as to get beyond the annual incursions of the Sangalli on its banks and wait for the chance of falling in with the great caravans from Tripoli or Morocco, said to pass from the Niger and Timbuctoo by Kassina and Sennaar to Suakem on the Red Sea, by which means I might escape to places directly connected with Europe, and after trying to recruit my finances from Venice, commence my journey provided for a voyage of discovery. But all these schemes presented endless difficulties, and long procrastination – and, in fine, my inclination to penetrate to the southward, by the White River branch of the Nile overcame all others, and at any rate I determined to cross the river and incline to the South west, in hopes of reaching the Kingdom of Darfur, represented to me to be inhabited by Mahometan merchants who correspond with Cairo, and through which I might easily, by a year's residence, procure some investments of importance to further my objects.

Accordingly we constructed a raft of palm-trees as well as a Kraal or cabin for security from the wild animals, and waited for a convenient occasion to transport ourselves to the opposite shore; for I confess I neither liked the near vicinity to the Sennaarites of Nubia, or the possibility of meeting some roving band of the ferocious tribe who claimed the river as their own. Yet during our short stay nothing could be more delightful to me than the sylvan scenes that presented themselves: a forest of varied and very ancient trees, divested of underwood, and whose gentle slopes were covered by a verdant turf, fed close by antelopes and goats, enamelled with small flowers and the humble and aromatic thyme, frequented by innumerable birds of all sorts of splendid plumage and sweet song, whose attraction was the copious waters of this noble river, transparent as glass, and flowing over shallow pools of the purest sand. Then again there were wild vines and variety of climbing plants exhibiting the richest festoons of gaudy flowers, and fruits falling at our feet in full maturity. The fish also were abundant, and so varied that scarce a day passed, that I did not see some to me before unknown, as well as exceedingly beautiful.

But perhaps my long confinement made everything interesting to me, as a child to whom all things are new. This sort of contemplative life could not however last forever, and as soon as I perceived the River expand I set earnestly about crossing it on my raft. With the crocodiles and hippopotami, we were now so familiar, that their haunts had no terrors for either of us, and in fact we had become so well acquainted with all the tribes of the forest and river, that they no longer became even objects of curiosity. My Negro companion and helper knew no fear, and often sought the wild animals of the most resolute character, to exercise his skill in archery, with poisoned arrows, and a powerful arm and penetrating sight, so that the result of his hunting frequently brought to my feet creatures I had not even heard of before, and it was in vain I entreated him, like me, to spare them, having been educated in a very different school – where the value of life never entered into the contemplation of his teachers – absorbed as they were in their own mere amusement – a degrading feature I fear among nearly all mankind.

Taking advantage of a moment when the stream flowed less rapidly than usual, we crossed to the opposite shore about two or three miles from our place of embarcation, steered by the Negro by means of a pole – and were by his skill conducted into a winding bay where the shore was shallow, and the landing easy. It was a spot encompassed by a grove standing on an elevation and backed by a mass of rocks, that seemed calculated to afford shade during the heat of the day. Having carried with us materials to form a hut, we halted our raft aground and before night were well furnished with shelter in a rural spot among shrubs.

CHAPTER III

My first object at break of day was to examine the neighbourhood, when I found the appearance of a cave with a narrow entrance, but so regular that it seemed the work of man rather than accident, and entering, after discharging my gun into it, with caution, I was surprised to see an apartment, adorned with figures elaborately sculptured and hieroglyphicks of no usual degree of finish. The whole erection was highly polished granite. The place was too obscure to enable me to view more than the entrance, although, as nothing had issued out but bats on my first firing, I had no reason to fear. I therefore returned and making Musumba advance with a torch of pine-wood commenced a closer examination. It had evidently been a tomb, for at the end of the first chamber a staircase was observable although choked with rubbish; but this first chamber was very interesting, the whole walls being covered as well as the ceiling with paintings representing fishing, hunting, and fowling, together with men employed in agricultural pursuits, the colours very fresh, and the outlines very decided.

I had seen the tombs of both Lower and Upper Egypt, and those of Nubia on my first travels, and little expected to find any traces of the ancient religion of Isis and Osiris in these high regions of the river Nile – much less to find the execution of these idolatrous monuments in a more elaborate, and, though dry and formal, correct manner. Yet so I found it, to an extraordinary degree, and if possible superior in neatness of execution to some of the finest fragments excavated at Thebes, where I always thought these fragments of their gods were anciently even then considered as antiques, from their fine preservation, just as the moderns esteem correct Greek sculpture of early schools, or the people of rank in Hindoostan, the early specimens of the Persian water colour paintings; the prototypes of the modern school, or as very exquisite specimens of the oldest china ware and antique Japan are esteemed by the degenerate artists among the Chinese. And thus it is very easy for any one, whose eye and taste have been corrected by long acquaintance with subjects of art, to appreciate the great superiority of the monuments at Athens or in Ionia over the best works of the Roman school, or of those of Thebes and the Temples of Lower Egypt, although the first is in a state of comparative decay to the other.

My education and travels, and above all my long intercourse with the discriminating and pure taste of Lycas, had made me, as we Italians say, an *Intendendi*, and the beauty of this chamber fixed my attention for so long a time, that Musumba, in astonishment at my curiosity, asked me if I intended to dine on those polished walls? in which case he would take the freedom to provide for an appetite that demanded something more easy of digestion.

"Do so,", said I, "only first bring me more splinters of wood for lights, and any thing will do for me, a few dates or so, and a pitcher of water at your return, for I find myself so well satisfied with this shelter that I shall for the present make it my abode, so you may at your leisure bring everything here."

Looking astonished, and shaking his head as he retired from the cell, he seemed quite at a loss to conjecture why I should prefer so dismal an abode to the grove by the river side, but he had been bred to obedience, and he soon returned with the articles I demanded; neither did I find it, after a good fumigation, by any means an inconvenient bivouac; as it was perfectly dry, and shaded by its situation from the sun's heat, which at noon was intense at this season of the year, I took possession of it. We made a soft pallet of long grass just within the entrance, and at night flanked it with heavy boughs to scare away all intruders, if any such were in the habit of making it a den, but we did not find any fresh indications of such occupants, and having swept the marble floor clean, lay down to sleep in perfect security.

The next day was wholly employed in closely examining the character of the paintings, which represented men of various complexions, but chiefly very dark ones, especially those apparently, by their occupations, of the lower classes – but having satisifed my curiosity in this respect, I could not resist the temptation, as we had time to spare before the great heats subsided, to pursue my discoveries into what seemed evidently a passage to the interior of the rock; for all I saw had been hewn from the solid mass, like the caves at Elephanta. The black was strong and I active, as well as willing, and we soon made a way through the rubbish that filled the second entrance to a narrow descending passage, by means of a staircase, into a small chamber, in the centre of which was a well open and seemingly not very deep. A stake and cord conducted us to the bottom, where a very small doorway, unincumbered by rubbish, opened an horizontal cavity just big enough to admit one man, if not of very considerable dimensions. The well was lined with hieroglyphicks very neatly and deeply cut, representing dragons and serpents in menacing attitudes, attacking men armed with bows and arrows or spears and round shields. And here I took the post of honour, and advanced with a torch in each hand, secure, from the rubbish-closed entrance in the first chamnber, that there was nothing within that could harm me – but Musumba thought otherwise, and assured me that there was more danger from goblins, than even lions. Yet he followed armed with his spear and torch, and talked loudly evidently to raise his declining courage.

At the end of the cavity, however, which was very long and very close and hot, I found the way obstructed by a wooden door that seemed to have been dropped like a portcullis from above, quite plain in its surface, and closely fitting the whole space except about the threshold, which it seemed never to have reached by some inches. I borrowed the Negroe's spear to try if I could lift it, in which, although I failed, I found the timber so rotten that it crumbled and gave way to great exertions, yet not so much as to give me any hopes of effecting an entrance beyond it. We were therefore obliged to retire backwards to the well, on which occasion I took especial care to examine the ceiling of the passage, lest other traps might also be suspended over our heads. But I found all solid granite throughout, and returned to the mouth of the cave to consider by what means I might penetrate the next day to the end of this chasm, which nothing could prevent me from attempting, not even the entreaties of my poor bewildered companion, who saw nothing but evil consequences from the experiments, and who a hundred times wished we had never beheld the enclosure, altogether boding misfortune, and perhaps only filled with dead men's bones, whose spirits would, he assured me, haunt and follow us in the desert in revenge for our molesting their quiet repose.

The ensuing morning early we entered armed with a stout long spear, which I made Musumba thrust between my legs when we arrived once more at the portcullis, and with one hand holding the brand and with the other the spear I converted it into a battering ram and soon found myself successful in demolishing the rotten door, but covered with a cloud of dust, to which my torch gave flame until it was extinguished, and glad we both were again to retrace our steps backwards to procure safe respiration, leaving our formidable ram behind. When we were recovered and could breathe freely in the well, and speak without fear of suffocation, I sent for new torches and, giving the dust time to subside, renewed my progress with alacrity, in despite of the remonstrances of the Negro, whom, seeing his apprehensions had nearly overcome his resolution, I ordered to remain behind and attend the lights, waiting my summons if I found mine extinguished.

When I came again to the door way, I thrust in my two torches over the ruins of the sill, which was greatly encumbered by them, and saw it led to a small vaulted chamber, on the back wall of which there stood, in a nitch, a soros of white marble covered over with coloured hierogliphicks, and in the form of a deep boat or vessel before which in the centre was a very small monolithic temple of black basalt exquisitely polished – and on the floor lay many little idols of *Isis* in porcelain and wood. The place was warm, but not excessively hot like the passage, and probably had been thus hermetically sealed from the time of its construction. Seated on the small temple, I collected my ideas and began soon to examine the soros which in point of form resembled a bulky vessel deep laden and without masts – being covered by a gently sloping roof. The rim was encircled with a broad band of incised figures, whose lines were filled with red, blue and yellow colour. It was closed down very correctly, and had at its ends two cavities which seemed to have contained the handles by means of which it had been deposited. The walls were every where white, covered with fresh paintings, and looked as if they had been recently finished, yet how many ages it must have been erected! when I considered the state of decay of the door, and doubtless it must have been coeval with the Theban cemeteries; or probably, from the chasteness of the ornaments, much older. It was impossible to decipher the images on the walls and ceiling, but according to my conjectures they all as pictures alluded to diluvian history, as there were boats, water, and men drowning, while others were seemingly separated from the falling waters and preserved in an ark. What a crowd of reflexions this circumstance brought into my thoughts, it is impossible to relate. I longed to behold the interior of a coffin, that doubtless contained some precious mummy as yet intact, yet I felt sensibly the indelicacy not to say indecency of indulging such an improper curiosity.

"What", said I to myself, "after the respect paid to these remains for so many ages, and from people of such different faiths, shall I, a way-farer and wanderer, a Christian and a moral philosopher, come from a far country, and be the first to violate this tomb? Shall I imitate the monstrous sacrilege practiced by the most degenerate of Egyptians at the instigation of the polished vagabonds of Europe? who roast their meats in the Thebaid with the coffins of princes, and exalt the fire with the precious balms and even the bones of priests and nobles? No. Ever sacred be the remains of mortallity, respected be at least the mausoleum, and let me wash my hands in innocency of such a violation!"

During these reflections my neglected torch expired, and left in total darkness I could not help feeling a sort of creeping horror at my situation. But not doubting that in so small a space, with but one entrance it would be easy to feel my way to the passage that led to it, I commenced by groping for the wall with both hands, and taking the cold sarcophagus for a fixed point, I turned to the right and soon found myself at an angle of the chamber, pursuing which, and stumbling over rude images of Isis with which the floor was sprinkled, I soon felt a cavity in the wall – apparently similar in width and height to that by which I had entered, but was not a little surprized not to see any glimmering of light at the end of it, as I expected to find Musumba there keeping up the lighted spears. I called aloud to bid him advance with one, but no answer was returned but a faint echo. I increased the volume of my voice, but only received a louder echo in return. Surprized at this, I advanced forward, suspecting some bend in the passage intercepted my voice, or the light. The walls were smooth, my footing firm below, and the height corresponded with the passage I expected to find, but judge of my feelings when, after advancing as I imagined as far as the outlet, I found the passage blocked up by some heavy body of stones, cold, damp, and polished. By my fingers I soon ascertained that it was not a door but an Idol, attached to the wall. After a moment's reflection I recovered from my surprize, judging that there must have been two passages, and that I had only to return by the way I came to be once more in a capacity to recover the clue, so strangely mistaken, and I lost no time in retreating, a little chilled in my nervous system, and somewhat, I fear, bewildered, and not so cool as I should have been. I however reached once more the monolithic altar on which I sat down with a sensation of weakness not common to me, and began once more to call aloud to Musumba. Still no reply came, or glimmering of light appeared – but I cheered myself by recollecting that the door was destroyed that barred the way we entered, and probably the stake lay there still by which we had forced it, and its fragments, over which I had stepped, and that by groping round the wall I must come to those obstacles and ascertain the right entrance leading to the well. I therefore collected myself, and proceeded, but again getting confused at feeling an entrance resembling that into which I had deviated, was somewhat disconcerted, until I reflected there might possibly be three, and that I was now opposite that which had so unpleasantly misled me, and which from the weakness of my light I had not at first noticed.

I therefore proceeded, not I must confess without a palpitating heart, not only on account of the embarrassment of my senses, but from an unhappy suspicion, which, in despite of my confidence in my conductor, crossed my disturbed mind, as to the possibility that he might have robbed, abandoned me and crossed the river to Sennaar, with some plausible tale that would there have easily found belief. I was soon however relieved from my first difficulty by encountering to my great joy the ruins of the old door, and (for in my situation even that was scarcely enough to satisfy my anxiety) touching the ram which lay along in the entry. I now therefore raised my voice once more lustily, seeing no glimmering of light, but no reply came but its own echoe. Onward however I pushed hastily, and was not long in reaching the well, where, finding all still dark, and no one answering me, my sad conjectures were renewed. Feeling nevertheless the beam of which we had formed the ladder, I speedily mounted it, and commenced crawling towards the entrance, on all fours, for it was scarcely high enough to stand upright, and rough with fallen rubble – and it was not long before a glimmer of day pervaded the deep shades, which resembled the blue of the external sky to my depressed sight. Not small was my rapture when I once more emerged to the interior of the cave, and saw the real day, which was of short duration, for, looking around, the chamber was despoiled to appearance, and Musumba was not there. A dreadful conviction now passed across my mind of his culpability, and I sank down on a stone unable to support myself, covered with perspiration, exhausted in mind, and overwhelmed with my acute feelings.

Nothing seemed left but what I carried about me, except a small crow bar and hammer with which we had accomplished our entrance to the staircase – and when, issuing out, at last, as my agony subsided, no one responded to my exclamations. What to do in such an affliction seemed difficult to ascertain. Then I called to mind the exalted precepts of the defunct Lycas, which never admitted of despair under any circumstances, and armed my mind with the remembrance of his piety. "The river," I said to myself, "is passable, the road to *Sennaar* not unknown to me, and better to fall into the hands of her citizens than perish here in the desert. I have one friend even there. Musumba has been treacherous, but he might have added murder to robbery, there seems to be no faith in man any where with certainty, but there is justice in providence, and at any rate I am undeceived." A slight thought also I fear arose in my mind, that if I could get back to Sennaar I might avenge myself of this injury. And thus meditating on my present condition I moved slowly towards the grove of acacias that covered the little mound by the river, possessed only of my arms, some powder and shot, a small compass, a map, and a few necessaries. Having given over hope I ceased to raise my Halloo – and had gained the top of the hillock and sat down on the grass, examining the stream flowing with an augmented rapidity that made me doubtful of ever being able to stem its current.

And now for the first time in my life I felt my total helplessness, for to construct a raft, and cross a flood which appeared to increase in volume, even while I looked on it, and at the same time to provide for my daily necessities, seemed beyond the powers even of a healthy and powerful arm like mine; and to proceed alone over a sandy desert was to meet inevitable death. I looked up to heaven, and thought only of succour from my maker and redeemer. I took out a small volume of devotion, from which, although a Christian in mere form, I had never parted, but used its invocations mechanically, and prayed earnestly and vehemently, that the being who had hitherto preserved my life, would now, in my extremity, vouchsafe to accept my supplications, and with his protecting hand conduct me out of my present apparently insurmountable difficulties. My thoughts ascended with my ardent desires, and I was so absorbed by my imagination, and fervour, that when I again came back to the afflicting view of the situation I was placed in, my forehead was covered with drops of perspiration and my body lay prostrate on the ground. But when I arose I seemed a new man, and felt conscious as of the divine presence, a renewed faith, a sense of humiliation, and deep conviction that my life had been one of passion and error, and that in placing my dependance on my own talents and weak reason I had laid the foundation of most of the misfortunes that had accompanied my well intended exertions in the cause of humanity.

CHAPTER IV

No words can express the perfectness of my resignation and confidence; with no evident mode of escape before me, I felt as already delivered from the jaws of death, and firmly inspired into a secure and silent hope of seeing better and more tranquil days for the future, or, if I was doomed to perish in this solitude, of a certainty of being translated to a better state of existence, secure in the love of my creator, and where one object would absorb all my thoughts, dutiful obedience to his will, and admiration of his goodness and wisdom. *"They also serve"*, I repeated, from the lines of the divine poet, *"who only stand and wait."*

Nor was it long before I experienced the realization of my hopes – for on looking round me, and listening to hear, if any nut or fruit fell from the date trees at hand, with which I might now satisfy my exigent appetite, an unusual note reached my ear like the groan of some person in distress, or under suffocation attempting to relieve his lungs, and stepping hastily towards the quarter from whence it came I could scarce believe my eyes, when at the foot of a tree I beheld *Musumba*, bound and gagged, and struggling to get free.

At this sight all the blood in my veins seemed to rush into my countenance, with a full feeling of my unworthiness, and in an instant I rushed forward to deliver him, when, disengaged, in his delight he embraced my knees with the symptoms of the warmest gratitude. But I felt a sensation by no means agreable to experience, or easy to describe, a mixture of shame and transport, which pride taught me to suppress, as too closely connected with selfishness to make it possible to disclose it to the harmless object of my unjust suspicions. We were both pretty well exhausted with fatigue and agitation, and I felt almost ashamed to enquire how he came into this situation, but after taking some refreshing fruit and water, he first began by telling me, that whilst he was tending the fires at the bottom of the well, and impatiently expecting my summons or presence, he heard voices in the cave above, uttering execrations in the language of the country, and began at once to believe we had been pursued by some Sennaarites who doubtless had my capture in view. He therefore advanced cautiously to the second entrance at the top of the staircase, where he beheld three or four men deliberately packing up all we possessed as if preparing to depart with it, and not being able to restrain his feelings, he made a rush among them with no other implement of defence, but the small crow bar we had used to enter by and his own dagger, striking right and left, with vociferations of his determination to defend my property to the last; – in which unequal contest he was over-powered by the robbers, for such they were, and after a fruitless struggle was bound as I found him, and obliged to see them mount their camels deriding his sufferings and making off with the booty. "Allah be thanked," said he as he ended his narrative, "that you were not present, for they were all I believe ruffians of the Sangalli Jagger tribe, and well armed, and had the contest ended by our mutual capture or by one of us falling, the other must have perished miserably by famine and by inches, as they fully intended should have been my fate. The mercy of heaven has, after all, preserved us both, I trust for a better end, and we must now look out for a safer place than this, which doubtless is the rendezvous of wandering banditti."

Another night, however, we agreed it would be best to take, in our forlorn condition, to the shelter of the tomb, and after a hearty meal, procured and cooked by the activity of my honest and injured guide, whose importance was now doubled in my estimation, I lay down with as much confidence and composure as ever I had done in my youthful age on the silken mattresses of Venice, surrounded by wealth and worldly splendor. Early in the morning Musumba arose, spread his garment on the sand at the mouth of the cavern, and performed his ablutions with the dust of the earth, whilst I repeated my orisons, full of peace of mind and grateful remembrances, only a few paces from him.

Our next business was to hold a consultation as to my future proceedings; and since to construct another raft was out of our joint power, we agreed to follow the stream upwards in hopes of finding some ford by means of which we might cross, and conceal ourselves in the forest, for on the side we were, there was little shelter but reeds. And now being lightened of our baggage we made great progress, I armed with my fowling piece, and he with a sharp pointed wooden lance, made for the occasion, and his attagan stuck in his leathern girdle.

The weather was favourable, and for three of four days we thus proceeded, but without any success as to our expectation of finding a favourable ford, during which journey we subsisted on the eggs of the inhabitants of the sands or marshes, and I shot some excellent game which all the way abounded, at night defending ourselves with fires supported by reeds and lances, which also kept off by the smoke millions of mosquitos, or sand flies.

The stream had now visibly decreased in size and depth, and the fifth day, invited by the shady appearance of the opposite bank, we were just prepared to attempt the passage partly by swimming and partly by wading, when to our great discomfit two men mounted on dromedaries appeared in sight making towards us, and were speedily followed by five or six more, to whom they hallooed and made signals by firing a matchlock. All resistance was now out of the question, and we were driven before them to a camp of their fellows consisting of thirty or forty tents surrounded by cattle. On being presented to the chief, an aged man of the Negro race, we were interrogated as to where we had left our Kofila or company, and where we were going? *Musumba*, who best understood them, looking at me significantly, said I was white physician whom he was endeavouring to conduct to Sennaar for practice, and that we had no companions, or any thing but what we carried about our persons, that he was my slave, and that if they would assist us to pass the river, I should be grateful to the utmost of my power. This speech seemed to be well received, and after a few complimentary expressions we were conducted to a tent and regaled with such food as they were themselves accustomed to, milk, honey, and bread, and that night, although evidently under inspection, we were not molested.

In the morning, a man entered the tent, and took away our arms and accoutrements, at the same time informing us that the chief would speedily see us, and soon afterwards we were again conducted before him and again asked to explain our objects and where we came from as well as where we were going to. This was somewhat difficult to comply with, and we were obliged to consult together as to the reply, which excited their jealousy, or so they feigned, and we were immediately remanded to our tent under a guard, our allowance diminished, and our treatment in other respects less ceremonious, and soon after the chief himself came in, and made me attend him to his tent, where introducing me to some females of his family, he said, "if you are a physician, exert your skill on them, and prove the truth of your professions." I now saw the folly of Musumba who had brought us into an unpleasant situation and desired he might also be sent for to explain why he had made so groundless an assertion, assuring them that I had no pretensions to such a talent, and which at my desire he contradicted, alleging that his object was to procure me more respect, and to promote their aid in crossing the stream, with other vague excuses.

"So then," said the honest chief, "you make no scruple of lying, whatever your master may do – and he perhaps was not aware that I should put him to the test or he would have contradicted it at first. We are simple people in this part of the country, following honest occupations, and have nothing to conceal. Your master is a white man, and is travelling alone without any either camels or merchandise, you tell one story and he another – and what should he go to Sennaar for, unless to report what he has seen among us, and how we live on this side the River. He may be a spy sent over by the Jaggas from Matamba who infest the opposite bank of this Bar-el-abaid and no good Musselman – wretches who are wandering everywhere, who at *Monsol* keep a market for human flesh, and where children are killed for the King's table, idolaters, and cruel, the enemies to all men. I must therefore detain you for my tribe's security. If you are honest men we shall soon discover it by your conduct. In the mean time as you appear to possess nothing but your arms, I shall give you both some useful employment in attending our herds, and a sufficient supply of food to preserve you in health. Go, my children – make no remonstrances, you shall receive both justice and hospitality."

It was in vain to reply, we were taken from his presence under an escort, stripped, and dressed in the costume of his servants, and sent immediately into the surrounding deserts to join others in this to me fatiguing and laborious employment.

A change of life like this at first seemed very afflicting, and we had leisure enough when at sun set, we entered our rude sleeping place to consider of it. In the situation to which we had been reduced I was obliged to confess a worse fate might have befallen us. Had we crossed the river we might have been seized on by the barbarians that infest it and murdered. Even had we succeeded in returning to Sennaar, there were great difficulties to overcome before I could pass out of the country into Egypt, or even Abyssinia, and a second captivity less salubrious than this which we were suffering might have lasted to the end of my days. One lesson, however, we might both derive from it, to learn a strict adherence to truth in all our commerce with mankind, and I trust I imprinted this conviction on the mind of the companion of my adversity.

"We have nothing," I said, "now to do, but to win the confidence of our chief by good conduct. Let us spare no pains in doing our duty, and heaven will hear our sincere prayers and deliver us in the end." As we pursued our occupations I spared no pains to instill moral precepts into the uncultivated mind of Musumba, and thus in a short time rendered him even an agreeable companion. The mind at ease, our severe tasks only contributed to our strength and health, so that the report of our conduct being praiseworthy, the old chieftain enlarged our indulgences, and at length ordered us to be brought up from the field to the tents, where our daily fare was not worse than his own, and I soon became a favourite with all the family, although an unbeliever, as I made a point of confessing myself. Having thus gained his confidence, I disclosed my adventures, some of which were of a nature to stagger the belief of a simple grazier who lived like a Bedouin and knew little of the world beyond Africa. His opinion however was that a man is best in his own country, and he very kindly offered me any assistance in his power to accomplish my return.

Mine did not very much differ from his, the wild wish to reach *Sophis* had vanished along with its improbability; and even Europe, with all its vices, seemed more tolerable after what I had seen and heard in this quarter of the globe. I had suffered enough to cure me of my impetuosity, and, my passions composed, all I sought was tranquility and retirement from the world.

I therefore gladly listened to his proposals, which were, to accompany him in his migration southward in the spring with his flocks, towards the high sources of the white river, which would give me a chance of meeting with the caravan of Tripoli or Fez, on their return, and by my services to the merchants thus get a passage to Europe.

To trace this unknown river to its springs had been among the early projects of my ambition, and from thence to ascend the Mountains of the Moon and behold the sources of other mighty floods to the south – but *Musumba*, who had no such ambition, preferred crossing the stream and returning to his old master. We therefore parted, and during some months I cheerfully accompanied the chieftain whose name, of Arabic origin, was *Fazzar*. Our route was from oasis to oasis, when we had ascended to the forks of two branches of a river diminishing in size almost at last to brooks, during which we always found pasture, and encountered many camps of various inhabitants – but never entered any town or city. As the summer advanced we ascended into a mountain country through extensive valleys, rich with the noblest trees my eyes had ever beheld, and fertile in brooks and fresh pastures, where we daily passed villages of a healthy population, who seemed to want for nothing which nature could afford, and lived a careless and indolent life, content with the produce of the earth without cultivation, and the result of the chase – infested it is true with many wild animals, but little annoyed by them, as their prey was abundant, and of course their ferocity limited to the destruction of their fellow quadrupeds. At length we came to a place of some consequence situated high up in these extensive mountains, which by no means answered my expectations of them as to altitude, where *Fazzar* flattered me I should meet with information relative to the track of some caravan, and we left the camp, a day's journey below, to make the inquiry, where he assured me I should find merchants resident who could speak Arabic, and from whom I might probably get all the information I required.

After a long and weary climbing journey we reached the gate at sunset. It was constructed of unburned clay, coloured brown and white in stripes, and its gates of strong bamboo were guarded by about twenty fine young Negroes, armed with bows and arrows, and spears and shields, the latter perfectly circular and small composed of stained leather, with thongs and fringes highly ornamental. They had daggers also or short swords of double edges in the form of an oblong leaf pointed with strong cross bar handles slung in their leather scabbards over their shoulders. On our arrival they all rose simultaneously, for all were seemingly at rest in their arms, and demanded our business with great civility. "To see the King," said *Fazzar* with great dignity; and immediately we were conducted through several well inhabited and clean streets to the Royal Palace.

It consisted of a mud wall enclosure of considerable extent, encircling another, where we found guards at every entrance and in the middle of the last enclosure many round huts surmounted by a more elevated mansion, thatched, with a long veranda of great breadth whose roof was supported by elephant's teeth at the entrance, and beyond, with pillars of polished dark wood, elaborately carved and ornamented. Before this house on a clean mat we were instructed to sit down, and wait, whilst from the veranda there came forth about a dozen guards who surrounded us, with looks of curiosity. The rest were I believe the band, as I noticed several rude instruments of music in their hands as well as large drums and flageolets with double stems.

As we waited some time, I had an opportunity of observing the surrounding scene. The house was richly coloured with figures in brown, yellow and black – barbarous forms yet still on the whole producing a good general effect, like the carpets of Turkey, that having no individual character, yet are agreeable on the whole to the eye. Presently a large mat was brought out by two black slaves, and placed under the veranda at the entrance, and four well armed Negroes took sentry on each side, soon after which the King appeared, a portly and well proportioned Negro, dressed in fine mats ornamented with circular spots, and his head bound by a turband of various coloured silks or a sort of shawl. Having seated himself in front of us, he asked if we spoke Arabic, and being answered, "imperfectly", he demanded our errand, and whence we last came from, if we had any presents &c – to which Fazzar said I had little to present, being a supplicant, a foreigner, and had been plundered of all I possessed, that he had afforded me hospitality hitherto and now he wished to transfer me to that of the King to procure me the means of returning by some Kofila passing by Timbuctoo to my own far distant country among the Franks – adding that although a Christian I had many good qualities and talents, and might be trusted as he had experienced my honesty and frankness.

"And what are these Christians good for?" replied the King. "They will neither fight or trade to any purpose. I know them well, for a nation of them exist near the borders of my country, who occasionally bring honey or coarse cloth here for salt. Shut up on one of the highest plains of these mountains, they hold no communication with the surrounding country, except when compelled by necessity to barter, inhabiting a cold region accessible only by a narrow defile, they exist probably in poverty and misery, and if this man is inclined to join them, he has only to wait to the next moon, when probably he may encounter them, and assist them in driving their asses on their return, by which means he may avoid a long and dangerous journey over the deserts, and find himself with his tribe, who however poor, are honest and hospitable although confirmed infidels, and lost in darkness."

I cannot express my astonishment at this speech, or the extraordinary curiosity it excited in my breast. Could it then be possible that a tribe of Christians had penetrated thus far beyond even the knowledge of our best geographers? and to what nation could they belong? I however lost no time in thanking him for his offer, and accepting it – for here at any rate I thought I should make at least a new discovery, and probably by this means lay the foundation for the return to Europe of these exiles from Christian society.

Alas! how little did I know the people I wished to befriend, how little indeed did I know myself, and the weakness of the human mind, its faults, its follies and its integral power!

Fazzar with a simplicity of heart, peculiar as I found to his family, and partaken in excess by himself, now produced all the articles which had been taken from me, on my first arrest, in the most perfect preservation, and, placing them before me, resigned them to my disposal, goodnaturedly suggesting that to procure the confidence of the King, who had thus offered me his services and hospitality, rather perhaps on his account, than my own, I should do wisely to present him with my arms, which as this was a city where no European had ever before appeared, would probably be estimated highly – and if retained be a source of continual jealousy and injury to my interests. In this council I saw a fresh instance of his parental care and kindness, but would willingly have made him accept my pistols or sabre, which he decidedly declined, alleging that it would tarnish in his own mind the merit of his protection to me, and leave him open to suspicion from these people with whom he occasionally had dealings previous to his return to the station where I first encountered him – "for," said he, "although the King is a chief of discernment, his people are rude and brutal, their customs cruel, and it is only by his superior mind that he governs them at all. Gentleness united by decision does much with such men and Allah has mercifully created such beings, to keep disorderly passions from overwhelming society." "Heavens," thought I, "what a pity this man should not be a Christian!"

CHAPTER V

Everything was now settled, the chiefs embraced, and a feast was produced, of kids roasted, boiled grain, fruits, and an intoxicating liquor which was liberally distributed among the soldiers and others, followed by wild dances of both sexes, and a concert of instruments that stunned my ears, but seemed to excite in my new companions transports of delight.

At midnight I parted from the good *Fazzar* by a clear moonshine, illuminating the grand African scenery around us, abounding in magnificent vegetation, whilst the receding stars of that high hemisphere burnt like the jewelled lamps of the firmament, set in a glorious blue without a cloud, as pure as ether, and fresh as the dawning day, or the reflections of conscious innocence.

I was now allotted a cabin within the royal enclosure, had an old slave appointed to assist me, and had my allowance regularly as if I had been an officer of the court – the return probably for the treasure I had presented in my double barrelled rifle, European pistols, and brilliant sabre and dagger of Egyptian workmanship, more gaudy than useful – things presented me by my friend and keeper at leaving Sennaar, and now no longer necessary to my preservation.

The King, for such he was called by his Mahometan subjects who preserved a large mixture of pagan institutions, and spoke a mixed Arabic, professed their origin to be from eastern Africa on the confines of the shores and to have been settled here for ages, attracted by some valuable salt mines, with the produce of which

ϟ and slaves they trafficked with Darfur, and the merchants who pass
annually in Kofilas towards Abyssinia, but, as the passage lay out
of the road and far below these mountains, they were obliged to
convey these articles of commerce a long journey to meet them, so
that it was not only very unprofitable from duties on the road, but
kept them from such intercourse with mankind. The country also
being chiefly forest, and little peopled, gave them few facilities for
agricultural pursuits. It was indeed truly magnificent in ancient,
lofty, umbrageous trees, which covered the hanging slopes of the
mountains, and pierced the tops of vallies of immense expansion,
and grandeur, well watered by crystal streams and murmuring
cascades; a mighty waste, ill peopled, but rich in palms, cocoa trees,
and lofty pines, whose abundant fruits supported multitudes of
monkeys, birds, and reptiles, as well as men. We were now on a
range of lofty hills thus flanked as far as eye could see, and above
rose almost perpendicular rocks that from their outlines seemed
to extend to vast table lands without end. From their bright blue
colour I conjectured they must have been very distant, and from
their nakedness barren – and such was the opinion of the people
I was among, for when asked about them they said they were the
ϟ abode of evil spirits, or a race of giaours who were supposed to
inhabit these heights, and who came yearly to their market for salt
– on which it was imagined they lived.

Every day increased my impatience to see these people, but I
could learn only that they were a poor, stupid, harmless race, who
paid amply for what they wanted, mixed little with the people, had
no arms, returning home speedily when they had accomplished
their barters. Very different were these mountainiers, fierce, war-
like, cruel, and superstitious, dirty in their habits, rude in their
manners, overreaching and treacherous – but on the other hand,
generous to their friends, and hospitable to all who confided in
them for protection. By their strength and hardiness they main-
tained themselves on a large portion of the country, and, wanting
nothing, troubled themselves little about extensive conquests. They
loved their chief, and were always ready to defend his family with
their lives, and considered exemption from actual service as a re-
ward, for indolence seemed their chief good, next to the indulgence
of the appetites and passions, so that it required no small man-
agement and skill to keep them at times in order, and good humour.

Foozoo, for that was the name of their captain and king, felt all
these difficulties, and often told me in confidence, for I soon be-

came a favourite, that he was the least happy of his tribe, since in more instances than one, they had in a spirit of equality deposed their governors.

I found this man to possess a great desire to be informed on every subject that related to other countries, and pleased with my communications, although he could not conceal his doubts as to the truth of many of them. "And why," he said, "should you travel thus far from your home, if all you tell be true, if Europeans possess such talents as you describe, wherefore are you come among nations that can boast of scarce any arts? If property is protected among you, what can induce you to seek at such risks a people where life is scarcely safe except to the strong? And how can you ever expect to get back again when deprived of even the means of communicating your wants? We live here surrounded by various kingdoms without a wish to observe their manners, and prefer our intricate range of forests with this healthy air, to all the riches of the plains which are said to abound in gold. If, like my brother Fazzar, you possessed flocks and wanted pasture, it would be some excuse for this rambling disposition, but even then it would be a necessity to be complained of. I must therefore conclude that your own land has some great fault about it, or that you have met with some more severe affliction than the loss of a woman's love. We like the sex, but never let them disturb our repose, much less ramble over the world in despair for a loss that can so easily be replaced, and finer females than ours I suppose are not easily to be purchased; the beauties of Paradise I should think can scarcely surpass them! Come, therefore," he would then add, "and take up your rest at last here, teach my people your arts, live with me as a friend, conform to our faith, and I will give you a wife that will soon make you forget all your former affections."

To such proposals as these, made in the generosity of his heart, it was not easy to reply without giving offense – especially when he added to them an offer of the best situation in his household, and the friendship of his bravest warriors. All I could therefore say was that my mission was first to *Sophis*, which he owned must contain a wise people, if Lycas was to be credited, and that I believed it to exist to the south of these mountains, and that it was possible these Christians he spoke of as inhabiting their summits might assist me in my research – all which it was evident he gave little credit to, "for," he added laughing, "aye, aye, try them, and I will answer for it you will soon return to me with joy and gladness."

And so we parted – but my dreams were all about these strange people, and every day seemed an age until I could satisfy my curiosity on that subject. In the interim I saw the country and followed the chase on a grand scale with my patron who delighted in dangers, and led us into the deepest recesses of these primitive shades in search of elephants, cameleopards, and lions – whom we subdued by courage and numbers and added to our provisions by the death of many antelopes. "And this," I said, "is what the poets call the golden age! – when every animal trembled at the sight of man, and man thought he had a *right* to destroy every species but his own!" My heart sickened at such a life, and I even ventured to suggest to *Foozoo* that there was a better mode of existence – but he cut me short by saying that time only could change the manner of living of his countrymen, or their way of thinking which depended, in a great measure, on local impressions, and that, when he was tired of life, it would be time enough to propose a change. He acknowledged their vices to be prejudicial to themselves and their country, but ended by saying, we must take things as we find them, or submit to die, for which he had no inclination – and thus concluded our conversation.

Among these wild and half heathenish people I was by circumstances compelled to reside much longer than I wished, and to witness disgusting scenes of depravity. It was in fact a military democracy, for their kings only reigned by custom, and were installed rather by acts of prowess and personal valour than by hereditary esteem, and, as for their religion, it was nominally Mahometan, among the leading men, but mixed with stupid and disgraceful pagan ceremonies. By setting the best example in my power of moral conduct, I made many friends and protectors among them, which increased my own security, but I had but few real disciples beyond the sovereign, although many confessed that the doctrines I wished to inculcate had a tendency to promote harmony in society, if they could be enforced. But discipline they had little; even their priests were suspected, and feebly obeyed, and, short as my stay was among this horde, it was long enough to witness more than one insurrection. To see such a fertile and gigantic range of mountains overrun thus by barbarians, who except in their superior forms were only one step above the wild animals that frequented their recesses, was a continual grievance to me, for nature here exists truly on the grandest scale, and with the aid of good principles, and a pure religion it might be converted into a terrestial paradise.

At length the hour arrived when their distant mountain traders were expected every day, and it was not without anxiety I heard they had been seen a few days back by some of the highest settlers, winding down the sloping and steep upper path with their flocks of goats whitening the bare faces of the lofty crags and rugged precipices. "Doubtless," thought I, "they will turn out to be good *Roman Catholics*, and then how great will be their joy to hear news from their lost bretheren, and the power of the papal chair in Italy? with the hope of by my means one day uniting the links of the broken chain – but should they be no better than those of Abyssinia, I shall still gain a step towards a further knowledge of this hitherto unknown region, and may perhaps ameliorate their manners and bring them back to a purer canon or, through their means, contrive some plan for further discovery of the interior of Africa." I even went so far in my imagination as to think it possible, that by crossing this immense range I might discover the sources of the vast rivers which disembogue themselves into the western ocean – or learn the actual situation of the lake of Zambre – once the sole object of my first advances.

CHAPTER VI

In such vague conjectures, I had passed a sleepless night, when one morning at day break *Foozoo* rushed into my cabin, and called aloud, "Rise up quickly, my friend, and go and embrace the giaours and the goats; these poor creatures are arrived alike wearied by their long journey, and not much unlike in their appearance; for the beards of some of the old herdsmen may rival that of their flocks. My people are highly diverted with the likeness, and I must order them into my own enclosure, or they will be overborne by the rude reception they will meet with from the crowd. I appoint you to be their conductor and interpreter, so be speedy and we will go to them together."

With a palpitating heart, I was soon by his side, and we had not proceeded far, when passing through a dense crowd of the black population, we entered an enclosed lawn filled with hundreds of white goats with their males and kids bleating in chorus, surrounding which were noble dogs keeping them at bay, and their Christian masters, clad in shaggy skins and caps, armed with long crooks, amounting to about fifty healthy looking men, grouped with as many asses and their packsaddles covered also with furs. These occupied the centre of the mass, some lads and the dogs keeping the whole body stationary. On our arrival a loud shout from the crowd announced it, and a venerable, and respectable chief from the travellers came forward, who embraced the knees of the King and claimed his protection. Not a word passed, but it was evidently understood that his claims were allowed, for, taking me by the arm, he led the way back to his enclosure, the whole tribe and their flocks following in a very orderly manner, guarded in the rear by a rude soldiery, whose jibes and taunts were loud, and laughter unceasing. At length the outer gates were closed upon us, and the King taking his seat under a shady tree, silence was commanded and the goat-herds formed a semicircle around his primitive throne – and never shall I forget their appearance. They recalled to my mind the times of the patriarchs of old. All were cloathed alike in white and shaggy jackets girt with broad leathern girdles fastened with thongs, goat-skin sandals also bound to their feet and ancles, their legs bare, and their caps in their hands or rather turbands of leather, plaited with great art and ornaments of a colour brown or black on a rufous ground. All had beards, some very bushy ones, generally black or very dark brown. All were stout men, with large dark eyes and fresh looking countenances rather ruddy than brown, with looks that bore the indications of simplicity and probity.

After the usual salutations, the chief came forward from the circle, and in pure Arabic which only *Foozoo* understood spoke as follows –

"Behold at your feet, your ancient friends and traders, who have according to our annual custom, with no small difficulty conducted this large Kofila hither, less in numbers by far than they were when we left our lofty station owing to accidents by the dangerous passes. We present them to you freely, only expecting in return such a portion of salt as your resources will enable you to afford, and we humbly add to our presents several beasts of burthen, reserving to ourselves, by your permission, as many animals as will be necessary to conduct our merchandise without loss up the tedious and fati-guing ascent that leads to our wild and solitary abode, of many days' journey, and full of perils and difficulties both as to the roads and the seasons, which makes it necessary to return with all possible expedition, the granting of which permission will be acknowledged as an addition to the many acts of friendship we have annually received from your powerful nation." Having spoken thus with a clear and sonorous voice, he bent his body in token of homage and slowly retired to his companions.

The King now rose, and having, as it were for form sake, put his consent to the surrounding councellors, who replied by a simultaneous clapping of their hands, he said with that dignified air he could easily assume, "All is granted!" and the assembly broke up among the clangour of such instruments as their poor notion of music enabled them to construct. We now mixed familiarly together, and whilst a grand repast was preparing to which the Christians' kids contributed the principal article, I was formally introduced to them as one of their faith and perhaps countrymen. At first I could not avoid noticing the great reluctance and shyness of the head herdsman to receive me – but on my making the sign of the cross on my breast and forehead, he looked round to his companions in astonishment and cordially embraced me, presenting me to them with the utmost kindness, and to my infinite surprize exclaiming in Italian *"Reguardato, anche que se trovo le creatura di Christo! grazia a Dio!"* At the sound of my native language, I started, and instantly replied, *"si, io sono christiano come voi altri"* and all ran to embrace me as a brother with joy and affection, thinking, as they afterwards informed me, that I was one of their stray countrymen, seeking the means of returning among them. In a few words when they found their mistake, they told me that they were all from an Italian stock, of few families, and unmixed with any other people, assuring me of their protection, and friendship, and a safe passport to the mountains whence they came, and to which, having finished happily their barter, they must commence returning the next day, according to the laws of their community.

We were now ushered into an enclosure especially assigned to us and our cattle, where a meal was provided of milk, bread and fruits – and having placed themselves in a circle, they began a hymn of thanksgiving, consisting of voices in three parts, so melodious and solemn, that it might have graced the Sistine Chapel, and gratified the first masters of Italy. This was followed by a prayer, when all prostrated their bodies, and after rising, and crossing ourselves, we sat down together to our refection like brothers.

When the meal was finished, preparatory to which and afterwards a short grace was delivered by the chief herdsman, he said to me publicly, that, if I united myself to them, I must prepare to depart the same day, and assist them in all they had to do, to which end I should be provided with a stout animal to carry me and every accommodation necessary on the road, faring as they did all the journey – there being no distinction allowed among them, except that each one was ambitious of being serviceable to others – that when I arrived at the country they belonged to, I should be put under the care of the elders of the village they first arrived at, and, if a lover of Christ and his doctrines, be readily incorporated among them as long as I was inclined to remain. I would willingly have interrogated him as to their peculiar tenets and origin, but he cut me short, by saying, they were herdsmen and not priests or historians, and referring me to the officers and deacons of their church on these matters. "But I can assure you," he said, "we have but one law for all men founded on the holy scriptures, and try to imitate to the best of our weak powers, our divine founder in all things."

At so judicious a reply, I was both surprized and delighted, and could not help entertaining a high opinion of a nation whose lower orders, as I then conceived them to be, entertained such just sentiments of their Christian duties.

CHAPTER VII

We were soon on our road after sun set, with our cargoes of rock-salt, I having first taken leave of the King and his family, who told me at parting, that the liberality, honesty and civil conduct of these people, had made a great impression on his subjects in general, and hence they were never molested on their return; that for his own part he felt a great respect for them, and wished some of them to stay behind and reform his servants, or act as his managers themselves, even their religion, he thought, could not be bad, which produced so many good men as he had always found these herdsmen to be. "And by and bye," said he, "I expect they will make some converts among us – rude as my people are and headstrong."

At daylight we made a halt in an open glade in the forest which clothed the sides of the hill we were ascending – and never shall I forget the beauty of the spot. A swelling knoll covered with the softest and shortest turf surrounded by a cool and rapidly flowing brook, that washed one of its curved and sloping extremities, was before us. Scattered here and there were flowering shrubs to me unknown, but rich in gaudy blossoms, on which many coloured butterflies and moths were reposing or flitting to and fro – the back scene opening up to a sequestered deep valley overhung with branching trees of great variety and beauty, and from the end of which fell a small brilliant cascade, the parent of the brook below. Many birds were on the wing from side to side of the gayest plumage, and antelopes were seen browsing on the promontories which protruded from the tops of the hills, richly gilded by the rays of the rising sun.

That was the signal for the morning hymn, commenced in low tones but terminating in the fullest and loudest chorus that ever waked an echo, and which, at this lovely spot, was heard reverberating from rock to rock until it died away in a hallowed and whispering sound. I need not add that I joined them with pleasure, for the words were from the poetry of David King of Israel and were as follows.

> O, send out thy light and thy Truth, that they
> may lead me and bring me unto thy holy hill,
> and to thy dwelling place.
>
> Psalm. 43.3

The good taste shewn in the application to our circumstances surprized me, and for the first time I began to think these my conductors could not be of the lowest class of this people.

From this spot the ascent became steeper and steeper and the road consequently more winding, bringing to view every hour new, fresh, and strange scenery, and thus we proceeded for many days through a sort of paradise where we found food for our asses, and fruits for ourselves, with sheltered spots, full of beauty to repose at every halt. But after about thirty days hard travelling the scene changed and we entered a region more lofty and barren than any thing I had expected – and here it became necessary to make a long stay to refit our packages, relieve our cattle, and prepare ourselves to support a change of climate produced by a greater degree of cold, the consequence of an increased elevation, warm haiks were distributed to all, and even the animals were covered with additional clothing, their skins examined and dressed, and as much attention paid to their security from annoyance or injury as we in Europe pay to our finest racers – at which having expressed some surprize, one of them said, "The same God who made us, made them for our succour and assistance, but at the same time endowed us with discretion to know how they ought to be treated in return. If on our arrival at home these dumb animals betrayed marks of suffering from our negligence, we should be justly punished and censured."

I could not help admitting the justness of the remark, or saying to myself, "what sort of people am I among? They must be I think quite equal to the Sophians!" At that moment there was a great stir in the encampment, and much concern expressed in the faces of several near me − the cause of which appeared to be that in calling over the names of the company a man was missing, who was however soon after brought in pallid, and apparently helpless, for he was borne by four others and gently reposed on a heap of goat skins, collected by the bye-standers in an instant from their shoulders. We soon learned from his own mouth the cause. The weakness of the animal he rode had induced him to retard his pace, well knowing that we should make a halt at the point we were arrived at, and thus he dropped off from the Kofila or string, − and being left alone, at a difficult pass, wanting assistance, both himself and his goods had swerved over a narrow path and fallen on a rock somewhat below, by which means he had got severely bruised and stunned, so as not to be able to call for aid, or rise from the ground, until those who had hurried back to enquire for him came to his relief.

He was immediately an object of attention to us all, and whilst some administered restorative cordials, which they told me were extracts from salutary herbs, others commenced giving friction to the injured and stiffened limbs, and a bath of steam was also pre-pared, by means of heated stones on which water was poured under a covering of skins. This accident my guide represented to me as singularly unfortunate, as bruises were more difficult to cure than broken bones in some cases, "for," he added, "it is of great impor-tance that we should as soon as possible pass over this barren and rocky part of our journey, and our brother's confinement may be longer than we expect, as he is not a young man." "Could not you," said I, "leave some one to attend him, who when he was recovered might follow our track at leisure?"

"O no," he replied, "that would not be consistent with our modes of proceeding. We have a law *to do as we would be done by*, and never abandon each other in cases of this kind, but rather all submit to inconvenience, as our concern is mutual, and the grievance to one is, when divided by all, much abated. And if this man were left behind with a small company, we should be under general uneas-iness during the remainder of our way, and be justly blamed by the elders of our distict at our return, as the road is now more difficult at every stop, and even water may become scarce."

I need not say I felt the truth of these humane observations, a little ashamed of my proposal, and that I learned my first lesson of caution, how I ought to conduct myself among these people, who evidently wanted no instructions from my Sophians.

During our long ascending traject through these woody mountains, which, although somewhat fatiguing to others, was not so to me on account of its novel appearance, and the strange things which often met my eyes, I observed with some surprize, that no one disturbed either animal or bird, although each man had three or four lances slung across his back, with which I also was accommodated although perfectly unacquainted with their management, and on one occasion, when some gazelles came immediately before our path had suggested the advantages they offered us of obtaining fresh animal food. "By no means," said my guide! "There is no necessity, we have plenty of better sustenance yet remaining, and even dried meat, should it become desirable or proper to use it. Let us travel on harmless of unnecessary injury to any living thing whose enjoyment is in its own life."

"Then for what purpose are these lances?" said I.

"For self defence", he replied, "from wild animals; when pressed by hunger they might attack our asses or goats, and fire is not at hand to repel their fury. We are Christians and are taught by our Lord to love all things he has created, and not to destroy anything wantonly or by way of sport as you call such a cruelty – which makes me think the community you acknowledge are not quite so perfectly instructed as they should be. Of such we have heard."

I was silenced by these words, for I knew we were not perfect, having long compared our tenets at Venice with even those of natural religion and suspected their purity long before I knew the venerable Lycas. Of course I became impatient to arrive among and see more of this people.

Our halt here was not long, for by attention and kindness our bruised companion soon was enabled to go on with us, assisted by his fellows, after a few days repose. Nothing very remarkable passed during our stay as we were all constantly employed about the packages and cattle, and I observed with satisfaction, that at three periods of the day, according with our Roman Catholic ritual, all said a short but energetic appeal to heaven, and that perfect urbanity was observed by all, so that no contention interrupted our general harmony, and, when our work was suspended in evenings, groups assembled to sing in parts national airs, to a species of guitar or rather Mandolina of a small size, which almost all could touch with skill enough to form a suitable accompaniment to the voice, and not a few as we travelled on could compose extempore verses descriptive of the scenes around us, which greatly beguiled the way, and seemed even grateful to the animals on which we rode – reminding me frequently of the muleteers of the Appennine, or the gondoliers of my native long lost city of Venice!

The space we were now tracing was a wild and rocky as well as barren region, a sort of Steppe nearly a plain, of considerable extent, with here and there a melancholy solitary tree cut by the winds and presenting a desolate scene almost without water, except when we halted at small but deep and dark pools, surrounded by yews and the thorny acacias, and which were generally at the foot of some scar that looked as if it had been blasted by lightning, or hemmed in by massive granite rocks piled on each other or plunging into the basin. Yet these wildernesses were not without sufficient herbage or bushes to shelter them, so that we found pasture nearly all the way. But I soon learned that we should find a very different country above these sloping plains, where was a table land of great extent, well supplied with water and every necessary of life, and that that was the end of the journey and the seat of the nation they belonged to who found the benefit of this sterile barrier in keeping off the scattered nations which surrounded them, and with whom they maintained no intercourse, except to procure objects of necessity. This wild range over which we were passing supported much life, for it was the summer haunt of the wild ass, the deer tribe, goats, and also eagles, hawks, vultures and ravens, together with several other animals to me at that time unknown – of which we saw abundance in the course of our march across it, which occupied, at our slow rate of travelling, about two European miles an hour, during fourteen days, for the paths were winding and sometimes very rough, and much time was taken up in halts to pasture the animals, whose wants were watched with that attention which they said was due from rational beings to irrational at all times, but most so when captured and employed in our service – and the effect was, as I clearly saw, that these services were better performed in consequences of this judicious conduct, for although the only stimulus allowed was the voice, we had scarce a restive beast among us.

"We never strike them or anything, but in self defence," observed my guide, "and being accustomed from the time they are foaled to tender treatment, they obey us with a sort of natural affection. It is the same with our dogs, who guard us against wild animals, that have not the benefit of such an education – for we know that even they can be rendered quite domestic, by a judicious course of training, as you will witness when settled among us."

Some of these ideas and practices were new to me, but I was

averse to confess it, lest I should lessen myself in the eyes of these good people, who acted, I daily found, on a principle based on sound judgment, and rooted by public instruction probably at a very early age. "If," said I to myself, "all the people I am seeking resemble these poor herdsmen, I shall have no occasion to enquire after the Sophians."

CHAPTER VIII

As we advanced, the country improved, the soil seemed to change, and the trees became more abundant, and soon we saw the country ascend gently, leaving this granite expanse, to advance on limestone hills, that overtopped it like a roof or hooded covering, the granitic rocks from the time we entered the region to this place appearing to be an immense fault, as geologists call a sinking in of a stratum. So rare an appearance a little surprized me, for it seemed as if the whole range of mountains to the east had slid side ways after being protruded upwards to throw off their coverings under some great convulsion of Nature.

And now the way became beautifully diversified with rounded and richly covered hills, resembling the great giants of Hindoostan, the roads more winding among park-like forests with little under-wood, and gushing cascades glittering at the head of every valley. On entering this stage of our journey, the countenances of our whole troop were dressed in sober and satisfied expression, an expression of gratitude, joy and thanksgiving. The hymn was raised with animated and loud sounds of praise accompanied by such instruments as they possessed, and it being in a deep gorge where there was an echo, the hills in reality seemed to rejoice, and the firmament to reply. After this the chief giving the signal, we all prostrated ourselves on the sod, and repeating after him the prayer of our Lord, we again pursued on our way, which had only been interrupted by this ceremonial service.

Thus advancing in silence a gentle ascent following the bubbling falls of a lovely winding brook, ornamented with slender trees and fine flowering shrubs, and whose bottom exhibited coloured rocks and waving plants through which abundance of splendid trout were darting at intervals, we made a grand halt at noon, in a grove, near the first building I had seen during our long traject.

It consisted of an extensive barn to appearance, remarkably well thatched and bound with canes in an ornamental manner having a deep veranda on either side, with oblong openings and wide entrances into which we drove our whole troop of loaded asses and instantly deposited our packages on broad shelves that surrounded the interior, after which the cattle were withdrawn, and the doors closed. It was, I found, a national depot for the salt, and the delivery ended the commission, so that afterwards each man was allowed to return to his own home. There was no agent to receive it, or fastening to secure the doors – on asking an explanation of which, I was told, it was now public property, at the disposal of the magistrates, and that robbery or embezzlement was with them a thing unknown – that after executing so important and hazardous a commission, the whole of its member would receive the public thanks as their best reward, and that he alone would make his report of their success before he returned to his family.

The venerable chief now took me by the hand, and seating me by him in one of the verandas on a long bench, broad and well polished, which extended its whole length, called two of his sons towards us, and thus addressed me. "My duty thus happily ended towards my country, I am called on by my religion to perform it towards you as a stranger and fellow Christian, whose confidence in me has placed you in my power and that of the state I belong to. I must therefore acquaint you that I am responsible for your good conduct, during your residence among us, and answerable to my fellow citizens for the step I have taken in introducing you to their notice. I am also bound to consider you as my guest, and shall receive you into my house and provide for all your wants, as far as our customs will permit me – and what I expect on your part is to be guided by our laws, habits, and manners, so long as you chuse to abide here."

To this having received my assent, he added: "It is sufficient. I have observed your conduct during our march, although we have not conversed much, my own serious duties having prevented that as well as the character I appeared to you in, but now you will in future see me in my proper rank and habiliments as as Elder, Pastor, and Deacon of our church, in which capacities I was appointed to this commission as one of the greatest importance, since a failure in it would subject a whole district to inconveniency and probably to sufferings, salt being to us one of the necessaries of life as well as to our cattle. At this season others also are sent in other directions for the like purpose to the pagan and Mahometan nations which surround us – who inhabit and have for many years been fixed on an extensive table land, of which we ourselves do not as yet know the extent eastward – the whole of which we have reason to believe is surrounded by such a rugged range of coasting boundary, separating this upper salubrious region from the forest slopes below, a happy circumstance which determined our settlements, and has afforded us that protection from the dark nations, who find the climate too cold, and the fruits of the earth not so spontaneous as to afford sustenance without labour.

"We call ourselves *Jovinians* from a Roman monk who, during the reign of the Emperor Honorius, being a member of the Church of Rome, early perceived its corruptions, and was considered as heretical by that hierarchy and the Council of Milan, for teaching, that complying to the baptismal vows, and living conformably to the Gospel made us equally acceptable in the eyes of the supreme being and equally entitled as Christian men to the rewards of a future state, with those who passed their days in solitude, celibacy, and mortification or any of the asceticks of Upper Egypt, however severe their self denials. Even Anthony himself did not escape his censure. For these and other salutary truths, he was sentenced to be banished by the Emperor, and collecting his disciples he bowed to the sentence, and migrated to Thrace and from thence to Alexandria and the Upper Nile, whence he entered Abyssinia. But finding persecution followed him even there, he advanced to Nubia where he died, leaving to his Church an injunction to advance into Africa if possible above the sources of the Bar-el-abaid, separating themselves from other sects, and endeavouring to form a community founded on pure Christianity, that when sufficiently numerous might, by the grace of God, go forth and convert the heathen nations of this vast continent. To these selected men, deeply imbued with his opinions, he left his writings, and counselled them to preserve themselves in retirement and seclusion until they had acquired the native languages, supporting their families by agriculture and the necessary arts, in a state as near equality as, consistent with human abilities, it is attainable. And here it was they set up their rest after long, difficult, and dangerous travels, in which it pleased God that few perished, being led as it were by the finger of providence to this new *Sinai*, where we are multiplied exceedingly, always keeping in view the object of our founder, the establishment and preservation of a reasonable church conducted on Catholic principles and concentrated on the maxims and practice of the apostles, whose creed we profess, and whose prayer we adopt together with their precepts according to the letter, having no other

Law but the commands of God through Moses and the Gospel of Jesus Christ, whom we worship and endeavour to please and obey, as a personification of the Deity emanating from him as a first cause, our Creator, our Redeemer, and our Judge."

When he paused here, I still listened with open ears, only wishing to hear as much as possible of their principles and conduct, so congenial to my own secret opinions, but which from what I had seen I never expected to find in profession or practice either in or out of my own country, whose dogmas were engrafted during my education, by our family confessor, on every lesson, of submission to the Papal decrees, and which I had imbibed rather than approved – yet dared not deny or enquire into.

While waiting in expectation he would resume his discourse, a loud shout met our ears, and soon I saw a crowd approaching with rapidity, consisting of men, women and children all habited differently from my conductor, at whose advancing he arose, when the people opening to the right and left, a venerable female surrounded by her family came forward to embrace him, first bending her head and crossing her arms respectfully. It was, as I soon found, his wife and children and grandchildren, who, having heard from others of his safe arrival, lost not a moment in setting out to welcome him home – accompanied by such of his neighbours as could learn the agreeable report. All were received with cordiality and sincere affection, and I never saw a happier set of faces or more decided proofs of heartfelt joy.

The matron was habited in long and dark brown vestments of cotton, girded by a scarlet silken cord under the paps, the ends of which with handsome tassels reached nearly to the ground, and her head covered by a white veil, which, contrasted with her dark hair and large black eyes, and a complexion of a warm brown, gave her an air of dignity and composed sobriety that was very impressing. The younger females were all in white garments, composed of short waistcoats with sleeves to the middle of the upper joint of the arm, short petticoats and long drawers, tastefully embroidered with silk of all colours, or sprigged with cotton flowers as needle work, their hair in varied agreeable forms or hanging down in plaited tresses behind, in curls flowing below their veils which were all white and tastefully ornamented, yet with remarkable simplicity.

The men wore turbans of various shapes and colours, close buttoned ornamented waistcoats of deep scarlet, or crimson, open at the breast, under which appeared a plaited cotton shirt, and the

rest of the body was covered by dark brown or black or blue pan-
taloons buttoned up the sides with light blue buttons as far as the
middle of the leg – the feet, among the young men, being always
bare. Whilst I was considering all attentively these unexpected
guests, *Stefanus* had retired into the store house, and returned
dressed like the rest arm in arm with his wife, only I observed his
turban was of twisted pure white muslin, without any ornaments,
which contrasted with his dark hair and beard and his white
waistcoat and pale blue pantaloons, surmounted by a scarlet girdle
– and his feet in handsome sandals, gave him an air of so much
importance that I could scarcely again recognize my rough herds-
man and conductor. He smiled at my surprize, and placing me on
his right hand we proceeded together, surrounded by the affec-
tionate group, to his habitation not far distant, the whole crowd
observing the utmost decorum and characteristic propriety. On the
way he related to his family the origin of his acquaintance with me,
who were not a little curious to know what country I came from,
that spoke the same language, although I must own very inferior
to theirs in accent and sweetness, less sonorous and less in the gusto
of our ancient poets and historians.

Leaving the grove in which the storehouse was erected, we as-
cended a rising ground by a well trodden shaded path and, emerg-
ing at the summit, came suddenly on a lovely scene of irregular
lawn, wood, rocks and a winding brook intertwined among them,
with a sort of farm house in the bottom, surrounded with trees,
under which appeared many small buildings as connected with it,
the chief covering of which was a neat and close thatch of a tan
colour, bound with regular bands of some dark coloured material
in highly ornamental lines.

On advancing towards what seemed the front of the house which
was surrounded with a deep veranda variously and agreeably col-
oured, and lined with gay yellowish mats, we came on a small
church, built in a style inclined to the gothic and of very just pro-
portions, whose gable end formed a deep porch, opening by great
folding doors to a simple interior lofty and well lit by openings in
the sides, and filled with rows of benches with cushions before each
to kneel on. We approached the gate with a solemn pace and,
halting in front of it, were received with gravity by two or three
priests dressed in white garments, who sang an anthem, to which
our leader responded with great solemnity, and then we all entered
the church, and, kneeling devoutly, joined in a thanksgiving for

the happy return of the expedition and resumed our progress to the house.

Here I was welcomed as one of the family, hospitably entertained, and shewn to an apartment, where a bath was prepared for me, and every comfort and accommodation they had the means of affording. My couch was broad and cool, my chamber airy and clean and, the windows opening to the west, I awoke at sun rise charmed by the songs of birds, and delighted by the scented gales wafted by a soft breeze from groups of aromatic shrubs and flowers to me unknown.

It all seemed like a vision from the time I joined these Italian Christians, whose heresy from the papal faith seemed to have been deeply rooted, by the pains they had taken to preserve it intact. Of their peculiar ceremonies I had yet to enquire, of their priesthood, dogmas and mode of government also – but I was forced to confess to myself that from the sample I had already had of their persuasions, customs, humanity, and manly conduct, there was as yet nothing to object by any reflecting and honest man. I was even reluctant to compare them with the inhabitants of Sophis, whose discoveries in morals seemed too deeply tinctured by the colouring of earthly enjoyment. Whilst ruminating thus, in a delicious train of sober reflection, not unmixed with humble gratitude to my Maker and Preserver, some healthy children of the family came to call me to the morning's meal, and brought me little garlands of wild and sweet scented flowers, with which they bound my arms in play, and pretended to draw me after them in their innocent gambols.

Their covering was only a single garment, of coarse stout linen girded about their loins with coloured cords of plaited wool that passed several times around their little waists, and the ends of which were knotted and tucked in, hanging down gracefully before.

At breakfast in the veranda I found nearly all the household, masters and servants, but in decorous order, seated to partake of a wholesome meal of milk, rice and honey, together with excellent bread of various forms and qualities, and pitchers from the purest, coolest spring which gushed out from a small fountain, and ran in a confined channel along the portico until it fell into a shallow stone basin that overflowed as it filled on a bank of salutary herbs below. I was placed in the seat of honour near the Deacon and some two or three of his grown up sons, a short but appropriate grace was repeated by all aloud and in harmonious expression, and then, though little was said, much was eaten, my host observing that all had earned an appetite, by the early labours of the morning – after which he invited me to attend him round his cultivated grounds which it was his custom daily to inspect, and although, on account of his age, he was allowed to indulge in some repose, he filled up the hours profitably by instructing the young during their laborious occupations. "For," said he, "there must be no idle person among us, there are no drones in our hive, and no situation exempts a man from being useful to society. Agriculture, and the raising animals useful by way of clothing or food, we hold to be the most honourable employment for mankind, next to that of instructing and educating the young, or teaching the important duties and offices of life by example and precept – as relating to prudence, justice, integrity, humility, fortitude, benevolence, probity &c, the practice of which virtues leads directly to the love of God, our neighbours and ourselves – on comparison of which all the wealth and wisdom of this world are as nothing. And these and other practices which are necessary to happiness constitute the most important concern in educating our children, not only commencing in their early infancy to lay the foundation with solidity, but following up the superstructure of rational and religious discipline in every stage of this existence, for we hold an opinion that we are reserved and placed in this sanctuary, with a commission to spread the genuine doctrines of our religion among the benighted men that surround us, and to lay the foundation stone of the conversion of Africa – provided we deserve so important an office, by our rigid attention to our duties, and do not fall away as other churches have done, and perished for their crimes."

I now began to see that providence had guided me to a spot where all my aspirations after virtue might be realized – where the light of revelation as much surpassed that of reason from reflection, as the direct rays of the solar orb those of refracted illumination, even when condensed, for then they are but exaggerated light. It became then my ambition to see more into the constitution of this people, and I failed not to confess my curiosity, and after a general statement of the history of my life, which on the principles of propriety and decorum was due to a man who, during all our travels together, had never made any attempt to pry into it, to solicit some account of their general state of affairs, for I felt, under my present impressions, that my first desire would be to reside with them to add to what I already knew of mankind such principles as their apparent wisdom might be able to impart to a mind only desirous to be guided in all things by that which is becoming and right.

A smile of grateful approbation and an unusual brightness lit up the countenance of my respected companion.

"There is not any thing you could have proposed," he replied, "which can be more agreeable to me, than to comply with your wishes, because it is a duty, and your whole history convinces me you are sincerely engaged in pursuit of truth and right conduct, and if it shall appear that our institutions are founded on an improvement of those you were educated in, there will be hopes you may adopt them on mature deliberation and add one more proselyte to a union which has no other end in view but obedience to the commands of God and submission to the councils of His compassionate and immortal son, whose presence, by the intervention of His holy spirit, we labour and desire to continue among us and direct all our actions and thoughts to humility and devotion.

"We know very well, from the writings of our founder, of how little value the discoveries of human philosophy were in comparison of revelation, and therefore are indifferent to the general pursuits of men in human science; but we have among us those who are allowed to addict themselves to the investigation of such as are useful – although none are exempt from the primary duties of piety and the love of our neighbour on that account – neither are the offices of life to be pursued to the prejudice of our faith and practical ceremonies of religion.

"But enough for the present; there is much to state before you will have a correct idea of us and our views. The hour of refection is arrived, the family are returning under the shades of yonder groves, let us join them, and when the duties of the day are past, in the cool of the evening I will endeavour to gratify your utmost curiosity."

So saying, we returned by the borders of a clear brook, full of musical falls, by a well trodden path, and soon found ourselves in a large, clean, barn-like building, where tables were spread, well covered with wholesome, ripe fruits, delicious bread, butter, cheese, milk both sour and sweet, honey, and fish fried to the utmost perfection. A prayer to consecrate the board having been said, and repeated by all present, each took his accustomed place, and made a short meal in silence, partaking modestly and moderately of what was set before them by the females who attended, after which all stood up and with great decorum united in a hymn of thanksgiving,

before returning to their several separate occupations or amuse-
ments, all of which I soon found constituted something useful to
the general society. After directing that what remained should be
carried to some infirm neighbours, and catechising a number of
children to whom he distributed rewards of fruit according to their
proficiency, the good deacon affectionately dismissed them to their
play and then proposed to me a walk to a plantation of dates and
figs in a secluded valley, where he said we should find a covered
building near a spring, whose perennial waters he was endeavour-
ing to convey to the roots of the trees for the benefit of an aged
neighbour that was too infirm to assist in the work himself – ob-
serving that we could save time by conversing on the way and when
there repose, and, if I was not tired of the subject, continue his
description of their motives and manners, uninterrupted by do-
mestic affairs, which, when at home, were almost incessantly oc-
cupying his attention – "for," he added, "it is thus with us; as we
advance in years, there are, very properly, more trusts imposed on
us of a public nature, in consequence not only of the experience
we have acquired, but on account of the wish every one must en-
tertain, as the end of life advances, to be useful to the last to those
objects of his affection he must so soon leave, conscious as we cannot
help being that when we have done our utmost to obey the laws
of God, we have been unprofitable servants of Him who has done
so much for us, and Whose presence the best of men must approach
at the Judgement with fear and trembling."

Whilst speaking, a loud cry was heard, and three or four females
rushed in, exclaiming that one of his grandchildren had fallen into
a deep well and was drowned – and the next moment the seemingly
lifeless body was brought in by its distracted mother, who laid it at
his feet and began carressing it, and calling on its name with all
the agony of a parent's feeling.

I saw the colour come and go on his cheeks, and the tear starting
in his eye, but he took up the boy, without uttering a syllable, and
ran within a chamber near, followed by the weeping mother who
clung to both with wild energy and uninterrupted sobs. Speedily
the door was closed, to all but those whose assistance was wanted,
and after half an hour's anxious waiting without, I had the joy to
see the affectionate grandfather come forth with a satisfied expres-
sion, to tell me that by proper applications the child was restored,
and that now we might proceed on our walk, and the object of it,
since, by the mercy of God, a great affliction had been removed

from his immediate household and if he were not now more cheer-
ful and more grateful than ever, he should be justly reckonned
among the unfaithful. His sincerity indeed was manifested in his
looks and gestures, for his steps were agile and firm, and the tear,
which lingered in his eye, was evidently that of gratitude and re-
joicing.

As we walked on he began as follows:

"I will not conceal from you, my brother, that had it not pleased
God to restore the child to us, both I and all would have been filled
with the deepest sorrow, not only on account of his amiable man-
ners and sweet temper, but because on that account we had, I fear,
indulged him in his wishes and desires more than for his interests
we ought to have done, but now no doubt all will be turned to good
— for it will impress us with gratitude, him with caution, and give
a flow of substantial cheerfulness to our society at home.

"With us, children are objects of great respect and attention;
when they come, we receive them as angels, and always conduct
ourselves before them, as if they were sent to inspect our conduct
from above — and thus whilst we guard, instruct, and attend to
their welfare as infants, they act with energetic force on our sense
of decorum, delightful companions whilst mutual love actuates us,
but fearful avengers if we neglect our duty to ourselves and them
— the solace of misfortune, and the lamps of consoling light, when
the darkness of declining age surrounds our couch, at that moment,
which must come, that our time of probation is completed, and we
witness, in their swimming eyes, that we depart accompanied by
their sympathetic and affectionate regards."

CHAPTER IX

There was no occasion for me to corroborate these just remarks
by my approval, for my looks of approbation must have expressed
it — and he proceeded.

"You have expressed a desire to be more fully informed of the
institutions of our community, being before made acquainted with
the general principles on which we are devoted to the letter and
spirit of Christianity, as far as we have been able by dilligent enquiry
to discover it — for even were it not of divine origin, it seems
indisputably to be the best code of laws for the government and
happiness of the human race ever promulgated. I shall therefore
for the present initiate you into our political morality as respects

all men, more especially our neighbours the heathen and half Ma-
hometan nations with which we are surrounded. As we have de-
termined never to use war as a means of conquest like them, and
have deprived ourselves of every mode of hostile resistance, which
we hold to be forbidden by the laws of God, it became necessary
to our first founder the virtuous Jovinius to study the arts of peace,
and practice them in order to arrive at this or some other asylum.
He therefore by the benevolent exercise of his skill in such medical
knowledge as was then extant, both for men and cattle, together
with a thorough acquaintance with the cultivation of the earth, and
some necessary and useful arts practiced by his enlightened fol-
lowers, contrived, with much patience and the practice of benev-
olence and justice, to make us a way through several barbarous
nations to this then despised and uninhabited table land, which
nevertheless by our industry and God's blessing has become a
Goshen to our persecuted race, where we trust the seeds of a holy
and innocent life may be cultivated and bear fruit, in due time, fit
to sustain the continent of Africa in just works, and a saving knowl-
edge of that word, whose immortal precepts He has assured us
shall extend to the uttermost parts of the earth – and on this
principle it is we entertain, with proper caution, a due intercourse
with such clans as you found us among, taking care, in all our
dealings with them, to become as it were benefactors, by making
exchanges which they know to be infinitely favourable to them,
thereby securing their friendship and regard. And this we are
enabled to do very easily, as our own wants are considerably less
than our industry might supply if we appropriated our productions
to ourselves, yet that it is which by employment preserves us from
idleness, the bane of society, and insures us a vent, for over pro-
duction that acts as a safeguard to our community, far more certain
than could be attained by arms, and which already spreads around
our settlements an increasing glory, which like the first rays of a
rising sun we trust will enable us to illuminate the horizon around
with that far exceeding light that is destined to brighten all human
Institutions, when pure Christianity shall prevail among the heathen
world, and the spririt of evil works be effectually subdued."

As he terminated these remarks, the amiable old men halted in
the path and turning his face towards me, with an ineffable smile
apologized for the length of his discourse, which he said might to
me who had come so far from a more polished society appear rather
vain and prejudiced, but he could assure me that with all their

peculiar customs I should find none without an honest motive, and that I should hear no untruths, or have to encounter any sophistry among them, that the least informed were taught civility, to all, and respect for the customs of other people. "And," he added, taking my hand kindly in his, "of the same nation, and I trust of the same general faith, I hope I may venture to call you Brother."

I had seen much of polished life, and something of courts, had associated with the well-bred Lycas, and heard of the suavity of the Sophians, perfect in the arts which embellish cities, but the air, the look, and the manner in which Stefanus, for that was his name, uttered his apostrophe to me, had something in it which spoke more to the heart than any thing of compliment I had ever before received – and I was actually embarrassed and at a loss to make a suitable reply. I however cordially embraced him, and assured him that I began fully to appreciate the soundness of their doctrines, as well as the purity of their motives and disinterestedness, and that if he was not exhausted already, it would much gratify me to hear him proceed.

By this time we were not far from the spot we set out to inspect, and soon came to the habitation of his friend, who received us cordially at the door of a long hut containing three chambers, substantially built of a fine pale sandstone, and covered by a projecting thatch of reeds bound tastefully with chequer work of bamboo, and at his request we took our seats in three cane chairs, resembling in lightness and construction those of China, which invite to repose by their depth and the cool matted cushions with which they are furnished, and here with the deacon placed on one side and myself on the other we were served by the wife with coffee and other refreshments, in a chequered shade, produced by branching climbers, the flowers of which emitted sweet odours, whilst water in clean vessels was brought for our feet, and the operation of bathing them performed by two females, the sisters of our host, who, advanced in life and widowed, resided under his roof in retirement, to administer to his comforts and make up an affectionate society.

To have discovered a native of Italy out of their communion seemed highly to gratify the old man since all they knew of us or the Papal government was only a matter of history. They knew not even if such a church was still in existence, not having even communicated with that of Abyssinia, so that my account of the then state of church government under the Popes was matter of great curiosity, and they seemed still more surprized to learn that so far from being now under anathema as hereticks they were entirely forgotten and their first schism only recorded in history as a matter of no moment. But I could see it grieved them that what they considered as a dangerous error had not been removed, and although they spoke to me of it in measured terms, yet they wondered at the patience of heaven in permitting such corruptions of Christianity to still exist. Yet all this was expressed with so much charity and good feeling that I could not help comparing their moderation and brotherly love with that fierce violence which had dictated their persecution and banishment.

When the business which brought us there was ended, and the young men engaged in the farm had received full instructions from Stefanus, the devotions of the evening were repeated, in which I now joined sincerely from a conviction of their propriety and congruity of expression in a dialect of our language as simple and pure as in our earliest writers – when we took leave of our obliging host, and returned lighted by one of the clearest moons at full to that peaceful dwelling in which I already seemed to feel at home.

"You have now seen," said Stefanus as we strolled onwards breathing the cool and refreshing breezes of evening in a climate rendered salubrious by its elevation, "how we live during one day, and I must inform you that with very little variation it is the same all the year. Temperance, sobriety of manners, labour, and affectionate duties, with the love of God, and His service, fill up nearly the whole round of our existence. We taste of no liquids but milk and water, and are true Rechabites in our abhorrence of wine, for although we cultivate the grape, our laws are unbending, in prohibiting its fermentation, neither are spirits allowed to be distilled even for medical purposes; spices alone are found adequate, and simple waters when stimulants are necessary. We have indeed no regular physicians, but remedies for sudden attacks and accidents are known to every family. Herbs serve for diaretics and catharticks, water in baths and sudatories is a great agent either by steam, or showers, or hot or cold, or drank in infusions of vegetables, and for wounds we find they never fail to heal when kept clean, and excluded from the air – for our temperance, a little exceeded, at all times reduces fever, and for broken bones we have very skilful hands at setting and splinting the limbs, beyond which it has been long discovered that no other manipulation is necessary, for time and the vessels adapted to that purpose do the rest, united with necessary abstinence, cooling applications and a patient submission to necessity.

"Neither have we any doubt of the efficacy of prayer as well as fasting in all cases of confinements when the want of necessary exercise is apt to accumulate humours in the body, even of a people as strictly temperate as we endeavour to render ourselves, for I trust there is not a man among us who is not as certain of the divine inspection as he is of his existence."

"But in cases of criminality," said I, "for where there are men there will be crimes, under every dispensation, what are the nature of your punishments?"

"That indeed is an afflicting truth," he replied, "and a subject we had better postpone until the morrow, for the very mention of such a grief, if canvassed now, may interrupt our repose, and destroy all the harmonious impressions which this glorious moonlight, and the glittering stars have made on our minds. No: let us cherish them as invaluable balms, shed upon our souls by ministering angels under whose guardianship we have returned from the performance of offices suitable to our nature when guided by reason and a proper sense of duty to our Maker and ourselves.

"By this time we had been welcomed with joyful faces, went through the customary ceremonies of the evening, and each retired to a cool refreshing repose, in a chamber which neither had or required any other security than that confidence which a quiet conscience diffuses over the couch of the innocent and pious mind.

And such I believe was the condition of this orderly household, but for my own part I must confess that what I had seen and heard since my arrival had conjured up a thousand inquisitive thoughts, as to what would be the result of this connection. Already it had dispersed several of my prejudices, and forced me to own that I had long wandered in error, in taking the professions of my own church for realities. For here in a very short space of time I had beheld more practical religion than all my residence in Venice had ever afforded me under our parental direction, and from the sample I might judge of the commodity. To what elevated benevolence might I not expect to see this fine discipline exalted? The serenity of the night, the silence and peace which surrounded my pillow, the sorrow for my past impatience and imprudences, in a word the deep conviction, that hitherto I had been a mere professional Christian, incapable of conceiving the efficacy of its practice, or the importance of its salutary duties and restraints, which here for the first time in my life I saw in action – these and a crowd of humiliating thoughts for a long time broke in upon my slumbers, and when I closed my eyes I whispered to myself, "hitherto I have lived under a great delusion in thinking philosophy and human wisdom were sufficient for man. I must see more of this people, for nothing but divine revelation could have made them what they appear to be, humble, happy, and completely resigned to the will of the supreme creator."

On these reflections my soul retired within me, and I slept soundly until awakened by the sun's returning light, when, on issuing forth to enjoy the fresh breeze of the morning, I found a young man busily employed in giving provender to two noble domestic asses who followed him like dogs carressingly – and from him I learned that having been brought up from foals with great kindness, and never having been struck or injured, they performed their necessary services mechanically and wanted only words to guide them, and that such was the system adopted in this community and many others towards all animals, having been found by experience to be effectual and attended by great advantages, both as to the benefits to be derived from their strength, and the avoiding of cruelty and excitement of the bad passions, whilst it encouraged those of gentleness and affection.

"We are taught," said he, "when children to treat every animated thing with generosity, and to use no coertion but in cases of extream necessity, when it may be as much for the benefit of the animal as ourselves, as in the case of accidents or injuries that must be repaired, and we find that although denied the powers of speech like us, they understand kind services, and even better than some of us respect and follow the hand that feeds them."

Again I was delighted with these just remarks from such a youth, and could not but admire their system of education that I perceived must have been adopted here, which increased my anxiety for further conference with Stefanus who, from the lad's account, was the fatherly friend of not only the district but of the whole nation.

Speaking to him on my return on the subject, he said as they were divided into districts, every district held some peculiar tenets but he believed it was generally allowed that to procure most peace and happiness to the greatest numbers of men and other animals was considered as the great end of civil government – that they constituted a federal union in which there was very little difference of opinion, and the fundamental basis of which was, equal justice, equal support, equal education – and a strict adherence to the law and the Gospel as found in the sacred scriptures to which all had access, and by which, both in this world and in the next, all were content to be governed, acknowledging no sovereign power, but in Him who died on the cross for their salvation. "For this," said he, "we are crucified to the world and the world to us – and of course no object of ambition is present here, where no emoluments are to be acquired by public services, but rather pains and labour, which was the lot of the founders of our faith, and no reward is to be expected for the longest services but the satisfaction of duty performed, and the testimony of a good conscience."

"And is this," said I, "a report generally applicable to your whole sect?"

"Decidedly," said he, "for, as a representative of my own community and district, I meet annually, to hear the reports of our numbers, experience, and affairs, I cannot be ignorant of the prosperous state and content which attends the disinterested principle of our constitution that has no earthly gain in view, or worldly honours, which disclaims all violence or war, and seeks only to extend its influence by hospitality, universal charity, and the good of our fellow creatures."

"Then," said I, throwing myself into his arms, "I am from this hour subject to your just government, and desirous only to be received among you on probation. Make me therefore, I beseech you, acquainted with all your laws, which I already perceive must be founded on equity, in order to my preparing myself to obey them. I have found, what neither my own countrymen nor the Sophians could teach, the value of humility and devotion."

The good and venerable man received this warm effusion with a complacent smile, and assured me he was flattered by the preference I expressed, but counselled me to well weigh my opinions and theirs before I decided to embrace a system of self-denial, which if not so strict as that of the Cenobites, had some repulsive discipline difficult to be reconciled to the habits of one not born or educated among them, and which, when the first impression of approbation was worn off by time and repetition, it might be found difficult to adhere to.

"Live therefore a little longer among us, and get a complete knowledge of our laws and manners, and the services we are preparing to undertake in order to spread our opinions through this continent, as well as the difficulties we may expect to meet with and dangers in the execution of the slow task of conversion of heathens, and then, if you remain firm in your opinion, we shall cordially receive you into our union. For already we have laid the foundation stone to our labours by cultivating an intercourse founded on a liberal diffusion of our superfluous products, if anything can be called superfluous which is applied to so useful an object as connected with the happiness of our species, and we hope by this operation to convince these ignorant people of the value of labour and to induce them to cultivate the earth, and perceive that human food may be obtained with much less risk and anxiety, than gold-dust or slaves, and if by the blessing and grace of God we at length arrive at this important result, we afterwards expect to have little difficulty in inculcating the principles of a Religion which alone could induce us to thus devote ourselves to their service, and which promises an ample reward to the just, honest, good and virtuous man – in return for his obedience to laws framed by infinite wisdom entirely for his advantage and well being, so as to insure his happiness in this life, and an eternity of bliss hereafter. For I am sure you and I can have no sort of doubt, that could we so perfectly subdue our natural tendency to evil actions, as to be incapable of disobedience any more, we should feel that even before we had paid the penalty of dying we had entered into a new state of being, and although deeply impressed with sorrow for what had passed that constituted sin, yet a bright lamp of glory would be illuminating our minds, and cheering up our jaded existence until that ever blessed hour, when the Son of Righteousness came and overwhelmed us with His own effulgence and merciful redemption.

"You must therefore," he added, after a pause, in which he bowed his head, as in prayer, "expect, if you unite with us, to be put to the test of your sincere belief in the end and reward of Christianity, by assisting our missions to barter, by way of forming a halo of connections around us – and some of them will not be so pleasant or easy, even when managed with the utmost precaution as that in which you encountered me. Yet even there you must have observed I did not think it prudent to stay, or to communicate with any one but the chief or King as they call him of this tribe, whose good will, when obtained by faithful transactions and liberal services, we expect in time to see communicated to his leading men, and through them to the people, for until this influence is secured, and it becomes the general desire to make agriculture the national concern, we cannot in prudence commence even that first important step towards civilization, and conversion – and of course it would be worse than useless to send missionaries among them."

It now became time to enter into the concerns of the morning, and I stayed and witnessed many clear instructions given to husbandmen, many appeals cordially answered, and many difficulties judiciously adjusted – all which served to confirm my already adopted opinion that these were *a wise people* – and at the breaking up of the audience when every one joined in the common prayer for the occasion, I stretched forth my hand to *Stefanus* and pronounced in the presence of all his united family – *"I am ready."'* The steady, firm and decided manner in which I pronounced these words seemed to be highly satisfactory, and I saw in the cheerful countenances of all this company that my pledge was received and appreciated with joy.

I now became only desirous to be put on my probation and to be formally initiated into my station as a member of the community, for their plans already seemed to me to be matured in profound reflection and sober calculation originating in a clear conception of man's duties. Neither was I long refused the object of my ambition. A general assembly was near at hand of the elders and representatives of all the several districts in a central spot, and, accompanied by my protector, I was formally presented and admitted to the honours of their fraternity, the particulars of which initiation it may be interesting to relate in its proper place, since it embraced questions of high import relative to the welfare of the species.

But first I wish to relate some circumstances which occurred during my residence with my friend, that will throw a light on the happiness which arises from moderation and a discreet use of the benefits which God and nature have provided for our sustenance and enjoyment. It had given me some surprize that from the time I encountered these people, I had neither heard of any disease, or remarked any bodily deformity among them. On the contrary, they were, generally speaking, strong, well proportioned, and of a healthy appearance, and what they were able to perform that required activity and muscular powers, the journey up these great heights had evinced. On making these remarks to Stefanus one day, as we were employed together in some useful occupation in the garden, he said he knew no particular reason why they should not be so, as their temperance alone would account for it. First, like the sons of Johonadab the Rechabite, they drank no wine; next their food was chiefly grain and fruits; and lastly, though never absolutely idle, they never worked to excess. Excess indeed in all things was positively prohibited, and as they considered labour as one of the chief pleasures of life, that of course was under the like restriction.

"Even when I seem at leisure, I am then most busy, for the mind supplies the place of useful action, and I am oftener fatigued with thinking than with manual labour. It even supplies the place of it, for it promotes digestion often, like sleep, by taking off our attention from the working of the internal machinery of our frame. But we are not without maladies incident to human nature, and oftentimes our extra duties induce them, such as securing our crops from the elements, attending to the parturition of our flocks, or watching the bed of our dying relations, whom age has reduced to decrepitude; for in general we wear to the last a good stamina, never pampered with luxuries, or enfeebled by over labour, as when we remark the progress of decay in the frame of our neighbours, we take care to administer to his support such restoratives as it becomes the office of the elders in rank to supply out of the general stock. For we have not forgotten the customs of the primitive Christians, in having all things in common, as far as is necessary for the general welfare.

"We have, as you must have observed, no hospitals, for we think it a shame to refuse any sick person a shelter in our own houses, and if we have few regular physicians, we have an abundance of domestic remedies, selected from herbs and roots, and those who have particularly addicted themselves to discover preparations of this sort are to be found in most departments, men who make it a duty, are always ready to attend when called on, without any idea of a reward beyond that which their cures afford them, and we respect them as some of the best members of society.

"Every house almost has some very aged people in it, who occupy the best and most convenient apartments, are attended with care and affection by our young females and children, and in return they acquire the lessons of experience and duty, together with the approbation of their superiors and parents, who esteem them in proportion to their exertions – for age is honoured among us, and always respected, and taken care of whilst life remains."

All this I found just and honourable, and that day was made witness to it in the lesson of an old inmate and assistant, who, in a state of entire debility, was the best dressed and best attended of any one in the family and scarce ever left alone. She was dozing on a soft couch, surrounded by vases full of fresh flowers, and fanned by children as lovely and as beneficent as angels, who were sent in rotation to amuse and divert her, chaunting, with their innocent looks and infantine voices, anthems in three parts to please her, in return for their lesson.

The females being almost always engaged in household affairs or works of mercy and charity, I saw less of them than the men, but when I did mix with them, they were always clean in their dress, orderly in their occupations, and modest in their demeanor, neither refusing or pressing conversation, and serious and sincere in their replies – without any affected shyness, or embarrassment when spoken to – and thus the plainest features became prepossessing and beauty doubly interesting.

"All our females," he said to me one day (on my remarking so many youthful mothers), "are married as soon as they become marriageable, and to secure this natural connection, we betroth them long before they become so, and thus suppress many evils, which might arise from unsettled opinions on that subject. They take to their husbands as a matter of course, and consider their parents as bound to provide one, to whom they willingly transfer their obedience; and by this method we avoid a great deal of embarrassment on that head, having been brought up together in expectation of this union almost from their infancy – so that celibacy is a rare thing indeed in this country, and is only embraced under peculiar circumstances – such as marital imbecility or personal defects."

And thus by degrees I gained, day by day, more and more acquaintance with their internal policy, all of which seemed to me to be founded on experience and reflection and all calculated to promote the happiness of man, for they seemed based on human interests and founded on openness of heart and the absence of guile.

The plainness of their manners, dress, and style of living, as well as the absence of the fine arts as well as poetry, at first gave me many a shock. I, who delighted in them all, could not well conceive that any society could be agreeable without them, but my friend, when I proposed to inculcate them among a select class, gave me solid reasons why it would be pernicious and destructive to their present plans to adopt my advice. "For", said he, "we are a separated people, whose objects are defined, and we have no precept in the writings of our founder to direct such pursuits, beyond music, of which we know enough to raise a few anthems only – and want no more. And for poetry, we feel it in the writings of the inspired psalmist and prophets and cannot expect ever to rival them by our feeble efforts. And what should we do with statues and pictures, among a people whom we hope one day to reclaim from idolatry? Or what among ourselves, who preach and practice humility? Would it become us to raise monuments of vanity according to the manner you describe, who have been told by our Lord, that he that humbles himself on earth shall be exalted in the kingdom of heaven, &c?

"According to your account, I admit, such productions must be very surprizing and cost much study to perform, nay even very amusing to the sight, as well as curious. But our object is to make men think and act usefully, and I can see no sort of use in these deceptions, for can any thing of human invention rival the forms of nature always before us, or the effect of a real moonshine on a group of noble trees or waterfall dashing down a precipice, or can art imitate successfully the brilliancy of flowers which we have continually before our eyes, or the insect tribe, or the full moon in all its glory?"

"Hold," I said, "I have done," seeing he began to warm with the subject, for he was a poet of nature without knowing it. "I see my plans are not for this meridian, and I feel the force of your observations. We will lose no more time on this subject."

Yet I own I felt some disappointment at his refusal, for I could not then discover all the force of his remarks, neither was I willing to resign my long cherished approbation of these studies when carried to ideality, more suitable, I must own, to a corrupt than a simple state of mankind, and the practice of which originated in the grossest idolatry, alternately sustaining its practice by the magic of ideal forms, or figures composed from an aggregate of fine proportions, and a symmetry so much beyond the general conception of the human frame, that even the well informed almost thought they were gods.

"At any rate," he would say, after I had explained these niceties to him, "it is not our business to seek for any such refinements. We profess and teach only the most essential and plainest of man's duties here, and cultivate only such arts as are necessary to his existence. To procure wholesome food, to construct convenient abodes, to manufacture necessary clothing is sufficient for us, and our leader brought with him no books that teach other sciences.

Plane geometry is taught, because it teaches us to form such in-
struments of agriculture as we require, among which the plough
you described to me one day has not yet been adopted. A little
astronomy suffices us to count time, and for geography we scarcely
know more than will help us to discern whereabout we are on the
great continent we inhabit. Our sole business is obedience to God
on earth, and we find it difficult enough to preserve the spirit of
submission to his decrees, and that profound sense of humility
which alone can enable us to receive the kingdom of heaven as a
little child, without occupying the valuable time he has allotted for
probation, with unprofitable speculations. What you call natural
history we certainly do in some measure entertain, for we examine
carefully every object which nature presents to our eyes, and have
from thence not only learned to adore His goodness and mercy,
but have derived from that contemplation a number of useful les-
sons in mechanics, as displaying also a provision against all exi-
gences."

Thus from every conversation, I gained new lights on their sim-
ple and innocent systems – and their ignorance of men and kings
might very properly be called, ignorance of evil – and I soon began
to ask myself, what more was wanted to contribute to a happy
association. For here I heard no disputes or clamours, was witness
to no insults or crimes, but all went on smoothly, for every one was
busily employed the quieter part of the day in gentle labours, and
if any difference arose as to the manner of executing them, a
reference to an elder settled it at once. Doors without locks, chests
without fastenings, and gardens without fences were things which
at first startled me, but I soon found that suspicion was no inhab-
itant of this district, and the good of all was a law engraved on
nearly every breast. Never did I behold a more cheerful population,
or more smiling countenances, and I may literally say there was
"no complaining in their streets".

"But this," thought I, "is under the advice of a wise elder, a good
and religious as well as indefatigable citizen, who lives and thinks
only for the benefit of the community. Perhaps it may not be so in
other places."

CHAPTER X

While making these reflections, I observed a great stir among the
people, and many running to and fro hastily – when I soon learned

that it was a deputation from the general conference of the elders on some public concern, to my friend Stefanus, and this bustle was occasioned by a desire to receive them with respect and honour, and this they accomplished rather by affectionate expressions than by ceremony, and surrounded by an eager crowd they were speedily ushered into the vestibule.

It consisted of two middle-aged men, dressed in the most perfect simplicity of costume in long garments, walking with plain staffs, and it appeared they had arrived on foot, having no scrip or purse, and, but that their habits were lighter, they much resembled some of the disciples of St Francis. Water was now brought to wash their feet, I was introduced to them as a stranger inmate, and a moderate repast was set before them − after which they announced their commission, which was to request Stefanus to attend them the next day to a general conference at the chief town, and to bring me along with him, in order to explain his motives for having introduced me to the community. I was much struck with the urbanity and gentle manners of these men, with whom I soon found an interest, and they seemed equally satisfied with my intentions. It was also conceded that we should return together next day, on foot, at early sun-rise.

There needed no preparation on either side, for like the apostles of old we were sure of a cordial reception, as I found, every where on the road, and our simple wants supplied with affection, so much was respected the character they travelled in. At the dawn of day, we were up and soon dressed and on our road, for it was a custom among them to take leave of their friends the preceeding night of a journey, with cheerfulness and affection, and to proceed to the first stage on a light stomach, uninterrupted by either greetings or good wishes, which they considered as want of good manners, and from the previous evening the traveller was considered as departed, when blessings and good wishes from all the company assembled at the supper sent them cheerfully to repose.

For my own part, I was absorbed in thinking only on the object of my introduction among them, and no small curiosity as to the nature also of this elevated country, its inhabitants, opinions, and customs. Although exceedingly high, and but moderately wooded, and separated by a region of crags of a volcanic character and forests from the vast plains through which the Bar rushes, yet it had its hilly inequalities which in most countries would be considered as mountainous, as was evident from the station I occupied, for it was surrounded by them, and which plain among them was distinguished by the name of *Dongala*, a name given it by the nations inhabiting its feet, by old geographers entitled the Mountains of the Moon, probably from tradition of the worship of Isis having been established there in early times. These and other thoughts kept me awake the greater part of the night, and when I joined my company in the morning, I believe I was the earliest of the group.

We entered a broad and well trodden path, all four in front, the two strangers in the middle, and all we carried was our stout pointed staffs and broad hats made of cane to keep off the direct rays of the sun.

The first part of our way might be said to be through a continued garden, in which, early as it was, we found many young persons employed, who gave us and received our blessing, offering fruits as we passed but never arresting us with enquiries, or being any way intrusive, greeting us also with extemporaneous songs full of good will and kindness. And this continued until we commenced a gradual ascent from a small and clear fountain where was a sheltered alcove surrounded with broad and commodious seats, as a resting place for travellers.

During our repose here for a short time I took occasion to ask many questions as to the country we were entering, its products &c, and was told that it was, although so high, mild and fertile in general, of an extent that they had not as yet perfectly ascertained, but abounding in noble fresh-water lakes, healthy open woods, and gentle rivers of the purest element, infested with few noxious reptiles or dangerous animals, or indeed any but the goat and sheep who came there in summer to pasture in abundance, with deer of a small species, and many of the hare and rabbit tribes, but that hawks, owls, eagles, and vultures of an enormous size also came with them and reduced their numbers greatly – retiring to the lower ridges, which bound this tableland in the severer season of winter, or perhaps to the immense forests below.

Whilst thus conversing, we ascended by a rivulet, bounded by a winding path overshadowed by acacias and other elegant evergreens, among which were many groups of noble hollys, such as in point of size I never before witnessed, and mountain ash loaded with their ruddy berries to profusion, for it was the autumnal season in a climate nearly resembling that of some parts of Europe; and

these elegant masses were interspersed with fragments long fallen
from the rocks above and covered by lichens of all colours, so that
the whole scenery might be pronounced truly picturesque, shady,
cool, refreshing, and in opening spots richly adorned with flowers
of every hue, most of which were to me unknown, as were indeed
the song birds which inhabited this delicious retreat, and which
from the close thickets of flowering shrubs, although at noon, made
the vale ring with their carrolling. As we ascended also little falls
appeared glittering between the leaves, and higher up formed rush-
ing cascades from accidental interruptions, and so interesting was
the scenery that we all as by tacit agreement remained silent and
ceased from our social converse, until we arrived at a spot so pre-
eminently lovely that it arrested us at once in silent admiration! A
little hillock covered with sweet scented flowers declining gradually
to the brook, and crowned by an ancient cedar, whose venerable
branches played like a fan on its summit, presented itself above the
path which approached and wound round the margin of a deep
pool of transparent water, whose sides composed of yellow sands
circumscribed its circumference. A little within the shade of the
cedar lay an oblong fragment of a rock forming a sort of bench,
as if placed there for the accommodation of travellers, and beyond
the pool the sloping sides of the valley, now much contracted, were
overhung with waving boughs of various coloured trees loaded with
their ripe fruits, or the bunches of wild grapes attached to their
arms as climbers. And as if to increace the attraction of this sylvan
bower, fish were seen darting from the surface of the sandy bottom,
and leaping to catch the gaudy flies which fluttered on its surface.

In a word, it was a scene calculated to arrest the steps of the most
indifferent passenger, and we with one consent threw ourselves on
the flowery bank to contemplate so enchanting a combination. For
some time we remained as if entranced, enjoying the sweetest re-
pose, when Stefanus first broke the silence, by ejaculating, "*Surely
God is here*" – and we all felt the divine force of his apostrophe.

"Yes," said I, "this is indeed nature in all her loveliness, a stimulus
to devotion, and a fit residence for innocence and wisdom."

"You have justly described it," replied one of our company, "for
it is in reality so appropriated, since not far from hence resides, in
a small cell of his own construction, a worthy aged member of our
community, who, having fulfilled all the duties his strength would
allow and filled many honourable stations among us, having lost

all his family, came here to end his days still usefully by devotion
to his own soul and to others passing this way in procuring them
refreshment on their passage.

"From his hands we received relief on our way hither, and prob-
ably his hospitality will e'er long renew the obligation, for his se-
clusion is only concealed by the woods in front of us, and knowing
its attractions to be irresistible, the sound of persons' voices halting
here generally reaches his ears if at home, or he hears or sees us
from the hill if out walking, and probably, by some winding paths,
to him best known, he will appear among us suddenly, and well
supplied with wholesome though humble refreshments."

Indeed he had scarcely completed these remarks, when a dog
or two came leaping into our circle, and soon after we heard a
rustling above our heads among the branching shades, and just
under the cedar came forth, like a vision, the venerable sage,
clothed in white with a large cowl and grisly long beard, one hand
grasping a rude staff, and the other holding a capacious basket.
He stopped short in the shade a moment to hail us with brotherly
expressions, and then invited us up to the shadowy seat on the
rock, as more suitable to the hour, to partake of the contents of
his wallet, whilst he crossed over to his cell and added to them such
additions as he had prepared for us, expecting our arrival about
this period of the day. Then, spreading a clean napkin on the stone,
he laid first before us his collection of the morning, which consisted
of honey in the comb and some mushrooms and truffles which by
the aid of his dogs he had found, and accompanied by me, as the
youngest of the troop, he conducted me to his cell to assist him in
bringing vessels for water and bread as well as some fruits, nuts,
cheese, and hard-boiled eggs. And here I found also mattresses
extended round the walls of goatskins laid on dry fern as a relief
for the weary, and the cot surrounded by a small garden containing
a neat arrangement of useful pot herbs, the whole refreshed by a
rill of the purest wave, which issued from a rock above his abode,
in one clear fountain, and fell, bubbling, into a natural basin,
sweetly, as with a garland, encircled by wild flowers and lichens of
glowing colours, which were reflected in its limpid vase as trans-
parent as crystal, and far too lovely for art to imitate them, or
description to portray. We were soon loaded, and seeing me rapt
in contemplating this scene of peace and beauty, he urged me to
follow him speedily, remarking that my companions were wanting
rather food than reflection, and he added: "When you are as old

as I am, it will be time enough to seek your road to heaven in such
solitudes, where necessity (*as it were*) has placed me, and where,
although feeble, I am not denied the pleasure of administering to
the conveniences of others, and sometimes of giving lessons of
experience to the young along with these agreeable services."

So saying, he led the way, and we returned across the brook,
wading to our knees through a safe ford and the parting boughs
which played like fans above it and soon stood before our company,
administering the fresh fluid in white earthen cups which he said
were all of his own turning from clays of the purest vein, and baked
in little furnaces with charcoal by himself prepared at hours of
leisure and retirement.

But I soon saw he was a man of profound understanding and
skilled to produce another species of admiration, for when the
repast was over, my companions with the utmost respect commu-
nicated to him the object of their mission, and took his opinion of
what ought to be done in a case of some difficulty. If he lived like
a Cenobite in the wilderness, it was not like them to macerate his
flesh, but rather like the prophets of Judea he retired to meditate
on schemes likely to produce the welfare of mankind, and to pre-
serve intact the purity of the Christian practice, which it was the
object of the nation to eternize.

When the repast was over, he rose up and conducted us by a
winding path to his residence, where, having placed us on thick
goatskin seats, he smiled and said, "I trust you will, considering
how rarely it falls to my lot to entertain such an agreeable party,
not refuse the earnest request of an old man to rest here until
tomorrow, and gratify the, I hope, laudable curiosity of an ancient
brother labourer in the good cause by first allowing me to under-
stand the motives and circumstances which have induced an Eu-
ropean to approach our resting place, and what were his intentions
in joining your company. A day's rest I know you have time for
before attending the conference, and I wish also to be informed
in what manner he can advance our objects, taking it for granted
that if he were not devoted to our holy religion you would not have
accepted him, or that if he were not an admirer of your general
conduct he would not have sought you out in such a perfect seclu-
sion."

When he paused, we looked at each other enquiringly, and I saw
at a glance that his polite request was not likely to be refused, and
thus it was settled by general consent, almost without a word being

spoken. It was now my turn to speak, and as they sat and listened attentively to my narrative, I divulged, without reserve, my whole history and patriotic views; together with my inflexible adherence to a religion whose principles are founded on justice and alone can insure peace and repose among the nations of the earth.

I had been listened to with profound attention by all whilst in my native tongue, which they well understood, although they used one of a simpler construction, and after a pause of some time, directed by the looks of his countrymen, the hermit of the valley took up the discourse, and with great deliberation in a sweet and silver tone that fell on the ear melodiously said:

"Respected stranger, the candour with which you have represented your errors, your misfortunes, and your designs, leaves no doubt on my mind of your sincerity, probity, and good will to your fellow creatures. Neither have I any doubt, notwithstanding your education in the lamentable errors of the Roman church, that you possess a mind ready to submit to truth whenever and wherever you shall discover it. Know then that it was owing to these ever to be regretted conceptions we are assembled here.

"After *Jovinian*, an Italian Monk of the 4th Century, we are called *Jovinians*, once a small sect oppressed, for a period, but now under God's grace his servants, and an independant church. Actuated by just principles, and feeling that the *service* of *God was perfect freedom*, he ventured boldly to adopt its liberal principles and write several treatises to prove that under the Popes its discipline was decayed and Christian men living as if they despised its ordinances – and humbly recommending the adoption of more purity in their lives, by abandoning, among other acts of immorality, the celibacy of the clergy, the worship of images, undue fasting, and other works of supererrogation. And for these other opinions having, without a trial, been expelled from Rome, he fled to Milan, hoping to find from the then Emperor Theodosius at least protection for freedom of opinion. But through the intrigues of bad men, his enemies, he found there a strong prejudice raised against him personally, and on being denied a hearing he was from there also expelled.

"Conscious however of his own innocence, and the importance of making a stand against the vices then prevalent in the capital, he returned to the vicinity of the papal dominions, where he united with his disciples and friends, men of pious habits and unbending devotion to the precepts of the Gospel of Jesus Christ, to whose service in obedience they had devoted their lives, and continued to advance his holy doctrines relative to practical religion until the year 398 – when he and his inflexible companions were, through fresh intrigues, and the accusations of Jerome, a father of the Roman Catholic persuasion, sentenced to be banished to some of the small islands of the states of Ragusa on the Adriatic, on the coast of Dalmatia, where it was reported he died on the Island of *Boas* by those who hated and persecuted him. But he escaped again with some of his chief followers, and they were secretly united once more at Alexandria, from whence they migrated into Abyssinia and Lybia in Africa, about 410 of the era. But here among the African churches he found worse evils to combat as to doctrine and morals, and seeing no prospect of being ever able to dissipate these heresies and abominations and even endangering the lives of his companions and their families by a longer residence among so depraved a set of men, he took his measures with much deliberation and, under the protection of God and guided by his own knowledge of mankind, ventured into the then unknown regions to the west, in search of an asylum from human persecution, in some mountainous and uninhabited country, carrying with them such presents as were likely to gratify the roving Arabs or petty states of Nubia, who then infested the borders of the Bar-el-abaid, in its descent from the Mountains of the Moon, now called those of Dongala, expecting from report that they must necessarily lead him to some lofty head above the sources of that mighty river where he might find a rugged country suitable to concealment and where they might, after their sufferings, remain and multiply until they became sufficiently numerous to form a nation of real Christians, united by one system of education in the principles and practice of Christianity whose poverty and numbers and unobtrusiveness would become a security from the aggression of their Negro neighbours and enable them at last to found a Propaganda-College capable in time of furnishing armies, not of soldiers, but of martyrs ready to go forth and, prepared by long attention, to acts of friendship to secure the regard and willing conversion of the Mahometans and pagans peopling this immensely extensive continent.

"Of the difficulties they had to encounter after his decease I shall not now enter into a description, for you, having trod the same ground, may easily conceive them, and had they not like Moses been guided by the hand of God they would probably never have over-come them. And this we consider as a testimony of our faith, and a proof that it was his reward, a species of miracle, that still holds our members together and especially increases them, for we now amount to eighty-thousand souls divided into ten communities or towns, all governed by the same laws framed alone on divine revelation, from the sacred writings of Moses, the Prophets and those of the *early disciples* of our redeemer. Of those laws, their motives and execution, the principles of our free constitution, and our general modes of life, you will not require a description from me, but will learn their tenor from your present associates on the road and more fully at the capital, if you chuse to conform to them and are elected at the conference by the deputies assembled for general purposes, as worthy to unite with the state as a member of our republican establishment."

Having ended, without waiting any reply he arose, went out, and speedily returned with both sour and fresh milk in calabashes, some honey in the comb, and white bread. A jug of pure water followed with nuts, and we were invited to partake of this primitive desert, with a cordiality that could not be mistaken, during which time, the sun declining, we had various conversations relative to our journey in advance, his tranquil mode of existence, and his contrivances to make his situation more and more convenient, some anecdotes of his faithful dogs and the progress he had made towards his next year's almanack — when, towards sun-set, to my surprize a bell tolled audibly as from the cave behind the cell whence the spring gushed.

At the sound of which, a prayer was said in terms in which no good man could refuse to concur, full of sublime expressions of gratitude to the creator and preserver, after which each man retired to his goatskin pallet, and no more sound was heard in the domicile until midnight, when the same bell was struck for the like purpose, and day-light awoke us in the morning to a hymn in general use, sung in parts, with which all seemed acquainted. After which, having joined in the morning service, we departed mutually delighted with the interview, and pursued our way, light of heart, to the next station about three hour's march onwards. But before we started, the good hermit of the woods, as he was called, satisfied my curiosity as to the bell, by shewing me that it was a contrivance to mark time by means of the perennial rill, by letting a given portion run into a bucket until it raised a cork or piece of wood affixed to a rod that lifted a plug, letting off the whole vessel's contents at once, so as to give liberty to a beam which struck the bell and returned by a counterbalance, replacing the plug, which remained stationary until lifted again by the floating apparatus, and thus he, by setting it as he wished, marked the proper hours for prayer or other offices in perpetuity.

"By this simple contrivance," said one of my fellow travellers, as we walked up the valley, in the cool air of the morning, "you will perhaps form a low idea of the state of our mechanic arts, and perhaps you will not be far from the truth. Our first settlers had suffered too much on such a long travel and found too many obstacles in the way of even procuring food to think much about any arts but those which properly belong to agriculture, to pursue which at first they had few tools. The spade, the hatchet, the saw, the hammer and the anvil were among their most precious treasures, and, but for the indiginous fruits of a high and temperate climate, their sufferings would soon have reduced the little church and colony to starvation. But He who feeds all fed them and saved them alive under the hardest labours and privations, until these very circumstances rendered them strong and confiding on that providence always manifest to them in every emergency. Defended by the natural form of the country from foreign intrusion, and as it were, nested in the ether, their spirits and their devotion to the principles of their faith kept pace with each other, and it was not long e'er the small supplies of different grains began in a rich soil to multiply enormously, the result of which was the augmentation of their numbers in the same ratio. Tools begat tools, and ovens led to furnaces with which they at first baked utensils instead of meat. Ploughs soon followed, drawn by animals which had carried the packs which contained all their little wealth and sacred writings – which guarded them from the errors of the Israelites and promised them a spiritual conquest of infinitely more value than the land beyond Jordan.

"When the tents they travelled with, after the manner of the Arab wanderers, were decayed, they resided long in rude and ill thatched clay huts, or such caves as the mountain afforded them but they were not long in forming rude looms to manufacture such coarse yarn as they could spin from the distaff, and to this day they know no other method, or wish it, since it employs all in useful industry, a great object in our conservative system, which will have nothing to do with any trade but barter, and admits of no idleness in any situation of life, neither mental talents, ingenuity, age or station being exempt from employ whilst they live among us."

"But what then," said I, "do you do with your superfluous productions? For if all labour as we labour in Europe, you will raise much more produce than you can consume with your frugal and plain modes of existence."

"In Europe," replied he, "(according to the account you have given us) all do not labour, but only those who are under a necessity to do so for subsistence, and they are aided by manifold improvements in the instruments of labour and accumulated powers of machinery – about which we as yet know nothing here. Yet still we produce more than our wants demand and without over exertion, for our work would seem play according to the account you give us of European industry. But we do not consider the superabundance of our food and flocks as unuseful, but quite the contrary, as it enables us, by generous dealings with our neighbouring nations, to secure their good will, and to supply ourselves with the only article of necessity in which this country is deficient – which is rock salt, important to our own health, useful to preserve provisions, and which we mix with the provender of our cattle whom we think are infinitely improved by it in their general health and regular digestion. This barter is all we know of trade, and this liberally conducted barter is a great agent in furthering our humane intentions towards the Negroes that surround us, for it has already been the happy medium of enabling us to inculcate, in some cases, the love of agricultural employment, and the breeding of cattle, by that means lessening in them the temptation to warlike enterprizes, and preparing their minds by civilization to embrace a religious life."

Every new colloquy in which we engaged during our march gave me a better and a more pleasing opinion of the sober virtues of this secluded community. Their readiness to communicate, their simplicity of language, their probity and disinterestedness, all recommended them to me; for I was by nature a lover of benevolence and a searcher after truth even when I suspected I should only find it in Sophis; towards the discovery of which a sort of blind instinct led me at all hazards, and now I seemed like one who, searching for silver, has discovered gold, and the gangue of precious stones.

Our progress this day was not very considerable, for, after attaining the summit of the valley, we halted some time to enjoy the prospect and inhale the fresh air of an elevated plain, in traversing which we followed a circuitous path round the margin of an irregular lake bordered with a variety of shades composed of trees of pleasing wild forms, and where evidently the hand of man had never interfered with their growth or the expansion of their fanlike branches, many of which played over the waves and some actually dipped into the waters – while at other places an uninterrupted path continued along the brim composed of fine soft sand, or continually washed gravel. It was early day, and the fish were leaping at the flies or fruit which dropped continually, some of which were brilliant in their colours as they sprang towards their prey, and met the sun's glancing rays, and this to me highly augmented the satisfaction of the scenery arising from its novelty and freshness.

In my turn also I made a point of informing them of the nature of many arts practiced by Europeans, but nothing so much attracted their attention as that of printing of which I shewed them a specimen in a small testament that I ever carried in my bosom, carefully preserved as a relict in a shrine. Nor was I less astonished to find a people to whom this valuable invention had not yet arrived and who saw in an instant the importance of the communication in promoting their object, the circulation of the scriptures among the heathen and Mahomedan nations, by multiplying the Arabic copies which hitherto they had circulated only in manuscripts on vellum, at the expense of much time and great labour. To explain the process and the method of applying it employed not only the remainder of our journey that day, but was the object of serious enquiry in the evening at our halting place; a solitary caravanserai at the termination of the plain, overlooking a spacious valley through which a meandering stream wound its snaky way until lost in the blue distances.

"Your surprize would be reasonable," said Stefanus as soon as we were seated and preparing our arrangements for the night, "if we were recently removed from European connections, but we have been a separated church for ages, and for ages lay concealed in upper Abyssinia, even there always a solitary congregation, and held together only by circumspect and secret intelligence. Our first founder Jovinus died soon after his arrival in Africa, but left his name and office to a faithful follower, and thus in succession each leader has assumed the title, until one more fortunate than the others, and who saw no chance of repose but in an absolute solitude, like this we have now for several centuries possessed, led us, like the Israelites of old, to this new Sinai, where our founder's views we trust will ultimately bear fruit according to the talent employed, and your arrival seems, by the very communication you have just made, to shew us a new light, and good signs of the times having at length arrived when the work we are engaged in may by this providential assistance make a rapid progress, if such be the will of God."

As the pious man ended his discourse, we saw some villagers arrive with baskets containing necessary provision for the evening meal, and other accommodations. They were a stout, healthy, and happy looking people, who approached us respectfully, and whom we as cordially received. And, after a repast in which we mutually joined, they sang an affecting anthem in three parts in which the youthful ones bore an interesting share with clear and sweet voices, they left us to our repose. In the early morning we were awakened with the same celestial melody, refreshed with a slight meal, and cheerfully departed in our way.

It was a lovely autumnal sun-rise without a cloud, when we entered the path on a fine down overspread with healthy flocks of sheep, goats and milch cattle, chiefly young heifers, who, grazing together on the gradual risings of the plain, enriched the landscape with their agreeable colours and pleasing forms. The dew glittered under our footsteps, and we seemed to push the world behind us by the rapidity of our healthful progress, until, entering a close wood as the heat became troublesome, we were enchanted by the strains of many sweet warblers, who thus continued our concert until towards noon we arrived at a village seated on an open space in the margin of a pool of clear water belonging to some herdsmen, when we were met at once by the aged men, who each solicited the pleasure of receiving us at their houses. And we were not long in chusing one rather larger than the rest, in the porch of which we seated ourselves, whilst they brought us speedily tepid water for our feet, and in clean calabashes an icy drink pure and sparkling from a gushing fountain that rose before our longing eyes.

Reposed, refreshed, and agreeably entertained with an extemporaneous song of welcome from the females, who thus ministered to our wants with kind complacency, we were next introduced to a shady and cool apartment, where all which they considered as luxuries were liberally spread before us by the whole family, who emulated each other in anticipating our desires, and after a short siesta we took a cordial leave of our obliging hosts and proceeded on our journey highly gratified by the reception we had encountered.

I was particularly struck with the cleanliness and order which seemed the characteristic of every house we saw, no less than the simple and elegant mode prevailing of dressing their thatched cottages with vines and creepers as well as flowers, whilst each separated dwelling seemed to be set, like a jewel, in a mass of useful herbs and flowering shrubs, and overshadowed by lofty and healthy trees. The people too looked healthy and happy, to appearance abounding in all the necessaries of life, for everyone brought some offering to the landlord, who seemed honoured by our company, and all took leave of us with affectionate expressions, in elegant language, which, when I noticed to Stefanus with admiration, he only said, "You will find it so everywhere. They have been educated as Christians. Courtesy and gentleness we teach them early to appreciate, we rank them among the first duties of life, and rudeness and incivility are censured among us as worthy of severe chastisement or reproof."

"You have excellent schools then I suspect," said I.

"You will see what we support," he answered, "tomorrow, when we hope to arrive at the seat of conference, and I trust you will approve of the system on which they are founded and the effects they produce. For the present I shall only say, we consider them as the most important of all our institutions, and watch over them with a care that is indefatigable, respecting and venerating the teachers who sow the good seed of moral and religious obligation, and, looking on them as the best benefactors to society, teach all the instructed to consider them as the fathers of the commonwealth."

"Then your government?"

"Is a republic," said he, "encompassed by democratical compensations. Every member of society is represented in our general assembly and knows the propriety of it – and is grateful to those who represent his wants in an assembly where talents and singleness of heart are the best qualification – where the most laborious offices are considered as rewarded by success and a clean conscience, and none hold their individual interest as any thing, when weighed against the services of the aggregate of the people – whose happiness alone forms the object of a government established by their voices."

"A hierarchy founded on representation, perhaps?" said I.

"Inasmuch," he replied, "as the maintenance of religion forms the leading feature of our association, and that our supreme *council* consists of men wholly devoted to its conversation on the principles delivered down to us by the apostles united with the precepts of Jesus Christ, and which consists of twelve men, elected by universal suffrage from the elders of each community, whose head is one chosen by the twelve and whom we consider as our bishop and who always assumes the name of *Jovinus*. But they are surrounded by no pompous titles or earthly rank or distinction, beyond that respect due to their exertions for the general service, in which they usually terminate their lives honourably and piously. But you will understand all this better by and bye when you come to the seat of government and depository of the laws, by which all our movements are regulated. And see, yonder are the first symptoms of its vicinity, a lofty tower surmounted by a cross. Let us pause and offer up our thanksgiving" – in which he took the lead in a position, voice, and manner, that evinced the sincerity of his gratitude, and his humility.

The spot was a grove of some of the loftiest trees I had seen in these mountains, evergreens resembling the cedar but more liberated in their branches and springing from a clean turf enamelled with many low white flowers small as our daisies, but if possible more brilliant. On the branches were many doves and grey squirrels, and in the distance among the trees gazelles were feeding as if unconscious of our approach, nay, some remained very near us. The middle ground below the hill was corn, vines and olives, and beyond rose the capital among trees, encircled by a silver winding stream, and backed by a long smooth range of blue hills that melted into the horizon, for the unclouded sun shews everything as under a delicate veil, rich in colouring, but soft and tender to the eye.

And here as at other places of our perigrination, we found people prepared to receive us and administer to our necessities. A stone table, with its surrounding seats of a breadth sufficient to extend ourselves on, was soon covered with wholesome viands and pure water in calibashes; and under the agreeable shade we sat down with our host to a hearty meal mingled with serious and pleasant conversation – so it reminded me of the tridonium of the Greeks, and the symposium of her ancient philosophers.

The chief town of a district was at hand, and the elders as soon as they were apprized of our arrival hastened to greet us. They were three or four venerable looking men, clothed in long white woolen garments, their heads and feet bare, and in many respects resembling the friars of the order of St Benedict – and this was the only distinction I found in the country, as it marked their proper offices as leaders of communities on days of ceremony. But when on journeys or engaged in their domestic concerns they dressed like other men, and no one continued always so habited but the *Jovinian Father*, whose duties were never interrupted, and who annually visited all the churches in the country, to see that order and the laws were obeyed.

When our meal was over, and grace said with due reverence, we were invited to see the place, and were first introduced to a school large enough to contain all the children both male and female of a certain age, who occupied seats in progression according to their ages, and, as I was informed, were teachers to each other in the same order, each class in subordination, a principle carefully inculcated throughout every branch of improvement, and thus one superintendent could with ease regulate a whole school, which was filled and emptied progressively as the population increased.

We next entered an hospital, one of the loftiest and cheerfullest of apartments, situate on an open and airy elevation overlooking the town, well ventilated, and exquisitely clean, in which the beds were separated by moveable screens, and each patient might be said to occupy a little chamber of his own, attended generally by one of his own family. The cases were few, chiefly inflamatory or contagious diseases, and those never placed there but by the advice of the elders, and consent of their relations, and none were aged, as it was, I found, a maxim to let the lamp of life expire under the roof where it had afforded light to the rising generation, with every attention to its nourishment and support, while a spark remained among the decaying embers – so that the patients in this hospital were only placed there for a temporary benefit to themselves, in the salubrity of the site, and a general one to the population. We did not stay long, but passed through it softly on clean and beautiful mats from end to end, as at both ends like a long gallery doors were opened of large dimensions, and I was delighted to see the gentle kindness of those in attendance, who had dressed the little tables of each chamber with flowers in vases, and fruits, on plates, of a refreshing quality, and some were singing in low murmuring tones as they knelt at the feet of the couches.

On our return to the caravansarai which was prepared to receive us, the moon shone on a little group of houses built in a semi-circle, with much taste and neatness, with each an arbour in front of it, and small paved enclosure resembling mosaic of black and white pebbles. "These," said one of the elders, "are the quiet retreats of some of our single and aged labourers whose infirmities are of a nature to require an insolated situation and hourly attention. The idiotic or the insane, by the blessing of God, are but few, and through his mercy they, like children, have all their wants carefully supplied."

Thus conversing, we soon returned to our place of lodging, and having taken leave of the elders, at break of day we resumed our journey, mutually pleased with the society of each other, on either side making communications of great interest, for I was, to them, they said, like one risen from the tomb of ages, so new and so surprizing were all my relations. Nor less was I interested to find myself among a people who, although surrounded by idolatrous and cruel nations, had so long retained the wholesome discipline of our religion and language in equal purity, the latter rather enriched by its amalgamation with the genuine Arabic imbibed during their sojourn in Abyssinia and ulterior Nubia. All seemed like a dream, and I often thought, should I ever return to Italy and relate my discovery, I should most likely be treated as a visionary or idealist, or perhaps be sent for my pains to end my days in the prisons of the inquisition. As we approached the capital of the Jovinians, if capital it might be called, that, as they told me, was only a collection of colleges and institutes, the country was more highly cultivated than any we had passed, and the paths more beaten, but the people to appearance always the same, in point of dress, cleanliness of person, and frank demeanor. Their houses also, although differing in dimensions, alike in construction and ornament; none had the character of wealth or poverty, yet all were of just proportion, agreeable tone of colour, and similar cheerfulness in external appearance.

Expressing my surprize at this harmony, I was answered that they were a Christian republic, and although goods were not quite in common, as in the first ages when the apostles governed the church, yet considering all as equally entitled to the common comforts of life, under their representative code of laws, it was not possible there could be much distinction of rank or fortune; for no one was allowed or indeed even thought of claiming more land then he could with the aid of his family cultivate, and as each individual was entitled to the support of the public in as far as he had not abilities or strength so sustain himself, so the public was again entitled to the surplus of his crops, over and above what was necessary to his own reasonable consumption.

"And are these laws actually acceded to by all? or are you only amusing me with a beautiful theory," said I?

"They are rarely infringed," was the reply, "and when they are we have methods of reclaiming the criminals from their errors that seldom fail of rendering them the most obedient of citizens, and better men than before."

"Then," said I, hesitatingly, for I began to doubt if these simple people had not systems superior to ours in the management of a common-wealth, "perhaps you can shew me some of your places of punishment, your prisons, your houses of confinement – or do you execute judgement at once by putting malefactors to death?"

At this they halted as surprized, and the eldest of our company, a very grave and serious man, addressing me, with a look of some astonishment, said, "It is time you should be delivered from such prejudices. We put not the innocent, or even guilty to death, as we might do if we had murderous institutions, such as prevailed in the days of Herod and Pilate, – for who but God can see the human heart? and who but Him has power to kill? Neither do we find it written in the scriptures of the second covenant that he has delegated this power to civil tribunals, and if men fell, in the first ages, by each others' hands, it was in the execution of *His* immediate decrees, not from their own. We trust we read the Gospel better than to set up bloody seats of human judgement, where truth can never be, with certainty, elicited. Our courts are limited to investigation, and the accuser and the accused are equally examined, with the strictest impartiality, neither being under any coercion or restraint, but that which arises from his conscience, and the influence of his surrounding neighbours at his trial. But when a criminal act is capable of direct proof, and the general opinion is obtained of its certainty, then the elders summon the culprit before them, and by remonstrances repeated in a spirit of love and pity, seldom fail of producing confession and repentance, after which and such restitution, if a theft, as is due, we generally return the faulty brother a penitent to the flock, and being under general inspection, and close superintendence from his parish priest, he sometimes becomes a valuable member of society.

"This to you appears rather strange, but it will cease to be so, when you know, that we watch from infancy the first inclinations to error, and inculcate in our schools, where all are initiated in infancy, by daily repetition the principles of duties and offices which appertain to humanity. But you will better undestand our principles of management when you have been introduced to our councils, and then if your heart corresponds with them, and you are willing to cooperate with us in our endeavours to promote peace on earth, we shall hail you as a brother with joy."

"I see, I see," said I. "But come, let us proceed. I am rather impatient to be among you, where I perceive new principles exist with respect to the operations of government."

To this they assented, as to the governments I had described among my own nation and those I had hitherto visited, and assured me I should find theirs neither founded on superstition or inequality of rights, but on the basis of general consent, whose service was perfect freedom.

This again increased my astonishment, as I had seen so many instances of deference and humility to my companions on the journey, such respectful attentions to wants, and liberal hospitality, that sometimes I could not help thinking them children of Loyola, who swayed the lower orders by an imposing air of sanctity, but this last declaration entirely eradicted such an idea from my imagination. "Well," said I myself, "let us go on. I shall soon, I trust, see my hopes realized and find myself at last among a just and wise people, a genuine republic founded on Christian principles, freedom of conscience, and equal rights, the imprescriptable privilege of man – civil and divine!"

In all the way I had seen no mendicants, no person whom from his apparel I could judge to be wealthier than another, no arms in the houses, or on the persons of passengers, observed no clamours or disputes either among children or grown persons, noticed no levity of action, nor remarked countenances of discontent, sullenness or pride. But songs I had heard, many sung in parts, in almost every field where labourers were assembled, in sweet harmonies that frequently arrested our feet, and cheered our way. And the kindness they manifested to us seemed to be so natural that it appeared to extend to all their animals, who never shewed any shyness as we approached, whether wild or tame – and their crops, or clothing or utensils we frequently found by the path side without any protection – that these new to me traces of goodness and

confidence made me often almost doubt if I were among men or
angels. But a circumstance occurred this day which dissipated a
little my delusion, and which I could see gave no little pain to my
associates.

On approaching a village where we intended to halt, on turning
a bend in the path near a spot where a small cascade fell into a
deep basin overshadowed with some cypress trees, a crowd of peo-
ple of all ages were weeping and lamenting over the body of a fine
young man stretched on a slab of stone covered with mosses. His
figure was comely, and his countenance, in death, full of manly
expression, his garments, drenched with water, adhering to his
person. Two young children were embracing his naked feet, and
an aged female bent over him wringing her hands with an expres-
sion of despair – whilst all seemed overcome with grief. After some
enquiries as to the mode he came by his death, which many seemed
reluctant to disclose, a young man advanced, and desiring us to be
seated on a fallen tree at a little distance from the spot, thus ad-
dressed us.

"My dear friend and companion who lies dead as the tree you
are now seated on, was only yesterday in health, vigour and beauty,
such as that he once partook of before the storm laid it low on the
cold earth. He was the joy of his parents, the admired of this village,
and the beloved of his companions. Married two years past only to
one of the most amiable of women, their mutual affection charmed
us all, and we thought none on earth could be more happy. But a
blight came suddenly over all their prospects! She was attacked by
a rapid decline in the bloom of youth and female beauty, and every
effort to restore her proved hopeless. In his distress on her account
every one partook, and by kind attentions sought to lessen his
concern. Unwearied by night and by day he watched over her
couch, and had the misery to feel at last hope abandon him, to
hear her last dying accents, and to follow and place her in her
grave. The spot he chose was near this fountain, there where you
see yon five rude stones, under the rock by the margin of the
deepest part of this pool.

"We all strove, but no one could console him. In vain the parish
priest exhorted him to be composed, and to reflect on the duties
he owed to his faith and to his children. From that fatal moment,
sorrow seemed to have absorbed his faculties, he neglected every
office of life, wandered about wildly by night, hid himself in brakes
by day, fled from his former associates, refused necessary suste-

nance, and seemed to have forgotton both his home and his children; employing his strength in removing those ponderous blocks only to form a monument over her whose ashes he seemed to adore. For there, if he was ever seen, it was in the act of wetting them with his tears. And here it was we used, when every other means failed, to place offerings of provisions, better than the wild fruits he sustained life with, in the vain hope of supporting his existence. And as at the approach of any one he fled, we cautiously ventured within his keen sight. But we often heard him at midnight chaunting in the wildest accents of impassioned grief, and calling on his deceased partner to return to his society. Still we cherished hopes, for he had many friends, and daily one or other inspected the spot with circumspection, lest he should irritate his feelings and procrastinate his recovery.

"But how shall I tell the sequel? May God forgive him! Surely he was at last bereft of reason – it must have been so – or he would never, no never – have – O dreadful to relate – No! – he was too good once to do any evil action – he would never have *destroyed himself.*"

Here he covered his face with his hands and sobbed aloud – and the tears trickled down our cheeks also. We learned afterwards that he had been recently found drowned in the pool, and the almost unexampled circumstance had drawn together all his friends and relatives, some blaming him, some themselves for not forcibly confining him, but all uniting in lamenting his loss, and the disgrace it would inflict on the community, to have had such a crime committed among them. The crowd now surrounded us, headed by their aged pastor, to know how they ought to act in this emergency, and after a long and serious exhortation on the unhappy subject, it was admitted that the act was done whilst deprived of reason, and directions were given to lay his body in the same grave with her whose loss had bereft him of his understanding. Their offspring was consigned to the public care, under the conduct of their affectionate relations, and on the headstone of their monument, of a weight that no other man could lift, was inscribed in deep letters – as a warning – "*The Pool of Despair*".

We pursued our journey, now, in deep silence for some time, which was interrupted by my friend Stefanus regretting that the deepest sense of religion should, in this case, have been obliterated by the violence of the human passions, "for," he justly remarked, "the mere effect of grief seldom produces such misery. It softens and humiliates the human heart, but here it required an intemperate attachment, united with disappointed love, to produce the sad catastrophe.

"You see," said he to me, "with all our attention to moral government, there will always be circumstances over which they have no influence. Man is still a mystery to himself – but, I assure you, this is among the rare instances of such untoward events with us, and although no one can fathom the decrees of providence, we are allowed to believe it may be intended as a warning to many yet unborn!"

To this my words and heart assented sincerely, and I could perceive they all took it kindly. But the impression of this event evidently grieved their minds, for in the evening, arriving at the summit of a smooth down which overlooked the city we were bound to, we passed the time till twilight taking our evening repast in sorrow and in silence.

In the morning however the gloom was dissipated with the rays of a broad refulgent sun, that gilded our couches, and shed a sweet influence over our prayers. "Tomorrow is the Sabbath," said Stefanus, "and this noon will end our journey, and place us in a situation to keep it holy. We keep it on what in Europe you call Saturday in compliance with the direction of our first Bishop, a matter perhaps, in your opinion, of little moment, but with us, a sort of Rechabites in our obedience, a species of pleasure, as shewing our respect for his ordinances whom for things of more importance we universally honour."

CHAPTER XI

After breakfast we descended gently into a plain and soon lost sight of the buildings we were advancing to, mingling among gardens and orchards and grounds replenished with fruits and flowers – labour carried on with gaity and songs, fields without weeds, habitations in the most perfect repair, personal cleanliness in all classes observable, in a word, apparent abundance, joyful faces and healthy aspects still accompanied our march, and cheerful friendly greetings rang from the most distant groups that saw us pass.

"They know," said Stefanus, "that we are a deputation to a conference on some national concern. They know we have no personal interests to serve, and experience has taught them, that all our deliberations have a tendency to advance the general happiness, and hence it is that their hearty cheers find a responsive echo in

our breasts, and the motto inscribed in the pediment of our council
house has not hitherto been invalidated – viz. *"The good of all the
community."*

"Now then," thought I, "the volume opens. It is a representative
government, and not a mere hierarchy" – and my heart beat with
anxiety to arrive at the denoument.

Towards evening we approached the place, accompanied by
many friends who had come out to meet us, and entered by a long
and shady avenue of ancient trees, bordered by a lively stream of
the purest water, on which boats that seemed constructed for plea-
sure, as being covered with elegant mats, were observable, filled
with many inmates and some loaded with provisions also. Beneath
the trees were abundance of convenient seats, filled with groups
of families, whilst the children followed their harmless sports in
their sight, and every thing exhibited the air of an holiday. When
near the town, a venerable man rose from one of the benches,
where he was sitting alone reading a manuscript roll, and embrac-
ing my companions, joined us and congratulated us on our safe
arrival. Although he closely observed me, he said nothing more
than that he was glad also to see their friend. His air was open, his
manner friendly, and his person interesting. I also observed that
his turband differed from the generality as its colour was green.
Our conversation was on common topicks, the weather, the scenery
around us, and numbers I observed stopped and spoke to him on
the way, to salute him, so that I concluded he must be a person of
consequence.

When we at length came to the termination of the avenue which
ended in a broad platform of variegated marble, he stopped, and
I was formally introduced to him by name. He received me with
much frankness and cordiality, and invited us all to his home, and
then I found he was *Jovinian, head* of the council of deacons and
elders, and had for some years been annually elected to the honour
of that high situation – no small distinction, as I found, since the
people elect the schoolmasters, the schoolmasters from their body
the elders, the elders the deacons, who are his councellors, and
from them are always annually selected one, by ballots, to take the
presidency. Nor was it without good reason that the public teachers
were so carefully selected from the general society, since on their
care, abilities, and zeal, depended the whole welfare of the people,
who received at their hands a knowledge of the laws, moral dis-
cipline, and religion, and who never were allowed to discharge a

pupil until they had proved by public examinations that they were
fitted for good members of the commonwealth, and deeply imbued
with the first principles of social order and justice.

All this I had learned during the journey, and of course imagined
I should be introduced with much ceremony and find him invested
with the distinctions of office and rank – at any rate that he would
be found inhabiting some palace or imposing mansion. What then
was my surprize when we arrived to see a house in all respects
resembling those of others, except in regard to size, for the vestibule
was calculated to receive a large company, and some other rooms
were of great dimensions, particularly one which was called the
hall of conference, and where I learned he usually met his coun-
cellors. The furniture also was as plain as the walls, substantial,
clean, and formed of woods of varied colours, well proportioned,
and whose ornaments were simple and appropriate, but all of which
seemed suited admirably to the uses for which they were intended.

It was a cool evening when we were ushered into the mansion,
and the vestibule was illuminated with lantherns of various colours,
and a table spread in the centre covered with milk, cream, lem-
onade, and pure water in clean white vessels, accompanied by every
sort of fruit in season, and others preserved or dried in honey, to
which was added, vegetables, both dressed and raw in salads, and
a great variety of biscuits and pastry. To this we were by the master
invited to partake of, and I had the honour to be placed at his right
hand. We were first however shewn into an outer room, where
warm water was prepared for our feet, and they were washed by
elderly servants – of whom for that evening we saw no more, as
during our repast we were waited on by youths and maidens, but
little above the age of children, and with the greatest modesty and
good will imaginable, who brought us every thing we desired with
assiduity and politeness. But here as on our travels no wine was
offered, but coffee for the first time made its appearance after the
meal, and, when ended, ewers of white china shed rose water over
our hands.

When this was over, and a grace had been repeated with great
seriousness and piety, to which we all assented by a distinct "Amen",
the children ranged themselves in orderly ranks, the males on one
side, the females on the other, and began a divine anthem in parts
accompanied by two or three harps, and something resembling a
bass viol – in which I found great science united by great execution,
and modulations of a peculiar sweetness. They then withdrew, after

passing the chair, and one by one receiving the blessing of the Father President – and conversation commenced after removing into another saloon amid the refreshing odours of some sweet scented climbers and other flowers which scattered their fragrance around on some large windows being opened at both ends of the hall so as to give us a view of the moon in her glory and to enable us to enjoy the music of many birds of song perched on the high trees and flowering shrubs that surrounded the dwelling.

As soon as we were again seated, leaving the remains of the feast to the attendants, who took our places, the President thus addressed me.

"As a European stranger, we receive you with pleasure, and shall gratefully accept from you any information you are willing to give us of the state of nations we have so long been separated from, and churches we were compelled to relinquish all connection with, on account of what we held to be their apostacy. If they have repented and are reformed, we shall rejoice. But if, like those of *Nubia*, they have become totally corrupt and are destroyed, we shall sincerely lament their downfall – and more ardently labour to continue and extend the pure faith of our own. At any rate we trust when you leave us, you will be a living testimony that we have not dissented from vain or worldly glory, or buried ourselves in this desert from vanity or pride or priestcraft.

"Our founder *Jovinus* was neither *Arian* or *Donatist*, but a humble and sincere disciple of Jesus Christ, who made the gospel the rule of his life, and knew no other law as a practical Christian. If he had not many followers, they were all men who knew no other rule than obedience, and who submitted to banishment rather than relinquish their belief in the necessity of imitating the life of their master in defiance of persecution, and considered it as impious to be Christians by halves, and took up this cross with the resolution of martyrs. In passing during many years through the ordeal of persecution from Alexandria and *Abyssinia* and through the upper Nubia, many fell away and were lost, but a remnant continued faithful followers of our Lord, and, that the good seed might not ultimately perish, under the guidance of the Holy Spirit, sought these then uninhabited mountains with great peril, as you can judge, who are the only European Christian that has ever approached our station, where it has pleased God to give us rest, and to cause us to multiply in one faith, fear and love and one doctrine, which is the imitation, as far as it is in the power of human nature, of the life of our great Master – thereby planting a goodly vine whose branches we hope will one day be extended over the whole of this ignorant and misguided country.

"The government we live under is founded on a constitution framed by ourselves, whose basis is pure Christianity, for all our laws must be conformable to that which is laid down in the New Testament – and neither code of government or cannon of the church is valid unless derived from the ordinances of Christ. So that we may be called, if you will, a Christian commonwealth, on republican principles, since every member of the community has a voice in the elections to offices, all of which must be gratuitously performed, and are considered as duties, the refusal of which would subject us to public disregard.

"I am only president of council of deacons and elders on this condition, and must be annually elected, if I serve more than one year, and, being a widower bereft of my children, have been considered as better able to endure the burthen of the station for a longer period than in general is customary. I am sensible of the honour, and that is my reward.

"You now therefore I presume have a pretty good idea of our colony, which, if much less perfect than we desire, is still, we trust, united in brotherly love, and unshaken faith. When you have visited our institutions established in this place and seen the tranquil manner in which we live together, I flatter myself you will allow that we have achieved something, and have established an advanced post against the enemy of mankind.

"And now we will part if you please to our several chambers; every thing will be provided for you whilst among us as well as our simple modes will allow. And as tomorrow is the Sabbath, which is kept with strictness, and will necessarily occupy much of my time, I consign you to the care of your early friend Stefanus, who, if you do not object to it, will attend you to our place of general worship, and initiate you into our ceremonial of devotion. On the next day I shall hope to have the pleasure of again seeing and conversing with you."

All then rose simultaneously and departed.

I was conducted into a small chamber, connected with a long gallery or dormitory, the entrance to a range of the same dimensions well lit by many windows, or rather doors, for they were all closed by shutters, and opened into a veranda of wood covered from the weather, but open to the west, and supported by rude wooden pillars ornamented by climbers, on which veranda there was a long seat next the wall or broad bench, and beyond it space enough for exercise in rainy weather.

The chamber was not only small but void of ornaments, unless flowers painted on the fawn coloured stucco could be called such, and a recess lit by a small window covered with talla was my bedstead. On a boarded bottom lay a mattress stuffed with some aromatic leaves, over that, if I chose it, a blanket, and a sheet of coarse linen, with its duplicate, and above a coverlet of woolen variegated with broad stripes of different colours, a large pillow of the same quality as the mattress, with a linen cover: and on a sort of rude rail at the feet hung a curtain, with which the niche could be enclosed if needful.

Beside this there was a wooden elbow chair, and a plain wooden table placed against the wall with kneeling place, and at the foot of the recess was a simple cross painted red. The floor was a grey stucco, ornamented by little cubes of black marble, in quincunx order, and, though plain and rustic, all was neat and clean, and well supplied with water and towels.

"You see here," said my friend in taking leave of me and placing a lamp of earthen ware on the table, which much resembled the small Roman ones, "one of the chambers prepared for visitors to the conferences. It is a specimen of nearly all the bed chambers in this country, although those for females are more ornamented according to their tastes or industry. But we are a plain people and cultivate no arts that are not absolutely useful. When we left our country, we left also its meretricious arts and even some of its sciences. Painting and sculpture, it was the opinion of our founder, had corrupted and led mankind into idolatry. At any rate it could be of no use to men who were exiled into Mahometan countries, and whose worship must be spiritual to bring about the conversion of the heathen – men who had to substitute temperance in the place of luxurious living, and prepare themselves to encounter various climates, by regimen, abstinence and exercise. Hence every sort of drink but water and milk was forbidden to his followers, or any food but that which husbandry bestowed on manual labour, or ever to raise dwellings beyond what is necessary to warmth and shelter. You will therefore see nothing here but what you saw on our travels. The arts of the Greeks and Romans were cast behind them along with the works of their poets and philosophers – content with that of the Hebrew Prophets, whose language is preserved in our colleges by studious men, as well as the Greek, and general grammars, because we find its use in enabling us to translate the scriptures into the Arabic for the Mahometans and idolaters around us, in which business our scribes are continually occupied, and in transferring them to skins, which our *Missionaries* carry among the heathen – a slow process and which demands abundance of parchments, and numerous hands. For this country does not produce the papyrus, and if we could procure it, we would be too brittle to trust such laborious works to. But I fatigue you. Tomorrow we shall have more time to talk of these things, when you will see how we keep our Sabbaths. A good night and heaven's blessing rest upon you."

So saying, without waiting for any reply he closed my door and departed, which, as it was numbered on both sides, I could not forget, for, as they were all alike and placed at equal distance, this became necessary as a guide to the occasional inmates, and to the two watchmen who remained in the gallery to execute the orders of the visitors, and to close or open the shutters according to the nature of the weather.

When he was gone, I could not but reflect on the scenes I had witnessed, and, as I closed my eyes, I ejaculated, "Would to heaven these people might be enabled to engraft their fruitful tree of life, on the healthy but wild stock of the Sophians of the lake of Zambre!"

At early dawn, I awoke and heard the tread of slow footsteps in the gallery, accompanied by a musical carol from the watchmen, expressive of a wish that we would arise and praise God. And soon after Stefanus tapped at my door to say the Sabbath was commenced with a glorious morning, and that he should walk in the veranda until I was prepared to join him in performing his duties.

When we met, the long shaddows from the early beams of light had beautified even the commonest buildings, and the veranda with its creeping flowers and transparent leaves seemed like a gilded paradise. All was still except from a gurgling fountain below us, and the distant hills covered with woods through which masses of rocky promontories penetrated, and silvery rills descending, lay in the clair obscure like visions of delight. In the midst of all this lovely stillness, and the sweet odours and freshness of the morning, the loud sound of a band of clear trumpets broke the charm, and announced that the Sabbath was beginning.

Then I soon saw numerous bands fill the streets from various quarters, all more gaily and neatly dressed than any I had before

witnessed during my sojourn among them, and on every door was
suspended a garland of flowers just above the portal. We joined
the crowd, who took but one direction, and soon found ourselves
before the gable end of the public place of worship, whose pinacle
was crowned by a stone cross, and whose entrance was arched and
lofty, the pavement beautifully formed of variegated marble, the
roof richly supported with bent timbers, and the body, for it had
but one very long aisle, thickly planted with carved benches, of
which the first rows were already occupied by the deacons, with
the *Jovinians' President* in an armed chair in front of all, before the
high *altar*, behind them the elders, and next the male inhabitants
according to their general ages, the oldest citizens in the rear rank,
next to whom came the females in the like order, and the cathedral
was soon filled. The high altar resembled in some respect those of
Catholic countries of the early centuries, but there was only a simple
silver cross upon it, and five or six priests robed in white linen to
officiate, with a dozen choristors. On each side the altar were two
manuscripts open, which I was given to understand were a Bible
and Testment, and a Psalter in the centre, out of which an aged
priest read the morning prayers – a copy of which was presented
to me as a stranger, and which I found were wholly extracted from
the Scriptures.

When all were seated, the choir sang the Hymn for Morning
very scientifically. To the last line of each verse, the whole congre-
gation replied by a long amen. Then at a signal by a bell all knelt,
whilst the priests by turns read some short Collects, applicable parts
of the Psalms of David, and ended with the Lord's prayer, after
which the high priest gave a solemn blessing to the assembly, whilst
the others incensed the building, and all retired as they came, to
the first meal of the day.

Having joined my friend in the throng, we returned to the Hall
of the President, and partook of a plain breakfast of coffee, bread,
and milk dressed in various ways, honey and fruit, the *Jovinus* and
his guests receiving me cordially and were pleased to find I made
no scruple in joining them in this their early oblation. On my
expressing my admiration of the simplicity, breadth and long and
picturesque lines of the building we had just been visiting, he said
they had builders among them, who had traditionary rules, long
preserved, founded on Greek and Egyptian grandeur, and that
they studied to erect their places of worship on the noblest prin-
ciples derived from simplicity and unity, so as to produce congruity

and a grave effect suitable to such purposes, in which proportion was rather sought than ornaments, but utility was never neglected even in their public buildings, or economy in their private houses.

After breakfast, he shewed me the public library, a very large, and a well-lighted room, with every convenience for the scribes to copy there, and furnished with valuable copies on vellum of the most ancient manuscripts executed by the early Christians – and among others I observed the original of the controversy between Jovinus the First and his opponents, also the life of their founder, and some fragments of Hebrew prophecies. After a short stay and a walk in the garden with his guests, he left us without ceremony to attend his duties in public, on the concert of trumpets again announcing middle prayer, which was conducted with the same decorum and attended with equal numbers. On this occasion, some portions of the Old and New Testament were read very emphatically, a few prayers and thanksgivings repeated, an anthem well sung and a sermon delivered by the President from the high altar standing up and delivering it extemporaneously, its subject the necessity and benefit arising from fulfilling our duties and keeping the commandments. His blessing followed, in which all the clergy united, and we retired whilst a hymn was sung by the choiristers employed at the same time in incensing the building.

At dinner which followed, we had for the first time a cold roast kid, dried fish, and a delicious salad, with other delicacies, of which all were allowed to partake on the Sabbath day which was always with them an high day. But no beverage stronger than lemonade made its appearance, only each man had a cup of coffee set before him at the end of the meal. On this occasion, being next to him, I took the liberty to ask my respected host, on what principle they had banished wine, the fermented juice of the grape, which even some physicians recommended, and the Psalmist spoke well of, and St Paul did not disallow? neither did Christ refuse, but on the contrary drank with his disciples at the last supper and spoke of as a beverage he should partake of in the kingdom he should inherit from his father?

After a short pause, in which it seemed as if he was collecting his reasons, he turned to me, and speaking so that everyone might hear him, he said, "You have put a question to me, that demands an explicit answer, and as we have no secrets here, I will give it one by owning that on that subject there have among us been different opinions. For we examine without scruple the dictums of our founder as we do those of other men, but the result of our discussions on this subject has been that we are agreed that there was wisdom in the ordinance, not because wine in itself is injurious to man, if partaken of with moderation, and doubtless might cheer the heart of a warrior like David, meaning probably with St Paul, if taken for the stomach's sake. Neither was it likely, in a country such as Syria was at the coming of Christ, that he would among his temperate disciples interfere to alter general customs, who did not come even to change suddenly any of the laws of states, but only to introduce a religion, which, if put in practice, would render man so perfect that penal laws or sumptuary decrees would be unnecessary. And he knew that among those who received his gospel as young children do the commands of their parents, there would need no law to forbid inebriety. And our founder having seen the evil effects of the use of intoxicating liquors among the Greeks and Latins his contemporaries, and the great falling off of the churches of Asia, probably from the abuse of their feasts and the old dregs of idolatry yet among them, he resolved to try to save a remnant of absolute Christians to go first as propagandists among the benighted people of Africa, and when he found that persecution followed their endeavours, and continually reduced and dispersed even his selected disciples, he considered it necessary to make strict rules by way of test, in order to keep a portion together of men devoted to a holy life and the preservation of the genuine principles of his Master's doctrine, men ready to go forth as martyrs, inflexible in their obedience, and willing to sacrifice the flesh to the spirit. To such men the rules of temperance could be no burthen, but they had to convert men of lax habits and insensate customs, pure idolaters, and some void of all good principles, and indulging in intoxication to excess. By example and precedent therefore he enjoined his followers to avoid every species of beverage that could disturb the understanding, no less than gluttony which also impairs the mind, and hence a moderate use of animal food was among his commands. And we now perceive his foresight and impress these habits the more on our children, as one means of giving them an influence on Mahometans, whose conversion would be greatly impeded by a wine drinking priesthood. If all men were Christians, then indeed the use of wine would be harmless or any other fermented liquor, because they would only be used medicinally, but we have, as a sect, seen in our travels and persecutions for the faith, both in Egypt, Abyssinia and Nubia, that inebriety has, as in Europe we read in our records, produced every species of crime, by the dreadful stimulus it affords to the passions, and that it has been the leading cause of every inhuman atrocity among nations by extinguishing reason. I therefore trust we are justified, inasmuch as we are able, extinguishing this fire brand of the evil one, and refusing to partake of what to us might be harmless, for the sake of the general society in whom its pernicious effects are manifest."

To these reasons, so candidly announced, I could not fail to testify my assent, at the same time that I apologized for the liberty taken in putting the question. But he interrupted me by observing that among them, freedom of discussion was thus charted, as being the only ready road to truth and liberal sentiments. "The dogmas of our schools," said he, "have all been the result of deliberation, and a sincere inclination to promote public and private tranquillity, the greatest blessing of social life, and on these principles it is we assume the right to dictate to our children from their earliest infancy certain maxims for their government, the reasons of which are explained to them as they advance in age and exhibit a cultivated understanding. Make therefore no apology for enquiries into the motives of our rules, but be assured that we take a pleasure in shewing our reasons for their adoption, in order that if wrong we may amend them, or if right afford a stronger foundation for their exercise."

It now became the hour when, according to their customs, every man on the Sabbath day retired to his chamber for an hour to meditate, after which they united in the public walks or where it was most agreeable, and the evening was usually terminated by visits to relations or invalids, acts of charity and kindness, and in harmless dances among the children, after which, at sunset, the whole community repaired again at the usual call to the place of worship, where after chaunting a litany, a solemn evening prayer was repeated aloud by the Jovinian President, and high priest, and after uttering a blessing on the whole congregation, every one retired to their respective homes, in cheerful groups of family connections.

When I returned to my chamber, it was twilight, and the long corridor that led to it, with all its doors open to the veranda, had a very solemn and imposing appearance, increased by the almost gliding shadows which in the distant end were seeking their different cells, all of which being accurately numbered, it was easy to discover even in that obscurity. Silence reigned throughout the mansion, the moon was rising in her fullest lustre and radiance, and invited by the loveliness of the evening I entered the veranda to observe her and the stars in all their glory. The town and all its buildings lay in softened shades before me mingled with the dark stems and lofty heads of cypresses and ancient pines impinging on the clear and almost blue depth of the distant atmosphere. The people seemed to have disappeared, and nothing was to be seen in the streets but a few dogs wandering here and there, or heard except the music of the nightingale and other solitary songsters, to whose refreshing strains my soul responded from the echoes of a satisfied breast.

All I had seen during the day came in my mind like an agreeable vision. There was nothing to blame in the conduct of any one; a peaceful pleasure seemed to have pervaded every face I had beheld, a decorum I had never seen before in the multitude of any country, no ostentation of ceremonies, yet all partook of a grateful and pious character. And as I leant on the rails of the gallery overlooking the suburbs, I involuntarily exclaimed, "Surely this is the rest of God! or is it the Millenium of the Saints?"

"I fear it resembles neither," repeated a voice behind me, "but I trust it is one of the landmarks on that narrow road which leads to His kingdom Who made the world, and came down from heaven to save it." And this was said in such silver and insinuating a tone, that I recognized at once the President *Jovinus* – and turned to receive his commands, for already I felt for him the profoundest respect and admiration. Our meeting was cordial, and, requesting me to be seated, he placed himself beside me and thus began to speak.

"My situation in this house and duties prevented me from attending you home from the evening thanksgiving, but those being fulfilled I called at your chamber in the dormitory to enquire how you liked our mode of celebrating the Lord's day, and to propose to you some visits for tomorrow with our mutual friend Stefanus and not finding you there soon discovered your retirement from the information of our nightly guardians who on their taking their stations saw you enter here. Your exclamation at once shewed me the light in which we appear to you, and renders unnecessary my enquiries. But although it was very flattering, truth obliges me to say, that we are still far from the desired ends of our institution, and although much has been done, much still remains to do before we shall have fulfilled the wishes of our founder. We have by his system of cultivating the virtues of the human heart, by early instruction, effected the labour of creating a population free from any gross vices, whose pride is in endeavouring to emulate the early Christians, and imitating the life of Jesus as nearly as they are able. And many are really praiseworthy on that account by the nobility of their actions, their love of their brethren, and entire disinterestedness. Of such we aim to compose our council of deacons and elders, and of such we endeavour to constitute above all our school teachers – in which we have pretty well succeeded. But as freedom must ever be the basis of honest constitutions and every man among us has an equal vote in all elections to the offices of government, and making of necessary revisals of such parts of our constitution as time has decayed, it is impossible but that some errors of choice must occur from ignorance, or prejudice, and thus it happens that we find impediments to the objects for which we have suffered such long persecutions. To make you understand me, know that although we all agree in the importance of converting the barbarians that surround us to Christianity, yet we have different opinions as to the right method, and zeal without knowledge but too much prevails in our councils, owing to men being selected as elders who, though prepared for martyrdom, have overlooked the persuasive system of their master, and go to their missions as to a certain conquest.

"Had we the power to work miracles, there might be some excuse for this impetuosity, but the most reflecting among us have long discovered that, before we convert men to our opinions, we must create a friendship in their breasts by disinterested services, and teaching them the arts connected with civilization. In short we must induce them to change their irregular modes of living and introduce order and wholesome laws into their communities – the work of time, patience, and perseverence. We have great difficulties to overcome with Mahometans and still greater with idolatrous nations, whose manners are so rude, that it is not easy or safe to go among them."

"I have experienced that," I said, "and saw by their mode of influencing the chiefs and kings of tribes that they were laying a good foundation of influence and interest."

"That," said he, "is my opinion of the safest method to attain our end. But I detain you from your repose. Tomorrow I am disengaged before breakfast, when I always take a walk for exercise, and if you like to accompany me I will introduce you to one of our Cenobites, who will tell you a different story." I agreed, and we parted mutually satisfied with the interview.

CHAPTER XII

On the morrow, at break of day we left the town and descended
into a deep valley, wild and overgrown, by a path scarce trodden,
and which led us down to a bottom overhung by dark rocks, and
terminated by a pool of stagnant water choked with rushes and
canes, from whence at our approach several water fowl rose with
clamorous cries and flapping wings. Having surrounded the basin,
we passed through a quagmire to some steps in the rocky back-
ground, where under thick bushes we began to ascend with diffi-
culty a rugged way, climbing by the roots of trees, and points of
stones for some time, until we came to a platform hanging over
the water, and my companion, out of breath, made a sign to me
to come and sit beside him.

When he recovered he said to me, "We have overcome some
difficulties, but have not accomplished half the way to the spot I
would willingly introduce you to, for besides the grand scenery it
displays, it would, if we could get there, exhibit a view of the state
to which a human being may reduce himself from a false zeal, and
the working of the imagination. Above these rocks, and somewhere,
not far from here, resides one of our brothers, in self condemned
sufferings, in solitude and sorrow, yet glorying in the mortification
he daily inflicts on himself. Should we discover him in his haunts,
to me he will probably speak as he respects my office, and is per-
sonally known to me, and you, under my protection, will be re-
spectfully received. But I advise you to be silent, as, not knowing
his peculiar way of thinking, you may chance to contradict some
of his received opinions, in which case he will instantly leave us.
To tell you the truth he is the object of our meeting in conference
to-day, to enquire what is best to be done to wean him if possible
from the errors he has adopted, and my visit is preparatory to
making a report of the state of mind at the present moment."

"Is he then insane?" said I.

"Not so," he replied, "but we think advancing towards that la-
mentable state, unless we can overcome his prejudices, and bring
him back to society, in which we are much interested, as, until this
abberation took place, he was one of the highest ornaments of our
community. His change arose from his excessive zeal and anxiety
to extend our missions for which he deems, fasting, penance, and
all sorts of mortifications are necessary preparatives, and accord-
ingly has chosen this dismal and barren den a fit place for probation.

But let us proceed. You see the mouth of a cave before us. We must enter it and trace its windings downwards, until we see a glimmering light, which will, after some climbing upwards, bring us to broad day on a shelf that leads to a natural gallery, as it were, on the surface of these rocks, very narrow and very dangerous of footing, where probably we shall find him, for at the termination of that groove he is said generally to sleep on the bare earth, and as we are early, probably he may be reposing."

We crept softly along, picking our way through the cave which was very slippery, and soon reached the shelf, a sort of bracket of granite, overhung by a smooth projecting continuous mass, but saw no one. Below us was the deep pool, and the rock was so perpendicular that we could see its water distinctly black and frowning. We however proceeded, as the President said he was sure he must be there, not having met him on the way, and there being no outlet from the end of the brackets upwards or downwards. The shelf or bracket bent a little farther on, in an angle rather acute where it was so narrow that it became necessary in passing the corner to take firm hold of a branch of a shrub rooted in a fissure of the rock, but we soon gained a broader shelf inclining rather dangerously of no great extent, at the bottom of which we saw a man extended on his back with his hands clasped and held up as in prayer, his eyes fixed, glazed, and his lips in motion. Yet he suffered us to approach him without exhibiting any sympton of consciousness. His bed was long grass, his dress a single dark coloured woolen garment girded with a leathern thong, no sandals, no turban. In a word he resembled the skeleton of a giant, or a monumental figure. His head was bald and lay against the cold rock, and his feet hung over the precipice. Above him were the boughs of a thick projecting shrub of the yew kind loaded with crimson berries, some of which had fallen on his bushy grey beard and clothing, which gave him more the appearance of a statue than a living man.

At the sight, when approached near to him, my friend's eyes were suffused with tears, and he uttered a sigh full of the expression of real suffering. And thus we stood over him for some moments, expecting he would shew some signs of recognition. At length he turned to me and whispered, "He is in a trance – shall I arouse him?"

I said, "Do" – and he in a kind and friendly voice, called him "*Antonio!*", at which the hands were dropped, the head turned, and with a ghastly smile he asked, "Who are you?"

"Do you not know me?" said the other.

"Yes," said he, raising himself suddenly on his hands. "You are Jovinus, but who is the brother with you?"

"A stranger, but one whom you may confide in. We seek you with affectionate intentions. It is my duty to do so, and his pleasure. You exhaust yourself too much; allow me to offer you some refreshment."

He surveyed us both with keenness for a while, turned his body forwards, and, leaning on his right arm, looked down as if thinking, and then in a sorrowful accent, said – "Who shall refresh my soul? I have suffered an agony this night, *Jovinus*, that was terrific – not more than I deserved but nearly as much as I could bear. All my sins came, and stood before me, accusing me, some with rage, some with bitter scoffs. I saw no angel near – no help! This whole rock was covered with fire – when I would pray, my lips became parched – and had not you awakened me, I had died!"

Still he looked down, and tears fell fast from his head which shook and trembled – his agony was great and we respected it. At last my friend ventured to speak.

"My dear, my good Antonio! Look up, and try to shake off this vision which so disturbs you. Be comforted – and take some restoratives," said he. "Let us lead you into the sunshine – allow us to console you."

He raised his head at this, and putting forth his bony hand, he cried, "God has sent you, as his angels. I consent, but bear with me a while, I am scarce recovered, my limbs are stiffened with the night dew" – and then he fell back into his supine posture, and fetched a heavy groan. In this posture we placed in his mouth some restoratives, and he shortly after sat up with his back to the rock, and again enquired who I was, that, although unknown to him, had shewn so much attention to him.

"He is a stranger from a far off land, and a new convert to our discipline," was replied.

"Ah! discipline! and what is our discipline? To live as you all do is easy discipline! But will he submit to mine? Will he be the companion of my hours of mourning? Will he macerate his flesh? Will he join me on my weary pilgrimage, and force his way to heaven?"

"No," said my friend, "no – we are not made for that presumptuous course, we 'stand and wait', – we serve. Our humility is of a different cast from yours, and I am come from the general council to implore you to return to society, where you once did so much good by your generous exertions. Come back to those who love you and live with them. If you will not give up your late unhappy prepossession, we will even build you a cell more suitable to your age and circumstances. But do not I beseech you by these austerities shorten the days of that life which both nature and religion have taught us we have no privilege to diminish. Reflect that in this you may, in this conduct, be unwittingly committing a sin, you whose course of existence has heretofore been so blamess."

"Hold, hold," said the Cenobite, rising up with dignity. "I dare not listen to such words. My life has been full of sin! inasmuch as I did not go forth in my younger days among the heathen, and there lay it down on the altar of martyrdom – but suffered myself to be persuaded that the doctrines we embraced were infallible, and our laws inexpungeable. Talk not to me of returning among men who are blind, I would sooner precipitate myself from this height into the dark pool below. Light surrounds me which you cannot see. Leave me therefore, leave me and drive me not to desperation. I had hoped when you saw how the hand of providence has thus long supported me under such extream privations, you would have relinquished the flesh for the spirit – but now I see there is no cure for the errors which have taken root among you – and all that is left me is to fulfil my duties *and die!*"

So saying, he walked from us towards the shade where we at first found him with tottering steps, and throwing himself on the ground, put back his hand as repelling any further intrusion, and we retired.

The good President shed tears at the ill success of his mission and turning to me said, "Behold the sad effects of superstition, and self complacency. We must now leave him, I see, but let us deposit our provisions near. It may be extream hunger will subdue his reluctance to accept relief.

"I know him well," said he, as we returned, "and know it is of no use to contend with him in these moods. May God preserve him! for with all his errors in doctrine he is really a good and pious man – but a false zeal has consumed him, and I fear he will die in its defence".

As we returned we spoke little, but I found his report was received with general regret, and I learned afterwards that in a few days the ascetic was found dead on the stone, where generally he slept.

The rest of the day I employed in surveying the place and, entering the school, was received with great politeness by the conductors of it – and observed, that it was so well organized that it went on almost by its own impulses. Competition was the prevailing maxim. The boys were divided into classes and half classes, so that the cleverest and best informed always became, of necessity, the teachers. Silence was preserved as much as possible by giving notices by signals of classes to be examined, and so much business going on, in learning or teaching, that there was no opportunity for idleness, and consequently punishments were almost unknown. But what pleased me much was to find each scholar was twice a day lectured and examined as to moral duties – and instructed on his leaving school as to what ought to be his behaviour out of it. The parents also were desired to attend a civic oration once a week in the presence of their children, explaining to them and enforcing their duties to their offspring; on which occasion prizes were distributed to the most worthy, neither was any idle scholar dismissed for faults, but only separated from his fellows. – Order the most precise reigned with respect to the disposition of the scholars, both as to age, talents and employments, and a thing which pleased me most of all was to find a falsehood was considered as the highest crime, and severely punished by solitary confinement and degradation to the lowest form, a space allotted for the purpose, at a distance from all the scholars, where a teacher, a priest, was appointed to shew them the vileness of the propensity, to reason with, and to reform them, and without a certificate from whom of their absolute conviction of the atrocity of the practice, they were not readmitted to their class – who were taught to receive them with joy when reformed and to make a feast on the occasion, called the purification supper. All lesser faults had equally appropriate punishments, and none could leave their schools without certificates, signed by the Master and Monitors, of general good behaviour. Not the slightest fraud was overlooked, and acts of kindness and generosity to each other were invariably rewarded.

Their hours of employment were those of close application, but they were not oppressive or of too long extent, and their plays were athletic, running, leaping, swimming and digging against time. Kites, hoops, and balls were also in request, but they were never without the presence of an inspector at any time, who, in difficult cases of dispute, formed a sort of jury of Monitors and decided as to proper conduct on the spot.

The building had been constructed with great care to answer the purposes intended, roomy, light, and strong, with covered ways against the seasons, and capacious grounds for exercise. And in the course of their daily walks with the Masters, every principle of mechanics was explained by actual inspection of the process in the hands of the manufacturers. Sacred music was also provided for the diurnal anthems, with which they opened and closed the school hours, in which all were taught to join properly. And temperance became a habit by the nature of their daily food, for all took the mid-day meal in the refectory with the teachers, and decorum was thus instilled into their minds practically. At evening, before sunset, all were delivered to their parents if young, or allowed to return by themselves, who were pledged to enter their own homes before sun-set.

These various details employed my whole day in examining, and I returned to the President's highly satisfied with my second day at *Jovinia*, for so the group of public buildings was called and not a city.

At twilight I met the President and my friend coming out to take a short turn or two before bed time, and to taste, as he said, the peace of the evening. I joined them at their desire, expressed my satisfaction at what I had seen, and we arranged that I should be admitted to the conference the next day. A bunch of delicious grapes, a cake of white bread, and a vessel of water quite cool and pure were handed to each of us as we sat in the porch on a polished bench, and thus we mingled with the latest meal the most agreeable and instructive conversation. The subject of our morning's walk and the incurableness of Antonio were discussed, and in the end we all agreed that there are infirmities which have in all ages attacked men of too studious habits, and which can only be prevented, by checking them, when observed, in the bud.

And now the porter came to warn us that the gates were going to be closed, that the evening anthem was commencing, and that the dormitory lamps were on the eve of being lighted. He was a man of such affected gravity and solemn deportment, that it was impossible to see him without smiling, or hear him with seriousness, and the good President set us laughing with some ironical questions which he put to him with much wit and good humour.

The second day of the week, for so they reckonned their days, I was introduced to the council, and accepted as a brother by all present, and in course permitted to be present at the conference, for nothing was done in secret among them, and any member of the state might if he chose be present at all their deliberations, none of which could have any other object but the public good. On this occasion I was seated next my friend Stefanus and near the President, who occupied an elevated chair, with a secretary on his right and left hand at their desks, at the end of a long table, on each side of which sat the deputies from the different districts, and at the foot was a reporter or scribe.

The subjects discussed related to the progress of the missions, the state of the schools, the wants of the communities, and the vacancies to be filled up, &c, and, among others, a report was made of the unsatisfactory state in which we had found *Antonio*, who was a member of the council, now on this account deposed, with expressions of real regret and a resolution to employ every kind persuasion to induce him to return to society, and to try every expedient to induce him to augment his sustenance and receive their offerings with complacency.

But what most surprized and pleased me was that, instead of taxes, they mostly voted bounties to the communities from the fund of *free offerings* of the superfluity in certain fertile districts, who sent into the depots only such articles as they chose, in support of the general distribution; and although no one was bound to contribute under penalties, yet there was always a superabundance for the purposes of government distributions. How different from the compulsive institutions of cabinets and kings!

"True," said my friend, "but here we have neither wars or foreign commerce, neither armies, or navies or colonies to support. Our disputes are settled by arbitration on Gospel principles, and above all we have no salaries for municipal offices, or even a revenue for our church, which is supported by voluntary contributions only. Yet no people can be better provided with all the necessaries of life than our pastors and curates are, and hence it is that by giving we abound. And ill should we think our shoolmasters did their duties, if any of them were to complain of want. In this respect we are taught to be moderate in our gratifications. Yet there is one class of beings who may be said to live in real luxury, a luxury we indulge them in, and are proud of so doing. This may appear to you a paradox, but it is really so, and I will shew you them to-morrow."

When we parted, I began to busy my imagination in conceiving who these favoured people might be. It could not be council or the elders, for they were very plain living people, or the females, for although they were decidedly restricted from all laborious employments, and habited more gaily than the men and treated with tender respect by all, yet they performed all their family duties with alacrity, and great attention to their husbands was a prevailing characteristic. And thus I went on guessing without any satisfaction, and really was impatient for the morning to solve this mystery.

"Have you found us out?" said he, when he came to meet me next day.

"Not at all," I said, "I am quite at a loss for any reasonable conjecture."

"Well then," he replied, "we will go among them at once. It is not a very long walk, and will prove I hope more agreeable to you than the visit to Antonio."

We set out, and he desired me to take a small basket in my hand, he had another in his, and after a delightful sail on the canal, which ran parallel with the avenue before mentioned, we came to a bend that encircled a swelling mount and were landed on the steps which led up to a rustic caravenserai of great dimensions, elegantly paved, and charmingly surrounded by easy benches, a sort of ottomans, covered with ornamented mats and soft cushions, low and open to the cool breezes at noon – and through which ran, in a marble channel, a stream of clear water, that in little falls discharged itself into the canal below whose contents were equally limpid and transparent.

Here we reposed a while, and then prepared to mount the little rounded hill dressed with flowers, and winding walks, concealed by healthy shrubs, and sprinkled with capacious seats at intervals, under some thickly leaved shades. We were long arriving at the summit, because the walks were so contrived that the ascent should be quite easy, and when we came there I was indeed surprized and charmed, for we came at once on a platform, converted into a perfect flower garden, the odours of which were very refreshing at the early hour we arrived, and, an alcove inviting, I was glad to accede to a proposal to repose awhile and enjoy the scene. After a short pause, I observed through the trees the appearance of some light coloured buildings, and noticed a handsome fountain. "Sure," thought I, "this may be the country retreat of the President, and it is to his office these concessions are made?"

But this conjecture was soon put an end to by Jovinus observing, that the persons for whose enjoyment this paradise was provided were yet probably at rest, as he saw none in the garden. "We will approach the buildings," said he, "however, in order that I may enjoy your second surprize, and a third is preparing for you.

We then advanced and soon, after passing through some dark cyprus and other evergreens, came in view of a circular orb of elegant white buildings that seemed a ring of cottages, of two stories, very neatly thatched, and paved in front with a broad footway. Each cottage had a little porch, and round the windows of the second floor ran a wooden gallery, covered both snug and shady. The windows were double cubes glazed with talsa, as he told me, and made to slide back so as to form openings of an oblong form, between which was a neat painted door, leading out in the veranda, that was furnished with two seats, one at each end, and I noticed that most of them had flowers in pretty painted vases in them, from which rich blossoms protruded and fell in links below the projection.

"What think you now?" said the President, stopping.

"Why I think," said I "these are the retreats of some of your philosophical citizens, who have by their labours earned this indulgence."

"You are far from the mark," said he. "These cottages are inhabited only be people who in general have little taste and no philosophy, who are little concerned with society, and are far from helping the world to go on. Yet many of them will probably be elevated to a high condition, at a future period, and several are indifferent to most things."

"You puzzle me purposely," I said, "for what can you intend in preparing such seats of indulgence for beings so almost useless as you describe them?"

"Not altogether useless," said he, "if they even did not care about these accommodations, provided they hold out a lesson to the public. But see, one of the inmates is coming forth."

At that instant a door was feebly opened, and a very aged man, aided by a staff, limped to a seat before the door and threw himself down as if exhausted. We approached him, and spoke, but received no reply. We touched his garment, and he looked up sideways at us, opened his mouth wide but said nothing – and we saw he had but one eye.

"Let us retire, we disturb him," said my companion. "His great age has destroyed his faculties of hearing and perception."

Whilst speaking, a middle-aged, very neat matron came out and brought him some milk in a vessel, which he took with a smile of pleasure, and she attentively waited his refection. "You see," said she to us, "how he declines, but I watch his wants, and although he can no longer instruct and amuse me, I feel a pleasure in administering to his necessities."

"Now then it is time," said Stefanus, "to inform you what all this expenditure of care and orament is made for.

"It is our agreeable mode of smoothing the declining path of life – it is a provision for the aged. We seek to divest their latter years of care and anxiety, by providing for every want and anticipating every wish, at a time when the burthen of domestic duties can no longer be borne without suffering. Age, the last disease, we cannot cure, but we can mitigate its pangs, and to those in health who know that such a resource is provided, if ever they require it, it makes the peace of the breast. All have not children to take the task on them of soothing the decline of life to those who bore their waywardness when in infancy. Some are left even without families, and many sigh for quiet and repose to prepare for their end, and gladly retire from the bustle of the crowd. Such, and others, whom I will not tire you with noticing, are always sure among us, in every village or town, of finding such a place of freedom from all inquietude. The less aged attend on those who are unable to assist themselves, and all are provided for, daily, with attendants whose duty it is scrupulously to supply not only to their common demands, but even luxuries unknown to general society are studiously provided and administered. We consider age united with infirmities entitled to every indulgence, and as *that period of existence* when society should pay the debt of obligation in full. It gives joy to every good heart to know that we not only thus diminish the evils of life, but even make the exit like a dream, subject only to the inevitable decay that by this means we render in some cases imperceptible. But come, let us look nearer, the happy inhabitants are stirring. See, all are not like this poor old man. Some are actively enjoying their walk, others with smiling looks and upright limbs conferring about little matters, and there I see one, although bent with age, endeavouring by aspersion to revive his flowers."

I now saw clearly the delicacy of their feelings on the subject, and blushed inwardly for our European reformers of Christianity, who with one hand relieve the poor, and with the other often repel them; but here the foundation being strong by means of a just system of instruction, early commenced, the superstructure was easy to elevate and lasting.

We found the buildings formed a circle seated on the top of a gradually swelling eminence whose centre was occupied by offices equally neat, a noble well of pure water in the centre and a soil remarkably dry, being chiefly gravel. From the outer ring of cottages, which were nearly all alike, the hill descended every way, and was surrounded by an artificial canal very shallow and very pure, by water procured from which, and the well, the gardens were irrigated when necessary. Beyond this canal, encircled by a wood, was a cemetary surrounded with a portico, in the centre of which was a flat pavement of black marble, each stone of which covered a vault capable of containing a single body, and which inserted in a smooth groove could be lifted by two metallic rings. On every stone was a number engraved, to denote the spot wherein was deposited the sad remains of a mortal being, and a register was kept of the name connected with the number.

On the north side of the circle of houses was also a chapel open all day, and even at night to those whose predilections led them to prefer it for the exercise of devotion, where the offices of the church were performed twice daily, by a priest attended with a sacristan – and the whole of the domaine had received the appellation of the *Gloria*. Having examined the exterior, we proceeded to the house of a friend, where we deposited our baskets, containing little presents of sweetmeats, and furred ornamental dresses for the winter. The first we visited was an old man who had for many years managed a school wisely and advantageously to the state, until infirmities obliged him to retreat. We found him and his apartment exquisitely neat, his air cheerful and composed, and our reception was perfectly polite and cordial. In the course of our conversation, he observed that, having arrived at an age when if he lived much longer, and his health further decayed so as to render him helpless, he should become a burthen to his family, he came to a resolution to end his long protracted days at the *Gloria*, which did not preclude him from being consoled by them when they had leisure, and gave him time to review his former life, and seek by prayer to be numbered with those who through faith and God's mercy are set apart for election. "I daily," said he, "take a walk to the cemetary and communicate in imagination with those whose mortal remains lay moldering in the dark cells below – and on my return through our lively gardens feel transported to paradise, when a ray of hope is shed over my mind. And thus my time draws tranquilly to the end. This is like a halting place between earth and heaven, and blessed be our founder who ordained this merciful institution, so consonant to the spirit of our belief, and so honorable to his memory."

Our next visit was to a person of a very different disposition, a female who had lost nearly all her family, and with a kind of misanthropical severity attributed all her misfortunes to her own misconduct, although it was generally known that she had fulfilled her duties with indefatigable attention. She was on her couch attended by a friend who never left her. Pale, emaciated, and sorrowful, she held out her trembling hand to my conductor and expressed great satisfaction in once more seeing *him*. "I an unworthy", she said in a low voice, "of all this kindness. I still live, but I live almost without hope. What can a worm like me expect at the hands of her all seeing Creator, whose heart never loved Him as was His due, but served worldly desires, and sometimes almost vibrated between faith and intrusive doubts of salvation. I fear to die, yet fear more to live under this uncertainty of pardon and mercy! Go – leave me, and when you depart, pray, I beseech and implore you, that my faint hopes may be realized, and that I be released." There could be no parleying with such sincere distress as she evinced, and we took our leave full of admiration at her timid and tender conscience and wounded spirit, not doubting that her faith would make her whole.

"This", said my friend, "this variety of the same feeling is a striking exemplification of the different temperaments of mankind. Both have lived to my knowledge most exemplary lives. He who made them as they are, no doubt sees and will respect their different modes of expressing affection. *Christ* was equally generous to the centurion who addressed him manfully, and the poor woman who sought only to touch the border of his robe."

"How well these people think," said I. "This is charitable and just discrimination!"

Returning, we met several people just arrived with their children bearing little baskets of fruit and flowers for the residents at *Gloria*; and this I found was almost the daily practice, and considered by the young as a holiday, no less than an indispensable duty, whilst they in return received lessons from their aged relations and friends, with little memorials of affection, executed by their own hands.

"Every town or village," said Stefanus as we were returning, "has a place of this sort, calculated solely for the indulgence of the aged, and which all seek to embellish with a sort of rivalry, as to pleasure and ornaments. Luxuries proscribed at our tables are in those retreats legitimate, and the cooks of these institutions study how to prepare dishes that are both light of digestion and savory to the palate, yet no way stimulating or heating, but purely nutritive, and thus it arises that our temperate habits procure a lengthened age in general, unaccompanied by chronic diseases."

"And the funds?" said I.

"Are voluntarily contributed from a sense of justice common to most of us, insomuch that we frequently have messages to the council, who distribute the necessaries, to desist for a while from their consignments, which consist of every thing that can be imagined to contribute to the comforts of age, and to smooth the downward path of existence, in which we make no distinction of family or talents, for none want for any thing necessary to the latter period of life."

The day had been lovely, in more senses than one, and I felt as much joy in the exhibition of this merciful and just establishment, as if I had been the founder. Nothing I had ever before heard of resembled it in propriety, or brotherly love, and we were near the avenue before I had ceased from my reflections.

We found the President there, with a few friends taking their afternoon's walk, for exercise. About a hundred young children, of nearly the same age, were united by festoons of flowers, running before them and performing a sort of Catena (or chain) dance, uniting their weak voices in an air of soothing melody. When we arrived, at a signal, they ceased, and only formed a ring around us in silence, in which they moved slowly like satellites.

We were received cordially, and on describing our satisfaction procured from what I had seen, the *Jovinus* turned to my friend, and observed to him, that having shewn to me their most happy society, he should also introduce me to that of what some believe to be the most wretched. "I mean," he said, "that place where we endeavour to soften the miseries of the insane, who, however few their numbers, in proportion to the mass of the community, are still objects of deliberate care and attention. We consider them as children from their habits and treat them with the same solicitude as to their wants, and even idle wishes, and if we congregate them together, it is solely for the benefit of their relations, with whom they cannot be so well managed as by those who are acquainted with their several propensities, and habitual restlessness.

"But see," said he, "the boat race has commenced on the canal, the colours are hoisted, the wind is fair, and we shall see some expert manoeuvering."

We hastened to the spot, and mixed with a great crowd assembled to try the powers of three new sailing boats, on a space which could be embraced by the eyes of the spectators, and in which were six sailors characteristically habited, one to command, one to the rudder, two to the sail, and two to the oars. A shout from the general spectators hailed their departure, they shewed great skill, and great activity, and the victorious mariners, after passing first by a fixed stake in the water, came on shore, and at the hands of the President received, with a complimentary speech, the reward, a gay silken penant, and a pair of painted oars.

"I thank you, President," said the winner, after he had shouldered the oars, "and I trust you will add to my satisfactions the happiness of taking you to the Gloria some fine day where I have a father whom it will gratify to see me so much honoured."

"Accepted," replied he, "and you may tell your father I shall have much pleasure in presenting him with so intelligent and able a son."

The losers were also praised for their exertions, and three "Vivas" ended the ceremony, after which we returned to the avenue, entered a semi-circular seat, and passed the rest of the afternoon in conversation on various agreeable topicks. I had a habit of taking snuff occasionally from a box which I had reserved, together with some tobacco, when I parted from the Negro-king, to whom I gave my store, from an idea that I should find the plant every where; but I soon found I had misreasoned, for among the *Jovinians* no such plant or such practice was known, and I took this occasion to enquire why they rejected this fumigation, or a gratification so common among mankind.

"We do it no less from principle than from command, for we are not unacquainted with the great use the Arabs make of this narcotic, first because we admit of no unnecessary habits, and think labour ill bestowed that promotes them; next because we abhor any thing which has the slightest tendency to inebriety; again as it must, we think, be injurious to health from the manifest effect it has on our neighbours the traders, whose teeth it stains, whose breath and whose appetite it seems to pall; lastly because it creates an unnecessary desire and is generally offensive to females. And with respect to the powder you apply to your nostrils, we only find it pungent, and likely to divest us of the enjoyment of the delicious odours of the flowers which surround us – and much less agreeable even than the fumigations from gums and aromatic plants used in our churches, which all can enjoy without staining our features, or offending our eyes, by particles of acrimonious powder, which the wind may convey to us unawares from the fingers of our companions.

"We respect however the habits of strangers, and but that you have mentioned it, you would never have had any notice taken of the subject. We think also that the circumstance of your being singular in the practice will in time cause you to relinguish it for want of a partner – for we have noticed among the Mahometans with whom the custom prevails, it seems to be connected with social intercourse".

All this was spoken with so much suavity and good humour that it was impossible not to feel that in combatting these reasons I should have made an ill return to their indulgence; but I do not think I took another pinch of snuff that afternoon, and soon afterwards, whether from the apprehension that I should not be able to supply myself, when my stock was exhausted, or for the reasons they gave, I, by degrees, laid aside a practice, of which I began to be a little ashamed, from the attention it always excited. Neither did I ever resume it when I found that my abstinence from tobacco acted as a recommendation to the society of some worthy females, who evidently avoided me, when in the indulgence of smoking. On our return I passed the evening with the family of the President, at the council house, and was entertained with some delightful singing in parts, by the females of his family and assistants.

The next day, accompanied by my friend Stefanus, I was introduced to the *Riposo*, a house where the insane were entertained and attended to. It was situated in the centre of an extensive enclosure surrounded by a belt of wood and lofty wall, which was laid out in walks under an open grove and fine turf, the wall covered by evergreen climbers of slight stems, and almost permanent flowers. The rest up to the house was grass except what was appropriated to gardens. A very shallow stream of clear water flowed winding through the grounds, and at its exit was an artificial lake or pond, paved with white marble, and sloping in depth gradually to the outlet where under an alcove attached to the walls was a low long seat over a grating which afforded a passage to the water as it ran off. The person who attended me shewed me some of the patients here sitting under the care of a keeper, bathing their legs in the running stream. And in different parts of the grounds others were employed in constructing little mounds of earth, or forming ponds, or building enclosures for poultry, or rolling the walks or turf borders.

"It is by these and other employments we engage their restless minds, each thinking he is engaged in a work of importance. We also induce them to attend to the common offices of religion", said he, "which with some has a very salutary effect, and the care of animals delights others. We invent also plays for them, and, when one tires, change it immediately for another – never refusing our assent to any request harshly, but rather either giving them hopes of our compliance, or proposing something different to call off their attention. Their diet is carefully attended to, and when inclined to indulge too far in foods proper for them, we remove the dish as from necessity, but never so as to appear like contradiction or unkindness. Free liberty is allowed to them in semblance, but when improper or carried too far, we recall them by some sounds of music or scenes of harmless pleasure, or indulgence in things they admire.

"And thus we have had the happiness to restore many to their homes and friends, and are never overwhelmed with patients – and indeed as none come here from blood inflamed by intemperance, or excessive indulgence when young, or pride disappointed, our numbers are always very few, and at this moment, we have not above fifty patients from the whole community."

"And what medicines do you find beneficial and how many are given medical professors?" said I.

He paused, examined me from head to foot, looked at my companion, and replied, with an air of surprise, "Really, Sir, in this place we know little of physic, except drinks from common herbs if recommended are reckonned such, and the bath and exercise in the open air, and diet. Our catharticks like those in the town, and emeticks are like many other curatives connected entirely with diet, and none are informed of our intentions in these cases of real necessity, but deceived like children with sweet cakes composed of materials beneficial to their constitutions. Indeed they are like children, all of them, even those prone to mischief, and might be as easily governed in their moody fits but for their strength, and that we are obliged to subdue sometimes by strategem or force."

"Still it must be painful to reside among such people," said my friend.

"Not at all," said the manager, "by no means. They are some times very entertaining, often amusing, and often amiable by their love of truth. Those who have possessed talents make them often available under this awful dispensation. We have good singers, musicians, and able mechanics here sometimes, and many truly religious from confirmed habits acquired in happier periods. And as we feel it a duty to lessen as much as possible their uneasinesses, some become our attached friends and help us to govern others.

"But is your personal safety never compromised among them?" asked I.

"Never," he said. "They cannot combine, or remember a fixed plan if they would, and as no conspiracy can be formed where there is no intellect, there is nothing to fear among them."

I next saw the house, which was composed of rows of chambers opening into pleasant courts with little mounts in them, or rills of water, or domestic animals running about, and only closed at night, to give them the form of liberty if they chose to go out at that time, merely for their own security, in rainy or cold weather, and to enable the attendants to accompany and persuade them to return. For the general principle of management was that of all good government, among mankind, not to repress or punish actions which in themselves can do no harm to society or the individual executing them. Thus, *much* quiet is introduced, and resentment avoided, and the good effects were evident, their minds, being engaged with trifles, turned less on themselves, and their peculiar real or imaginary distresses, and, as I mixed with and talked to them, I heard no complaint except that of a desire to return home and be at entire liberty. Much pleased with the novelty and good sense of this management, on my return I asked Stefanus, what were considered as the chief causes of insanity in a country so sobered by Christian discipline, and so orderly. To which he re plied, "They mostly originated in bodily disease or the loss of re lations, but some from tender consciences and the effects of overstrained duties. In general however nearly all are cured in time, or rendered so manageable as to return to their homes, where by affectionate attention they are rendered often useful in their retired circle of domestic employments."

CHAPTER XIII

We now were passing through some well cultivated fields where a late harvest of various kinds was gathering in and people of all ages were actively employed, with cheerful countenances and cheerful voices aiding each other. All bore the marks of robust health, and were cleanly though coarsely dressed. The separate fields had separate owners, but on some occasions I found they called in the aid of their immediate neighbours, and this was one of those. But I remarked there were no females among them and was told that although some females were occasionally employed in the cultivated and separated ground, yet in these general congregations, it was not thought proper – and that, except for gardening in their own peculiar plots, few females were at any time employed, as they made it a point of discipline never to subject the softer sex to any species of hard labour.

"God has given them to us," said my friend, "for the solace and comfort of our domestic circles. The tender carefulness and love which he has planted in their hearts was not bestowed to be exposed to robust labours, but chiefly I think to soften our sterner feelings, and warmer passions. They, and our children, are the ministering angels of our habitations, their kind smiles the reward of our toils, their lively affections the solace of our sick beds, and their indefatigable attention the consolation of our maturer age."

I had now seen so much of this sober and moral people, as not to doubt that I should find fresh subjects of satisfaction in the pursuit of my enquiries. But although I had passed through much of the country, I had not a clear idea in what manner the land was divided, for I beheld fewer fenced fields than I had observed in any other country, and neither in their houses or the surrounding space did I remark any great distinction as an index to wealth or poverty. On this occasion, as we had many cultivated spots to pass over, I requested an explanation of the system of division of the soil, and the nature of tenures.

"Those fields," said he, "which you see without enclosures are held in common by each separated village or community, and those so neatly enclosed are private property, which have descended in succession to such males of the family, as, by the decision of the elders of the place, were deemed most worthy of the succession. For we do not conceive ourselves privileged to dispose arbitrarily of our property as fancy shall direct, or partiality incline us, and the law, administered by the elders, makes our wills. But whichever son succeeds, he only occupies his father's office during the life of the mother, which, if he is himself married (as is almost always the case) and provided with a piece of ground, he bestows it on some one of his family who may be unprovided, always with the consent of the elders of the district. And thus it generally happens that some one of the same blood is resident in the same habitation. But beside this, every grown up and married man has an allotment either on a vacant lot or on the frontier of the general enclosures, which he is to cultivate and bring into the common stock, or farm, where a general barn is provided to receive the fruits of the harvest, and overseers appointed to deliver the produce with a just equality. And as we do not allow above a certain number to congregate in one village, it is a task easily performed, especially as we are appointed to it in succession, unless unable by disease, age, or want of natural talent."

"But when your numbers encrease?" I said.

"Then," he answered, "we go on until we trench on a neighbouring community, after which a new district is carefully allotted by those best informed of the value of the soil, and this once indicated, and prepared by the general assistance of clever men, colonists are sent from all overpeopled districts, and a new community is soon formed, resembling the works of certain insects, from parents, to families, to colonies. Such is the general outline of our civil polity. Comprehending the order and arrangement of these national transactions would demand a long conference with the President, who directs these movements, under the advice of his councellors, but on our first settling we had wise and well informed men, who, foreseeing the probability of our rapid increase in numbers when once established in a free commonwealth, judiciously marked the boundaries which prescribed the distance which every village should be from another – from whence it is that hitherto we have found no hindrance in settling. But there are those among us who say, that at a future period we must, in consequence of pressing on each other's bounds, be obliged to form a new constitution. That however need not trouble the present generation, who have room enough to multiply on the existing system, and are content with the laws as they are.".

"And what are the laws?", said I, "and where are the lawyers that administer them, where are your courts of justice, and how do you settle your law suits?"

"Pardon me, you make me smile when you talk of our law suits! Our venerable, pious and liberal founder thought the Bible was the best law-book for a Christian people – and recommended us always to make it our code when deciding on criminal cases, if such should hereafter occur he says (for during his administration of justice it is said none appeared). And having on that principle framed our constitution by general consent, in early times, we are not now disposed, generally, to alter it. Here then is the fountain of our law. And for lawyers to administer it, we substituted a jury of citizens chosen by ballot, to enquire into all complaints, guided by the parish priests, who point out the passage which defines what command of God is infringed by any criminal act, and the sentence of punishment is laid before a general council, who, with the approbation of the deacons, increase or diminish it, and then the President gives order for its execution. But in common cases the elders recommend arbitration, and, the parties having consented, their award is final."

"Happy people indeed," I exclaimed, "who have no necessity for professional lawyers, and whose disputes are so easily adjusted, by the councils of their neighbours, and the probity of their priests. Above all great is your felicity to be judged by the *morality* of the sacred writings; and blessed are ye if ye know how to conform to it! But when criminality is made manifest, what are your general punishments, and where do you place the criminals to receive it?"

"For trifles," said he, "they are reproved privately, and, shewing a due sense of their faults, are dismissed on a promise of amendment. For serious faults, they are placed in confinement in an enclosure from whence they cannot escape and employed in labour in the quarries, where they are always under inspection day and night, and constantly admonished until brought to a sense of their shame, and thoroughly reformed, until which time they must remain, however long the period may be, after which they return to society amended men, and often the best of citizens, the stern promoters of virtue in others, and all is forgotton in the joy of their regeneration."

"But for high crimes," I said, "such as assassination, robbery, incendiaries? &c?"

"Let us not talk of horrors which are rare. Any such wickedness would indeed afflict us all, and, God be thanked, in my time no such deeds have been perpetrated. Who should steal where all things abound and are almost common property? For who is there that will deny his neighbour what he earnestly solicits and wants for his family? And what but madness would induce a man to set fire to his brother's barns, who refuses him not a share of its contents when necessary? But with respect to murder, that indeed has occurred in the heat of some inordinate passion frustrated, and a quarrel carried to blows; and we have some criminals of that sort, who have long been under severe solitary confinement; and which will probably not extend to the end of their lives. But even for the recovery of such, Christian hope is not extinguished, neither are they treated with cruelty, but constantly exhorted to repentance, the fruit of which will be evident when they shall no longer desire again to sully society with their presence; but rather be enclined to expiate their offences by penances and daily labour for the benefit of others and the good of their own souls."

"You put then no criminals to death," said I, "however great their enormity?"

"Certainly not," said he, "for we are of opinion that great and heavy transgressions against morality and religion demand long suffering and full repentance, and dare not extinguish the life of a depraved man in the very heat of his depravity, leaving such judgement to God, who alone can tell if he is entirely given over to wickedness. For when He said whoso sheddeth man's blood, by man shall his blood be shed, we do not know if the sentence had not the same meaning, as when it is said, those who take to the sword shall fall by the sword, alluding to the criminality of man."

By this time the sun was setting, and our rural walk coming to a close, when, passing through an olive ground where a group of neighbours, who had been assisting each other, were assembled, we found ourselves compelled by their cordial entreaties to repose a while and partake of their hospitality. Under the shade of some tall trees they had made a circular turf seat, in the centre of which sat the village pastor, and the teacher of the school, coadjutors always in any scheme that can contribute to the pleasure of their children, as they called them. The children had made neat crowns of olive branches and placed them on their heads and were dancing to some stringed instruments before them. We took our seats close to the elders, who rose up with much civility to embrace us, and were served with such refreshments as they could command, during the partaking of which we had some good village singing and when that ceased, we were told the reason why they intercepted us in our walk, which was to decide a question that had been propounded, and in which they were not all agreed. It regarded the trees under the shade of which they were seated.

They were very ancient tall pines, on the nuts from the cones of which they had been feasting, when a young lad had observed that if these trees which so long afforded food, demanded no cultivation, it would be well if the country abounded with them, and it would be wiser instead of eating these kernels if they were to plant them, and so provide food without labour. The parish pastor had been struck with the ingenuity of the boy, to whom he explained the obstacles to such a mode of subsistence, but could not deny that looking to the future provision of emigrants, these rare trees might be cultivated on the borders of the settlements with advantage, as the timber alone would repay the loss of time necessary to bring them to maturity; and observed that it has been a great error in the first settlers to destroy so much fine wood as they had done, without encouraging the art of planting to supply ultimately the deficiency. And this led to a general discussion of the subject of planting and the question whether it was not in itself the most productive branch of agriculture, a point on which, not being agreed, they decided to abide by the opinion of the first Elder that passed that way. And hence my friend on coming in sight was called on to settle the subject in dispute.

This he readily accepted, and being all seated round him he thus began.

"The honour you confer on me, by this reference, I will not decline, since I think the subject of infinite importance, and well deserving of every good citizen's consideration. And although we may not be able to settle the point on this occasion, it may serve to stir a very important enquiry, and one ultimately fit to be brought before a special conference.

"When this colony was first established, we were unprovided with the tools and artificers to construct habitations of timber; and after long residing in tents like the Arabs, substituted, when settled, houses built of clay and stones in cases, rendered hard by compression with blows, and covered with a rude thatching of boughs of trees and long grass. Hence timber was considered as of so little value that it was only used for firing, and its destruction was accelerated to gain open space for the cultivation of grain. And as soon as we had acquired the means of making iron tools, and that of applying wood to the construction of houses and furniture, that which remained undestroyed possessed an artificial value, and is now become comparatively scarce every where except in distant forests, to which at a great expence of labour we are compelled to have recourse. The question then which this thinking lad has accidently started, and you have discussed for amusement, is not a trivial one – but seems to be of great importance to the happiness and welfare of our future society.

"Planting trees is of all the occupations man can be engaged in the most profitable, when we contemplate the produce and compare the means. It is like building a cottage that instead of decaying and being consumed should in the course of fifty or sixty years, during all which time it had afforded shelter to the builder, have become a palace of great value. You insert into a shallow trench some acorns, which appear the same year above ground and give assurance of their future growth. You protect them a very few years from injury, and after that, left to themselves, they continue to advance in size annually, until returning to them, after years of absence, you find them aspiring to the heavens, with extended branches to afford shade, and dropping fruits every year for the sustenance of your cattle. You neither attend to them summer or winter, the air and the earth support them, and in your old age, they are, if cut down in maturity, an estate to your progeny or, if you leave none, a benefit to your country – not to speak of the young poles you get by thinning and firing afforded by their loss. It seemed to me therefore always to be a duty to plant, and one that like other duties is its own reward. To raise corn also is man's duty to himself and his family, one to which our immediate necessities impel us, and therefore not necessary to be insisted on, but considered as a profitable employment of time and land, it can scarcely be considered as equal to the other, for we have to prepare the land, to find manure, to obtain seed, find labour, both for planting and dressing, weeding, fencing, reaping, thrashing, and grinding, before the crop is available; and in the mean time the soil deteriorates, the fences decay, and the field must be again dug, again dressed, &c, e'er it again yields its produce. It therefore seems to me clearly that I ought to decide in favour of planting trees where wanted, and that our little brother should be honoured for having by his observation started the subject. And if such is the opinion of this company, let us vote him a rural crown, and place it on his head."

The proposal afforded some mirth, but it was put in force, although the modest youth would fain have escaped from the com-

pliment, and took to his heels on hearing of it, but he was soon
brought back, by his young companions, and sportively covered
with crowns and garlands from their own brows. After which we
left them and returned to the town, he well pleased with the flat-
tering distinction paid to his short oration, and I still more and
more admiring the simplicity and humility of this people.

After a temperate repast at the President's table with the rest of
his visitors, to most of whom I had to reply to some of their inter-
esting enquiry, the female branches of the house joined us in their
sober costume, with smiling faces, and after friendly enquiries as
to my health, and a wish that I might find my accommodations
agreeable to me, the eldest matron took her place by my side, and
in her turn put many sensible questions as to the present state of
the countries I had travelled over. Above all she seemed curious
to know if I had left a wife behind me, and what were the customs
of my country as to the state of wedlock. On all which subjects
having satisfied her, she expressed great astonishment to hear that
I had never been married, and seemingly some dislike to me on
that account – for, she said, it ill became the character of a Christian
nation to permit a state of celibacy, of long continuance, a state
that could only be founded on avarice, misanthropy or libertinism,
and above all wondered how the lady I loved so well, could have
suffered herself to be incarcerated in a monastery, which she in-
sisted was a prison, or that parents could be found wicked enough
to propose it to her. She however parted very cordially with me,
and, having set the example of chaunting the evening song, in
which many sweet voices joined, they departed, and we all retired
to our dormitories.

The next day I determined to sift the matter of their matrimonial
engagements; I will own, in some degree influenced by the impres-
sion made on me by the presence of one of the most exquisitely
proportioned and open countenanced maidens, that had joined us
that evening, and who, although at a greater distance than I wished,
seemed to view me with curiosity if not interest. And notwithstand-
ing it smote my heart as the first instance of infidelity to one long
lost to me, I persuaded myself before I slept, that I should never
gain a good reputation among this people, if I stayed among them
and neglected to take a wife.

Accordingly, having turned early into the veranda in the morning
and finding Stefanus not there, I knocked at the door of his cham-
ber and proposed to him a turn before breakfast, to which he

readily assented. And in a short time we were in the great avenue by the side of the beautiful canal, where it being a soft dewy morning the fish were leaping in abundance, and the early birds twittering on the branches of the trees, we took a seat facing the water, and on the first opportunity I expressed my wish to him to favour me with the character of their matrimonial engagements, which hitherto had been to me a mystery, as I had scarce, since I had been in the country, observed any but married people even united at a very early age and heard some so addressed whose apparent ages made it quite impossible that they could be connected by such ties.

"I do not wonder," said he, "that you should in the latter case be a little astonished that in appearance people who aim at so much purity should talk to mere children as of their husbands and wives. But I shall soon put an end to your surprize when I explain to you that, intending to promote early marriages, from a variety of laudable motives, we betroth our children in infancy almost, to the children of such families as we wish to ally ourselves to, and by accustoming them to consider themselves from their early years as intended always to live together as friends, we beget in them, frequently, a habit of regard, an animal friendship, by association in all their youthful amusements, which never wears out; and thus their union at a proper period, in which we are governed by their own indications or wishes, their marriage seems but a continuation of that associated friendship contracted by habit, and reciprocal services during their minority.

"Another reason for contracting early connections of this kind is that we know the force of the passions, and endeavour to restrain their power by shortening the duration of their tyranny and the force of imagination by complying with the sacred dictates of nature. But we do not object to the virtuous union at any later age, considering it as an alliance entirely dependant on the will of every one who is desirous of contracting it, and out of the reach of human legislation, yet founded on the principles of our holy religion, a sacred bond not to be rashly entered on, but which the contracting parties are only answerable for if they turn out ineffectual. And as we consider the end of marriage chiefly to be a spiritual alliance, no less than an association for mutual support and consolation under all the difficulties and cares of this life, we condemn celibacy in our sermons and discourses. And hence it is that you see so few single people, and so many happy families of very youthful partners. And this is all the mystery."

"But my friend," said I, "although you are speaking generally of a good and virtuous people, you will not I am sure tell me, that there are not among so many connections some unhappy people, who have for want of judgement, or governed by intemperate passions, found themselves deceived in their expectations, and so ill sorted as to feel the sacrament, if such you call it, a tie of wretchedness and intolerable to be borne. Do you insist on such people lingering out a life of contention and woe? Is the bond indissoluble, which constructed on principles of misconception as to the tempers and talents of the parties it binds?"

"No, my friend," he exclaimed, "we are too well read in the scriptures not to know that Moses allowed in certain cases of divorce, and that God who created woman as a companion for man to soften his solitude and be bone of his bone and flesh of his flesh, a consolation and a comfort to him at all times, never could have intended to constitute her an incurable disease, instead of an homogeneous and real union of souls. And when it was commanded that what *God has joined together,* no man should be allowed to put asunder, it could only relate to those proper unions founded on pious principles, and not on worldly connections based on fraud or error. In such cases, when it is proved that there can be no happiness for either in an unsuitable engagement, but that rather a continuance of association leads inevitably to disappointment and disgust, we allow the parish priest, the elders of the community, and the teacher united to examine into the complaint and grant a divorce, in which case each is allowed to remarry. Fortunately however these cases are very rare indeed, as our system of early associations, where the parties are betrothed, which gives them the means of thoroughly knowing each other's tempers, leaves no grounds for mistakes, and few who have thus early been united ever disagree – or are known to be unfaithful. Their youthfulness enables them to bear the cares of matrimony cheerfully; their equal ages is another link of security, and as they grow old together, neither notices the change in person but bears alike each other's infirmities, with gentleness, arising from confirmed friendship and habitual association. And this is with us almost always the blessed result of marriages commenced with the full consent of both parties after sufficient acquaintance, and a mutual agreement in the doctrines of primitive Christianity as taught among us from an attentive examination of the two testaments, whose word forms the body of *all our laws,* and is the basis of a constitution agreed on as a rule inviolable after baptism.

"Another reason why we seldom are driven to the unhappy necessity of sanctioning these hateful disruptions is, that beside that the civil contract is entered into by both parties as a spiritual union and so solemnly accepted in the celebration, our manners, as you may have observed them towards married women, are calculated to insure deference and respect, rather than familiarity and indecorum. An affianced woman is in her own house held as sacred as a priestess in a sanctuary, taking a sober but dignified habit, suitably to adorn her person, in which purity prevails rather than enticing ornaments, best calculated for the young and playful, obedience to the husband of her mature choice, duty to society in holding forth a worthy example of steady conduct to the world around her, attention to the bringing up of her offspring in healthy exercises, and a holy life – these, and a relinquishment of promiscuous male intercourse beyond sober conversation on moral subjects in the presence of her husband, render it very improbable that any unlawful attachments can be formed, whilst under such friendly inspection. For we hold prevention to be the best link of security, and observation the bond of social perfection, as well as the anchor of truth.

"It is true, and we lament it, that no human precaution can exterminate evil, but that ought not to hinder us from endeavouring to impede it, and if this *liberty of divorce* in cases where marriage has become a curse in lieu of a blessing, from being erroneously accomplished, is consonant, as we believe it is, to scripture, we leave to the consciences of the parties the result – for who but God can penetrate the recesses of the soul?"

CHAPTER XIV

Here we parted, and I retired to my pallet to meditate on the subject of our conversation, a subject of grand and lofty import, which, if it has divided the opinions of divines and philosophers, has by all legislators been treated as necessary to be conceded to human frailty by the best institutes they were able to frame to diminish the evils arising from matrimonial dissensions, so as to secure the peace of communities and avoid the scandal of licentiousness. I could not therefore deny the soundness of this doctrine, so modestly advanced from so strong a foundation, the basis of which was both natural and in accordance with revealed religion. And thus I became daily better inclined to give them credit for wisdom and consistency, founded on a humble desire to conduct themselves and others according to the commands of God. But I sooner than expected had an opportunity of witnessing that their practical piety was parallel to their professional declarations and doctrines – for in the middle of the night, a confused noise in the dormitory, and lights passing backwards and forwards, awakened me, and a moment after my friend Stefanus opened my door without the usual ceremony of knocking, and recommended me to dress as soon as possible, as my chamber and those of others would speedily be in requisition for some distressed persons who were expected soon to arrive at *Jovanina*. And then in a few words he related that a partial flood had suddenly swollen a small river from the mountains, which the canal we before noticed was excavated to drain, and, coming down with rapidity in the night, had overwhelmed the lower part of the town, swept away several houses, and was now actively producing more mischief hourly.

"The President and leading men," said he, "are now as near the scene as they can with safety to their own lives venture, and the hardiest of our young men, under their directions, are actively engaged in taking out the helpless from the houses surrounded by the foaming waters, which easily penetrate our mud cottages, and have already I fear drowned many of the inhabiatants, who were taken suddenly and unprovided."

We hastened to the scene with torches, for the night was cloudy and dark, and found from report that the waters had isolated a lower part of the town so as to enclose several habitations and their surrounding walls, cutting off all means of escape. They could see our torches, and we could hear their cries of distress, but they were hid from our sight, and all we could at first do was to encourage them to keep together on the highest part of their insular situation. to connect their furniture as a raft, in case of the rising waters flowing over, to depend on our every exertion to get them off, and to trust in God for a deliverance.

The first person I encountered was the venerable President and his friends and guests, accompanied by some young and able bodied men, on the brink of the stream, who were uniting several long poles together at their ends by cords, the bottom of the first and stoutest of which was firmly lashed to a stake but so as to give it play like a hinge. He then directed that others should be added to them and firmly united by bands end to end, until a sufficient number were connected into one rod or mast to reach across the stream, and then by their united efforts launched at once, with a buoy at the extream end, furnished with loops and grappling hooks. By this time the moon had given us some light, the storm seemed abating, and on the opposite side we had persons ready to assist in mooring the buoy.

And now came the trying moment so anxiously waited for by those on each side the floor. A hundred youths aided at once to place the long mast in the water, and those at the furthermost point of this instrument, which resembled a jointed cane, first entered to launch it off with the tide, the others following in succession; so that by great efforts and the aid of long poles they pushed it towards the middle of the stream, so as at length to get the water to act upon it and with a great shout we saw it carried over, the end still held by a venturous youth whose father received him on the bank, where they lashed it firmly to a sunken tree. We had now made a weak bridge and saw with pain that it bent like a bow on the surface, but all the joints held firm, and several attempted at separate intervals to cross by the aid of their arms, who conveyed cords back again in the same way, and thus we were enabled to get over something like a cable bridge, just before our first conveyance broke in the middle and was carried away down the stream in two parts only attached by the fastenings and playing against the bank.

The joy, the shouts of satisfaction now expressed, I shall not easily forget, or the rapidity and skill with which our young assistants strengthened our connection. Suffice it to say, all the inhabitants were after many anxious hours, and united exertions, safely landed. Few however saved any property, and the houses were entirely destroyed, for before day-light the waters rose with such impetuosity that the whole islet was covered and nothing remained when they subsided but a surface sprinkled with ruins. Even trees were rooted up and carried away by the stream. In the memory of the oldest people, such an accident had never before been known, for the small river thus swelled was seldom altered by the seasons, and was so manageable that the canal and the moat surrounding the *Gloria* hill had been supplied by its waters on account of their gentleness, clearness and equal volume at all times flowing. It could therefore only be accounted for by the bursting of a water spout on the hills and its attendant autumnal storm.

When the people were safely landed, it was affecting to behold the general joy, and the self satisfaction of their deliverers. It was now a struggle who should first receive them into their houses, and the good *Jovinus* very soon peopled our dormitory. Wet, harrassed and alarmed as they were, their first thought was to return thanks, on their knees, to the merciful providence that had sent them deliverers. And the meadow on which they were assembled was with the aid of the President and his deacons and elders speedily converted into a chapel. The Te deum ended, refreshments were brought in profusion, clothes and every necessary, and the crowd departed with those they came to aid in this great misfortune.

By this time it was broad day, the sun shone out, and the waters subsided as fast as they had arisen, insomuch that the islet was left dry on the side where the rupture had been, and we found it not difficult to pass over, in which our bridge of cords still was serviceable. And this enabled us to inspect the opposite side of the river, where we learned with pain that on the first onset many lives were in danger and some actually lost. Among others a miller with his whole family had been swept away with their mill whilst in bed. Their cries had been heard long after the fragment of the mill had passed down, lessening on the ear, till it was heard no more. A rick of corn too had been seen floating down at day break, with a child asleep in it, whose life was saved by its getting entangled between two tall trees in a meadow below the town, from whence it was recovered by the aid of a powerful and bold swimmer when the waters began to subside, who returned with it on his back amid the cheers of hundreds of spectators – who carried him home, quite exhausted, in their arms, and rolled a large stone to the door of his parental mansion by their united efforts as a monument to his honour.

When the water had fallen to its usual level, a deep trench remained where it had burst through to gain a speedy vent, almost dry, for now, having two channels, neither was navigable even for the smallest boats. It became therefore necessary to place a dam to the entrance of the new cut, with an overfall which made a picturesque cascade at all times, headed by a wooden bridge and a sluice, so that it afterwards turned to account for a little mill and restored to them their unusual navigation, and kept the little useful river of its previous size, augmented far below the town by the accession of the canal which surrounded the Gloria mount, serving to irrigate some rice grounds on the common fields, which for that purpose had been opened higher up on the river.

The greatest misfortune that ensued from this sudden flood was, that the banks of the canal having burst, these fine rice grounds which lay below the canal in a hollow basin had been inundated and converted into a lake, a loss which seemed irreparable, and created great alarm and anxiety at the Presidency, for no one could hope ever to drain it, as it was surrounded every way by higher grounds. To pump it by a water wheel of which they well knew the use from having learned it in Egypt, seemed impossible, from the immense body of water collected, and much of their food depended on this valuable portion of cultivated land. So that when I returned to the house of the Jovinus, I found him lamenting the accident, and preparing to call a council of all the intelligent people around him to consider what was to be done under these unhappy circumstances.

"It is not," said he to me, "that we entertain any apprehension of a refusal of supplies from all the districts round, but I know not how it is possible to drain this lake in many years, or where to find a spot suitable to the purpose it has been applied to, and which originally was the inducement to settle here. We cannot expect always to be supported by our humane neighbours, and shall probably be obliged either to greatly lessen our numbers, or remove to a new settlement far distant on the frontier of this high and extensive ridge, which now separates us so providentially from the barbarians of the plains."

We went together that evening to view the spot, where I found the canal repairing at its rupture by hundreds of active people, and I observed that its channel was conducted along the side of the hill which bounded these extensive rice grounds, and went on in a straight line for a considerable way, banked with stone, and resembling an aquaduct – and in an instant I saw the remedy.

"There is a means," I said to the President, "to make this very canal, which has been the cause of so much mischief, perform the cure".

"By making it turn water wheels?" he said.

"No", I said confidently, "by its own stream, I will make the work be performed, without any other operation whatever."

He looked as doubting, shook his head, and with a deep sigh said, "I *wish you could.*"

"Give me but hands enough," I said "and it is done."

"The whole country is at your command," he said in reply, "and I would work among the rest, if it were only to see such a miracle performed."

"Be then assured", I said, "I am serious when I state that I have myself witnessed such an operation in my own country, and can answer for its success."

"Then you can explain it to me," he said. "I am no great hydraulist, but I think I have sense enough to comprehend a simple proposition, and God knows how grateful we should all be to the man who, under His good providence, we may be indebted to for such an invaluable benefit."

"You doubtless know that water will find its own level. It is on that principle I have seen this operation performed of draining a lower ground by means of a higher stream. You have only to pour this canal before us into a tunnel and make its waters pass in a semicircular dip below the lowest part of the flooded ground, and by its constant rapid action it will take up and convey, to its outlet at the other end of the semicircle, all the water of the lake, let into it by a sluice at the base of the curved tunnel – after which, you, by closing the sluice, leave your rice fields as dry as you find convenient for the purposes of raising crops."

I had scarcely concluded my description of the general principle, when, his eyes sparkling with delight, he clasped me in his arms, and exclaimed, "I see, I see we have been too long absent from Europe, and its improvements in arts would exhibit our ignorance, were we to return. Africa is ages behind you. Tomorrow you shall lay your plans for effecting this great and necessary work before the council of deacons and elders as well as the most intelligent men of our town, and may the blessing of God attend your disclosure, by which you will prove yourself a true brother in Christ, and become at once an efficient member of our holy union – disinterested, loyal and free.

On our return, we found every chamber of the dormitory occupied by the female sufferers who had accepted our invitation, and the gallery strewed down with straw for a number of men who had no other home. People were running backward and forward with warm cloths and provisions in abundance, and every one was cheerfully performing his duty with alacrity and zeal. In this way we were employed until morning, deferring our own repose until day, when we took our turn for a little refreshing sleep – keeping as it were watch until larger accommodations could be provided. And it was several days before some of the females and children recovered from the colds and fevers caught during the dreadful

night of the water-spout as it was afterwards named. No time how-
ever was lost in rebuilding the houses demolished, refurnishing
them even better than before, and so well did their neighbours
acquit themselves of their duty that there were few who were not
better supplied for the winter than they could have been, had the
misfortune not invaded them.

The next evening, after every one had ceased from his daily
labours, a grand meeting was convened, and no one being able to
propose any effectual plan to drain the rice fields – I was called
on to offer mine.

By the profound silence of the assembly, I could not doubt that
the President had dropped some hint of my being able to suggest
something likely to be effectual. And thus encouraged I explained
every particular of the process with the utmost precision, exhibiting
also a diagram of the whole, and ending with an assurance that on
a smaller scale I had seen it, in the country I was born in, tried
and proved completely successful.

At first, a murmur of incredulity was heard from some to whom
the principle was even unknown, and I was obliged to reply to
many ingenious questions, but when the *Jovinus* arose, and
avouched that he had no doubt of my succeeding if the waters of
the canal could be turned into the river during the operation of
making the siphon-like tunnel, and that a sufficiently strong under
ground channel could be constructed, with the aid of every spare
hand in this or the neighbouring community – they, with one voice,
hailed the project, and it was agreed that it should be instantly
commenced, and every man present undertook to do his utmost
to procure labourers for the great undertaking. For, as to turning
the canal, no one doubted the possibility.

I will not detain my reader with the history of the process, but
content myself with assuring him that, by the united exertions of
all the able bodied people, we found means to turn the water off
the canal into the parent river, and of solid stone constructed a
round tunnel which, dipping in a regular semicircle, so that the
lowest part of the arc descended to a level with the bottom of the
inundated land, there received and caught up the water, introduced
by a sluice, and carried it forward by its own velocity to its exit at
the other end of the arc, from whence it flowed on in a gently
declining plane, and was ultimately discharged over the country
for the purposes of irrigation.

The excavating the deep cavity into which the stone tunnel was inflected required the aid of many hands, but here all could labour in removing the soil, which fortunately was a strong clay and rubble, so that at no future time was there any danger of the channel leaking from decay, as, our stone being sandy, might have occasioned, or we might have been put to a great deal of trouble in procuring clays to ram the bank with. I leave any one to conjecture how much anxiety all this occasioned me and my assistants, but fortune crowned our endeavours, and I came off triumphant. The work was finished before the spring, and I had not only the pleasure of seeing the flooded land daily emerging, but of being considered by this intelligent but unpretending people as a national benefactor, and worthy, if I would accept it, of the office of even the Presidency.

But what endeared me most to my situation was to find that my success excited no envy, from any quarter, and that I was regarded with the same affection as if I had been born among them. This transaction also convinced me, that they were sincere in their practice of retrenchment on the article of external shew, for I found their artizans to be capable of executing any species of ornament in the course of my intercourse with them, and that they were possessed of all that geometrical knowledge and laws of mechanics, which relate to proportion, and which only demand a taste for architectural composition to carry it to its highest pitch.

It was therefore on principle that they adopted simplicity in all they constructed or manufactured, admiring only utility and convenience – and hence *proportion became the source of beauty* and shed a calm splendour around their dwellings, like that soft and mellow illumination of the full moon when at midnight she sheds a shower of pale and silvery glory on the plains of Egypt, and makes a solitary block of granite resemble the mansion of a king. A native taste they undoubtedly possessed, and being prevented by their principles from expanding itself in the productions of what in Europe we call the fine-arts, it broke forth in a display of symmetry united with simplicity in every thing they constructed, and if they had no paintings or sculpture, their houses, their habits, and their utensils, as well as plantations, offered groups and combinations of congenial forms which the most tasteful artists would be delighted to copy. Their houses never exceeded one floor on a raised platform, which was ascended by a gently sloping, and sufficiently wide, path for two to pass at a time; the colour of the stone of which this plinth was composed always harmonized with that of the habitation. The roofs always projected handsomely and were bound down very elaborately with cane which assumed agreeable lines on the surfaces. The tints with which the walls were finished were ever blended so as to relieve each other, and by their gravity gave repose to the eye. Their habitable rooms were seldom large, but generally lit by only one oblong capacious window, which could be closed at pleasure by rolled mats, wove with varied colours, and at certain seasons changed for materials stronger or lighter, some of which to keep out flies or mosquitos in the hot weather were of a fineness equal to European gauze composed of silk, for which purpose alone they manufactured it, and for sashes to surround the loins, an article which all persons were accustomed to wear, and which was found to contribute to the general heath at every period of the year, preserving the intestines from cold, increasing strength in action, and effectually assisting digestion.

Another peculiarity in the furniture of their rooms gave them always an air of order and repose; instead of moveable seats, the walls were surrounded by a broad cane bottomed bench of a breadth sufficient to sleep on if desired, covered by mats or skins, and, in the case of workshops, of plain boards, beneath which were boxes on little wheels, calculated to contain any articles which were wanted, and which were easily with drawn, when daily swept under, and, when not used, completely out of sight. Even their workshops betrayed no disorder. Tools, always bright and clean, adorned the walls, and the floors were as pure every evening from litter as the tables at which they employed themselves. For no man had occasion to make business a slavery, and every mechanic was enabled to enjoy his afternoons with his family, according to his taste and inclination. In fact there was, in consequence of their reduced wants, no occasion for hard labour in this country, where there was no army, no navy, no foreign commerce, no court establishments, or tythes, or taxes, or official emoluments. The people had only to employ themselves in the production of food and clothing, and as the climate was mild and the land not in general unfertile, that operation demanded no more exertion than was compatible with health. And in the culture of their fields, their gardens, and attending to their flocks and herds they seemed to enjoy rather a pleasure, than partake of a labour, and when a man had sons and daughters at home, he had little to do but to inspect and direct the industry of others.

CHAPTER XV

Education, indeed, in the moral duties and offices of life, as well as the practical performance of the ceremonies of religion, gave constant employment to those advanced in years, who were never considered to be too old to be useful to society in that respect, and the reverence for age which their usages promoted rendered people of that class the most useful part of the community.

Having now become one of the initiated, and looked on by every one as a true brother, I found every door open to me, and had free accesss to not only private society, but to their councils and conventions, and was the object of several plans concerted to promote my establishment with comfort among them. Among others, a proposal was made by my friend Stefanus, who was now about to return to his own district, to form a matrimonial alliance with the widow I before mentioned, whose attractions, they had observed, had led me often into her society, and whose portion of land would amply suffice for a moderately large family. But to this scheme, although I listened with some pleasure, I could never bring myself to finally assent, for it seemed like stirring the embers of an expiring attachment now nearly extinct. He then suggested to me that I might return with him, and, after preparing myself for it, assist him in promoting a mission which he had in contemplation among the tribe where we first met at their annual expedition for salt. "For," said he, "your European education and manners, together with your knowledge of the Arabic, might, after a short residence, give you influence enough with the chief to prevail on him to join you in endeavouring to civilize his followers, by teaching them to depend on agricultural pursuits, and thus then become as it were stationary – in which case we might act together and by rational means attempt their conversion."

After many conferences on this important subject, and submitting our plans to the Jovinus in council, it was decided, that in the spring I should be sent over to him for instructions, passing the winter at the Presidency, and acquiring, during these months, a perfect idea of their constitution and principles of government, above all their system of education. To this end, I formed an intimacy with one of the most intelligent teachers of the place, and went to reside at his house.

His custom was, after the common instructions of the morning were ended, which consisted merely of reading, writing and the first principles of figures, to call his scholars together, after their dinner meal was finished, and to exercise them in the public grand avenue – after which he placed the younger ones under a monitor of fit age and influence to continue his lessons there in the presence often of their parents, who also came there for recreation; taking the elder ones around him to proceed in a long walk which lasted till evening, along the canal, over the Gloria, and sometimes towards the head of the river, in the course of which peregrination they were at times discoursed with on moral topicks when they reposed, or taught to swim, to climb trees and rocks, to run races, to leap, or to trace in the wood the haunts of wild animals, or the construction of their concealment; to learn the names and forms of useful plants, the mechanism of the insect race, and in a word the principles of mechanics from nature.

In the course of these long, and sometimes fatiguing rambles, they often visited the habitations of the cleverest citizens and observed the arts of agriculture, and the advantages to be derived from labour, and were occasionally employed in the practical part on the spot. His views were to make recreation conduce to utility, and the very exercise itself the main benefit, as while it tended to invigorate the body, it induced that sound and healthy sleep, which best prevents the lapses of the mind, and renews the spring of our animal construction with the morning.

The sun was the chamberlain of the whole race, and his setting or rising indicated the hour of retirement or employ – so that clocks were little necessary, but dials there were in the school gardens, and the sand and water ones were not uncommon among them. Habit and observation had made most of them expert at finding the hour of noon, wherever they were, and for very nice divisions of time it was not necessary in a country where when awake no one was uselessly occupied.

He used to say to me, "My academy is a little world. In children I see the germs of men. All the natural infirmities of man, in them at a certain age, are exhibited without disguise, and as we teach them afterwards not to disguise them from themselves but to labour to suppress them at all times, a habit of candour and a love of truth are by degrees inculcated and acquired. We recommend no secret confessions, lest two persons being convicted thus of some evil habits, it should lead to mutual apology, and confirmed practice. On the contrary, we recommend open confession of errors, as the surest pledge of amendment – and instead of indiscrimately punishing early lapses into error, we only express sorrow to the patient and shew him, by its reality, that his fault is great. Those whom I find constitutionally careless, I take to my especial care, and conquer the evil heart by persevering in kind services. It is not in human nature to resist this system long; it must finally succeed, as water wears the stone, and the earlier it is resorted to the better, for the young mind has a strong bias to good and generous actions, long before the temperament of the body can exert its influence to mislead. So that when once peace and happiness are found to depend on right action, there is little or no difficulty, with good examples before us, of restraining and keeping under the evil propensities, until we can completely master them."

I found his theory also in harmony with his practice, for not only did his pupils commence and end their labours with an highly appropriate address to the deity to implore His assistance in reforming their faults, and correcting their evil dispositions, so as to enable them, each day, to fulfil their several duties as Christian children, to the satisfaction of their tutors and parents – but he regularly and daily lectured them, with kind and affectionate expressions, on the necessity of guarding their minds from the first impulses of passion, and in the most trivial actions to conduct themselves so as by no means to infringe on the happiness of others.

"You think," one day he said to the schools, "perhaps, that I too often repeat the same advice – but you are wrong if you so think. Let the strongest of you take this hammer, and give his most powerful stroke to yon stone, and it will resist the blow. But I will shew you how by a repetition of gentle tappings to produce a vibration on its inward particles that shall shiver it to atoms."

And thus it was by palpable images, by proverbs, and by tales suited to the moment and the age of the scholar, he won them to good purposes rather than by reproofs.

"If," he would remark, "you were running thoughtlessly towards a precipice, the danger of which I knew, and I did not recall you from it, should I be worthy of your friendship, or fit for the office I assume? Shall I not then intercept your tendency to error with the like care? And is it not my especial duty to interpose my voice and authority if necessary, for my own sake as well as yours? For it is alike my office and pleasure to present you to your parents daily without blemish, and to your country at your last examination as healthy plants well trained, strong in a determination to excel in the moral and religious doctrines of your forefathers, and fit to produce wholesome fruits in a community where the highest station is only to be obtained by disinterestedness, probity, and the love of God and your fellow creature."

And thus it was he won them over to the side of virtue, by incessant exhortations to liberal conduct. Line upon line, and precept upon precept was his wise maxim, until, as he often said, he had so amalgamated, and mixed the good principle with the evil as to refine the mass, and, in the crucible of public opinion, produce a pure metal by the fire of the Gospel truths.

Yet it happened here, as it always will among mankind, that, in some, the evil propensities are hard to master, a source of grief perfectly reasonable, and a subject which called for the most serious consultations among the deacons and elders, whose system of conversion, ever reasonable, and conformable to the precepts of their Master, led them to long forbearance before they employed the severity of the laws against the incorrigible offender – which consisted at worst of solitary imprisonment for a limited time, accompanied by intervals of probation, under inspection, and tests of good behaviour, a circumstance which I was witness to one day when, on a visit to the school accidentally, they convinced me of their moderation patience and justice. For these institutions for education are jointly managed by the deacon, the elder, and the parish priest, if I may so call the officiating clergymen of the village or hamlet.

On entering, I heard a shout of satisfaction and saw a very good looking lad of about sixteen years of age surrounded by a crowd of his companions, who were cheering him cordially, in the presence of the three persons above mentioned, who seemed pleased with the applause bestowed, and on enquiring the cause I was told, that he was the son of a very excellent man, who had betrothed him to the only child of a neighbour, and, as was customary with them, thinking their attachment secure, but that they were too young to marry, had caused the girl to be sent off on a visit to some relations who resided at a distance, in order to gain time for each to finish their education, and become more mature and steady under such a relation. A strong and passionate regard having already taken place on both sides, it was soon found that a sudden change took place in the youth's manners, habits and health. He performed his tasks vigorously, it was observed, and was not wanting in his family duties – but he became silent, unsociable, and seemed always plunged in deep thought.

At length it was discovered, that during the night he absented himself from his father's house, at several times which discovery was made by the yelping and joy of a favourite dog who always welcomed him on his return before daylight. In vain did his father, in vain the priest, reason with him on the impropriety of this conduct. He refused to tell his motive, or where he passed the night, but always returned haggard, wasted in strength, and sullen. Yet still he persisted in completing his lessons and attending the school, as well as performing his domestic services, until at last nature gave way and, his strength failing him, he was attacked by a severe fever, that afforded little hopes of his recovery. Every remedy was applied fruitlessly, and, all hope failing him, the priest was sent for during an interval from delirium to afford him the last spiritual consolations, when his father, who was a widower, with tears streaming down his cheeks implored him to confess what was the cause of his frequent absences, where he went, why he had broken the commands of both parent, tutor and priest, and offering any sacrifice he could ask, to satisfy his wishes, within the compass of propriety and justice.

"It is now too late," said the youth in a faint voice, "I fear I am dying – when you took from me!" – and here he burst into tears – "when you took from me!" – and again he paused and covered his face with his hands.

"Took from you!" said his father in an impassioned tone, "my dear boy, what did I ever deprive you of that I could indulge you in? What is there that I possess that I would not now give you to save your life?"

He shook his head – embraced his father, shed tears on his neck, and whispered in his ear – "*Martha!* Were we not brought up together?" said he. "Did not you promise her to me? – I loved her like a sister, I had no other to love. Why then did you separate us? Why take from me more than my life? I shall I know never more see her, I shall die and she will be inconsolable if she feels like me!"

At this disclosure, which astonished and grieved the father, light broke on the parent's heart; he saw he had acted by them unkindly and without reflexion from being incapable of penetrating the depth of a pure affection, which modestly concealed its tendency even from its object – and he hastened to assure him, that nothing could be further from his wish than finally to separate them. And in a word he promised to send for his betrothed immediately in proof of his veracity.

From that instant the youth revived, was restored, and soon had the extatic joy of receiving his Martha in his arms recognised as the intended companion of his future life. And the moment I saw him was when his father had conducted him back to his tutors, full of joy and health at receiving the pardon and congratulations of all around him.

"You see the simplicity of our manners," said my friend, when he was gone. "This lad revered his father, loved me as his tutor, and obeyed his spiritual instructor, until this event took place, suddenly and in his absence from home, by the advice of one who neither intended or suspected such a fatal result on the youth's feelings, who only then discovered how much his fair mistress was necessary to his existence, and in his modesty and innocency wanted the resolution to disclose it to his father and his friend, whose grave demeanour was ill calculated to discern her affection towards his son, or the father's serious heart, to conceive the force of that of his son's to the beloved Martha. And thus brooding over a misery which he thought inevitable, plunged in hopeless despair, he sought, by exhausting himself in wild rambles during the night, to procure that repose which fled from his pillow, until at last nature gave way, and that disease siezed on him, which had so nearly extinguished his life and love together.

"This you will say is the result of our ignorance of the human heart, and it may be so – but such effects of passion are exceptions, not rules to go by. And the honest simplicity of this affectionate father is I think more creditable to our system of education than a keener penetration would display. Sagacity may be useful in a busy world, but we prefer native simplicity and the docile bosom, the parents of faith, humility and brotherly love."

"How then happens it," said I, "that yourself, the President and others possess so much penetration, since all are educated alike?"

"Ask me rather how it comes to pass that trees are not all of the same size, when all are equally nourished by the soil. Men like plants are I apprehend not all alike endowed with a stamina fit to receive the nutriment or accretion of ideas, or all alike provided with that healthy and perfect brain, that possesses the power to arrange, store up, and distribute facts of importance in the conduct of the mind. All are capable of perceiving their general duties and believing in a ruling power, and obeying his laws; but it is only given to a few to combine these feelings with the talents necessary to direct and govern for the general good by persuasion and reason, derived from those sacred writings open to all, but seldom fully comprehended except by those whose inclination and leisure enable them to make them a continued study."

"You allow then," said I, "the communication of the sacred volume to all?"

"Yes," he said, "and to that end we teach every one who is capable of it both to read and write. Nay, none can be passed out of our schools, as complete scholars, who have not copied on parchment the whole of the new Testament. But there is a wide difference in their copies, owing to circumstances past control, and of the best we make scribes who after a certain proficiency accompanied by a vehement desire to take upon them the office, we constitute deacons, priests and lastly elders with the voice and approbation of the whole community, only to be obtained by a life of moral decorum and zealous piety."

On this we parted, and, as I returned, musing on what I had seen and heard, I repeated to myself, "*Surely the grace of God is here!*" Temperance and frugality I saw were the pillars of their commonwealth, labour the practicable impediment to evil, truth the basis of their morality, and discipline the head stone of the corner in church government. I saw also in what manner they made the influence of talents take their proper station, and now became only more anxious to examine their liturgy and religious rites, an opportunity for which was soon afforded me when I was introduced to the chamber of scribes, where several were always employed in preparing such manuscripts as were necessary for the public service.

This was an establishment common to every district, the members of which were also employed in preparing the public annals, and writing marriage and other civil contracts, for which services they had apartments provided with a maintenance at the public expence, and the hours of attendance so arranged, by rules, as not to interfere inconveniently with their domestic concerns, for, being many, they served in rotation. And what I could not fail to approve among their institutions was, all were like this in a liberal scale, free from drudgery or dependence. The highest offices sustained the hardest labour of necessity, as few could be found able to fill them, but those who devoted themselves to such useful situations as the *Jovinus* and the *deacons* were men who were sure to act faithfully, since their election arose from public admiration, and their sole reward was public respect and an approving conscience.

One day in the spring, for that was generally the period at which they commenced their espousals, I was invited to be a witness to a marriage contract with the son of the President, and the daughter of the priest of the place where he resided. At early morning she was serenaded with bridal songs by the maidens, as the bridegroom was also by the young men, and soon we were assembled at her father's house, in number not less than twenty, consisting of the bride and bridegroom's relations, friends and neighbours, who each brought some present for the feast, consisting in what they considered as delicacies, together with flowers in garlands and little presents of useful articles. And when all were assembled, previous to the refection, we formed a circle into which the parents of both parties led their respective children, and having joined their hands, on which occasion they gave them a solemn blessing, a scribe read, from a parchment roll, the names of the bride and bridegroom, their ages, and the date of the time from which they had been betrothed, the names of their parents, and the date of the instrument, after which they were called on to sign their marriage contracts, and all who were present witnessed it, with the addition of their place of abode, age, and employment – after which the ceremony was concluded by a short admonition from the parish priest, and we all reassembled at the dinner table, at the head of which sat the bridegroom and at the foot the bride. Afterwards, for their meals were never long, there were several national dances by young children, dressed with garlands of flowers, who went round to the visitors and received little presents of sweet meats, concluding the whole with a hymn and chorus by themselves. And then we all dispersed to our several occupations or pleasures, the bride being attended by her nearest relations as well as those of the bridgroom to the habitation prepared for them, of which they took possession, and leave of their friends, and attendants, appearing the next day as married people.

On my return, I explained to my friend the difference of our mode from theirs, and expressed my surprize at its not appearing a religious ceremony, or being performed in the church.

"As we do not consider it as a sacrament, we see no necessity of calling a church together on these occasions. But surely you will allow it to be sufficiently religious, when solemnly contracted by so public an agreement, and so generally witnessed to on a public document, ever after placed in the archives of the commonwealth as a testimony of the union? We know of no sacraments but baptism, and the Lord's Supper, the first of which is always bestowed before the whole Christian congregation, twice; once after birth, and a second time when the young persons are dismissed from school, after a public examination in our catechism. With respect to the administration of the Eucharist, that always preceeds marriage, for at least one year every Sabbath day, and is taken monthly afterwards without exception, by every one, who has any proper sense of religion as a means to preserve the impression, the priest taking the cup and wafer for all, who acknowledge the acceptation of it kneeling, and openly assenting. For we do generally believe in transubstantiation, and are of opinion that if all literally partook of the cup and bread it would be a hindrance to the general receiving of it, by the unnecessary time it would take up, by the indelicacy of the operation, and above all, as real wine is never drank among us, by a violation of a sumptuary law."

"What then does the Priest drink," said I, "as a substitute?"

"A little honey and water," said he, "for as it is a consecrated form of commemoration of the death and suffering of Jesus for our sakes, the material is of little consequence to the spirit of the action, and if it was necessary to record the whole process of that solemn parting and injunction, we might, with like propriety, partake of the paschal lamb, and eat the passover — for that according to scripture must have preceeded our redemption."

As I had nothing to object to this reasoning, I desired him, if he had a copy, to put their whole liturgy into my hands, and having received one, very beautifully transcribed, as a present, I took it home with me, and set about examining its contents with no small degree of curiosity. For although I had now been long an inhabitant of the place, no one had particularly pressed me to adopt their creed, in all its parts. On the contrary, they seemed to wait patiently to see if their practical Christianity would not bring about in me a spontaneous conversion to their exterior rules and forms, on which they placed evidently much less value than on their general conduct in relation to charity.

The work consisted of a very few leaves, containing the Lord's prayer, the apostle's creed, the ten Commandments, and that law of love, which enjoins the love of God and man as absolutely necessary to salvation — the form of baptism according to the Roman Catholic ritual, and the form of prayer to be used at receiving the Lord's Supper — in which the rules were laid down by which the wafer should be consecrated, as well as the cup, and the necessary preparatory prayers, the substance of which evidently implied that the communicant verily and truly believed that when the priest received it for them, they all literally and truly received the spiritual body and blood of the Redeemer. This, except a few collects and a short litany, was all it contained.

The Gospels they read as well as the Psalms of David. Almost the whole of the Psalms indeed were chaunts, and sung, as well as others of the composition of their ablest scholars, at times, during even the operations of husbandry, and always at commencing and terminating religious worship. And although they had brought with them no rules for composition, their voices being in general good, they sang in parts as it were by a certain sympathy or affinity, such as one musical string receives from another in its octave, and formed often chords so harmonious that the mind in a transport embraced the associated tones. And for my own part I declare that whether from the distinctness with which they were pronounced or the sublimity of the poetry, no singing had ever before so much affected me as theirs often did.

But I shall not attempt to give the world their whole system of theology, as my stay in this blessed country unhappily did not afford me time to thoroughly examine it. Yet it must have been good, since it produced so much moral goodness, and had nothing in it of reserve or mystery, every member of society having received the same advantages of education. For here the service of God and man might with truth be said to be perfect freedom, their political and religious code being founded on one principle – the desire of arriving at truth alone. Rectitude in government, probity in dispensing the public wealth, temperance in the use of all things, were the leading features of their code. But infallibility was a term unknown among them, and annually they held a general council to revise their laws, and to reform any errors if such had crept into their practice – and in all their prayers *"Deliver us from evil"* was the leading feature.

During my short stay, it appeared to me that temperance, which was universally adopted, was the main spring of the happiness they enjoyed, not only diminishing the amount of necessary labour to sustain life, but by its good effects on the general health, and the support it afforded reason, no less by repelling the passions, than by inspiring cool and deliberate discussion on all debatable subjects.

"We consider intemperance," said my friend to me, as we were noticing an instance of it, in a child who had eaten too much for its stomach to bear, "as the great leading vice which overthrew our ancient churches in Asia – and we guard against its appearance here, with the utmost vigilance, by rendering it nearly impossible that property should be very unequal. We think it to be the parent of all the diseases that afflict human nature by hereditary contamination, and like other damning vices never mention it in our discourses from the pulpit or altar but with marks of abhorrence, *and images of terror*; or ever at all, but when absolutely wrung from us by necessity. For we think the display of debasing crimes within hearing of the innocent and good to be imprudent, and rather always paint in glowing colours the beauty of right action, which may lead to imitation, knowing that man is a creature often subdued by habit, and who may be corrupted by too great familiarity with evil images. The touch of impurity defiles – and the greatest happiness we enjoy is to be attributed to our ignorance of the corruptions of the heathens that surround us."

After this conversation I was careful on all occasions to avoid, in answering their enquiries, all relations of the horrors of what is called social life in cities at the present day, the sad source of penal laws, and valedictory ordinances, confining my discourses to subjects of useful improvement in education, the arts, and morals. For I knew they would have listened with disgust to pictures of war among people calling themselves Christians, as well as the mode of supporting such butchery by taxes leveyed alike on those who abetted and those who abhorred it – of the frauds by which commerce is supported, to obtain contaminating luxuries, and the coercions instituted to prevent them, together with oaths and penalties – in which church as well as state joined. Could I have defiled their ears with a relation of the iniquitous and disgusting practice of ecclesiastical or chancery courts of law, or laid on them the affliction of hearing that the inquisition and all the abuses of popery still existed? and that legislatures, after promoting crimes by neglecting to instruct the people, put them calmly to death in open day, and called it an example to others equally ignorant? No! But feeling the beauty of the system around me, and knowing that here I might learn but could not teach, I began seriously to think, if by conveying this picture to my countrymen I might not do good where it was wanted, instead of remaining for my own comfort and pleasure among a superior race of men who could gain no improvement from my example, and would condemn my principles as soon as they saw they were founded only on selfish and exclusive motives.

I therefore lost no time in laying my reflections before the *Jo-vinian* and his council, who saw at once, he said by them, that I had already imbibed their principles, by my offer to act up to them. "You no doubt," said he, "with your amiable qualities, might here form connections conducive to your individual happiness, and after your sufferings find some excuse for engaging in them. But man was not created we believe for his own sole enjoyment, and you no doubt embrace that conviction taught by adversity, and the sad pictures you have beheld in your extensive pilgrimages. But among all your sufferings and wrongs, those inflicted by the passions have been the cruellest. Yet like strong medicines they have purged your intellects, and a heart of flesh is substituted for one of stone. If our example has had its share in it, I rejoice inwardly, and thank God for it, and I therefore heartily embrace your proposal to leave us, whatever I may suffer by the privation of your society, friendship, and experience, and, if I may be allowed to advise, should rec-ommend your returning with our next salt cofila to the chieftan Foozo, accompanied by a well instructed missionary, there to aid his objects in an attempt to improve the condition of that little kingdom, and in the mean time to contrive some plan for joining a caravan of merchants who are trading towards Darfur, in which it is not unlikely, you will find a friend in the chief, whom we think our visits and open conduct have prepared for this experiment of civilization."

Of the candour, good sense, and friendship of this council I could entertain no doubt, and my heart told me, by its responsive beatings, that it was the best I could adopt. I therefore from that period abandoned all my golden dreams of a settlement among the *Jovinians* and indulged in other thoughts than those of mar-riage. I often pictured to myself the felicity attending my return to Europe, the knowledge I should have gained, the discoveries I should have to report, the important news I should convey of the progress of Christianity on the African continent. Then again I figured to myself the joy of my remaining relations at my return, but above all the possibility that her, for whose beloved remem-brance I had endured so much, might yet be even in a convent recalling my memory. I figured to myself our meeting after so long a separation and relating with complacent minuteness our several adventures and griefs – the mutal sacrifice, the mutual affection, our sorrows, and our joys. And then I used to resolve that I too would devote my remaining hours to a religious life, and make the cloister my home – from whence to send abroad my systems of reform, and teach the wise, by the example of the simple hearted, to be good, and to be happy.

But when, awaking from these pleasing trains of thoughts, I found myself as it were alone in a wide world, and could figure to myself no probable means of ever returning, I felt of all men the most miserable, and in one of these reveries it was that Stefanus came to my chamber, gently lifting the latch, and invited me to a conference then sitting, where the subject of a mission had been decided on to the African chief and to which I was invited as a coadjutor and superintendant. The moment was favourable, and I made no hesitation, on my entrance among the elders and deacons assembled, to accept the office – so that every thing was soon settled as to my fitting out and rank in the mission.

CHAPTER XVI

In this and every other movement, I found them prompt when once decided, and it was not long before having, with tears in my eyes, taken my leave of such men as I never can expect again to encounter, we were on our route to the Chief Foozo and prepared for our pious enterprize with firmness and devotion.

As our route lay through the same places, there is little worth relating. In a country where inebriety has never entered, and war is not known, few must ever be the disorders of society arising from passions inflamed, or resentments long nourished, and nothing but the failure of a harvest could disturb that hilarity, which seemed innate among these felicitous beings. So that we arrived at the salt depot without meeting one obstacle or accident, so well were we provided for by the natives. On our arrival, we were met by all the family of Stefanus, who welcomed us by a chaunt, and an offering of cakes, fruits, and flowers, each placed in elegant little carriers made of cane, and carried by young children, who were taught to value the honour less than the hospitality. By all we were welcomed with open arms, and led through their gardens instead of the highway, to shew us what improvements they had completed in our absence. To produce the greatest abundance of human food in the smallest space was one of the objects of rivalry, the result of which was extreme neatness and order, for not a weed could be found in *those* enclosures which were most successful, an effect always observable, I have remarked, where industry prevails in all countries alike, and that very love of order again producing not only advantages in point of economy but even beauty and elegance, of which it is the legitimate parent.

"You tell me," said one to me, "of sculpture and painting, its grandeur and imposing impression. Of these we are ignorant, but we feel something like what you speak of even in the agriculturist's cottage, when we see on the walls symmetrically arranged his well constructed and daily polished tools, suspended with tasteful simplicity, and nothing around him out of repair. We even think where this correct feeling for propriety exists it carries with it an external certificate of the purity of the owner's habits and calm reflections, a test of his improved understanding."

Nor was it long before I witnessed the effects he described, realized in the habitation of my conductor, whose chambers were evidently constructed from proportional parts of the cube, judiciously applied to length, breadth and altitude; a harmony of proportional parts we might call it, executed by a mind naturally susceptible of a mathematical impression, from intuitive taste, whilst the apertures for giving light and egress were geometrically constructed, so as not to offend the eye by any disporportion or excess – the floor and walls of a sobered even tint, the curve of the ceiling taking so agreeable a segment of a circle as to insure in appearance its stability – and the ornaments sparingly, but richly invented. But one thing which highly delighted me was that at a moderate height, all round the room, on a narrow bracket, the females of the family had placed a row of small, elegantly formed vessels, each of which contained, in water, a single specimen of the flowers of the season, or ferns, or grasses, or tender branches selected for their freshness and verdure – at seeing which I could not avoid remarking the genuineness of these rudiments of refined art, and assuring my friend that they were not far from its utmost perfection as capable of enjoying all its satisfactory results, on a scale at once natural and refined.

Add then to this imposing effect so easily procured, the sight of real symmetry in the persons I was introduced to on my entrance, the graceful simplicity of their demeanour, and the choral chaunt which broke out on our arrival, whose harmonies were redoubled by the reverberation of its chords, from the smooth, and well polished surfaces of the walls, and you will not be surprized that I preferred the impression made on my mind to any I had experienced in the lofty and splendid drawing rooms of princes.

When our mutual congratulations were ended, and the object of our return explained, refreshments were brought in, after which we sat down in groups on the ottomans of matting that encircled the walls, and either reposed or conversed during the heat of the morning, inhaling the delicious odours produced form the expanded flowers which so naturally ornamented the border of the apartment.

For my own part I slept, not alone from fatigue, and a saturated appetite, but from a sort of happy content and carelessness for every thing but the present enjoyments. And when I awoke I found myself surrounded by my friend and his wife and two eldest daughters, to whom he had been he said relating my adventures at the capital, so that now they were all as well acquainted with my conduct and destination as I could be myself. And I saw, in their kind looks, how much it had increased their former friendship and familiarity – as a proof of which, the mother, taking me by the hand, confessed that during our absence she had formed a wish on our return to endeavour to ally me to one of her daughters (alluding to one not then present) and whom I had never seen, provided I could make up my mind to let my wanderings end with them. Neither in that case had she much apprehension of a refusal, as the maiden was the flower of her flock and equal to any of her children, in mildness, modesty, person and talents. "But now," said she, "she must, like the rest, consider you as her friend and brother, and I as a lost but esteemed son."

To such unsuspecting liberality, what could I reply? but that I should feel the misfortune which prevented our alliance, when all hopes of ever being again associated were by my superior duties prevented. And in thus expressing myself, there was indeed no falsehood or flattery, for I will not deny that a gleam of reflexion came then across my mind, that but for my positive engagements and duties, such an arrangement might have contributed to my lasting felicity. For I had, on my first interview with this charming family, noticed with admiration the maiden alluded to, and felt the full influence of her irresistible charms as well as interesting and amiable manners. Neither have I to blush when I confess this momentary deviation from my first inextinguishable attachment; for what mariner after long and perilous voyages, when cast on shore on an unknown paradise, will not give way to nature, and pause to admire? forgetting in his transport his native home? Besides, it is not always in man to refuse certain for uncertain happiness, and

I well knew that my present undertaking was sure to be attended by both difficulty and danger, and that I had need of all the stern virtues taught me by *Lycas*, to put it in execution; whilst the result must be a life of anxiety, terminated by a sacrifice of all its lawful pleasures, and its end solitary retirement, accompanied, I doubted not, by the approbation of my own conscience, and the hope of a blessed reaction, in that state, which no man can describe, and only genuine faith can feel or imagine.

But a truce with reflections; we were now about to enter into action, and we lost no time in preparing for the undertaking; like faithful believers we girded our loins for the combat. In a few short days, all was ready at the store, and we parted affectionately, but without painful ceremony, from this intelligent family on the frontier, with one of whom I left a sacrifice easier to feel than to describe.

As every undertaking among this decided thinking people was conducted with perfect order, we met with nothing to disturb it but the common occurrences of all travellers, and arrived safe at the hermit's cell in the beautiful valley, who was now no more to be seen following his daily duties and charities, but, in his stead, a young novitiate attended us who was to join our caravan after we had taken the necessary refreshment there.

I went immediately to his honoured cell, now solitary and gloomy; the fountain flowed as usual, his pallet was there, and his seat; nature was unchanged, for the birds sang sweetly, and rich were the chequered shades with the beams of the evening. But the miraculous machine, the animal font of thought, which flowed with wisdom from the mouth, now forever closed, of our admired friend, had disappeared, and the fragments were deposited before the door of his cell, in a grave which he had dug with his own hands, as a premonition of his approaching end. As I stood over the depository of his bones, I dropped a tear for his mortal part once so active, ever so useful to others, so honoured, so beloved. But the intelligent soul, the aspiring mind, the humble, patient reason, where shall we find that or its counterparts? "Thy body is mixed now with the sods of the valley. Its work is done, its sufferings are over, it is withered and dissolved! The elements from which it was formed receive it again, nothing is lost – but where is thy etherial part now silent to all our enquiries? Does it ascend to a purer atmosphere, or hover round us awhile ere it ascends towards the empyreum whence it came, the 'Harmony of exulting mental light'!"

Such were my reflections, on viewing the few traces left of what had been that compound being man, chained by generation to a changing form and doomed to fourscore years of residence with contesting elements, in sad probation, earthly toil, and mental sufferings! And the effect was a deep submission to my future duties, and His will who placed me here – so that it gave a fresh spring to my, already formed, resolution of giving up self and studying to be beneficial to mankind.

"Come," I said at length, to my friend Stefanus who with me was musing on the disappearance of a being refined by age and reflection, "let us on to our work. Every thing beside is insignificant; we are all alike merged in a material covering, capable of good or evil, of happiness or degradation. It is the will of the supreme; let us obey his commands and be at peace."

The next day we all advanced on our journey in serious order, cheered with the reflection that our object was honourable, and although the harvest might be distant, we were preparing the ground for good seed. And thus at length we came in sight, once more, of the dwellings of these half civilized Africans under the influence of their King Foozo.

I shall not swell my narrative, with an account of some little accidents which impeded our progress on our descent from the mountains, but let me not forget to state that these generous people had, by a vote of their assembly, ordered that a considerable portion of the provisions was to be placed at my private disposal as the means to support me during my residence among the tribe of whom Foozoo was the name of the chief, or to enable me to reach some European port, if I decided to return. The same attention was also paid to the necessities of the missionary who accompanied me, and who was to be left behind until the next year's expedition – at which time, if such was his choice, he was to remain to promote the instruction of the heathens.

The country was well wooded and very grand to the eye as we approached our destination; a country full of mountain torrents bursting from rocks among forests could not fail to be so, especially as the season was after summer, and, of course, the springs moderately full. Neither did I ever in my travels behold so many delightful waterfalls or lovely irregular rills, as then irrigated this neglected country, whose innumerable fountains replenished the White river and head of the Nile as well as other rivers to the South to all unknown, except by report, of which the Niger was one spoken of generally by travellers in this region.

CHAPTER XVII

It was in one of these most enchanting spots, under groves of the tallest forest trees, near a fall of water, whose sounds were music to our ears, and afforded a delicious refreshment to our senses, that we made our last halt, preparatory to entering the district we were bound to; our animals relieved of their burthens, scattered around us feasting at leisure on the freshest herbage, and all, with hymns of praise, returning thanks to the omnipresent God of light and life for our safe arrival, when a man, whose countenance bespoke the effects of some sore malady, ill clad, with a raucous voice, and great debility of utterance, came suddenly among us, and, bending to the earth with profound humiliation, implored an audience of the chief of our band. He stated, with tears and the profoundest expressions of grief, that he came as ambassador from Foozo the chief of his nation, being himself a priest, to relate to us that troubles and afflictions of a most awful nature had been inflicted on his countrymen since our last visit, commencing with an unprovoked war with a neighbouring district, which war had been followed by a famine, and that by a pestilential disease which now raged among the survivers. And knowing that this was the period when we might be expected to visit them with our provisions, he had been waiting some days on the road to instruct us in the danger of coming among them, and to entreat us to forward, through him and his companions, who were convalescents, the relief usually bartered; assuring us of the largest and best return, as the article we sought was, in consequence of their diminished numbers, become of little value to them.

I need not say how cordially we received his generous proposals, or how liberally we supplied the immediate wants of him and his followers, who kept aloof as under his direction to do so – and that we lost no time in lading him a string of asses with abundance of corn, speeding his return with alacrity, and assuring him we should remain at our station until every thing relative to our business was finally settled.

When they were gone, we held a conference, at which all were present, as to what our course ought to be under all circumstances, and the result was, that we had a duty to perform towards these people, which their present conditions rendered more imperative than ever, and that we should now find it less difficult to impress on their rude minds their true interests, from the effects of their

sufferings; that no danger on our parts should deter us from avail-
ing ourselves of the happy opportunity of serving them, and that
myself, our chief, and one more attendant should, after settling
the usual transactions of barter, go among them, as physicians for
both soul and body, sending back the rest of our cofila with the
goods, and to explain the reasons of their so hasty return.

Many insisted on accompanying us in this work of Christian
charity, but we contended that to us alone belonged the honour,
and reward, not doubting that, under their present depressed state,
we should be willingly and hospitably received. And so indeed it
turned out, for the chief came himself to bring us in, and with him
a sorrowful train of people, among whom were many women and
priests, who now all approved of the councils we had formerly
given him to reform his subjects, adopt agriculture and arts, give
up the slave trade, and receive Christianity; for which these severe
inflictions lately suffered seemed to have prepared the way, by
softening their hearts, as they one and all admitted that they had
merited them by their irregularities and contempt of justice. That
we should stay with them under such circumstances seemed to
excite their wonder and affection, and we were ushered into the
courts of the palace as men of God come to bestow wisdom and
piety on them, with great ceremony, having a separate house and
establishment allotted us, and guarded from all intrusion from the
ignorant natives, Foozoo himself only being allowed to visit us with
his prime minister.

The next day he came alone, and seating himself thus addressed
us with great seriousness. "When it pleased the supreme god to
send among us the followers of his Prophet, to convert us from
our idolatry to the serpent, our fathers were not backward in sub-
mitting to the divine will, and we became believers in the unseen
deity who is said to be everywhere present. We worshipped blocks
of wood no more, but we did not discard altogether our magicians
or their charms, the Fetice. To you *Jovinians* I owed the discovery
of a more rational faith, in a redeemer, the sent Son of God, not
his prophet only but his son. Those disclosures made a strong
impression on my heart, and that of some of my leading people,
but I thought the populace too rude to receive such doctrines, and
waited the time when some of you should arrive and commence
teaching them both domestic habits and even letters, being opposed
in council by the wealthy part of my subjects, who feared lest,
becoming well instructed, the lower orders would discern the fallacy

of our system of governing them by their passions, and throw off our yoke with turbulence. Your religion however is of so mild a character, and so benevolent, as your presence under our calamity proves at this interview, that I have now no doubt when proposed by me and our chiefs it will be accepted, and bring with it those fruits of felicity you so evidently enjoy. Accept therefore my adherence to its doctrines, and teach all its precepts to our people, since I have been by you fully satisfied that I govern only for their advantage and that Christians will never refuse their willing support to such a mode of government, since it proposes only their security for persons and property, and yields the same to those whose wisdom and humanity naturally place them in the arduous situation of guides and directors."

To this open evidence of the impression already made by our predecessors was added that of his companion, who assured us, that the most ignorant and turbulent of the population having been swept away by war and disease, the remainder were looking up to the chiefs for directions, and ready implicitly to obey their orders, and thus our introduction had commenced with a happy augury. The first thing we recommended was to provide hospitals for the sick, which, under precautions, we attended ourselves; the next to employ the healthy in preparing land for corn cultivation, of which we were both able and willing to direct the form of the necessary instruments; next to destroy the infected houses; then to build others on a more habitable plan; and lastly to construct a place of worship and for a school in which the *Gospel* was to supersede the *Koran* – of which indeed they knew but little, and its good precepts we took care to preserve as far as they related to the duties of humanity and the love of God, incorporating them with our own, from which indeed many of them had been derived. And this gave us great weight in the commencement of our introduction of the new covenant.

In a word, providence so prospered our labours, that before the end of the first year of our stay among them, we had established most of our benevolent reforms, and among the chiefs found willing proselytes and teachers, whose authority gave weight to their new doctrines, and importance to this reduced community, so that, every thing advancing towards a Christian establishment, the *Jovinians* had even proposed an incorporation of some more of their members, and the king had consented to be considered only as their president.

Thus situated, and our object happily attained, I began to think of what ought to be my own proceedings. To settle with the *Jovinians*, however agreeable, seemed only a selfish determination. To stay here was now unnecessary, as I had already contributed from my little stock of science all that could be useful to a people who required only the arts necessary to subsistence, and who had an example before them of the inestimable importance of mutual aid, mutual affection to render man as happy as this world can make him. To tempt the desert therefore now seemed to be my task, and the trial of my sincerity in the profession of a faith which has no other end than the welfare of mankind. And although I did not flatter myself that, even if I arrived safely in my native city of Venice, I should be able to stem the current of bad manners so prevalent there, yet it seemed an indispensable duty to attempt it, and above all, in that hope, to shew to my countrymen, that Christ has not abandoned His church, or left His divine doctrines without a testimony of their efficacy when practiced through a *faith* founded on the pure principles of *brotherly love*; thereby laying by my narrative, however slightly, a foundation on which to build by degrees a reform, at least among the afflicted and humble. For as drops wear the stone, it has ever been my decided opinion, that the heart of man is only instructed and softened by degrees, and that the course of amendment can only be laid by reiterated reflection, example, and the divine aid.

It now therefore became necessary to consult Foozoo in the proper steps to be taken to render probable my success, and I accordingly took an early opporunity of explaining to him my intentions. "To go back with the tribe," he said, "who introduced you to my little dominion would only be, for any thing we know, to meet with the same difficulties you formerly encountered, and I should rather advise you to bend your steps towards Darfur, a nation of the Great Desert, which affords a sort of central communication to all the caravans that traverse it, and from whence you may take your departure in that direction which best suits you. It is a great undertaking and worthy of your principles, but I do not despair of finding the means to forward your noble design, by means of some of those wandering tribes who occasionally visit us to procure a supply of salt. They are Mahometans, but many of them men of probity and, if once pledged, will fulfil their engagements to the letter as well as spirit. We must therefore make you an agent to traffic in our staple article of which we can afford you abundance without any loss to ourselves, and consign it to you as our factor, in which casae you will be quite sure of a safe conduct to *Darfur* and when there will, by the sale of it, find sufficient means of both living and continuing your journey. If you leave us, it will be to us all a subject of regret, but you have too well taught me my duties not to induce me to forward every just desire of your heart, for my own sake, for yours, and for the advantage of others. Go therefore in peace by the first favourable opportunity. And if we never are destined to hear of each other in this life, let us hope that in futurity we shall be permitted to renew that friendship which commenced in esteem, continued through mutual good offices, and which will never be erased from my memory."

So speaking he hurried from me, evidently to suppress those tears that already impeded his voice, and my own emotions were too much like his to allow me to detain him.

Nothing could be more suitable to reason than his proposal or more likely to forward my objects, or more generous than the means he offered to accomplish them. On this all were agreed among those to whom they were communicated, and I now only waited for a convenient season and opportunity to commence my arduous undertaking.

These Africans, though rude and ignorant of most things beyond their own district, were men, and as such their minds were, like others, accessible to acts of kindness, of which we were beginning to reap the fruits abundantly; for every one shewed a willingness to contribute his aid in my assistance. One offered a camel, another a young and vigorous ass, a third salt, a fourth corn, and although it was not necessary I should accept of these offerings, since the good will and abilities of Foozo had provided me from his own stores sufficiently, yet I felt rejoiced by all these manifestations of good will, as an evidence that our doctrines had made their due impression, and that the result of their heavy chastizement would be salutary and effective. My principles also were now confirmed, I had braced up my mind to the task of dedicating my life to the benefit of my species. No longer a slave to selfish enjoyments, I was emancipated from fear, my health stable from temperance, my strength increased from exertion, and my soul at peace.

Thus fortified, I hailed with joy the arrival of a small cofila of Arabs, and was doubly rejoiced to find them, providentally, the same company who had originally conducted me to this mountain pass. The same motives induced them now to leave the road, viz.

to procure a supply of salt, "but," Fazzan added, very affectionately, "I also had some curiosity to enquire what had become of a man who to me seemed unlike all I had ever encountered, and for whom from your honest, open conduct, I could not but conceive a regard and interest."

CHAPTER XVIII

When Foozo communicated to him my intentions, he shook his head, and after remaining silent for some time, as deeply considering it, thus spoke.

"You are one of the most extraordinary men I ever met with. When we first became acquainted you were wandering the desert on the borders of a river that we Bedouins, even when in numbers, fear to approach except at certain seasons. You had then with you only one black slave, who seemed to follow you from pity and affection, but that we prevented you, would soon have seen the end of your journey and your lives. He from a love of country, and because he could not fall into a lower situation, left you, when you resolved to take our protection, and to proceed on a scheme the wildest I ever heard of. Your confiding conduct produced in me so much esteem that I would willingly have united you, had you embraced the law of the Koran, to my family. You refused even this generous offer, and chose to be left a stranger among the wild race where I now find you. But with them you could not stay, and sought a people whom report says are all Giaours and inhabitants of the most desolate region on earth. You discover their abodes as by miracle, join them, adopt their manners, yet leave them also, and return to this desolated tribe of Africans – and now again wish to embark on new difficulties and tempt the distant lands of Darfur.

"To them no doubt, if you have any merchandise suitable to such a market, I can direct your steps, but where will be the end, my child, of all these wanderings? At Darfur, even if you accomplish the journey, you will find only selfish merchants, slave dealers, and an arbitrary government, who will rob you of your gains, and impede your rambling progress. Once more therefore accept my hospitality; we rove sufficienctly free I trust to suit your inclinations, I esteem your talents, and intelligent character, your love of enterprise is not unsuitable to some occasions which occur among ourselves; we like brave men. You have been tried, and evinced

your courage. Lay aside therefore, at my entreaty, the vain sug-
gestions of your imagination. I will do everything for you your
heart can desire, you shall be my son. All my family esteem you.
Come then once more among us, and addict yourself to our habits;
we ask only your attachment, your probity and your alliance."

Here he paused and embraced me with open arms, and I will
confess, from my former knowledge of his noble character, and
real regard, as well as obligation, I should, had not his faith stood
in the way, have felt inclined at any rate to incorporate myself in
his tribe, had not higher motives swayed me – such as I could only
communicate to him by saying my country called for my services,
and that, however distant, that and my family had claims superior
to all others.

"Why then," said the sagacious Arab, "did you leave it to search
for that happiness which can only be found in domestic society and
the increase of progeny? But you are a singular man, and we must
not I see reason from your example to our race. God is great, he
has had men widely differing. Come then, I will again do everything
in my power to serve you. Your faith in your own Prophet, and
contempt of ours, does not seem to me so criminal as it does to my
followers; I will even conceal that weakness, you can pray silently
when we pray aloud. But take care of the Darfurians if you get
there; they make no allowances, and to be known to be a Christian
may subject you to be massacred by the populace."

In fine, this good old man took me under his especial care once
more, and being provided with several articles suitable to the trade
of Darfur, we left the mountains together, attended by his servants,
who were generously paid for their trouble, and I entered a second
time a Bedouin camp among people who knew and regarded me,
his whole family coming out to receive me as if I had constituted
a part of it, particularly that amiable daughter to whom he had
once proposed to betroth me, and whose modest demeanour and
blushes indicated even something more than esteem. Of the pri-
mitive manners of these inhabitants of the desert it was impossible
not to approve and admire. The simplicity of their lives, the sin-
cerity of their professions, their activity, their temperance, their
courage, I can vouch for, as well as sincerity of religious faith, which
they so publicly maintain; in which few of us have the consistency
to imitate them. But there are recreant tribes of whom the reverse
of all this is notorious, robbers, merciless and cruel; these are the
exception not the rule, and are avoided by the honest Arabians of

family with abhorrence. We entered the flat country even in fear ourselves of these marauders.

"I can only conduct you safely," said Foozo, "to a certain point. There I must leave you, with your guides whom I will carefully provide, to pursue your way to the capital you are bound to, for I never mix with the traffic in slaves, some cofila of which you will probably be obliged to join to get there, and with whom you must make your agreement to pass towards Europe by Fez, Morocco, or some other of the many routes of the merchants. I abhor the trade, which is connected with every atrocity; my family slaves constitute my support, and I provide for theirs; one faith, one feeling unites us, and many of them are admitted to my blood.

"But report says you Europeans tear them from their relations to work them like cattle, give them no instruction as to moral conduct or religion, abuse their females and make drudges of their mixed breed, even sell them (the spurious offspring of their own loins) to others, and work many to death. If this be true, which *Allah* forbid, some grievous misfortune will follow it, for they are men like ourselves, and under the care of the supreme – but after what I have witnessed of your gentle temper and sincerity, I will never believe this; and after all, God is just!"

The first days of our journey were all alike; we were descending the River *Bar* by the western banks and had many tributary streams to ford, and many precautions to take to preserve the herds and flocks, but patience, numbers, and interest overcame every difficulty, and I saw no difference on these occasions between the master and the bond slave.

"Man lives not," said Fazzan to me on one of these trying occasions, "more dependant on the existence of the sun, than on his fellow creatures; let his rays be withdrawn, and all creation dies; let our fellows refuse us their aid and we perish. God has so willed it!" "God is good!" was his phrase on all difficulties, and this descendant of Ishmael might I think have vied with any of the Patriarchs for resignation. I loved the man so well before we parted for this and other virtues that had he been my father I could not have quitted him with more regrets.

He told me he was of the ancient tribe of *Mahmid*, who have long occupied the borders of the Kingdom of *Darfur* towards *Kardifan* – raising stock for sale, such as camels, horses, bullocks, and sheep, and occasionally visited *Cobbe*, a great mercantile mart, to dispose of these and salt, an article of considerable value to the *Joovians*, to whom, and to other chiefs, they occasionally paid tribute for the use of lands for grazing, and annually made excursions to the mountain sources of the *Bar il abaid* for salt, ivory and for herbage, passing at no small risk the country of free and independant Negroes, many of whom, like those I was left by them with, were half pagans, and very warlike, collecting slaves for the traders by force but that none of his family were slave dealers, excepting in the purchase of such as were absolutely necessary to their existence, whom they always treated as their own children, and valued in proportion to their services, restoring them often to their parents and to freedom after their deaths, and in many instances, uniting them to their children on accepting Islamism. Neither do they use any violence in their conversion, even when Christians of Egypt or Coptic stewards, among whom there are in *Darfur* many of honest character and well versed in accounting, far safer to trust than the natives, "and one of whom, an old and respected men," said the good Arab, "I mean to place you with at *Cobbe* in whom you may confide, for, as a Christian merchant, you would by no means be safe with a bigoted Darfurian. For," said he "I see, if only on your account, I must accompany you there or send one of my sons, and as soon as we arrive at our last encampment under the government of the Sultan, I will select some salable articles and introducing you as my agent going to *Kahira*, or hit on some contrivances to forward your escape from a kingdom, by no means fit for the residence of such a man as you are."

That this noble Arab kept his promise no one will doubt, who has noticed our first connection, and it was not long before, passing through the country as his dependent, I found myself in the centre of Darfur at *Cobbe*, and lodged with all my merchandice in the house of an old Coptic Christian, who, having been long resident and highly esteemed for his probity, enjoyed universal respect and protection. His house like all those of that country was enclosed in a considerable area, with a fence of thorns and a mud wall within, where low rooms, whose walls were clay and the covering the same supported by rafters and brushwood, were constructed at a small expence, suitable to every use, and scattered according to convenience within the enclosure, their doors a hewn plank, their floors the soil, covered by very elegant mats of which their couches were chiefly composed. Under this man's protection I enjoyed great privileges, was introduced to the *Sultan* to make my presents, and in his company several times, during my stay, visited different parts of the country; which, although arid, possessed much grand scenery, some elevated mountains, and might be compared, from the sterility which surrounded it, to an oasis of the desert.

Having acquainted him with my former travels, I found he was also an observing traveller, he had spent much time at *Thebes*, and seen with admiration its stupendous antiquities; that he had, or pretended to have, some knowledge of the hieroglyphic language – and one day, after we had been speaking on this subject, he took me into a small building near his habitation, where he said he would shew me a monument long preserved with care by his ancestors, who had a superstitious veneration for it on account of its representing, as they imagined, the true symbol of the ark of Noah, and which they had extracted from a royal tomb at Thebes. "But although," said he, "this invaluable relict of antiquity has descended to me from ancestors who were once perhaps idolators, and is, I believe, inestimable from its workmanship and preservation, I have never ventured to shew it publicly, but keep it in a chamber which I consider as my chapel covered carefully with a pall; and as we have no church here, and are few, none but Christians are allowed to enter, and the implements we use in our ceremonies are always carefully deposited, within this Soros."

At this relation my curiosity was greatly excited, and it was with no small pleasure I heard him one day say, "Although you are not a believer of our community, I shall have no scruple to unveil to your eyes this relict of antiquity, because you, like us, admit the authenticity of the Mosaic account of the history of the world. Come then, it is now night, and all is quiet around us. Follow me, and satisfy your curiosity."

He then took a lamp, and conducted me softly to a little door way connected with his own chamber of repose, and removing a plank from the wall ushered me into a little cell of about twelve feet square where was an altar and a crucifix, in a painted niche. And in the middle of the floor, on a fine mat, and covered by another, was a wooden sarcophagus, large enough to hold a man at full length. It was of sycamore like the mummy cases, and beautifully coloured within and without, representing at the bottom a hieroglyphical figure of Osiris surrounded by innumerable figures on the sides on a white ground, representing birds, fish and animals, included between grooved lines, to me unintelligible, but which he assured me he understood well the recondite meaning of; that they contained the sacred history of the antediluvians – and that from his knowledge of the ancient Coptic he could easily comprehend them.

The Soros he said was the ark, hollow within and of the form of a coffer or coffin, and the internal paintings were intended to represent a calendar of events previous to the flood as well as the object of their worship. But the external delineations related to that sad event, and according to the rude style of the revival of arts by *Ham* the son of Noah exhibited that catastrophe. In one compartment there was represented by zigzag lines water, and men drowning in it, whilst others, not yet covered by it, exhibited antediluvians dancing as regardless of the danger. But the most extraordinary picture was at the broad end outside. It comprized a square or plane moulding dotted all over with very small punctures, which he assured me represented the air or atmosphere, the interior of which was covered by descending zigzag lines intended to express water falling from the skies, and which covered every part of the space within the frame, except a portion, on which floated a boat, supported beneath by a protecting power, who with outstretched arms sustained it, being himself beneath the waters and consequently invisible. In the boat is the sacred Beatle or Sun, adored by two deities which might be *Isis and* Osiris, to the right of which are three men, the sons of Noah, with thrones above their heads, and on the left are five more persons which are Noah, his wife and the three wives of his sons.

This Beatle extends his fore feet upwards, supporting a large disk, representing the globe of the earth, which is connected to a figure of a man, an Ethiopian, who springs from the head of a female figure with the tail of a fish who is also descending through the waters, and whose fingers, held up in adoration, are formed of zigzag lines to shew that she is the genius of humidity and pours herself out.

The figure of the Ethiopian represented, he said, the human race as preserved and again connected with the earth. And all this, he declared, was explained by nine hieroglyphical figures enclosed in the circle created by the curve of the fishy tail of the female genius of the waters.

The two prows of the boat ended in lotus flowers, and the whole is an engraved picture, whose lines are filled up with some blue mineral colour.

How far this old Coptic merchant read these hieroglyphicks by the aid of his own language I cannot pretend to say, but his explanation seemed probable, and he added that he spoke from a very ancient tradition, and that the whole of the Egyptian monuments were emblematical pictures. His opinion also was that the ark rested on the sandy countries which extend over Nubia and Egypt, and that the temples of the Theban deserts are constructed from a recollection of the works of the same kind of the antediluvians, whose language was doubtless connected with such a measure of art as was then known in the world, the invention probably of Tubal Cain and his descendants, for what other prototype could they have had recourse to, and there is reason to believe *Ham* revived the ancient idolatry, the adoration of the sun and moon, together with the fixed stars.

To find a man, in the Sudan country, in the midst of the deserts, who, among Mahometans of the most illiberal class, was by profession a Christian, and protected, greatly surprized me. But he explained all these anomalies by relating the history of his family, which was, that when, as Nazareens, they were proscribed during a persecution, being then at the head of the Coptic priesthood at Thebes, they fled, and commenced merchants with the nations to the south, and having acquired wealth in the country he now was established in, they settled at *Cobbe in Darfur* under the protection of the Sultans, to whom, as general merchants, they had become so serviceable, that a peculiar privilege had been granted them to exercise their own religious rites in private, on paying a small tribute. But under such circumstances, being proscribed from attempting to make converts, except of their slaves, they had declined in numbers, and now consisted of a very small body, among which he, as chief, retained their traditions, and faithful records, on papyri, together with the language of their sacred books, derived from the writings of the patriarchs and prophets of the Hebrews.

"Am I then to understand," said I, "that by means of these languages you read the hieroglyphick sentences inscribed on the monuments of the Thebaid?"

At hearing this he smiled, and, setting down the lamp with which he had been illuminating the ark to shew me some of the exterior engravings, replied, "No such thing. We only view the Egyptian hierogylphicks as pictures representing events of their history, and principles of their worship, together with records of political events. But we do not pretend to decypher them, without an alphabet. Even if they were a written language, it was probably a sacred one, only accessible to their priesthood, from whose communications it is likely the picture I have been describing originated. And we preserve it with care rather as a monument of our ancestors, than from any hope of ever being able to read its inscriptions by the aid of our own language, although a great many of its roots must have been derived from the vulgar Egyptian. And to what end should we search out their meaning, since a complete knowledge of their sculptures could only bring us to be more acquainted with their idolatry? Idolatry, with which they have infected Greece and India, and to put an end to which, Christ was revealed to the only nation that had preserved a knowledge of a spiritual creator."

And thus it was I became satisfied that the secret of the hieroglyphick writing was a vain endeavour with our present means of enquiry, and that even its pictures could only be explained by ingenious conjecture, or oral tradition handed down by Christian converts who abhorred their religious ceremonies.

Still these vast monuments of art are interesting as exhibiting its early attainments, derived no doubt from the ingenuity of these talented men who lived before the flood, whose knowledge of the arts of painting, sculpture and architecture appears to have been founded on plane geometry alone. And the progress of the fine arts can evidently be traced back to their principles, as well as the disposition of mankind, to this day, to vie with each other in erecting temples to the deity or first cause, whom all acknowledge as the being to whom all hearts are open, "all desires known, and from whom no secrets are hidden".

And now being thoroughly satisfied, from the candour of this man's communications, that his heart contained no guile, I opened mine familiarly to him, narrating my adventures and soliciting his advice with respect to my European expedition.

"You are come hither," said he "as the mercantile agent of the honest Bedouin and must depart with the next caravan to *Kahira* as mine; for here were you to reside all your days there would be no possibility of propagating those doctrines which you call pure Christianity. Nothing is listened to here that does not promise gain, and your *Jovinians* were they to appear with their philosphical precepts would be torn to pieces.

"The law of the strongest reigns here as among wild animals; men who live by ensnaring and selling their fellow creatures and who consider fraudulent dealings as a proof of talent, and the doctrines of the Koran as the word of God, will not easily countenance the divine precepts of the Gospel, under any form, still less in that of *disinterested love*, a self sacrfice. You are an enthusiast for promulgation, or you would never have quitted such a people as you have left. For my own part I must own, if what you relate be not founded on prejudice or partiality, I should be very glad to exchange the dangerous and dependant state of life we lead here in Darfur for such a home, and such noble associations. And if our mutual friend Fazzan will insure me a safe conduct, such as he has procured for you, I do not know, being now devoid of family, if I should not try to escape with the remains of my fortune, to a spot where I might be sure to die in peace."

With such conversations we passed the hour of noon under a canopy of cotton cloth supported by four sticks within the enclosure of the mansion, and it was agreed that, my merchandise being disposed of by the Copt along with that of the Arab, I should depart for Kahira as agent to the Christian merchants and settle the account there.

After this affair was concluded, I observed great agitation in the Arab chief (strong expressions of regard), and at parting he could scarcely conceal his tears. He gave me his solemn benediction, with cordial embraces, and his last words were – "May Allah prosper you, honest Christian, you have cured me forever of my prejudices against your sect."

The next morning I rose early to wait on my benefactor and friend, and to my astonishment found he had departed in the night, leaving behind a letter for me, in which, after paying me many undeserved compliments, he relinquishes his share of the merchandise to me, saying, he left it as a father's portion although I had resolved not to be his son, and to shew me that an Arab would not be outdone in disinterestedness by any one. When I returned home to my host and shewed it to him, he was under no surprize. "It is like the man," said he, "I have known him perform many such acts. We must make no distinction of faith among noble minds. God alone can judge the heart!"

The sales were very advantageous, and I found myself soon possessed of good bills upon Kahira sufficient to enable me to travel from thence to my home with every convenience. But I will not trouble my readers with every particular of my journey under the escort of a considerable caravan augmented by one from Fez – with which the writers of travels have entertained the world already. Suffice it to say that our route to Dongala on the Nile was through a country always exposed to danger, but afterwards embarking in

ॐ ॐ a Cangia with some pilgrims who were going to Mecca, I after the usual interruptions, arrived safe at that capital City.

When I parted from the intelligent and humane Copt, I made him suitable presents from purchases made in the market of European goods, both for himself and the Sultan to obtain a safe
ॐ Firman; for these petty sovereigns of the desert, paying tribute, like to assume the manners of Constantinople, and thus we severally fulfilled our duties of benevolence, for although what I had been furnished with by my Jovinian friends cost them little, in that distant market, it availed me much, and enabled me with ease to accomplish a journey, under adverse circumstances nearly impossible.

Among other kind attentions, the merchant presented me with a Negro lad from his own household, an orphan, generally liked from his cheerfulness and docile disposition. Treating him with
ॐ kindness, he soon became attached to my interests and was easily fashioned to virtuous habits and by good instruction, in after life, became intrinsically useful both to himself and to me.

Thus provided with a good camel driver, and three young animals to carry ourselves and necessary provisions, I accompanied the caravan, disembarrassed from the care of any merchandise, except a few articles for presents on the road, in case of interruption, for every Cofila in passing these oceans of sand, must depend on its own precautions, where borrowing or lending is out of the question, few being provided beyond their absolute wants.

Of this kingdom I can say little, from the shortness of my stay there, except that it is independent, Mahometan and ruled by a negro Sultan, whose sway is absolute and dominion extensive, surrounded by independent tribes of Negroes and the kingdom of *Kordofan* generally at war with him. However, they are able to keep up a communication with Fez, Morocco and Egypt, being situated in Latitude 14, Long. 28, as I learned at Kahira, and that they have from time immemorial carried on some trade in slaves with that place from Central Africa.

ॐ Of Kahira or Cairo, as by some it is spelled, I need not enter into any description after the volumes that have been written on that subject. I found a Turkish garrison there, and a Cangia to carry me to Alexandria, with renewed bills on Constantinople, and finding a Venetian vessel in that port bound for home, I with joy and gratitude secured a convenient cabin, and set sail with a fair wind for my long deserted country – not unprovided with the means of support, for a time, should my family inheritance be unattainable.

What were my feelings during this short voyage it is impossible to express. Resentment there was none, it had been extinguished by reflection, and suffering. Lycas had taught me to know my own failings, and the examples I had beheld of true philanthrophy had purged my heart from prejudice. Love alone remained, and a sense of deep humility from reflection of my early follies and their consequences. That which could not be extinguished, of affection for one to whom I had caused so many sorrows and who for my sake alone had sacrificed her liberty, still reigned paramount in my breast; but it was no longer the violence of consuming desire, but a mild although inextinguishable attachment, a tender inclination to contribute to the felicity of the adored object, pity and love blended in the softest sentiments of the heart – such as, I conceived, would have been our mutual regard had we, after a happy union, lived to an advanced age together. I fancied I was on the wing to repair all her regrets, not to interrupt her serenity. I even anticipated the calm, sober joy of our first interview, prepared arguments to prove that we might both draw consolation from our trials, that a friendship like ours, which had stood the test of time, afforded all the consolations this life was capable of receiving. In a word, I gloried in the thought that she would rival in goodness and sweetness the Laura of Petrarcha, and I am not sure that, in estimating my own sacrifices, I did not for a moment compare myself to something like that exalted poet.

But on the other hand I was fortified against the reverse of these calm but pleasing visions, and, humbled in my own eyes at last, had I not been an attentive observer of the patience of the Islamites in sustaining with fortitude the severest reverses on the mere strength of a creed embracing fatalism, it would have made me indeed ashamed of the meekness of a religion, I now began to understand the value of, I had not been able to subdue my passions.

I had no sooner got my foot on board the vessel than I seemed like one waking from a dream. I had quitted my country in a ferment of rage arising from disappointed love and fierce resentment against those who imagined they had received equal injustice from me. My very patriotism was tinged with selfishness. I knew little then of mankind and still less of myself – neither did I stop to weigh the feelings of my family, a father acting from principles, perhaps prejudices imbibed with his milk; governed by custom, and the habits of his countrymen, he saw nothing but disgrace in an unequal alliance for his son, and, in the severe chastizement he inflicted on me, was supported by his own conscience, and the approbation of all around him. Perhaps I had shortened my parents' days or broken my mother's heart by my violent evasion of my home! All these, and many other painful but just reflections, now broke in upon that tranquil resignation which the example of *Lycas* had first inspired; which the habitual torpor of my Asiatic and African connections had increased, and the reasonings of a Christian society had confirmed. My reveries were profound, they turned inwardly on my soul, and I felt like a dying man approaching the seat of final judgement, as I contemplated my return to my country.

What intemperance, what follies had I not committed, through giving way to excitement, and self will? And my almost miraculous escape from their just consequences was equally surprising! Again, all was uncertain as to the situation of my worldly affairs. My absence and long silence might, according to our laws, have exposed my lands to litigation, or subjected me to outlawry from political suspicion, being no favourite with a government that looked with jealous eyes on the friends of freedom, of which I was well known to have been a leader.

CHAPTER XIX

Such were the reflections which forced themselves upon me, on my first embarkation, but the charms of nature and the glories of the open sea in a fine climate and vernal season soon dissipated them and called my attention to the action going on around me. We left the port of *Alexandria* with a fair wind, and soon lost sight of the flat shores of the delta, whose fertility has been the admiration of all ages, and where man still contrives to exist and multiply with little labour even under a despotism the most coercive. Everything favouring, our progress was rapid, delightful, and prosperous, until, having ran under the Island of Patmos, we were suddenly becalmed and compelled to cast anchor on one of the most glorious summer evenings my eyes ever beheld. The sea was like a mirror reflecting a million of tints of the richest variety of golden, silver, rose coloured and blue tints imaginable. The sun was retiring behind an enamelled cloud, whose edges his phosporic rays inflamed, and the island seemed a gaudy diadem rising from the smooth waters. It perfectly burned at its illuminated extremeties, and in part looked like an emerald or noble opal. Without being enthusiastic I may be allowed to say, that all the glowing images so luminously painted by the saint who wrote his revelations there, came as it were before my eyes, and dwelled on my spirit, and I was so transported by the celestial glories of the moment that I felt as if I also could have prophesied. But the joy was like other exquisite joys transient, and as the mariners commenced their evening hymn, all was transformed to a neutral grey.

To this soon succeeded night, a pure ether impregnated with holy lights, and a moon half horned whose substance seemed to be molton silver.

Such pictures even the crew were affected by, and I saw in the flickering lights and shadows among the tinted tackling more than one beating his rude breast before the Madona near the mast and exclaiming "Misericordia!" But the gravest man on board was the captain, a native of Ragusa, bearded and whiskered like a Turk, a man indeed who never smiled, but carried care in his rugged countenance, and was always watching the winds. He saw, he said, nothing to admire in the gaudy finery of the island. It boded only storms, and the calm face of nature was, he said, deceitful.

In this at least he spoke from sad experience, I suppose, for never did a morning break with more fearful threatnings. We were all aroused by a wild singing in the wind to which the shrouds responded by a trembling murmur, and the masts by groans. All now was uproar and confusion, we broke from all our anchors, whose cords snapped like threads, our sails, though furled, bent the yards like bows, a stream of wild hissing wind poured behind us, and before lay an ocean all froth. The sky was black with dense clouds, which yet opened at intervals as if rent, closing again and shewing a velocity of motion that their huge bulk made terrible. We knew we were among dangerous islands, driving onward without compass or helm, for that was unshipped speedily after the commencement of the storm, the conviction of which accident was soon announced by the stentorian howl of the captain, and a volley of execrations, but too well known by the crew – a trembling set of genuine Italian mariners, too often unprepared in danger, and trusting to vows rather than exertions.

I had long discovered the depths of our superstitions – long seen how far we were in our civilization removed from the true Christian character, but I should have doubted, if I had not now beheld it, to what a state of debasement human nature can be brought, by ignorance and priestcraft. Perfectly sure I now was that if we escaped being wrecked we could only owe our lives to providence, for not even an attempt was made to save the vessel, and all was one mingled note of despair, except from the brute who owned her; who, nothing daunted by the lightning playing around him, or a smaller vessel rushing under our lee, who hailed him to ask if he knew his tack, and would spare them, answered, with a volley of oaths, being just able to discern them by their lights – "Put your helm aboard, or you'll all be in Hell in a moment". Lashed to the mast, I and my faithful African could only offer up our prayers for deliverance, for all my efforts to inspire the crew with activity had long been found ineffectual. And thus we rushed on, without even disencumbering ourselves of the masts, with a velocity probably beyond what we could any of us calculate, through a dark and murky atmosphere, occasionally being struck by fragments of spars which we knew could only have belonged to some other vessel that was dismasted. And once I heard, at a moment when the wind was lulled, the piercing cries of some drowning mariner – followed by the deep roll of distant thunder, and soft lambent gleams of lightning, that seemed like floating fire. But even this, horrible as it was in our helpless state, afforded some hope of abatement, and proved the harbinger of joy – for soon after the wind lowered, the wrack dispersed, and, when we could see our way, we had the happiness to discern no land before us and, summoned from below by the loud voice of the Ragusan, the sailors came up from the hold to humble themselves before his savage reproaches, and resume their duty.

A temporary spar was substituted for a rudder, by great and dangerous exertions, the sails were with difficulty unfurled, and once more we were floating under some command. Where we were no one knew, but the pilot, an aged man, the most collected of all, guessed by the direction of the wind when we broke away that we must have made a great progress westward, and so it proved, for a vessel we encountered soon after and hailed, assured us we were not far from the cape of Spada in *Candia*, and had not the storm abated it is evident we should have inevitably been wrecked on that island. So many miraculous escapes, among so many dangers as the archipelego presented, was very striking, and I took advantage of it to suggest to both the captain and crew a suitable feeling of gratitude to God. But the result was little suitable to the event, or honourable to human nature, for they appeared to be, by their indifference, among the very lowest grade of civilized Europe; and the owner, viewing my Osmanlic garb with scorn, asked me how long I had been a renegado from the Port? and Mahomet? using such blasphemous expressions as evidently to terrify his superstitious dependants, who certainly placed some little confidence on certain amulets fastened to leather thongs on their bosoms, crosses tatooed on their brawny arms, and a little image of St Antonio attached to the binnacle.

"And this is Europe," I exclaimed, "and this European government! And in what is it better on the seas, than in an Indian forest among savages? and Venice? Venice my birth place, the pride of Italy, the Mistress of the Adriatic, the polished corner of the temple of politeness – in what is she better? A depraved moral government, whose roots are nourished by crime, and watered by deceit, and whose branches bring forth nothing but impure fruits – the paradise of priests and tyrants, where the multitude are sacrificed to the few – a republic in name, but a despotism in reality – temples inscribed to God, polluted to superstition, the garb of holiness covering a golden idol, and vice stalking openly abroad under the banner of aristocratic protection.

"Yet there am I bending my course, in the company of men whom to know is to fear, and all to secure a patrimony among men that the *Sophians* and *Jovinians* have taught me justly to abhor – to reclaim whose manners an army of martyrs would lose all hope, a people devoted to false principles, yet who persist in calling themselves Christians, whilst they reverse all the holy precepts of the divine ordinances of Christ! and instead of brotherly love, and equal privileges, are divided into casts, and are a community of slaves and tyrants, mutually detesting and detested."

Whilst these sad reflections were passing in melancholy review, and I thought of what Venice and indeed all Italy was, when I left my country in disgust, anticipating the difficulties I should encounter on my return, the door of my cabin slowly opened, and a dark hand holding a small lamp was intruded very cautiously, followed by my affectionate African boy – who as soon as he had satisfied himself that no one was near, extinguished his light, and advised me to do the same by mine – came near my cot and in a whisper told me he had just overheard a conversation between two of the seamen, by which it appeared that the captain had formed a resolution to destroy us both, as soon as a convenient opportunity occurred by throwing us overboard, in which these two men were to assist him and share with him my property, putting into some port in Dalmatia, instead of going to Venice, and if any enquiry was made on his return to Alexandria, asserting that we were lost during the great storm which had so disabled and nearly foundered us. The poor lad I believe trembled more for me than himself, but very resolutely assured me, that since we were to die, he would die by my side.

"The tale is not improbable," I said to him, "by what we see of this captain and crew, but we must trust in God, and in such a dreadful emergency use our coolest endeavours to escape. Return therefore to your berth if possible unnoticed, and by morning I may perhaps have been able to contrive some invention to avoid this frightful conspiracy."

I need not say I slept but little that night, or that I was uneasy until I saw the young African again, to be assured he had returned unnoticed. Convinced I was in the lion's lair, I looked well to my arms to be ready to resist in case of a sudden assault, and under pretence of indisposition kept my servant near me all the next day, whom I soon inspired with a resolution to defend ourselves to the last if necessary. And in hopes to procure some friendly aid among the sailors, I announced that, as soon as we landed, I intended to distribute among them a handsome bounty, in gratitude for our remarkable escape. This report seemed to give general satisfaction to all but the commander, who assured me it would be throwing my money away to do so, as there was not a man among them capable of any gratitude, and who would not cut mine or his throat the next day if they had a convenient opportunity; and that as soon as he was refitted and at the end of his voyage his intention was to discharge them all, and probably get them punished for their neglect of duty during the tempest.

We were then beating up for the gulf of Venice, under our ill constructed helm, without yards or sails that were not in tatters, and forunately the following day came in sight of a port, which a pilot boat that put off informed us was that of *Otranto* in Italy, and to which they offered to conduct us in safety, where we might in some measure repair our damages, if not yet completely refitted. Such an advantage in our condition was not to be overlooked, and a bargain was soon made, and as soon executed; for before the next morning I had the happiness to find we were securely moored, and a boat waiting to take us ashore.

The Ragusan now assumed an air of urbanity towards me, and proposed that during our short stay we should reside under the same roof, assuring me that the *Otrantese* were great rogues, and that it required the tact of a Ragusan to avoid their schemes of plunder. I thanked him for his offers, but assured him that, being an Italian, I should be enabled to defend myself, and immediately went up to the Podesta, to whom I communicated my grounds for suspicion of the captain, and obtained from him a government boat to bring my property to the custom house, in which I went myself to secure my trunks and my servant's things, taking care to fulfil my promise to the mariners before I departed; several of whom applauded my conduct in quitting the vessel, and broadly hinted that in their opinion I had thereby saved our lives.

But I shall not easily forget the rage of the corsair (for he was no better) when seeing me coming on shore before he suspected I had left the port, with all my goods around me, in a custom house boat, and thus making a perfect clearance, the object of which could not be doubtful. His colour came and went, he gnashed his teeth, he could scarcely breathe.

"And what is all this?" he said. "Who had dared to break bulk on board my vessel e'er the freight is paid? Where is my mate? I shall not discharge these goods you may depend on it before I arrive at Venice, to which place they are consigned. I will have my mate on shore also and imprison him."

All this while we were coolly landing our things on the quay, regardless of his rage and menaces, and having consigned them to the proper officers I turned to the master and owner, with all the courtesy I could assume, and desired him very civilly to come with me to the Osterea and receive his freight and charges according to our written agreement for the whole voyage.

"You intend them to remain here I see," replied he, with a sardonic smile. "You are very quick in your measures, but I wish I had only known them an hour ago. Perhaps I should have been able to persuade you to accompany your boxes to the end of the voyage. I shall however complain to the governor of this infringement of the maritime laws in landing, perhaps contraband articles, without the consent of the commander."

"Come along," said I, "you will find me with him when you arrive. I love open dealing. He is an honest man, and I shall send for two of your crew, whose clear evidence, joined to that of my servant, will satisfy you as to my motives for quitting the ship."

At hearing this and observing my coolness, he turned pale, and after muttering some curses, and placing his hand on his dagger, he called for his boatswain, and immediately embarked, swearing vengance on all on board, and bidding me be ready the next morning early to meet him at the governor's levee, rowed away

Knowing the man, I expected a stormy encounter, and went early to the port, to be ready to attend him, when I found, to my no great surprize, from the officers, that he had sailed during the night, crippled as his ship was, and probably would no more return, as from the conversation of some of his crew who had come on shore with him, he was suspected to be a pirate and an order was issued to arrest him, which but for his sagacity would have taken effect.

Thus was I delivered, providentially, from a monster through the vigilance and affection of my Negro boy, for he was never more heard of after he left the Bay of Manfredonia, either here, at Venice, or Alexandria.

This change in my destination made a change in my sentiments as to going straight to Venice and made me resolve to take Rome on my way. Accordingly I hired mules and a guide, and proceeded by the way of *Lucera*, *Molise* and *Tora*, crossing the Apenines to that city, encountering some difficulty and nearly as many dangers as in the ill governed Africa, although fast approaching a city which, according to its pretentions, ought to be the strong hold of Christianity and the pure source of order and good regulations.

After a pleasant journey through a picturesque country, among the splendours of Italy, I arrived by the way of the lake of *Nemi* at *Rome* and immediately presented myself to the Cardinal Vicar for an introduction to the Pope, who received me with perfect cordiality as soon as he was informed of my family and connections.

"You, my son," said he, "a true scion of the venerable stock of the *Memmos*, have been long regretted as lost by your countrymen, long invoked through the prayers of our holy church, and many masses have been said for the repose of your soul, under an idea that you had perished in foreign climes. But now I hope you are returned a wiser man than when you absented yourself from our church and communion, and, after due confession, she will receive you to her arms again with a parent's affection, and your country will rejoice in it."

I then, after receiving his blessing, at his requests, faithfully narrated the history of my perigrination, to his great astonishment. But when I came to give an account of the *Jovinians*, his brow darkened, his lips expanded, and, colouring warmly, he lifted up his hands, as shrinking with horror, and exclaimed, "The Heriticks!

The vile Arians! So then they have escaped our thunders, and are corrupting themselves, and the southern world! But we will reach them still, we have faithful missionaries in Egypt, and you my child are I trust destined to increase the glory of our legitimate authority, and aid us to exterminate these corrupted children. Go, fly to the president of the Propaganda fide, give him a clue to their retreats, and share with us all the honour of their extermination."

How little I felt inclined to such an office I need not I believe declare – but with the horrors of the Inquisition before me, I was cautious of committing myself, by disputing his orders, and retired from the audience, accompanied by the Cardinal Vicar, to obey his holiness's commands, well knowing, and rejoicing in knowing, that, for all I could communicate of an itinerary, the good *Jovinians* were far out of the reach of the most sanguinary or bigotted missionary they could employ.

The Cardinal and the President were men of the world; satisfied with their own emoluments, they cared little about such unprofitable commissions, as hunting heriticks, among the Mountains of the Moon. They invited me however to partake of a sumptuous dinner at which some Indian missionaries were present, on their return from Bengal, who brought coins of gold, and jewels as presents to their superior, which were displayed with no ordinary admiration, and among other offerings, a pendrous gold fillagree neck ornament from a rajah who had been converted; and on which, to my utter astonishment (who knew something of these men before I travelled) the lingam was, by a little management, substituted for the cross, and, on my expressing my surprize, it was said, by way of apology by the President, that, we *must* give way a little to ancient customs if we expected to make converts to Christianity in India.

I had now sufficient evidence of the impossibility of any effectual reform in our Roman Catholic Church. Yet I felt I might abide by the original faith, without a formal renunciation of her errors, unless prepared for a fruitless martyrdom, or a solitary cell in the Inquisition which would effectually extinquish my power to benefit my species in any way forever. I therefore made a speedy retreat from the Holy City, and prepared myself to encounter the legislatures of Venice, in defence of my paternal inheritance – resolving to be reserved on the score of my adventures in Africa, until I could find the means of disclosing them usefully; for I had learned, at Rome, that I should have to contest at law for my patrimony, which in consequence of my absence, and withheld claims, had been assigned to other branches of my family.

I had a sister however whom I loved and on whom I relied for affectionate council, and decided first to disclose myself to her, before my arrival was publicly announced. And my thoughts were employed whilst crossing the Appenines, and inhaling with joy my salubrious native air, in preparing myself for the affectionate encounter. At Loretto I was obliged to halt on account of the mules, who were exhausted in crossing the mountains, and was kept long enough to witness the most disgusting idolatry and superstition, mixed up with the vile impositions of the traders at that holy-fair.

CHAPTER XX

And from Ravenna, after a short stay, I embarked in a felucca for the port of Venice, with a farmer who was carrying some provisions for the market there – so that we landed early in the morning on the Quay of the Rialto, and I took up my quarters at an inn that faced it. When my trunks were disposed in my chamber, and I first looked out of the window, as the sun was just rising from the Adriatic, it is impossible to describe my mixed feelings of gratitude to heaven, joy at seeing my native place, and hope as to a cordial reception by my countrymen. The beauty of the scene, as the early rays disclosed the preparations of the dealers with their daily supply of the choicest fruits and flowers, their gay apparel, and the crowd of gondolas which cut the waters with their silver prows – all conspired to induce reflections long absent from my mind, some painful, some pleasing, but which all ended in the absorbing thoughts of her who once shed a lustre over every image that came before me, and whom I now beheld, in my mind's-eye, as precluded forever from my embraces, pining in seclusion, and performing her monotonous services perhaps with apathy, or possibly with a wasting fervor, the forerunner of an unnatural and early decay.

To see her first I however decided, for I felt persuaded that if all other beings abandoned my interests, or had dismissed me from their affections, in her I should, whilst life remained, be assured of a tender and lasting friendship. But how to present myself offered some difficulty as to the decision; my person was altered by time and travel; my dress was Asiatic; and my beard increased in me the appearance of advancing age. I therefore resolved to appear before her as I was, to see if first love possessed eyes to penetrate my disguise, and on failure in that case to pass for a stranger who came to inform her of my decease, as a trial of her faith and affection, before I disclosed, if she still loved me, the voice of one in whose heart she lay buried and enshrined.

When at last the conflict of feelings was over, and I had a little calmed my beating heart, I put on my most becoming apparel, and choicest turband, and with firm steps approached the Convent of the Ursilines. But when I lifted my trembling hand to pull the bell, it fell repeatedly from me, and it was not until after some time I could overcome my irresolution. "She will be," I said to myself, "altered, doubtless, in dress and complexion; constant vigils will have rendered her pale, disappointment divested her of her sweet smiles, and hope long deferred have made sick her constant heart. And am not I trifling with her regard, to put on any disguise? Is it not ungrateful to one who has sacrificed all the enjoyments of this world to me, to even hint at a doubt of her fidelity by this experiment?"

My hand was once more on the handle of the bell when a sad thought intruded itself. May not religion have taught her that it is her duty to reject me, for women are sometimes resentful; may she not have changed her love to hate, from my long abandonment of her, and the evil reports of others? "No, no!" I cried emphatically (for men are all at bottom vain), and I drew the cord with vehemence.

The die was cast, and it was not long when a venerable porteress presented herself to answer my enquiries. "I want to see," I said, with a hesitating accent,"the Sister Nazure."

"There is no Sister Nazure here," said the nun.

"My God," I exclaimed, "she is dead! And I shall never more behold her."

"You," said she, "seem a strange man; you look like a Turk, and speak like a Venetian, and, a Mahometan no doubt, pretend to have an interest in a Christian recluse. Tell me who you are? and that speedily, or I shall close the gate against one who seems to come to mock us."

"Pardon me, my good lady," said I, "if my language offends you, for I am not what I seem by my dress, but the affectionate friend of that lost lady I enquired after. But she is dead, you say, and I am dead also, for the news will dismiss me from human society. I cannot brook the thought that she expired with an impression of my disregard – I loved her to distraction, and for that cause have been long a wanderer on the face of the earth for many years. But now my course is ended, and we shall soon be united in the grave."

So saying, I threw myself on the floor of the parlour, in an agony of disappointment and momentary despair – and she not a little alarmed departed to inform the abbess of the strange adventure.

In a short time I heard the folding doors of the opposite side of the grille opened, and heard a voice through its bars calling me by my name, in an accent that I could not be deceived in – it was the voice of one whom but a moment before supposed to be dead, owing to the stupid accuracy of the old Porteress. "Rise, rise," she said, "unhappy man, if you are, under this disguise, that *Memmo*, whose affections I have long renounced for a station not mortal."

At the well known sound, I was instantly on my feet, and would have thrown myself at hers but for the interposition of the grating. "And are you then alive, and do these eyes once more behold those which so long enthralled me?" I said, in an impassioned tone.

But she with dignity repelled my enthusiasm, and suddenly replied, "Hold *Memmo*, I know and affectionately esteem you, but do not open again wounds long healed. I am here no longer the object of earthly affections such as you seem to feel. I am enshrined in an office that admits only of spiritual consecration. I am sacred from all human prepossessions – and on no other terms than pious regard can we ever meet again. If you really esteem me, you will still seek my happiness, and rejoice in that change, which has delivered me from a world of troubles, and follow my example by discarding from your breast the remains of that infatuation which your reason will teach you to reject, now that its early objects are unattainable. On these terms and these only I can be allowed to retain your friendship. And now therefore leave me. We both want time to overcome this surprize, and my duties and character will allow no longer conference. Tomorrow I will receive you, in the presence of one of my sisters, when I hope you will appear more like a Venetian. For although I am better acquainted with the danger that awaits you here from your enemies than you are, you should know also that to escape notice under disguise is impossible in a state governed as this is, and if I so receive you I compromise this house and myself. Go therefore quickly, my valued friend, present yourself to the proper authorities, avow your honourable station, and all will be well. Adieu, Adieu, my *esteemed* Memmo!" she said in an affectionate voice – and vanished by a side portal.

I stood for an instant like a being spell bound. All she had so sweetly said rung in my ears like music. I felt at once its force, and her regard – and slowly obeyed her wise commands, scarcely knowing how I got back to my inn.

It was now near noon, and I resolved instantly to see my married sister, from whom I doubted not I should obtain all the necessary information relative to my situation, my title and my property.

I accordingly went at once to her palace, for she had married a noble of the ancient house of Cornaro, and sending up my true name by the Camanire, who viewed me with astonishment and doubt, was announced, after waiting some time until she had left her bath.

The instant she saw me she started and exclaimed – "Santa Maria, who have you brought me here? *Memmo!* it cannot surely be you?" But my voice and familiar address satisfied her I was no impostor, and she flew to my embrace with her accustomed affection. After first looking at me, at arm's length, with amazement, then bursting into a loud laugh, she cried, "You have not verily turned Turk, Memmo? You cannot have been so absurd. It is quite a ridiculous faith, even for one so romantic as you have always been. Come, come, this will never do in Venice. It may have forwarded your intrigues abroad, but here at home there is no nation more despised. You have lost much by your adventurous spirit, but this would sink you forever."

I soon satisfied her on that head, and assured her that all my wild schemes were over, that I was not only still a good Catholic, but trusted one on principle, and that the next time we met it would be in a very different costume.

"Well," said she, "but you look so handsome in this – that I would not have you throw it away – it will do at our masquerades, excellently, and insure you the glances of all our most fashionable women. And indeed, my dear brother, you must now look out for a fortune, as I am sorry to tell you, you have little left to support your rank, our father having, in resentment of your absence and other indiscretions, disposed of all he had any power over among his other children. And you know, my Memmo, rank without fortune makes but a poor figure in a gondola. But never mind, I for one shall always be glad to serve you, and you will have still I trust enough to enable you to act the part of a gay bachelor. Your long travels alone will recommend you to society, and at my casino I shall call on you often to describe the beauties of the Turkish and Egyptian belles.

"But how long is it since you arrived? And where are you at present? I can't ask you to dine to day, as I am engaged to a large party, and there is no one at home but my stupid husband, and who besides is not very well disposed towards you, from a foolish notion that it is not his interest to promote yours. So go back as fast as you can, and get into covering befitting the importance of our family, and come to me tomorrow, when I shall have time to shew you how to steer your bark, among the quicksands of our political lagoons; which I can assure you menace you dreadfully by what I hear. Go, go, my dear brother, or I shall not have time to dress for the casino party, to which I dare not carry you thus caparisoned.".

So saying with a smile, she rang the bell with one hand whilst she presented me the other to kiss, and, the doors thrown open, I was conducted with great respect by her valets into my gondola at the front of the great entrance.

"And so," said I, to myself, whilst gliding on the smooth canal, shut up in my sombre box, "I am not likely to find much sympathy on my return where I might have most reason to expect it! – or to make any converts to Christian principles in my native home? Home, did I say! When was it one to me? A blight has fallen on my blossoms, and now my earthly branches are withering. But after all, I have obtained wisdom by sore experience, and no one can take my discoveries from me. As to fortune, what is it in the way men abuse it? and what is Venice and its honours under a despotic oligarchy, and a bigotted church, and am I not a Christian?"

The boldness of this apostrophe at first startled me, it savoured too much of that confidence in myself which had so often been corrected by reverses – and I instantly ejaculated a prayer that I *might be one on trial*. The difficulty of the task was I felt diminished, by the humiliating situation to which I found myself heir; and that zeal, which had been kindled by experience of the possibility of promoting the principles of our great teacher with no other means but his grace. "On then," said I, "to duty, on to happiness!" as the gondola came ashore – and I mounted the stairs of the Locanda with a species of gaity very different from that I had formerly experienced in ascending the noble flight of marble steps which led to my father's palace amid a crowd of vassals who humbled themselves to the dust in anticipating my future greatness.

Assured and strengthened by these reflections, I assumed that day my native dress, composed with a gravity suitable to my intentions, and sending for a notary, whose respectability I had known before my absence from home, I empowered him to make the necessary enquiries with respect to my remaining property. The result was that I found nothing to which I could make immediate claim, but a small annuity secured on the family estate, to be paid to me with interest should I ever return to Venice, and a landed patrimony left to me by my grandfather in the Eganean Mountains above *Belluno* and beyond *Feltro* and *Cadore* called *Aronzo* at the source of the River Piave. The annuity and the accumulated interest was an immediate resource, but the estate he said he feared would be only a burthen to me, as the buildings had been long neglected, and the lands unproductive, and he ended his commission by recommending me to throw myself on the generosity of the Senate, whose feelings towards patricians were always favourable. This I knew, but I knew also my altered situation and opinions would soon put an end to their republican partiality. Had I not heard of *Sophis* and seen the *Jovinians* to teach me to bow my neck to the yoke of this corrupted oligarchy? I however felt it was for my safety to dissemble my intentions, and to assure him that my humility was perfected by sufferings, and that I did not mean to disgrace my family by any mean and unnecessary submissions, being at any rate first resolved to visit my little territory, and see if that which, I knew, had sustained my grandfather would not support me – that I needed repose after my travels and obscurity. I therefore requested him not to even mention my arrival to the people in power, as I felt myself by no means in a condition to attend councils, and he took his leave, evidently with but a mean opinion of my talents and understanding.

I had now only one more trial to encounter, and only one being to part with whom I could leave with regret. The morning was at hand which she had appointed. I arose that day before the sun had penetrated with his early beams the serrated tops of the towers of the city, and was rowed through a soft mist to a bathing sand where I had often when a youth indulged in the delightful exercise of swimming, and the circumstance brought back to my reflections, as I undressed, a thousand agreeable remembrances. "It is the same sun," I cried, "and the same water, the same glorious golden beams, and the same invigorating air, the same Venice – but where are the feelings of my youthful joy, when I played in the waves of the Adriatic like a fish, and sang with exhilarated emotion, as I buffeted the pure water, and raised a cloud of spray around my head? I am now come like a sick man to be healed, of a wounded heart, and seem alone amidst a multitude; instead of encountering a crowd of professed friends on my return, I have only one left, who cannot seek me, and whom I must seek in captivity."

With such reflections, I completed my refreshing bath, which however braced new nerves to endure the encounter for which I requited some previous preparation, and as in gliding back, listening to the cheeful matins of the hardy goldolier, the warm rays of a nascent sun-shine playing on the rich outlines of the embellishments of St. Mark's place, the living Canalettes passed before me like a changing vision of beauty, and I stepped on shore with a much lighter heart than I had embarked with at rising from my agitated repose.

Having completed my toilet, I will confess with something more than usual care, I attended to my appointment at the Convent to a second, and found a ready admission to the private parlour of the abbess, for such was my adored Veronica become, having been unanimously elected on account of her good sense, misfortunes and urbanity.

She received me with all the warmth of old friendship, but with great gravity, and was accompanied by a sister of her own age, who did the honours of an elegant collation, evidently prepared in compliment to my introduction, with even more than Venetian taste. She began by congratulating me on my return, and having resumed the costume suitable to my rank and country, cordially avowing her regard for me, which she assured me would end but with her life. "We have both," she said, "made great sacrifices to propriety, and we are mutually thereby pledged to live with decorum. But my vows do not debar me from doing justice to merit, or to suppress the dictates of gratitude to you who have suffered so much on my account. Had I not lived, you would e'er now have been a wealthy ornament to the senate.

"It has pleased God however to call us both *'cin altro impresi di altro virtude'*, and we must bow down with humiliation to the decree. For my own part, I am thankful that the duties I am vowed to fulfil are distinctly marked out, and am only anxious to know what future path you have chalked out for yourself – since I know but too well the disappointments you are likely to encounter here."

Here she made a pause, yet her sweet voice still sounded in my ear, and I arose, somewhat agitated, to take her hand, which she offered me with a sobered dignity that convinced me that I should offend if I expressed the warmth of my tender admiration, for she had lost little of her former attractions. I therefore resumed my seat, and correcting my emotion, I related to her, in as few words as possible, the whole of my travels, as well as the situation in which I was placed, by the disposition of my father's effects, together with my determination to retire to the old family mansion in the mountains, there to seek that peace which the world cannot give, and to endeavour to imitate His life, Who died for all, by living for the good of my dependents, and seeking, in their happiness, my own.

"Yet we may correspond," I said, "and sometimes meet perhaps. You shall be my Laura and I your Petrarch. Will not that be allowed?"

She nodded assent, rose from her seat, and taking the hand of her attendant nun, before she departed expressed great satisfaction at what she called my generous and rational resolutions, and we parted, rather as ancient friends than separated lovers. Yet I could not help observing, that her colour came and went from her cheek at bidding me adieu, and that she seemed at quitting the chamber to need the aid of her companion's support. For my own part I must confess it was a trying interview, and although I wished to conceal it if possible from my own bosom, the embers of my faithful attachment were still glowing beneath their grey whitening ashes, and it needed all my firmness to resume my practiced philosophy.

This trial over, I felt fortified against the outward world, and its annoyances, and resolved to cultivate the philosophy of Christianity in retirement. I accordingly lost no time in arranging, with the aid of my notary, every preliminary dependent on taking possession of my little territory, during which time I kept myself strictly to my chamber, neither did I take leave of any one but my sister, whose astonishment at my resolution, however great, never once induced her to endeavour to impede it, and this last parental tie severed, "the world was all before me, and providence my guide."

CHAPTER XXI

On a very fine morning in the spring, at break of day, I landed from my gondola on terra firma and, mounted on a choice mule, with my Negro boy Cuba on another and two of my future tenants conducting my baggage on a car drawn by two buffalos, I proceeded to the foot of the hills by Caneda – where for the first evening we took up our rest, and beheld the most glorious sun-set gilding the rich shades that it was possible to see. The rocks were like gold from the furnace, the woods like emeralds, and the sky a blaze of glory. What a contrast to the tumultuous streets I had left, the hum of human beings, and the vile odours of the narrow canals. We seemed to inhale the breath of roses, and imbibe life at every pore. A clean country wench at the osterea brought me sparkling water from the pure fountain, instead of the filtered, flat and insipid beverage of the city. Milk and honey and fresh oranges crowned my desert, and my chamber was fragrant with flowers clustering around the casement. That night I tasted freedom and repose, and dreamed of the innocent and affectionate *Jovinians* – and from that hour I may date the commencement of a happy existence.

My grandfather had been a man of simple habits, who lived among his tenants like a father among his children, his patrimonial estate having been enjoyed for many generations by men like himself, and whose only vanity was the boast of having descended from Roman blood – patricians of that state, and uncontaminated, of which the ancient part of the castle bore evident monumental inscriptions. It was seated on a rock, embattled, and overgrown with ivy, and surrounded by a foss of considerable depth, now filled with fig and olive trees – its situation, the head of a promontory connected with the termination of a deep and well wooded valley by a narrow road, each side of which was clothed with a variety of ancient trees, many were evergreens, towards the bottom and between which a perpetual stream tumbled over broken rocks, anciently fallen from above, uniting at the termination of the promontory, and descending after a considerable fall in one clear winding stream though some fertile pastures enclosed on all sides with irregular forests, and open groves of olives and mulberry trees – a site poor in produce, but picturesque, the haunts of painters and poets, and connected with a dependent village, whose humble church half buried in shades occupied one side of the valley above the fall, and was celebrated for the antique tombs of my long line of ancestors.

To arrive at this venerable mansion, it was necessary to make a considerable tour among the mountains to avoid the necessity of ascending by a very steep acclivity, so as to enter by a saddleback of narrow dimensions guarded by a gate and double bastion which through a long a shady terrace conducted to the great gate of the castle, whose enclosure encircled the rugged sides of the promontory, and encompassed a considerable space of ground, well laid out in pensile gardens and orchards, and watered by a living spring that flowed in a stone channel on one side the terrace, irrigating every court and plantation, as well as supplying the mansion with delicious water, and ultimately, after sustaining some noble fountains, trickling in little divided rills to the stream below.

The building was a mixture of many species of architecture, and a combination of many conveniences the result of the demands of a variety of owners; in one part rich with classical ornaments, in another sombre with gothic gloom. Many good but neglected pictures covered the walls of the galleries, and some Mantegna and Jan Bellino's works were there, as well as some rare portraits by Margantone, Cimaber and Giotto. Like all old houses it has its faults and deformities, but its dining hall was truly cheerful, as one pair of folding doors looked out on a fountain in the front court, and the other on a gay but trim old fashioned flower garden. There was a library also of choice books for the times (containing the works of Dante, Petrarca, Boccaccio, Crysolaris then in his glory, Mat Paris, Joinville, Gerson, a divine Wickliffe, Jerome of Prague, Piedemontanus &c.) connected with a long gallery whose walls was covered with maps, plans, prints, geneological trees and old armour and some Roman antiquities which had been disinterred in the neighbourhood and let into the walls. I found also both summer and winter chambers, prolific fish ponds, and a lofty square tower whose summit commanded the whole country, well furnished with telescopes and other optical and mathematical instruments, placed there by my grandfather, whose scientific pursuits had given him the reputation of a necromancer among the surrounding villages – and in an ebony chest there, I found the works of Roger Bacon, Lulle, and Albertus Magnus, with Scotus and Companus &c, for he was a collector of curious books. The furniture was in general massive of a half German construction, of dark oak, walnut tree, and ebony, richly ornamented and carved in the best dwelling rooms; and there was no paurity of chests of linen, with some ancient plate &c. But everything partook of the utility and frugality of the good old times.

Here then I found myself installed with a mind prepared to recede rather than advance in the career of the luxuries of my times; and found the house in the care of a few aged servants, pensioners and tenants – among whom was an old *Cachiatore* and his wife, with his middle-aged son, his wife, and two youthful maidens his daughters. They had not expected me or been any way prepared, but every thing was clean, orderly, and proper. The old huntsman well remembered me, and came forward cheerfully to pay his obedience with tears in his eyes. The son and the rest of the domesticks were drawn up before the folding gates, which were opened for the first time since the death of my grandfather, and all were regularly introduced by name. Each possessed, in virtue of my grandfather's will, some portion of vineyard land and a few mulberry trees, and they remained in their different offices as heirlooms on the estate, and occupiers under the trustees – regularly collecting the produce, and remitting the profits to the family annually, when called on by the proper authorities.

I had long been considered as lost, and my brother-in-law had availed himself of the product, never very valuable, and now, from his neglect, considerably lessened; but the land was there, capable of great improvement, the tenants at easy rents, the house in good repair, and a considerable sum due to me for arrears.

Thus situated I began to look about me, to consider it as my ultimate home, and the people about me as the fit objects of my care. To gain their affections was therefore my first concern, to which end I called them all together, and, having installed the old huntsman's son in the office of bailiff and steward, in which his father was to assist him, I confirmed all the tenants' grants, offering premiums for improvements, and assuring them that I considered them as my children whose welfare, by residing, I should attend to, but at the same time I should expect from them that deference to my instructions due to a father, since my intentions were not so much to improve my own estate as to amend their condition, and to make this little community a pattern for the surrounding country, in morals, industry, and religion. To those who know what Italians are I need not relate the enthusiasm with which my address was received – their *Vivas* were long and loud, and after giving them an entertainment suitable to their expectation, the evening was terminated with a dance and all returned before dark to their respective homes in a state of hilarity and happiness renewed, such as they had always enjoyed under the mild and parental yoke of my venerable, pious, and reflecting grandfather.

And here it will be proper to relate some peculiarities of my ancestor, a tranquil, home-bred man, of sound mind and simple manners, inflexibly just, well read, a scripture theologian, a good Catholic but secretly inclined to the reformation of Wickliffe, the friend of Gerson, and as pious as Tho.⁵ Acquinas of later times – who as far as a Venetian of rank dared, under Pope Urban 6ᵗʰ, extended liberty of conscience to his village, gently probing the wounds of superstition and error, and just uniting political freedom with the freedom of God's worship – insomuch, that I remember my father was apprehensive I might from him imbibe doctrines subversive of the sway of the church and senate, and that the opinion of the family was that he was safer in his country house than in the streets of Venice. For my own part all I remembered of him was his great kindness to me whenever I was allowed to attend him, and his indulgence to his vassals, who all loved and obeyed him from affection; and that he loved me, the pains he took to reserve for me this small estate fully evinced his regard.

"Well," said I to myself, when I had arranged my little menage, "I suppose I was born to carry on his plans of emancipating the minds of all around him, and *I will do so*. The work is prepared, the times are favourable, I have neither the talents of Jnº Huss, or Jerome of Prague, but I am a reformer," and both these divines as well as J. Gerson, had, I found by my grandfather's manuscripts, been in correspondence with him; men, who certainly understood and aimed at recovering the spirit of Christian doctrines, however they might differ in some points of discipline. By a careful perusal of this correspondence, which was sealed up and addressed to my peculiar care, I found that a generous and liberal feeling had inspired all of them, and that, advancing with that caution which the state of the times and his own utility rendered necessary, my good grandfather had, by degrees, enlightened the understandings of his tenants and surrounding neighbours, so as to make them almost united in a desire to examine the Scriptures for themselves; to which end he had, long before he died, established schools in which reading had been so industriously taught that very few indeed about him were ignorant of its advantages, and although he did not dare at that period openly to put the Scriptures into their hands, he had instructed his school master to communicate portions of the Gospels to them as lessons for many years, and had himself, in his constant visits to their cottages, read the Gospels to those who desired it in a regular series of chapters from his own translation. In fact he lived among them always, and when pressed by his friends to come to Venice, his usual reply was that he could not be spared from his curacy.

With such an example handed down to me, under existing circumstances, it seemed that providence had destined me to fulfil his views, and I cordially embraced the office, good for me and good for others — for the promotion of brotherly love is ever the right hand of industry, which benefits all.

I therefore had no scruple to turn my spare apartments, coach-houses, and stables into a spacious manufactory for winding and weaving silk, in which all the surplus population found immediate employment, and my spacious gardens were made the means of raising mulberry, fig trees, and vines for the cottagers. In a cool and capacious servants' hall I established a school, giving the curate, who fortunately was an efficient man, the superintendence of it, and, as good taste is ever favourable to virtue, I gave premiums of flowers and shrubs to the best ornamented cottages, and, enforcing cleanliness, laid out the village like a pleasure garden, by making neat and regular walks to every house from my own, in which I employed many useful hands among the aged, conducting them by winding and easy descents from the old castle gardens, through an irregular wild park adorned with very ancient trees, which encircled the termination of the promontory on which it was constructed. In this peculiar department, my duty became my greatest pleasure, I found society among some of the most intelligent of my tenants, and an opportunity continually occurring to inculcate the best feelings with the most liberal way of thinking. I also gained, from the experience of the aged, a considerable degree of information relative to the natural history and statistical state of the country, gave them also importance in promoting my just views of the general interests, and, by proper familiarity where it was most due, secured their respect and affections. Thus in a short time we understood each other, and I had nothing to disturb my peaceful and prosperous establishment, but the apprehensions of the inroads of curiosity from my relations, or countrymen, in their hours of ennui, when, driven by the great heat of the summer, they seek in the cool shades of a villagiatura a listless relaxation. But here the state of the high ways was in my favour, for many miles round, and not a carriage had in the memory of the oldest inhabitant of Aronzo ever reached the secluded spot.

With my sister I rarely corresponded, as she was so lost in a vortex of city amusements that of her recovery, from this species of monomania, there was no hope whilst youth and adulation lasted, and I allowed her to believe me an ascetic, a hermit of the desert, morose from disappointed passion, and one who could do no harm to any one but himself. But my greatest consolation in my hours of study was in cultivating an intercourse by letters with that better half of my being, which to have lost the friendship of would indeed have been to be annihilated. To her it was my delight to communicate my adventures and my thoughts, and all my plans were submitted to her cool judgment and approbation for revisal.

She was indeed my *Beatrice* and my *Laura* united, a guardian angel, whose presence, in my imagination, accompanied all my projects whether forming or executing, or chastened flame to try my virtue by, and the summit of all my ardent hopes was, that having by arguments brought her to my sense of our mutual duties, the day would come when, matured by time, she should think it no impropriety to come and personally behold the result of a system of good will to all men, and its reward internal felicity.

CHAPTER XXII

My decision was to take up my rest near the ashes of my forefathers, to lead a life of celibacy, and to dedicate the remainder of my days to the improvement of the mental conditons of those around me as well as their temporal prosperity. I had learned from the history of the Sophians the influence of moral causes in promoting the peace of society, but I had since witnessed the far superior results from the practice of pure Christianity, a blessed ordinance, the compliance with which is capable of rendering even this life a source of unmingled tranquillity, whose doctrines are spiritual, and at enmity with the uninstructed natural man, but, when embraced from conviction founded on impartial examination, are demonstrably infinitely superior to the highest sensual enjoyments of the passions or appetites – insuring to the humble and devout that peace which surpasses all imaginary description, subduing fear, and lending grace to every occupation whether important or trivial, whose object is love to all, and its end eternal joy.

To carry these points I did not feel it necessary to enter into a contest with the Church or the Inquisition, but rather, by a system of education, to enable my people to receive and comprehend the principles of true religion, and moral conduct, so as to prepare them to accept from my hands such portions of land as they could conveniently cultivate both for their own advantage and mine, my intention being finally, as I had no relations who wanted it, to place every deserving family as tenants on such a portion of land as would be necessary for their support after my decease, and to leave them ultimately in full possession, as my heirs, in reward of their industry and good management.

Of course I reserved this part of my plan secret, for the consolation of my own bosom, in order to prove their fidelity and good conduct.

Thus I became by easy means, a patriarch and legislator, and, having first procured the affection of my countrymen, I had little difficulty in leading men who soon saw I was acting for their interests. Swearing and drunkenness had been stigmatized by my grandfather, so that I found it more easy to institute rules of strict temperance on that foundation. We had premiums for proper economy, and honours for generous actions. Cleanliness was insisted on, and the improvements of their habitations as to space made the object of their extra labours, with occasional assistance from my purse, for I have ever held it as an incontrovertible truth, that the crowding poor families in too small a space tends, by lessening their self respect, to debase their moral feelings. Freedom was my pole star, and under our regulations I could no more have entered the habitation of my poorest tenant, than he could have intruded on mine. But if liberty was our beacon, love was our palladium; no act of unkindness was ever overlooked, and cruelty implied disgrace.

We did not however banish the evil minded, but considered them as the especial objects of our pity and regret – and with the help of the good curate, backed by his best communicants, and some unmerited acts of kindness, we generally overcame by perseverance the criminal subject, and by our combined exertions restored him to society, not only a penitent but a useful, active member of the community.

For my own part, I shewed them by my example, how little is necessary to our personal wants, and had no other valet than my faithful Negro, by this simple means overcoming the prejudices of some against his colour, which was entirely destroyed when I conducted him to the baptismal font, after due preparation and a public examination.

I had thus become a manufacturer and agriculturist, to the great horror of my Venetian cotemporaries and countrymen, who on that account had less inclination to interrupt my tranquillity, and had it not been for some church ceremonies, omitted by joint agreement, I believe I might have proceeded, under their contempt, in

my useful plans, to the end of the chapter. Among other remnants
of ancient superstitution, we had a few relicts that neither myself
or the curate thought worthy our care, and they were suffered
silently to go to decay – no one thinking them worth enquiring
after even among the least instructed of the congregation. But there
was an old and impious ceremony that had been annually per-
formed, in which a man was procured for wages to lie all day in
day in a tomb behind some iron rails representing the body of the
Redeemer. And so clear was the light elicited by the reasoning
against this blasphemous practice by myself and the curé, that the
second year after my arrival no one offered himself as a performer
in this impious drama.

This gave us great satisfaction, and we added to the attractions
of the day's service on the interment an invitation in the evening
to the castle, where some refreshments were provided suitable to
the festival and that part of the Scripture which related to our
Lord's crucifixion and burial was read by the curate and com-
mented on before they departed.

All were satisfied except one very aged female, who saw nothing
but impiety in the change, and had refused to attend the invitation
– and she found means by the aid of the carrier, who occasionally
came with parcels from Venice, to report us a set of hericticks, and
my worthy curate was summoned before the ecclesiastical consistory
at Venice to answer as he might the old crone's charges.

Something like this I had expected, and resolved to go with him
as a protector, well knowing that the subject would only be em-
braced as a matter of levity by the leading magistrates, who would
not have suffered such a pageant to be exhibited in the city. And
on this occasion I saw again my sister.

"Well *Memmo*," said she laughing, "here you are again. What new
embroglio has your eccentricity created? I am told you and your
lamb-like curate are to be subjected to an auto-di-fe. But really we
have droll customs in the villages, my dear brother – and it is
scarcely worth while to get into scrapes with the Pope about them.
Here we never let our gaity be interrupted by such trifles, and I
advise you to let every farce go on, civil or ecclesiastical, if you wish
for ease or enjoyment. What has a broken hearted lover to do with
theological disputes or profitable impositions? Do you not know
that the Council of Constance are now sitting, who have just made
a Martyr of Jerome of Prague, and burnt the bones of Wickliffe,
that mad Englishman, whom our grandfather had a strange par-

tiality for, although he never saw his heretical Bible. Take care they
don't hear of this frolic of yours and your curator and secretary.
For should they send for you, it would require all the interest of
your family to save you from pains and penalties – and they have
dungeons I hear more dismal than your solitude among the rocks
at *Aronzo*."

Her husband now entered, who embraced me with an artificial
cordiality, and with a sort of protecting air of compassion, assured
me that he trusted he had silenced the enquiry, by pledging himself
to the proper authorities, that the charge was unfounded and that
the woman was mad.

"You may now therefore consider yourselves as exculpated and
return in peace, but I do advise you not to meddle with that scor-
pion the Church of Rome, and to clap the old sybil into some of
your caves in the hills for the remainder of her life."

My utter contempt for these unfeeling and artificial people pre-
vented me from making him any reply but my thanks on account
of the worthy curate – who with me was at that time in correspon-
dence with those truly reflecting, learned and virtuous men Poggio
Braccioline and Leonardo Bruno of Arrezzo, and the respect of
such men gave us little inclination to flatter power in Venice. But
like them we saw no good to be derived from an open rupture with
blind bigots, and contented ourselves with the peaceful intercourse
between reflecting minds who knew how to meet the times, and
silently forward freedom of opinions where their tendency was to
ameliorate the condition of humanity, by promoting good will to-
wards each other, and the love of virtue and of God.

The good curate, who loved his flock and his sheepfold among
the sources of the Piave better than all the splendor of the capital,
lost no time in turning his mule's head towards the Castle of *Aronzo*,
but I again in the city could not so easily shake off the attraction
to the walls of the Convent of the Ursulines, where, enshrined and
beloved like a saint by the sisters whose welfare she incessantly
watched over, forever sealed from the world's intrusion, reposed
the only friend, within the circumference of Venice, on whose
sincerity I could confide.

We had occasionally corresponded during my retirements, and
she knew all my plans for purifying our little congregation, among
the recesses of Montibello. She had improved her leisure and could
read the Latin language enough to enable her to consult the vulgate
Scriptures, and peruse the writing of both Huss, Wickliffe, and

Jerome of Prague. These great divines had convinced her that a reform in the Church of Rome was become necessary, and the conduct of our profligate prelates had confirmed that opinion – but on this subject we were obliged to be cautious in our correspondence, under a government the essence of which was deceit and treachery. A personal interview for both our sakes was desirable, and I lost no time in requesting one, which was immediately acceded to. This time however she received me alone, in the common parlour, behind the grille – and we met, as I trust we shall in heaven, on both our parts weaned from the world's intrusion, and actuated only by a refined and spiritual regard. It was the last conference I ever had with her, and it left an impression of her wisdom and goodness that will never be erased. She received me with an affectionate smile, heard all my plans of reform with attention and complacency, and then addressed me as follows –

"Memmo – my friend – my dearest only friend! for so I must be convinced you are, after the light you have, since your return, shed on my before bewildered senses – the darkness of Romish errors had never at any time had complete dominion over me. In your virtues I find a stay and support, against the oppressions that encircle me. As a woman, I dare not, could not, take an active part in the reform our holy church so much requires – but if I cannot purify her sullied robes, I can adjust them with decency. In my office here I can, like you, promote true piety and disinterested love among my children, and gently remove the veil of superstition which has so long obscured the light of truth. We have different tasks, both attended by personal danger, but both attended also with self conviction of its paramount duty. It is our best patrimony on earth, and must be our sole reward. Understanding each other's views, we can act as well apart as together, in the promotion of that change of heart which time only can ameliorate, when it shall please heaven to bring men to love and benefit each other, after dispelling the delusions of priestcraft and opening the gates of glory to all believers. Let us therefore act separately to the same end by the different means appointed us, and part like apostles going to different quarters on the same errand, you to your strong hold amid the rocks and torrents – I to my little Zoar from these plains of Gomorra – and may the Almighty shed his merciful influence on both our labours."

I would have willingly prolonged the conversation, but she prohibited it, by passing her hands through the bars to take mine with a cordial pressure – saying "Adieu, *Memmo*. This interview has already continued too long for my station – we must part" – and she disappeared to my eyes like light extinguished suddenly.

Whether it was the tone of her voice, or the forebodings of my heart, I know not, but I felt as if I should never more behold her, and after taking leave of my relations I set off that very day alone on my return, with a depression of spirits that not even the beauties of the country could relieve.

The vigilance of the Papal spies had been made evident, by this attempt at persecution, and the high interest employed to evade the blow proved that the obscurity of my residence was no protection from the Council of Constance, then sitting under the influence of Pope John XXIII, who beheld only the danger to his temporal power in any reform of the Holy See, who feared the high independence of the Venetians, and the storm gathering in the northern part of his territories against the regular orders of monks extended through Germany, and already thundering in England and Bohemia. These reflections increased my sadness, for although, as a reformer, I had no views beyond the correction of spiritual abuses, I could not be unaware of the colour artful men would give to our good intentions, and the immense influence of the Conclave with foreign courts in preserving their worldly domination. I trembled also for Veronica, whose just views of the errors of Popery laid her open, in her isolated situation, to every species of persecution – for even my correspondence, if intercepted, was dangerous, as it was evident that I was already suspected to belong to the liberal party of the Hussites. Thus communing with myself, I pursued my way leisurely, and as evening advanced ascended a steep hill, through a broken way, in a forest of ancient trees, leading to *Caneda*, where I intended to lodge for the night.

At this period the states were at peace, neither Genoa nor Constantinople disturbed our aristocracy, and men were corrupted by wealth and luxury more than at any other time. At the same time religious principles lost their hold from the same cause, and the vices of the clergy were so notorious, that they become a scandal even to laymen, and excited in the sober part of the community a desire for reform, without any organized plan, yet sufficiently evident to arouse the jealousy of the Pontificate, and men who spoke or wrote freely, on the subject of religion, were oftentimes arrested and disappeared without being ever more heard of. We had our dungeons of oblivion for political offences, and the church also had her impenetrable cells. I knew this by report, and I felt that suspicion had reached me – and although no proceedings had been instituted, I doubted if it was extinguished, so that the greeting of a stout, well-looking horseman who at this moment overtook me created some alarm.

When he halted by my side and asked me if I was going to sleep at Caneda, "Doubtless," said I, "for we are within a league of it, and the sun is setting."

"You will find indifferent accommodations there, Eccelenza," said he. "Will you accept my offer of a clean bed at a small farm, which I rent in this vicinity?"

"I thank you, friend," I replied, "but it is not my custom to lodge with strangers."

"Pardon me, Signore," he said, at the same time placing his mule before mine in a narrow way – "If I am a stranger there are those at my house to whom you will have no objection to be known."

"How?" said I, "Do you intercept me by force? You will find you have no timid person to deal with."

"No, Eccelenza," said he, "I have no such commission, but to warn you against entering *Caneda*, and since I see you are inclined to refuse my invitation, I must request you, for your own sake, to read that paper," pulling out a small note and offering it me.

It would be difficult to describe the various conjectures which passed across my mind as I unfolded the paper and still more my astonishment, at seeing the hand writing of Veronica. It only said, *"Follow the bearer and he will bring you where you ought to be"*. This contained an enigma, but it decided my compliance; had she bid me enter a lion's-den it would have been equally obeyed.

I followed the man, in silence, who after conducting me through many obscure windings arrived, as the sun was exhibiting the twilight, at the closed gates of a small farmhouse, and having knocked gently, they were opened by an aged female speedily, and on our entrance as suddenly and silently closed. He took my mule and bags, and she, after making me wait whilst she entered to light her lamp, led me up the stairs of a small turret to an upper chamber door, at which she tapped softly, and to the question of *"Chi e?"* replied *"Amici,"* when the door was unbolted both at top and bottom, and by the light of her lamp I saw before me a venerable man habited in a gown and square bonnet, who took me by the hand, and led me to a seat by a table covered with a carpet, which occupied the space of an oriel window. Bidding me welcome, he returned to the door, took the lamp from the female. And giving some directions to her, with a low voice, closed the door again with the bolts, and placing the light on the table took the seat opposite me.

"It demands some apology," said he (placing his cap on the table, and thereby disclosing a noble and ingenious countenance), "for the liberty taken on thus interrupting your journey, and I humbly make it; but when you shall be informed that both your interests, mine, and those of the saintlike abbess of the Convent of the Ursulines are served by it, you will I am sure readily pardon the intrusion. My name is *Giovanni Gerson*, and I am but lately escaped from the Council of Constance, where you know doubtless my business as ambassador from France has been to enforce the doctrine of the Council's superiority to the Ecclesiastical See, thereby making some enemies of no common abilities. But that which made it at length prudent to retire for safety was the execution of an imperious part of my duty to my conscience by maintaining that the murder of the Duke of Orleans was unpardonable, against John Petit who defended that atrocity. So that to avoid the vengeance of the Duke of Burgundy, I am advised not to return to Paris, and am seeking some concealment from his agents, until I can procure a safe conduct to Lyons, where I can be secure in a Benedictine convent of which I have a brother who is the prior. I came hither from Germany, where I first retired, by the direction of our joint friend the good abbess, with whom I have long been in correspondence on the subject of those reforms all good Catholics more or less embrace, as the only safeguard of a corrupted church. The farmer who stopped you is a tenant of the Convent, who supplies them with wood, and was sent after you by her orders, being on his return when you departed, having gone to Venice expressly to announce my arrival. And I find her wish is, that I should retire for a short time with you to *Aronzo*, as more out of the notice of travellers, from whence I may take my route to Lyons at the proper season – and where we may confer together as to measures of safe reform."

Delivered, by this communication, from a host of suspicions, I cordially embraced the Christian Doctor, and readily acceded to the proposal, assuring him that I considered it as a great honour to contribute to the preservation of one so generally esteemed for his learning and courage in maintaining the good cause, and that having no other view on earth but to promote among my neighbours a *rational Christianity*, I could not but be happy to unite my exertions with a man who writes and speaks always so well on that subject. In a word, we agreed to proceed before day break towards a *Aronzo* together accompanied by the farmer who knew a bye road to avoid *Caneda*, where, by his account, there were spies of the church ready to introduce themselves to travellers, and to lead them into improper conversation.

After a temperate collation of fresh fish, cheese and eggs, we each took a little rest in our chairs, and before the dawn were mounted on our mules on the road to *Aronzo*, where we arrived safe before night fall and found good and convenient quarters.

Secluded from all interruption, among forests and waterfalls, we here had leisure to communicate our ideas, which were very similar, and with his pious aid I completed my introductory schools, and constructed a catechism, which if not exactly corresponding to that of Wickliffe, was on the broad principles of the doctrines and discipline of the New Testament, in which the mild and humble curate assisted. And thus sanctioned by such high authority, I more easily introduced our amendments to the enlightening people, who in that remote and secluded station, were easily guided by men who they saw had no pecuniary interest in any change of manners that were suited to promote the general welfare – for the fact, is, I in a manner shared my lands among them, and instead of seeking to live apart and in luxury myself, gave every family a home by allotting them leases on easy terms, and waiting for my returns of rent, when they could pay it from improvement. And thus legitimately acquiring their real regard, I found it not difficult to persuade them to amend in their habits and spiritual concerns, and to induce them to live according to the ancient discipline of the church, in the bond of peace and brotherly love, and if I could not make them as bright an example of true Christianity as I had found the *Jovinians*, it was not long before we were quoted as a pattern to all the surrounding country; and our neighbours of Cadore solicited an alliance with us. Industry supported by intelligence soon brought us wealth also, and the population, increased from the comforts arising from industry, supplied labourers for our forests and mines, so that when we had doubled our population, we had not a poor man among us. As for my own estate I found it a wilderness, converted, by making its interest a general concern, into a principality; and as I still threw my surplus into the common stock, my advantages became the interest of all around us. We improved our roads, enriched our pastures, drained our lands, and increased our buildings, and the result was that all lived in comfort and cleanliness, and there was no room for envy where none wanted the necessaries of life in super-abundance.

But the basis of all this happiness was a proper education in which moral principles and religious obedience formed the ground work of every establishment; and in the institutions of our schools I was greatly asssisted by the wise and cool advice of *Giovanni Gerson*, whose deep knowledge of man, and the practice of useful science made him, during his short stay with me, a very valuable acquisition. For we both agreed to conform to the times, and lay the foundation of a gradual reform by degrees – and by this means we effected a great victory over superstition and idleness among a simple and well meaning people.

Science also had its share of our attention, and with his aid I converted my grandfather's observatory into a school for astronomy, his library to a source of instruction, and even the old picture gallery with its maps, plans and antiquities served e'er long as an introduction to the fine arts among our mechanicks, in embellishing their habitations.

Having at length completed several benevolent establishments, which were of great utility in perfecting my grand scheme, of subjecting all my tenants to a system of pure morality, accompanied by industry, and making their improved comforts the result of their own exertions, it next became my *higher* object, as well as that of my two friends, who delighted to assist my endeavours, to establish, on a permanent basement, Christianity *in its original and utmost purity*, for I had all along looked to this as the crown of all my labours, and the goal to which my various experiences had furnished the golden clue. Neither will I conceal from my readers, that I owed my own conviction of the necessity of this proceeding to the luminous conferences which I had so often, since my return to Europe, held with my friend and the abbess of the Ursulines. My former intemperate passion was now resolved into the purest friendship, and from her subdued mind she had taught me a righteous affection, and to ascend from particulars to generals, ending in the genuine love of God.

"You see," she would say to me, "how a good providence has made your very errors contribute to your reforms – the intemperance of your passions to sober down themselves by disappointment, your exalted imagination has been corrected by experience, your impetuosity subdued by inevitable circumstances? And although your life has for a great part been subject to delusion, yet as your intentions have been always noble and humane, you have not been suffered to sink into atheism, or to adopt a system of faith that would have made you a pure deist. Lycas no doubt was one on principle, and evinced the depth of his understanding, considering how he was educated. God will not look for fruit where no seed has been sown, but even his persuasion awakened your reflections, and retarded the danger of your losing all recollections of the scanty portion of religious instruction bestowed on those nobly born by this our corrupted church and country. But how mysterious are the ways of heaven? What you considered as a misfortune so intensely, and I also as a cruel event, has been the blessed means of benefitting us both, for it led me to a deep examination of the grounds of the religion of Jesus, and soon converted my regrets into thanksgivings, when, appointed to the superintendence of this convent, it enabled me to instil into the minds of my companions in seclusion the real principles of the early and holy Catholic Church, by means of which I have been enabled to convert a cell into a paradise and purge away the errors of our sadly abused creed upon the reflecting principles of our mutual friend and fellow reformer.

"Let it be therefore our joint effort to bring about, with out noise or ostentation, among your people, as I have done with mine, a sound, inflexible, real love of the Redeemer, and the strict practice of His inestimable precepts, which will promote unspeakable harmony, gentleness, tenderness, kindness, and, in a word, that love, which descending from the Father of mankind, is productive of a peace surpassing human understanding."

Whilst thus she spoke her countenance beamed with brightness, and her eyes glistened with the rising tears of joy, and her voice, sweetly tremulous, seemed to my senses like the music of the spheres – so that from my own acute feelings, it brought to my mind those exquisite stanzas of Petrarch, for I must confess that although I venerated Veronica as a saint in glory – I could not but be impressed with recollections of her beauty and virtue united.

But to return from this involuntary digression, let me add, that by such interviews and discourses I was fortified in our resolution to bring about a reformation in the little district where it might be said I now almost reigned, by the aid alone of common reason and common justice; and where by setting the example of that humility and affection I wished to establish for the general good, I had less difficulty in bringing it into universal practice. What obstacles I encountered in my progress, what help I received from private as well as public prayer, for the aid of the Holy Spirit – how circumspectly I was obliged to guard against my own deficiencies, and the intrusion of others to my hindrance; what repulsion I found in the pride of the human heart, the prejudices of the aged, and the volatility of the young – none but a determined reformer can well understand. Suffice it that truth triumphed at last, and that I am now surrounded by a beloved society, who consider me as their father, and whom I esteem as my children, where peace and good will have taken deep root, immoral actions are nearly unknown, and the duties of genuine Christianity seem to be graven on all hearts, to the bringing forth of universal love and joy.

A remarkable combination of circumstances has contributed to enable me to perform all these salutary changes – my being in possession of this territory in fee and by hereditary right, my having declined any contest with my relations about other family possessions, my known fixed character, the present indifference of my countrymen to any forms of religion, my total separation from general society in Venice, which has caused me almost to be forgotten there, and a sort of contempt for a man who has acquired unfeigned humility, have all, under the blessing of God, enabled me to create a new church in the heart of these mountains – where their inaccessibleness befriends us, and their vicinity to the Swiss Alps is a protection for those who think for themselves. Beside all this, I am careful to prevent, as much as possible, my people from leaving their happy homes in vain speculations, the danger of which I am continually inculcating by my own example. And although we consider ourselves as allied to the Protestants, we never call ourselves by that name – but are content with the building of the Old Church as we found it, only stripping off the garments of superstition where they had a criminal tendency to idolatry, and by judicious changes in the obsolete liturgy of the Roman Pontiff retaining all that was pious and sublime in the construction of its formula. So that although we have removed the images which had very improperly been the objects of worship, we have not thought it necessary to discard the crucifix from the altar, since it is the chaste hieroglyphic of our persuasion, and serves continually to recall to our minds, that Christ thus suffered and died for our sins. Yet we do not consider this mere building as by any means His Church, but refer it always to the assembly who meet there, whilst we pay due respect to its venerable antiquity when we unite at stated hours to sing forth His praises, to Whose service it is dedicated. Among other changes, all my people now can read, and everyone is furnished with a Bible in our native tongue, of which every day not only an instructive portion is read in our schools, but also when the whole district attends at the dawn of day, on the ringing of a bell, that all may not only be sure to hear the word, but the improvement of the texts is taken up by the deacons chosen by the general consent, when, at nightfall, the inhabitants are again assembled to prayer before resigning themselves to repose, or carried on by the heads of families at their return to home. And thus it becomes impossible for any one to be ultimately unacquainted with the Sacred Scriptures, or their primitive precepts and commands.

Now all this procures them a cheerful and a happy life, and music and singing, as far as it is consistent with our duties, is cultivated very generally, its beauties heightened by its propriety, and made effective by the enthusiasm it produces in a virtuous cause; so that when we hear the song of reasonable mirth, we feel a double pleasure from the certainty of its propriety – and the hearts of our young people are not less touched, with their songs of Zion, full of religious expression, than the effeminate Venetians are with the sensual ones of the city.

When the time arrived that my friend could with safety continue his journey to Lyons for the security of a convent, I felt his loss indeed, and strove by every means in my power to postpone a privation to me irreparable. I even used my interest with Veronica to prolong the advantage of his valuable association, where he had hitherto remained a long time unsuspected and unknown to the active agent of the Duke of Bordeaux, who had sworn his destruction. But he knew too well the Venetian state and its intrigues to be quite easy within their territory; and finally I was obliged to accede to his conviction and name the day of his departure. On that, to me lamented day, he came into my breakfast room early prepared for his journey – and thus addressed me.

"At length, my dear Memmo, we must part, but not entirely, for we shall correspond ever while life remains, and Veronica will be the happy channel of our secret communications. We have unitedly but one object to impress on our followers, the necessity and utility of endeavouring to imitate the life of our Lord and Master. That end she has had the advantage of time and leisure to further, within the pinfold of a small flock it is true, but permanently there; and good principles we know, well planted and watered, extend their branches far and wide. She will eat the fruit in another world with joy.

"For yourself, I am convinced, and you should be so also, that every thing which has happened to you has been for the best end, and your eternal salvation.

"Had you complied with your father's wellmeant views, no doubt, and abandoned that amiable woman on whom you had, unconsciously perhaps, in the heat of youth fixed your first affections, you would now probably have been a Senator sworn to promote the objects of a remorseless and intriguing government, chained to a misalliance, and stung with repentance for your infidelity and injustice. Your passions repressed flung you violently out of a vortex of crime by their own eccentricity, and the Castle of *Sennaar* by its coercion restored their equilibrium. But there it was your guardian angel in the person of Lycas first impressed on your mind the importance of moral worth towards the conduct and felicity of life; a lesson you could never have attained in your native city among statesmen and an aristocracy. And next, what a blessing, when in that wilderness, you found, where it was least to be expected, one of the copious springs of the well of life of whose waters they who drink may truly be said never again to thirst. Lastly when adverse fortune, as she is called, had done her worst to deprive you of that worldly patrimony, on which most men place their unstable repose, she could not impede your restoration to your valued friend now restored to herself and purified from worldly interests: a fit associate for you both here and in a better state. Weaned from the world and its sordid enjoyments in your spiritual alliance, you will be helpmates to each other, and find at last that you are most blessed in being enabled by the grace of God to fulfil the proper duties of man in promoting obedience to His inestimable commandments among your adherents and dependents, thereby insuring to yourselves and others as much happiness as can be obtained by man on earth – and the best hope hereafter of pardon through His intercession with His Father, Who died for our transgressions and knows whereof we are made.

"For myself, I too have been a highly favoured being; born among a frivolous and amoral people, advanced to a chancellorship connected with princes, and employed as an ambassador – taught to venerate even the palpable errors of the Pontiff, – the love of truth and justice never abandoned me. I beheld her pure and simple torch shining above the splendours of a court, and now am, by the result of my very worldly vocation, led back to the sanctuary of peace."

When he ceased speaking, his countenance was irradiated with a smile of contentment which seemed to say, "it is finished, I am no more man of the world, my new duties shall be executed with zeal, and they shall be my reward." We embraced cordially without a tear at parting, for we each restrained ourselves; and all I could utter was, "the sun is now rising to gild your path. May it be an emblem of your future days, and this the advent of our mutual endeavours to fulfil our several duties."

As a faithful and unsuspected companion, I gave him my hardy, young and zealous African convert Cuba for whom I contemplated, some future day, an attempt to reunite ourselves with the *Jovinians*, and at his return I had the satisfaction to know that they arrived safe at Lyons without any one noticing them on the way, where, placed under his brother's wing, our good Benedictine found peace and protection – and still assists me by his councils in affecting our reestablishment of the discipline and worship of primitive Christianity. We shall probably never again meet in this world of probation, otherwise than by occasional correspondence as we have hitherto done in mind and in spirit, but we have both calmly and without undue enthusiasm pursued our assigned employments in our several paths; he by his writings and exhortations; she by her reformed monastic discipline and prayers; and I by my secular exertions to amalgamate the interests and affections of those around me into an aggregate of human society, free from absolute want, alive to universal charity, pledged to their religious duties as the bond of their union to God and to each other, and humbly prepared to receive with humility that sentence which infinite wisdom, goodness and justice shall, in mercy, award hereafter.

Neither do we object to any recreations that are in themselves innocent, and productive of either bodily strength or mental amusement, preferring always such as are neither injurious to health, or subversive of good temper, for cheerfulness and innocency are considered among us as twins of a sane birth – the offspring of disinterestedness and the liberal feelings of a subdued heart.

My little territory, which is dedicated to the public good, as it is now cultivated is sufficient to support in moderation twice its population, but already, so efficacious has been the result of our improvements in agriculture and the useful arts, that there is no demand upon it for subsistence, and my rents are made available to so much general improvement that the whole district will soon resemble rather a garden than a farm, and all we have to fear is the envy of our neighbouring states – to repress whose jealously we seek every occasion of serving them, thereby hoping to in time enlarge our boundaries, and soften the line of partition, by converting them to our institutions.

Have I not reason then to be thankful to providence for the trials I have been subjected to, and the experience they have produced? Instead of being a proud and overbearing Venetian Senator, I have been taught humility in the school of adversity, to know myself, and value my fellow men – to despise riches, except as applicable to useful purpose by benefiting others, and finally after subduing the passions by the aid of our holy religion to bow myself humbly at the foot of the cross.

Notes to the Text

PART 1

Titlepage: In *Original Tales* (1810), there is no separate titlepage for *The Captive*. Instead, there is a kind of half-title which reads:

AN

AFRICAN TALE

> You have amongst you many a purchased Slave,
> Whom like your Asses, and your Dogs, and Mules,
> You use in abject and in slavish sort,
> Because you bought them. –
> *SHAKESPEARE'S MERCHANT OF VENICE.*

The first page is headed "THE CAPTIVE, &c." and there is no running head. In fact, there is no indication in the 1810 edition of what "&c." represents.

The brief title "An African Tale" is also the title of a quite distinct short story in *Original Tales* Volume II, apparently first printed about 1780.

Advertise- The Advertisement served as an introduction to the 1810
ment: *Original Tales* in general and not to *The Captive* in particular. The 1798 edition of *The Captive* had no introductory matter at all.

p.5, l.2 See The Geography of Parts 1 and 2, pp. 306–16.

p.7, l.6 It seems anomalous that Lycas should have "a small gold ring in one ear", for we learn later (pp. 65–6) "that every male, and every female [*in Sophis*], received, on arriving at a state of puberty, golden ornaments of an equal value, though not similar construction: the males, a plain ring for the middle flinger; the females, a small single ear-ring...." Lycas received a finger-ring when he was naturalised (p. 90), which he perhaps turned into an ear-ring.

p.8, l.3   1810 reads "fancy", probably in error.

p.17, l.35 The "considerable port" is probably Suakem on the Red Sea; see The Geography of Parts 1 and 2, pp. 306–16.

p.18, l.37 "Caffre" (spelled also "Caafra" and "Caffree' by Cumberland) is an Arabic name for an unbeliever, that is, for all non-Muslims. It was applied generally to Negroes and specifically to South African Bantus. However, I do not believe that Cumberland intended the word to mean Bantus, even though Ker changed "a Caafra" in his 1798 text (p. 328) to "a native of Caffraria" in 1810, for there are "hordes of Caffrees" near the mouth of the Zebee River, well beyond Bantu territory.

p.21, l.10 The 1798 edition gives "rainy season", which Cumberland crossed out in the Printer's Copy but did not replace. Perhaps it should be "the summer", for on p. 22 he speaks of "the rainy months of summer". In Sennaar, the rainy season was April to June.

p.25, l.27 "juncs" are rushes.

p.32, l.5   There seems to be some confusion about whether "no one ever carried any worldly gain from us" or whether the Sophians had "no commerce whatever with the rest of mankind," as Lycas's master the old Jew says (p. 79), for Lycas later explains that "my old master['s] ... profit arose from an exchange [of gold] for [Sophian] pearls of a considerable size."

p.40, l.3   For "using it otherwise than as conveniency dictated," the 1798 edition read "misusing it, so as to throw an odium on one part more than another." The change was evidently made by Cumberland's friend Ker without Cumberland's authority.

p.40, l.7   For "and in their active and athletic images, a Phidias would have found an endless number of the finest models of the human structure," the 1798 edition read: "and would have spurned at the unnatural depravity that affixed ideas of shame to the most necessary, wonderful, and noble organs of the human superstructure." The change was probably made by Ker without Cumberland's authority.

p.60, l.11 "sherbet" is a Persian or Turkish drink made of sweetened fruit-juice and water, not necessarily chilled or frozen.

p.62, l.12 A vina is an Indian instrument like a mandolin (see p. 327 below).

p.62, l.28   "chastity" in 1798 was changed to "female chastity" in 1810, evidently without Cumberland's authority.

p.73, l.35   "Gratitude to that omnipotent being to whom they are indebted for every earthly enjoyment should also in a more special manner be inculcated" was written on this page in the Printer's Copy but was not included in 1810, partly perhaps because the two clear indications on the MS of where it should go are both impossible.

p.85, l.7   Cumberland's words in 1798, "painted her, quite naked," were altered, evidently without his authority, in 1810.

p.86, l.25   "The injudicious application of cold & wind is highly dangerous," which was added to the Printer's Copy, was not given in 1810, perhaps because there is no clear MS indication as to where it should be inserted.

p.93,   This list of works "by the same author" appeared at the end of the first printing of *The Captive* in 1798. The first five works listed there by Cumberland were then in print, the most important of them being his *Thoughts on Outline* (1796) with twenty-four plates, eight engraved by his friend William Blake. His *Six Moral Tales*, which was "*Speedily ... [to] be published*," never appeared at all in this form, although it may have been transmogrified as his *Original Tales* (1810) in which *The Captive* Part 1 was reprinted, and *Letters from Italy*, which was "*preparing for the Press*," may never have acquired text, for it seems to be the work without letter press called *Scenes Chiefly Italian* (1821) with lithographic views.

PART 2

Titlepage   At the top of the page is "[new Title of new vol *del*]."

Titlepage   Part 1 refers to the printed *Captive* (1798); Part 2 is the present text.

Titlepage   I have not traced "Molyneux letters XCV."

p.100,   Cumberland's Preface is for Part 2 only.

p.103, l.9   "The feast of reason and the flow of soul" is from Pope's "First Epistle to the Second Book of Horace," l. 128.

p.104, l.22 "bina": a vina, a seven-stringed Indian lyre (it appears in Thomas Moore's *Lalla Rookh* [1817]).

p.104, l.39 The passage "And during a week ... effect my escape" is added on the facing blank page, with a memorandum at the foot:
   Note.
   At the above should commence the Second part of the

work – if divided into Two Volumes, omitting the connective word And

p.104, l.41   The "Bar-el-abaid" river flows North from the Mountains of the Moon; it is the White River or White Nile.

p.105, l.24   In the copy of *The Captive* (1798) in the John Rylands Library, Cumberland wrote a note about the inserted sketch of "The Castle of Sennaar, as seen by Major Felix in 1828 – when there with Lord Brishoe[?]. it had bronze windows of elegant workmanship brought from India it was supposed but is now a mere ruin – and the only large building left there, since the invasion of the Pacha of Egypt."

p.105, l.39   Globe and wings are Persian (Zoroastrian) rather than Egyptian symbols.

p.106, l.18   "Kofila" is a cafila (variously spelled), a caravan.

p.106, l.31   Sangalli – evidently the Shangalla Negro tribe (as they are named by Bruce and Salt) living to the East of Sennaar.

p.109, l.8   Suakin (Suakem) is a caravan-terminus and port on the Red Sea (now in the Sudan) North-East of Sennaar.

p.109, l.14   The White River branch of the Nile is the Westward branch.

p.109, l.16   Darfur is the kingdom to the West of Sennaar.

p.111, l.28   "Intendenti" is Italian for one who understands.

p.112, l.18   "the caves of Elephanta" are on a small island in Bombay harbor; they contain massive Hindu statues hewn from the living rock about the 10th Century A.D.

p.113, l.33   Soros – Cumberland used the word to describe an alabaster sarcophagus is a letter to *The Monthly Magazine*, LIX (1 May 1825) 315–17, in which he interpreted it as "*a true ark or Noahtic monument.*"

p.114, l.4   "two" cavities is a doubtful reading.

p.114, l.27   "Thebaid" is a doubtful reading.

p.115, l.2   "spears" is a doubtful reading.

p.117, l.34   "They also serve who only stand and wait" is anachronistically quoted from Milton's sonnet "On his Blindness."

p.119, l.20   "attagan" may be related to the African weapon called an assagai.

p.119, l.29   "bank" was apparently converted to "Country."

p.120, l.37   Matamba was a kingdom (and town) an enormous distance from the Nile at Latitude 5–10S, Longitude 13–19E, now mostly comprehended by Angola.

p.123, l.18   "elephant's teeth," i.e., tusks.

p.126, l.1   Darfur is "a nation of the great desert" (p. 247) west of the Nile and south of Kordofan.

p.126, l.21   "giaour," a Turkish term of contempt for infidels (generally Christians), given currency in England by Byron's *Giaour* (1813).

p.129, l.18   Lake Zambre in Central Africa surrounds the island of Sophis, the setting of Part 1 of Cumberland's *Captive*.

p.132, l.32   "Were flowering" reads "with flowering."

p.133, l.13   Psalm xliii, 3 is paraphrased; the King James translation gives "tabernacles" for Cumberland's "dwelling place."

p.133, l.28   "haiks" are all-enveloping Arab garments.

p.137, l.12   This "immense fault" may be related to the Great Rift of Africa.

p.137, l.18   The "great giants of Hindoostan" are, of course, the Himalayas.

p.139, l.8   For Jovianus, see The Historical Contexts, pp. 316–20.

p.139, l.91   Flavius Honorius (384–423 A.D.), Emperor of the West (395–423), used his feeble energies to support the Roman Church and persecute its opponents.

p.142, l.39   "I was" is omitted in the MS.

p.147, l.35   The text reads "human *nature* [prospects *del*] *Institution*]."

p.149, l.27   "we taste of no liquids but milk and water" means essentially that "they drank no wine" (p. 154), for later we hear of them drinking lemonade (p. 181), coffee (p. 186), and herb drinks as medicine (p. 207).

p.149, l.27   Jonadab the son of Rechab commanded his sons "saying, Ye shall drink no wine, neither ye, nor your sons for ever" (Jeremiah xxxv.6).

p.151, l.38   This sounds strikingly like J.S. Mill's greatest good of the greatest number.

p.152, l.33   Cenobites are monks who live in a community under a rule and superior (e.g., Basilians and Benedictines), as opposed to isolated hermits.

p.154, l.40   Johonadab should be Jonadab; see above.

p.155, l.22   For a description of the "hospital" near the capital, see p. 173.

p.156, l.25   "marital," an uncertain reading, is a revision of "mental."

p.157, l.23   "Prophets" is an uncertain reading.

p.158, l.32   "no complaining in their streets" adapts Psalm cxliv. 14.

p.160, l.2   For Dongala and other places, see The Geography, pp. 311.

p.161, l.10   "rushing" is an uncertain reading.

p.164, l.20   The MS gives, erroneously, "3ᵈ Century."

p.164, l.32   Theodosius I (c. 345–395 A.D.) was Augustus from 378; his grandson Theodosius II (401–450) became emperor in 408 A.D.

p.165, l.6   Ragusa was the name of Dubrovnik (Yugoslavia) when it was the great rival of Venice.

p.165, l.25   "where" is omitted in the MS.

p.165, l.34   For "by acts" the MS reads "to acts."

p.167, l.30   "packs" is substituted for an illegible word in the MS which looks looks "aves."

p.167, l.31   "which guarded" and "of which I": Cumberland deleted both "that" and "which"; I have restored the latter.

p.168, l.2   "talents" is preceded by an illegible inserted word ("should"?).

p.170, l.10   The MS reads "may be by this providential assistance make."

p.173, l.21   The school system described here is very like the one which Joseph Lancaster (1778–1838) instituted in Bristol and North America (and elsewhere) and with which Cumberland assisted vigorously in 1808–34, collecting subscriptions, writing letters to newspapers, and so on.

p.173, l.22   This "hospital" is difficult to reconcile with Stefanus's statement that "We have, as you must have observed, no hospitals" (p. 155).

p.173, l.41   "some were singing" appears as "some we singing" in the MS.

p.175, l.16   Cumberland was much concerned about criminal law and prisons; he wrote to *The Bristol Gazette* on such subjects, inter alia on 20 Feb 1815 (Bristol needs a new gaol), 10 April, 4 May, 15 Oct 1815 (about the state of Bristol prisons), and 4 March 1825 (the excessive severity of the laws requires "an *entire revision of our Criminal Code*").

p.176, l.21   The Children of Loyola are presumably (and anachronistically) Jesuits, the order founded by Ignatius of Loyola (1491–1556).

p.182, l.22   "dissented" is an uncertain reading.

p.182, l.24   The Arian creed held that the Son was not of the same substance as the Father. It was rejected at the Council of Nicea in 325 A.D. and declared a heresy at the Council of Constantinople in 381 A.D.

p.182, l.24   The Donatist Controversy, which arose in 311 A.D., divided the Empire as successive emperors persecuted and re-instated the sect, until at a great conference in 411 A.D. the Donatists were declared heretics. The Donatists wished to exclude from the Church all who had committed mortal sin.

p.183, l.33   A misplaced caret in the MS makes the text read "initiate you to in our ceremonial."

p.184, l.6   "Talla" or "talsa" is an uncertain reading.

p.184, l.40   The MS reads: "The arts of the Greeks and Romans, [we have *del*] we cast behind [us *del*] them."

p.185, l.1   The MS reads "colleges of & by studious men."

p.191, l.21   The MS reads "master, and and go."

p.201, l.7   The MS reads "said he [Jovinus *del*] Stefanus."

p.201, l.24   The MS reads "who whose."

p.204, l.8   The MS reads "arrives arizes."

p.206, l.26   The MS, linking two pages, reads "avoided me avoided me,."

p.208, l.39   The MS, linking two pages, reads "rendered rendered." Elsewhere there is no catchword.

p.209, l.23   The MS reads "this these."

p.210, l.23   The "certain insects" Cumberland had in mind are indicated in a deletion: "the Coral."

p.212, l.25   "whoso sheddeth man's blood, by him shall blood be shed" (Genesis ix. 6); "all they who take the sword shall perish with the sword" (Matthew xxvi. 52).

p.214, l.22   The MS reads, perplexingly, "a ∧ no ∧ benefit."

p.214, l.28   The MS reads "∧ and ∧ or land."

p.215, l.8   The MS reads "to some to ∧ of ∧."

p.221, l.3   The MS reads "on their faces ∧ knees ∧."

p.224, l.16   The MS reads "smaller scale it had [been *del*] ∧ seen ∧."

p.226, l.18   "of moveable" – "of" was omitted in the MS.

p.238, l.15   "whatever I" – "I" was deleted in the MS.

p.241, l.37   The MS reads "momentarily."

p.243, l.25   The MS reads "of [Salt *del*] of the provisions."

p.245, l.33   "Fetice", i.e., "fetish."

p.249, l.19   The MS reads "so so much esteem."

p.258, l.8   In Cumberland's time, Fez was a separate kingdom to the North of Morocco.

p.251, l.4   "Joovians" is an uncertain reading.

p.252, l.23   "Kahira" is Cairo.

p.252, l.30   The MS reads "the house an old Coptic Christian."

p.253, l.5   Thebes is in Southern Egypt on the Nile, now called Luxor.

p.253, l.21   "Soros" is a sarcophagus – see p. 113.

p.255, l.9   Tubal Cain, great-great-great-great-grandson of Cain, was "the instructor of every artificer in brass and iron" (Genesis iv, 22).

p.257, l.40   Dongala is on the Nile in the Sudan.

p.258, l.1   Cangia is a light boat used on the Nile.

p.258, l.1   Mecca is, of course, across the Red Sea in Arabia.

p.258, l.6   Firman – passport.

p.258, l.15   The MS reads "treating [him rather as a son than a Slave *del*] with kindness."

p.258, l.34   The MS here and elsewhere reads "Cario."

p.260, l.16   "increaced" is a doubtful reading.

p.260, l.31   The text reads: "on one of one of the most glorious summer evenings."

p.261, l.1   The Saint is John who wrote the Book of Revelation on the Isle of Patmos, which is south-west of Samos, just off Turkey.

p.261, l.14   Ragusa (the modern Dubrovnik, Yugoslavia) was the ancient rival of Venice for dominion of the Adriatic, which may help to explain the malice of the Ragusan captain towards Memmo, who boasts of "Venice my birthplace."

p.262, l.33   The Cape of Spada is at the north-west point of Candia (the modern Crete).

p.262, l.35   The MS reads "so almost ∧ many ∧ miraculous an escape ∧ s ∧."

p.262, l.41   "Osmanlic" (written "asmanlic") is Turkish.

p.263, l.41   Dalmatia – that is, into one of the ports friendly to Ragusa.

p.264, l.12   The MS reads "I was easy."

p.264, l.32   Otranto is on the heel of Italy, South of Brindisi; it was made famous in Cumberland's time by Horace Walpole's *Castle of Otranto* (1765).

p.265, l.4   Podesta, a magistrate in a medieval Italian town.

p.265, l.26   Osterea – inn.

p.266, l.13   The Gulph of Manfredonia is below the spur of Italy at the south-east on the Adriatic.

p.266, l.18   Lucera is inland from the town of Manfredonia, and the district and town of Molise are north-west of Lucera.

p.266, l.24   Lake Nemi is just a few kilometres south of Rome.

p.268, l.12   Ravenna is just south of Venice.

p.270, l.9   "I supposed" – "I" is omitted in the MS.

p.271, l.8   Camanire is an uncertain reading.

p.272, l.23   Locanda – an inn.

p.273, l.6   Belluno is a town north of Venice in the Alps; Feltre is west-south-west of Belluno; and Cadore is the name of a district and town north of Belluno. The Piave rises north and east of Feltre. Aronzo (also spelled Azonzo (p. 280) and Arronzo (pp. 288–9) is a real village at the source of the Piave River in "the recesses of Montibello" (p. 284) at the extreme limit of the Venetian state's power.

p.274, l.8   "Canelettes," perhaps scenes of Venice like those painted by Canaletto?

p.274, l.32   "cin altro impresi di altro virtude".

p.275, l.31   *Paradise Lost*, XII, 646–647: "The world was all before them, where to choose Their place of rest, and Providence their guide."

p.277, l.11   The Italian painters are Andrea Mantegna (1431–1505), perhaps Giovanni Bellini (1430–1516), Giovanni Cimabue (1240–c.1302), Giotto (1267–1337); Titian and Tintoretto are deleted.

p.277, l.18   The authors are Dante (1265–1321); Petrarch (1304–74); Boccaccio (1313–75); Manuel Chrysolaris (c. 1350–1415), Greek scholar; Matthew Paris (d. 1259); Jean de Joinville (*1225–1319*); Jean Charlier de Gerson (1363–1429), prelate and reformer; John Wycliffe (c. 1320–84), English religious reformer; Jerome of Prague (c. 1380–1416), a follower of Huss, burned at the stake on 30 May 1416; Roger Bacon (?1214–44), philosopher and scientist; Raymond Lully (c. 1234–1316), philosopher and mystic; Albertus Magnus (?1206–80), Aristotelian prelate; John Duns Scotus (?1270–1308), scholastic philosopher; Campanus of Novara was the (posthumous) pen-name of the twelfth-century scholastic philosopher Abelard of Bath. Unlike the painters, they are all chronologically appropriate.

p.277, l.38   Cachiatore – hunter.

p.278, l.40   Thomas Aquinas (1225–74), theologian; Pope Urban VI is Bartolemmeo Prignano (?1318–89).

p.279, l.15   John Huss (c. 1370–1415), reformer, was burned at the stake in July 1415.

p.283, l.39   The "Council of Constance ... now sitting" had just martyred Jerome of Prague and burnt Huss. It was summoned to suppress the schism of the west and succeeded in doing so when it met from 5 Nov 1412 to 22 April 1418.

p.284, l.20   Giovanni Francesco Poggio Bracciolini (spelled Baccioloni in the MS) (1380–1459) was a papal secretary, classical scholar, and controversialist.

p.285, l.37   Zoar – sanctuary.

p.286, l.13   Baldassare Cassa (?1370–1419) as John XXIII (1410–15) was one of three simultaneous Popes; he was forced to abdicate at the Council of Constance.

p.288, l.10   Jean Charlier de Gerson (1363–1429) verbally attacked John Duke of Burgundy and his councillor John Petit for the murder of the Duke of Orleans; in retaliation, Duke John sacked Gerson's house, tried to have him assassinated, and drove him into exile in Germany until John's death in 1419, when Gerson returned to Lyons.

p.289, l.19   The MS reads "men whom ∧ who ∧."

p.289, l.31   The MS reads "an [example *del*] a ∧ pattern ∧."

p.290, l.20   The six paragraphs beginning "Having at length" and ending "the sensual ones of the City" are written on four unnumbered leaves (eight pages) bound at the back of the MS. They commence with a large "X," apparently as a cross-reference, but there is no corresponding link in the text, and their position in the text here is an arbitrary one for which the editor is responsible.

p.291, l.35   "virtue united": In the MS, a footnote reads:
    *here insert the interesting and impassioned lines so full of nature and fine devout feeling [*illeg words del*].

p.293, l.1   For "its venerable" the MS reads "it, venerable."

p.293, l.30   Duke of Bordeaux presumably should be Duke John of Burgundy.

p.295, l.24   The MS reads "have both ... have persued."

Epilogue

The Geography of *The Captive* and the Historical Contexts of the Sophians, the Jovinians, and Memmo

THE GEOGRAPHY OF *THE CAPTIVE*

The Captive of the Castle of Sennaar begins (Part 1) and ends (Part 2) in obscure parts of the known world, but most of the action takes place on sites in central Africa scarcely known to cartographers of Cumberland's time and quite unknown to those of ours. Lake Zambre, where the Sophians live in Part 1, and the Mountains of the Moon, the home of the Jovinians in Part 2, appeared on contemporary maps but have disappeared from ours. Cumberland has deliberately taken his characters beyond the borders of verifiable geography, but he has taken them farther than he knew.

Africa

Cumberland's hero Memmo was fortunate in possessing "A tolerable good map of Africa" (Part 2, p. 106), but he does not display it much, and he does not apologise when he says "I will not trouble my reader with every particular of my Journey" (Part 2, p. 257). Indeed, he seems to be somewhat uncertain of what "I could communicate of an itinerary" (Part 2, p. 267). Memmo is the only European ever to visit the Jovinians (Part 2, p. 180) near the headwaters of the Blue Nile, and Lycas was one of the very few Europeans to go to the island of the Sophians far South of Abyssinia. Memmo and Lycas would have saved readers some uncertainty if they had been rather more liberal with the names of the places they visited.

Sennaar was the capital city of the black kingdom of Sennaar on the Upper Nile, which was visited by only a few of the most exotic travellers in Cumberland's day and is scarcely better known today – as a matter of fact, neither the Castle nor the city of Cumberland's novel survive.[1]

---

1 The Castle was in ruins by 1828, and the modern town of Sennar is several miles up river (south) from the old site.

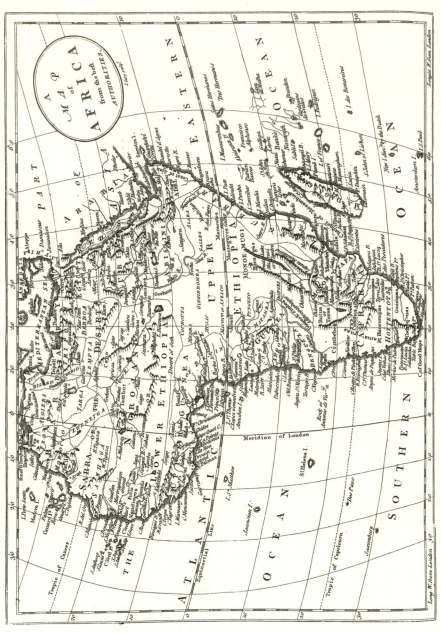

Map of Africa, from John Seally and Israel Lyons, *A Complete Geographical Dictionary* (?1784), Vol. I (GEB).

It was situated on the west bank of the Blue (Eastern) Nile south of its junction with the White Nile[2] and some 170 miles south of modern Khartoum. In his *Travels to Discover the Source of the [Blue] Nile* (1790), James Bruce said that it was on an insalubrious and godforsaken spot, with temperatures rising to 119°F in the shade. The populous, mud-built city of Sennaar was founded in 1504 by a "brutish" Negro tribe which still ruled it when Bruce was there, and he liked neither the site nor its citizens: "War and treason seem to be the only employments of this horrid people, whom Heaven has separated, by almost impassible deserts, from the rest of mankind, confining them to an accursed spot, seemingly to give them an earnest in time of the only other worse which he has reserved to them for an eternal hereafter."[3] In Bruce's time, at least, the city was almost entirely cut off from the rest of the world: "no caravan comes now from Sudan to Sennaar, nor from Abyssinia[4] or Cairo. The violence of the Arabs, and the faithlessness of the government of Sennaar, have shut them up on every side but that of Jidda, whither they go once a year by Suakem."[5]

The palace in Sennaar was made of sun-dried brick,[6] not of "Egyptian granite" as Cumberland says (Part 1, p. 5). It did not have an "immensely massy tower" (p. 325) nor a "high turret" (p. 32), for it was a modest building only five stories high built round a seventeenth-century mosque which had "bronze windows."[7] Its real appearance is given in the sketch "by Major Felix in 1828" which Cumberland laid into the Printer's Copy of the 1798 edition of Part 1 (in John Rylands Library) and which is

2 It's not on the "peninsula of an island," as Lycas says (Part 1, p. 33).

3 James Bruce, *Travels to Discover the Source of the [Blue] Nile, In the Years 1768, 1769, 1770, 1771, 1772, and 1773 In Five Volumes* (1790), IV, 454, 460, 476, 481; the account of Sennaar is general is in vol. IV, pp. 418–81. (The contemporary impact of the book may be seen in the 113 page review of it in the *Analytical Review*, VII [1790].) As late as 1902, Bruce remains ... our sole original [*English*] worker in this field" (R.S. Whiteway, tr. and ed., Miguel de Castanhoso, *The Portuguese Expedition to Abyssinia in 1541–1543* [1902], xviii). A long paragraph is devoted to Sennaar in J. Seally & I. Lyons, *A Complete Geographical Dictionary* [1787], II, and doubtless it is described in other similar contemporary works.

4 This is confirmed in W.G. Browne, *Travels in Africa, Egypt, and Syria* (1799), xx.

5 Bruce, *Travels*, IV, 486; "whither" is misspelled "whether."

6 M. Poncet, *A Voyage to Æthiopia Made In the Years 1698, 1699, and 1700 Describing Particularly that Famous Empire; as also the Kingdoms of Dongola, Sennar, part of Egypt, &c. With The Natural History of those Parts* (1709), 19, and J. Seally & I. Lyons, *A Complete Geographical Dictionary* (1787), II.

7 H.C. Jackson, *Tooth of Fire* Being Some Account of the Ancient Kingdom of Sennaar (1912), 1, 83.

reproduced here (facing p. 2). The accompanying pencil note says, "it had bronze windows of elegant workmanship brought from India it was supposed but is now a mere ruin – and the only large building left there since the invasion of the Pacha of Egypt [*in 1801*]." There was no "Castle" in Sennaar apart from this palace. All other buildings in the city were made of mud and reeds and were only one story high.

In describing his early travels, Lycas says, "We passed up the Red Sea to a considerable port; and travelled, with few accidents, through this accursed kingdom of Sennaar (under whose intolerable tyranny we now groan), meeting with every accommodation we could wish for in the Abyssinian domains": we passed above the fountains of the Nile, and descended the river Zebee (Part 1, p. 17). The "considerable port" is probably Suakem on the Red Sea, the chief Red Sea terminus of caravans passing through Sennaar. The "fountains of the Nile" are those of the shorter Blue Nile, which James Bruce believed he had located in Abyssinia. The Zebee River flows south from the Mountains of the Moon on the western border of Abyssinia across the Equator to the Indian Ocean, according to John Thomson's *New General Atlas* (1817).

Lake Zambre and its Island of Sophis are located by Lycas "a few weeks farther journey to the south-west" from the mouth of the River Zebee.[8] They are therefore in unexplored Central Africa south of the Equator, beyond "some very high mountains" at the headwaters of "a mighty river" (p. 19). The lake itself is of "vast extent," like "an unbounded ocean," requiring more than "a fortnight's journey" to traverse one side.[9] Indeed, Lycas says that "no European had ever before reached" Lake Zambre (p. 21).

The lake is apparently a real one. Great Lake Maravi or Zambre is shown on the map of Africa in John Sealy & Israel Lyons, *A Complete Geographical Dictionary* [?1784], Vol. I, and Cumberland's Lake Zambre corresponds roughly with Lake Nyasa in Malawi – "roughly" because the distance, marked in days of travel, and the directions given are very approximate. Lake Nyasa was apparently first visited by Europeans three-quarters of a century after the date of Cumberland's novel.

In the novel, "The Island of Sophis [*is*] at the head of Lake Zambree" (p. 20); it is, however, not just one island but a suite of islands, separated

---

8 Part 1, p. 18. In fact, the journey to the lake takes over "two months" (p. 19), for the old Jew had "miscalculated the distance" (p. 20).

9 Pp. 19–20. Later it is said to take "two months" for the journey (p. 19; see pp. 24–5). In the novel, the lake is evidently named after Zambre, the wife of Sophis.

from each other by "some miles" of shoal water (pp. 19, 40). I have found no other contemporary account of such islands.

Most of the places which Memmo encounters after his escape from Sennaar and on his return from Jovinia are real. "The River Bar" (Part 2, p. 251) or "The Bahar" (p. 159) or "Bar il abaid" (p. 252) which he crosses to the west on leaving Sennaar[10] is the Bahr il abiad or White River (Nile). Memmo once said that he wanted to trace it to its source (p. 122), and in fact he did so. On returning from Jovinia, Memmo descended at first on the west bank of the White Nile (p. 251), but evidently he then turned into the desert. Darfur (pp. 125, 247), with which the Arab chief traded salt and slaves (pp. 249, 251) and towards which Memmo returned after his stay with the Jovinians (pp. 249, 249), is to the south of Kordofan (now in western Sudan). Cobbe, "in the Centre of Darfur" (p. 252; see p. 255), is accurately described as an oasis town (p. 253), "a great mercantile mart" (p. 251) in the middle of the desert at latitude 14, longitude 28 (p. 258). The Kingdom of Kordofan, through which Memmo returned to Alexandria (p. 258), is just west of the Kingdom of Sennaar. The town of Dongola, in the province of the same name, is on the Nile (in the Sudan), south of Sennaar, and was the terminus of an important caravan route. Memmo arrived there on his return with a party of pilgrims bound for Mecca (p. 257). Kahira "or Cario, as by some it is spelled" (p. 258), to which Memmo was sent as a merchant by his Bedouin patron (pp. 252, 257), needs no "description after the volumes that have been written on that subject" (p. 258); as it is just up the Nile from Alexandria (p. 258), it must be Cairo, as by most it is spelled.

The Mountains of the Moon are the most obscure area in Part 2 of the novel. After the Jovians had lived for "ages" in Upper Abyssinia (p. 169), they migrated so far across the Nile and to the west that they lost communication with the Church of Abyssinia (p. 148). They settled on a "Table land" (pp. 138, 147) among the mountains "by old geographers entitled the mountains of the Moon" (p. 160), apparently in Nubia,[11] and Memmo is "the only European Christian that has ever approached our station" there (p. 182). Among the Mountains of the

10 "The distance between the *city* Sennaar, and the *Bahr-el-abiad* ... [*is*] three and a half days," according to W.G. Browne, *Travels in Africa, Egypt, and Syria* (1799), 449.
11 P. 139. Once it is called "ulterior Nubia" (p. 174). Nubia was a very elastic term among the ancients and among Cumberland's contemporaries, and it is therefore of little use in making equivalences with modern places.

Moon arises the Bar-il-abiad (p. 104), the White Nile, just as Ptolemy and the ancients had said it did.[12]

The lands of the Upper Nile and the Blue Nile were roughly known in Cumberland's time, thanks to such extraordinary travellers and writers as James Bruce, Henry Salt, and C.S. Sonnini.[13] However, the centre of the continent, the heart of Negro land, darkest Africa, was almost completely unknown, and, if contemporary cartographers did not populate it with anthropophagi and hippogriffs,[14] they did belt it almost from sea to sea with an equally fictitious range of mountains called the "Mountains of Kong," Donga (called Dongala by Memmo, p. 160), or the "Mountains of the Moon." These were placed just above and below latitude 10 north (5–15 North) and from longitude 5 west to 35 east and had been so placed from the time of Ptolemy onward – apparently no European traveller had been to this enormous tract of land to report that the Mountains of the Moon do not exist. On the maps of Browne (1799) and Thomson (1817), the White Nile is shown as rising in the Mountains of the Moon (at about latitude 7 north, longitude 23–28 east),[15] just as Memmo and the ancients described it. Cumberland therefore had good reason to believe in the geographical reality of the Mountains of the Moon, though they are just as fictitious as his Jovinians and Memmo. The probable site of the Jovinians' rich and fertile table land was in what is now south-western Sudan or the Central African Republic.

African Sources   In Cumberland's time, there were few sources of information about the lands near the headwaters of the Nile, Among the

12 This is contradicted in "A Report on the Kingdom of Congo, A Region of Africa, and Of the Countries that Border about the same Wherein is also shewed ... That the River Nile springeth not out of the Mountains of the Moon," Drawn out of the Writings and Discourses of Edoardo Lopez, a Portuguese, by Philippa Pigasetta, Translated out of the Italian by Abraham Hartwell, in *A Collection of Voyages and Travels*, Some now First Printed from Original Manuscripts, others Now First Published in English, vol. VIII (1752), 575–6. The map at p. 519 shows The Mountains of the Moon bordering a large lake at 20–25° East, 3–7° South labled "Zaire Moras Zambre Moras."

13 James Bruce, *Travels to Discover the Source of the [Blue] Nile* (1790); C[harles Nicolas] S[igisbert] Sonnini [de Manoncourt], *Travels in Upper and Lower Egypt* (1800); Henry Salt, *A Voyage to Abyssinia, and Travels into the Interior of that Country ... in the Years 1809 and 1810* (1814).

14   So Geographers in *Afric*-Maps
        With Savage-Pictures fill their Gaps;
        And o'er unhabitable Downs
        Place Elephants for want of Towns.
           (Swift, "On Poetry: A Rhapsody," ll. 177–80)

15 W.G. Browne, *Travels in Africa, Egypt, and Syria* (1799); John Thomson, *New General Atlas* (1817).

few in English were *Purchase his Pilgrimage* (1613); Father Jerome Lobo's *Voyage to Abyssinia*, translated from the French by Samuel Johnson (1735); James Bruce's *Travels to Discover the Source of the Nile* (1790); W.G. Browne's *Travels in Africa, Egypt, and Syria* (1799); C.S. Sonnini's *Travels in Upper and Lower Egypt* (1800); and Henry Salt's *A Voyage to Abyssinia* (1814). A very few attempts were made to use the uncertain resources of these lands in fiction, notably in Johnson's *Rasselas Prince of Abyssinia* (1759); in Anon., *Memoirs of the Nutrebian Court* (1747, reissued in 1765 as *Nutrebian Tales*, a kind of Nubian Nights); and Charles Lucas, *The Abyssinian Reformer*, or The Bible and Sabre, A Novel (3 vols., 1808), none of them with much concern for Abyssinia or Nubia. None of these works, nor any other relating to central Africa, was listed in the "Catalogue of the Library of G. Cumberland Collated in 1793"[16] or in the catalogue of the sale of his books at Christie's on 6 May 1835.

The relatively sparse geographical data in Part 1 might have been largely derived from such a popular work as John Seally & Israel Lyons, *A Complete Geographical Dictionary*, 2 vols. (1784?), in which Lake Zambre is actually named on a map. Part 2 of *The Captive* is a good deal more detailed and its facts more verifiable. The book which seems to supply most information relevant to Part 2 is Browne's *Travels* (1799). In particular, Browne gives an extended description of Darfur (esp. pp. 180–313) and of its capital city of Cobbe (pp. 234 ff), which was twenty-four days from Sennaar (p. 448) and thirty-one days from the source of the Bahr-il-abiad (p. 472). Like Memmo, Browne had hoped to travel "along the banks of the Bahr-el-abiad, which he had always conceived to be the true Nile, and which apparently no European had ever seen. To have

---

16 Manuscript in the John Rylands Library of the University of Manchester, added to in later years. The only works in W.S. Ward, *Literary Reviews in British Periodicals 1798–1820: A Bibliography* (1972) related to Africa (besides Lucas above) are: 1) Eusebie, *Elegy on a Much-Loved Niece; with a Hymn from the Ethiopic* (1798); 2) Royall Tyler, *The Algerine Captive*, or, The Life and Adventures of Doctor Updike Underhill (1802); 3) H.W. Tytler, *The Voyage Home from the Cape of Good Hope*; with Other Poems relating to the Cape (1803); 4) [William Dunlap] *The Africans*, or Love, War, and Duty (1808); 5) Anon, *Yuli the African*, A Poem (1810); 6) Constantine Williams, *The Campaign in Egypt* (1811). There is a plausible parallel to Cumberland in the short novel called *The Life, Voyages, and Surprising Adventures, of Mary Jane Meadows* ... who ... in the unfortunate [ship] Grosvenor ... was Cast away in [1782] on the dreary Coast of [South] Africa; where, after travelling through vast Deserts and the kingdom of Caffraria in the most imminent danger, arrived on the borders of the South [Indian] Sea, she was again Cast away upon an uninhabited Island ... for several years ... Written by her own hand (London [1802]). It is presumably based upon the accounts of the loss of the Grosvenor such as those by Alexander Dalrymple (1783), George Carter (1791), and Edward Riou (1792), but it proves to be as unrelated to Cumberland's novel in geography as in story.

traced it to its source was rather to be wished than expected" (p. xvi). In an attempt "to bring back [*Arabic*] proper names to the original pronunciation", Browne uses "*Kahira* ... for *Cairo*" (pp. xxvi, xxv), as Cumberland did (see Part 2, p. 258). Most strikingly, his map shows that "Mountainous district called Donga in which are said to be the sources of the Bahr el Abiad", also called the "Mountains of the Moon". Most of the geographical information about Africa in *The Captive* Part 2 could, I think, have come from Browne's *Travels* of 1799.

However, at least part of Cumberland's information about central Africa probably came through acquaintances. In his Commonplace Book [17] is an account of the travels in Africa of Mr Bruce, probably made while Cumberland was in Italy, about 1789, and before Bruce's book was published in 1790. Whatever the sources of his African geographical information, it seems to correspond well with other accounts of the time, except of course for the purely fictitious Island of Sophis and the table land of the Jovinians.

The fabled wealth, superstitution, and mystery of darkest Africa had, of course, always fascinated Europeans, but there may have been a more specific and current reason for Cumberland to place a race of uncorrupted Christians far from sight in central Africa. Emanuel Swedenborg wrote so emphatically of a surviving race of primitive Christians preserving the Gospel in all its purity in the heart of Africa that one of his first Swedish followers set off to discover them — and died in the attempt. Cumberland's early friends John Flaxman and William Blake were among the first adherents of Swedenborg in England, and Cumberland could well have heard of such a long-lost colony from them or from other Swedenborgians. Cumberland's Jovinians are, of course, quite unlike the followers of Swedenborg's New Jerusalem Church. The coincidence is important chiefly as indicating the persistence into the late eighteenth century of the legend of a paradisal or true Christianity flourishing in splendid isolation in the heart of darkness.

Italy

The Italian portion of Memmo's journey in Part 2 is fairly plain. From Alexandria at the mouth of the Nile (pp. 258, 260), Memmo sailed north to the Island of Patmos (p. 260) off Turkey, where his ship was becalmed. They were then driven westward by a great storm to near Capa Spada at the north-west corner of Candia or Crete (p. 262). The ship put in to

17 F. 10[r] (with the Cumberland MSS).

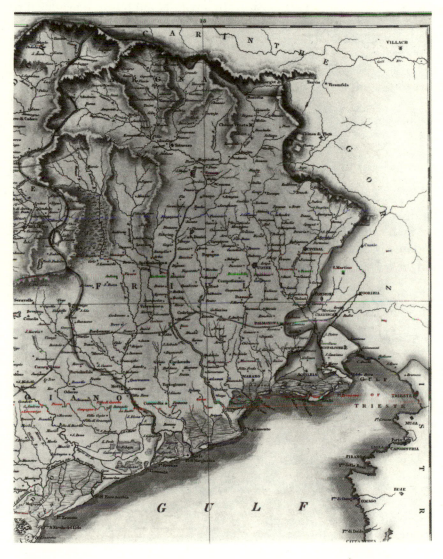

Map of Italy, from John Thomson, *A New General Atlas* (1817) (Bodley)

repair at Otranto (p. 264) in the heel of the boot of Italy, where Memmo disembarked hastily (p. 264), and then with equal haste the ship sailed north to the Gulph of Manfredonia on the spur of south-eastern Italy, the last point at which she was seen (p. 266).

Memmo proceeded north by land along the Adriatic coast, presumably as far as Manfredonia, where he heard of the Ragusan ship, and then turned inland, across the Appenines "by the way of Lucera, Molise and Tora,"[18] past Lake Nemi[19] to Rome (p. 266). After his alarming and disillusioning interview with the Pope, he recrossed the Appenines, pausing at Loretto (p. 268) and at Ravenna (p. 268) by the sea, and finally arriving in a felucca at Venice, queen of the Adriatic (p. 268).

From Venice he retreated due north, through Belluno, past Feltre, through Cadore (pp. 273, 289), all real places, to his patrimonial estate "at the source of the River Piava" (p. 273) in the hamlet and castle of Aronzo.[20] This hamlet was by the watershed of the Alps, close to the German-speaking lands, and presumably as remote and safe a place as Memmo could have found in the Venetian dominions.[21]

The Italian geography of Cumberland's story is presumably based largely on Cumberland's own experiences when he lived in Italy for several years in the 1780s and travelled through the Italian Alps and as far South as Naples.

THE HISTORICAL CONTEXTS OF THE SOPHIANS, THE JOVINIANS, AND MEMMO

George Cumberland tells us little about the background of his beautiful Sophians, and the origins of his virtuous Jovinians seem almost equally mysterious unless we have some information about the early years of Christianity. History is not important in Part 1, but it is strikingly relevant in Part 2.

The Sophians

The Sophians are clearly an ideal race – "they were the happiest, the most beautiful, and the best people on earth" (p. 28). However, it is not

18 P. [266]. I have not located Tora.
19 Lake Nemi in 1789 is depicted in Cumberland's *Scenes Chiefly Italian* (1821), pl. 35.
20 Pp. 273, 284; the name is sometimes spelled Arronzo (pp. 288, 289), or even Azonzo (p. 280; today it is spelled Auronzo.
21 The source of much of my Italian information here is John Thomson's splendid *New General Atlas* (1817).

so clear what race they are. Certainly they are not Negroes, for they came from Asia. At a time of unspecified antiquity, Sophis, "our ancestor, accompanied by his numerous family [*and by their characteristic sheep, with their fine yellow fleece (p. 75)*], ... descended from the springs of a river called the Indus [*in the Indian Himalayas*], on the other side of the world; after crossing a great water [*?the Indian Ocean*], suffering inconceivable hardships, losing many of his people in passing large spaces of sand [*?Arabia*], ... he came at last to the borders of this lake of Zambre" (p. 74). Sophis had been driven out by religious persecution, "for his own countrymen had banished him" (pp. 74–5, 343): "he endeavoured to overthrow the dark superstitions and idolatries of the times in which he lived;[22] but men calling themselves the priests of the Gods drove him from his country with his family and followers, here to establish a select nation, who, by restraining themselves to the proper enjoyment of their mundane natures, and following up the system of universal benevolence, have attained that peace, health, and longevity, which is denied to the cruel, rapacious, and unjust part of mankind" (p. 83). Sophis and his followers eschew clothes (they are "nearly as adorned by nature" [p. 29] and "live strictly ... on the most simple food" (p. 84), and they are apparently vegetarians, for they "kill nothing that breathes and lives" (p. 41); their sheep and cows are kept for wool and milk, not meat. These naked, vegetarian philosophers from India[23] with their "dark complexions" (p. 29) and "black hair" (p. 35) are much like the gymnosophs whom Alexander the Great encountered on the banks of the Indus river in the Fourth Century B.C.

However, the Sophians are clearly not Asians either. They have "short curling hair" (p. 29). Mica has "ivory" skin (p. 71), and Lycas, a Greek, is like them in race and language for when they first see and hear him they call him "one of our children" (p. 37).[24] Their loose, toga-like robes (p. 39), their simple, rectilinear architecture with its abundance of white marble, their devotion to music, dance, theatre, painting, and poetry, and especially their speech indicate that they are Greek. They seem to be classical Greeks in race, language, and cultural heritage.

22 These "superstitions and idolatries" are also found in Europe, for when Lycas "recounted all our [*European*] hymeneal system, ceremonies, and laws," Chilo replied that such "customs he had often been told, were the reason of the Sophians separating themselves from the world" (p. 67).
23 Cumberland was much interested in India, and in his Commonplace Book (among the Cumberland MSS) are desultory notes and sketches about India, mostly based on objects in the British Museum and on books.
24 He is "one of our stray children" in the first edition (1798).

The sparse evidence suggests, then, that the Sophians are descended from companions of Alexander the Great who settled in or near the Vale of Kashmir in the Fourth Century B.C. and adopted the diet and costume of the naked holy men they encountered there, while maintaining their own language and arts.[25] At an unknown date Sophis and his followers were driven forth for impiety by priests, perhaps Hindus, to embark upon their hegira to the Island of Sophis at the head of Lake Zambre in Central Africa. Since that time, ages have passed, but there are few indications in the novel as to the century in which Lycas found the Sophians and returned to Sennaar.

The Jovinians

The historical origins of the Jovinians in Part 2 of *The Captive* are established rather more precisely than those of the Sophians. Not only is history more important in the background of Part 2 than in Part 1, but at the conclusion of the novel it becomes part of the foreground.

The Christian Jovinians are of course a mythical people, but they are descended from the followers of a real man named Jovinian of the fourth century A.D. Jovinian (called Jovinus in the novel) was a monk of Rome who was profoundly distressed by the extravagant asceticism of many Christian hermits and orders and by their claims of moral superiority. He did not oppose their extravagance; what he opposed was their claim of superior virtue for such masochism. He argued that total abstinence, for example in sexual and dietary matters, is no more virtuous than moderate, legal indulgence, and he taught that each leads equally to God's grace. God's reward for the faithful in heaven is of one kind; there is not one reward for the virtuous, fruitful mother and another, greater one for the ascetic, barren hermit. Further, all disobedience to God, i.e., sin, is of one kind — sins are not graduated in wickedness. About 388 A.D. he published his arguments, the chief of which were that:

1 Baptised virgins, widows, and married persons are precisely equal in their domestic states;
2 Baptised Christians in full faith cannot be overthrown (or, according to another reading, tempted) by the Devil;
3 Abstinence from and enjoyment of meat are equally praiseworthy;

25 The Kingdom of Gandhara fits this description.

4 All who have preserved their baptismal grace shall receive the same reward in heaven;

5 "All sins are equal."

For these views, Jovinian was condemned in 390 A.D. by a Roman synod under Bishop Siricius, he was passionately denounced by Jerome[26] in two books Adv. Jovianum (393 or 394 A.D.) in whose invective is preserved almost all we know of Jovinian,[27] and later he was excommunicated by a synod under Ambrose at Milan.

With the definition of Jovinian's argument as heresy and his exclusion from the Church, Jovinian disappears from history; only extrapolation from later obscure references to him by Jerome permits us to conclude that by 409 A.D. was dead. So far as I know, Jovinian and his heretical moderation have since then been of no significant interest to anyone in fact or fiction, except in the second part of George Cumberland's *Captive of the Castle of Sennaar.*

These facts about Jovinian have always been accessible in the writings of Jerome and elsewhere, and Cumberland has built upon them imaginatively. According to references scattered through *The Captive* Part 2, Jovinian emigrated with a few followers from Italy across the Adriatic to Dalmatia, probably about 400 A.D.,[28] after his views had been declared heretical and he had been excommunicated. Presumably he and his followers found sanctuary there for a time until the pursuing anethmata from Rome drove them on once more, from Dalmatia to Alexandria at the mouth of the Nile, and thence to the Upper Nile and Abyssinia. In Abyssinia Jovinian died, about 409 A.D., and his followers settled there for "ages," during which time "many fell away [*from the faith*] and were lost." Perhaps because of these defections, the Jovinians migrated one last time from Abyssinia Westward across the White Nile, across barren deserts and inhospitable mountains, among savage beasts and savage men, to an isolated, fertile tableland in the midst of the Mountains of

---

26 C. 340–420 A.D., the translator of the Vulgate Bible, later canonized.

27 St Jerome, *Letters and Select Works* (N.Y., Oxford, London, 1893) (A Select Library of Nicene and Post-Nicene Fathers of the Christian Church, Second Series, tr. under the Editorial Supervision of Philip Schaft & Henry Wace, Vol. VI), pp. 66, 78, 81, 109, 175, 246–449; Jovinian is "a dog returning to his vomit," "a real Antichrist."

28 Pp. 139, 164–5, 169–70, 182. References on pp. 139, 164, 182 to Flavious Honorious (Emperor of the West 395–423 A.D.), to Theodosius I or II (Emperors from 378 to 395 A.D. and 408 to 450 A.D.), to the Arian Creed (declared a heresy in 381 A.D.), and to the Donatist Creed (declared a heresy in 411 A.D.) consistently and skillfully support the historical context implicit in the migration of the Jovinians.

the Moon,[29] near the headwaters of the White Nile. There they flour-
ished exceedingly "for several centuries," with 80,000 persons in ten
communities, but they were apparently quite cut off from Christianity,
even from the Church of Abyssinia; they made contact with the outside
world only through a little annual barter for salt with Arab traders. They
preserved their independence in part by their remote isolation and in
part by the appearance of abject poverty which they presented to the
Arab traders.

Memmo

This, then, is the situation when Memmo encounters the Jovinians, deep
in unknown, unexplored Africa, and nothing in the tale thus far would
set the scene more precisely than some time after about 800 A.D. – "ages"
plus "several centuries" after 410 A.D. Before this, while Memmo is
incarcerated in the Castle of Sennaar listening to Lycas' narrative about
the Sophians, when he escapes from Sennaar, and when he discovers
and lives with the Jovinians, the story is essentially timeless. It is only
when Memmo returns to his native Venice and tries to effect its refor-
mation that the year, or even the century and millenium, become clear.
Cumberland evidently intended to surprise his reader with the discovery
that this apparently timeless tale in set in a precise year among events
which were shaking all Christianity.

At the end of Part 2, Memmo returns to Italy, is shocked by the in-
humanity of the Pope and of Venetian society, retreats to his ancestral
estates on the limits of the Italian Alps, and undertakes the reformation
of his villagers – and only then does the historical context of the action
of the novel become clear. Memmo's grandfather had granted some
liberty of conscience to the villagers in the time of Pope Urban VI
(d.1389); he had been a friend of Jean Charlier de Gerson (1363–1429),
an admirer of John Wycliffe (c.1320–84), and a correspondent of John
Huss (c.1370–1415) and of Jerome of Prague (c.1380–1416) (see
pp. 278–9). These last are Memmo's contemporaries whom he wishes
to imitate: "I have neither the talents of Jn.° Huss, or Jerome of Prague,
but I am a reformer" (p. 279).

Yet more precisely, "the Council of Constance are now sitting" (p. 283).
The great Council of Constance was summoned to suppress the Schism
of the west, to dispose of two (at least) of three simultaneous popes, and
to deal sharply with reformers. It met from 5 November 1412 to

29 At this point, the geography becomes as fictitious as the history.

22 April 1418 and generally accomplished its objectives. Most particu-
larly, according to Cumberland's novel, Jerome of Prague has "just [*been*]
made a Martyr" (p. 283), and Jerome was burned at the stake on 30 May
1416.

The action of the novel occurs, then, in the first years of the fifteenth
century, near the beginning of the Reformation, and concludes not long
after 1416. Memmo himself is an inconspicuous but valiant reformer.
His great adventures in Africa, in Sophis in Lake Zambre, and in Jovinia
among the Mountains of the Moon have been preparing him socially
and spiritually for his role in the great events which were wracking
Europe. He values the arts, freedom, and fundamental Christianity be-
cause of his experiences with the Sophians and Jovinians. In Part 1 and
most of Part 2 of *The Captive*, the date and historical context seem of
little consequence, but the last, the Italian portion of the novel, is gov-
erned by the spirit of the Reformation.

When we know that the novel is set about 1416, we may perceive a
number of minor anachronisms in it. The Japanese (lacquer) tray
(pp. 34, 43) and the concern for the "picturesque" (p. 54) are essentially
eighteenth century phenomena in Europe, and Lycas' double-barrelled
fowling-piece (p. 29) seems improbable if not impossible. For that matter,
the City of Sennaar (founded in 1507) did not exist at the period when
Lycas and Memmo are held captive there. Most such anachronisms are
visible in Part 1, which was perhaps written before Cumberland had
decided to give the novel such an early date.

The period in which the novel is set may have come as much as a
surprise to George Cumberland as it does to the reader, for in describing
how long the Jovinians had been settled in the Mountains of the Moon,
from about 450 A.D., he first wrote "about 2000 years" and only later
emended this to "several centuries" (p. 170). A number of anachronisms
in Part 2 may betray carelessness, ignorance, or Cumberland's change
of the date of the setting. Some of the painters such as Mantegna and
Bellini, whose works hang in the Castle of Aronzo (p. 277), were not
born until some years after 1416, though the authors (p. 277) and re-
formers cited are all quite appropriate. Memmo need not have been
"astonished to find a people to whom this valuable invention [printing]
had not arrived" (p. 169), since printing from movable types was not
invented until about 1450. The Jesuits, who are referred to (p. 176),
were not established until long after Memmo died, in the sixteenth cen-
tury, and smoking tobacco, which is said to be "a gratification ... common
among mankind" (p. 205), was unknown outside the Americas before
the return of Columbus from his voyages eighty years after the time of

the novel. It is very unlikely that much "genuine Arabic" was spoken in Abyssinia in the fifth century A.D. (p. 174) when the Jovinians settled there, long before the Arab conquests. The "classical ornaments" of the Castle of Aronzo (p. 277) are appropriate to 1810 but not to 1410, and the Christian missionaries to Bengal (p. 267), the weaving of silk in Aronzo (p. 280), the holy fair at Loretto (p. 268), and the Ursuline Convent (p. 269 ff.), founded in 1572, are all chronologically impossible for 1416. Most of these anachronisms are very minor inaccuracies – almost any other order would have done for the Ursulines, for example – but Memmo's stress on printing is of some importance to the narrative. For the rest, the reader need not be disconcerted by the anachronisms.[30]

In its last portion, Cumberland's *Captive of the Castle of Sennaar* is in a sense an historical novel – and an early example of the genre.[31] Most of the novels of the eighteenth century, particularly the good ones, were set somewhat vaguely in the present; Clare Reeve's *The Old English Baron* (1777) was one of the first to deal seriously with the past. The form was made sensationally popular by Sir Walter Scott, beginning with *Waverley* (1814), and his methods were thereafter enthusiastically imitated and extended. But Part 1 of *The Captive of the Castle of Sennaar* was printed in 1798, and Part 2 was probably completed before 1810. In attempting seriously at the end of his book to illustrate the spirit of the early Reformation, Cumberland was apparently almost as original and remarkable as he was in the geographical, social, and cultural contexts of the preceding sections of the novel.

---

30 The occasional echoes from later authors such as Milton (p. 275) need not worry the reader, since they are not identified by author or date.

31 Cumberland was doubtless encouraged by the historical novels *Arundel* (1789), *Henry* (1795), and *John de Lancaster* (1809) by his distant cousin Richard Cumberland.

Appendix I

Substantive Emendations to the
Text of *The Captive*
Part 1 (1798) Found in the Second Edition (1810)

I have tried to give sufficient context to suggest the motive for the emendation. This list of course omits the frequent alterations of punctuation from 1798 to 1810, the correction in 1810 of typographical errors (e.g. "agreeble" 1798 p. 3, "uncooth" p. 24, "suuject" p. 33), and the creation of new typographical errors in 1810 (e.g. "al" 1810 p. 6, "accommedation" p. 137).

*	indicates that the emendation to the 1798 text found in the 1810 edition also occurs in the Printer's Copy of the 1798 edition (in the John Rylands Library). 1810 emendations to the 1798 text not authorized by the Printer's Copy were presumably made by C.H.B. Ker.
[his] *the* soul	Words in the 1798 text omitted in 1810 are given in square brackets; words added or substituted in 1810 are *italicized*.
§	indicates corrections also noted in the 1798 Errata list, which, however, only goes as far as p. 27.

*p. 5,	l. 13	*that they may* perhaps even fall
*	l. 17	[to] *for with* such [an one]
*	l. 17	[his] *the* soul
	l. 18	[feeds] *feeding* on her gathered fancies, [and] realises
	l. 20	That merciful *first* Cause
*	l. 21	*has* cheered me
	l. 33	[with] *by* fatigue ... [with] *by* disappointment
*	l. 36	any thing *very* interesting
*	l. 37	excellent in most *things*
*p. 6,	l. 8	on the [solid] *marble* pavement
	l. 12	which [had] *in a* friendly *manner had* taken hold

*p. 6,   l. 23   in tears, [I] exclaimed
*   l. 36   yet, *to my afflicted soul* as they were spoken [to my afflicted
                       soul]
*p. 7,   l. 2   [and his garment of] *a* fine white woollen *garment* reached
                       to his feet in many folds, [tied] *fastened* beneath the chest
                       [with] *by* a narrow black girdle, and [clasped with], *clasps
                       of* gold[1] – His feet were bare, but [under] *beneath* them
                       were light wooden sandals. – He had a [large] *small* oval
                       gold ring in one ear
*   l. 7   the [graceful] *interesting* figure
*§   l. 8   an [act] *air* of benignity
            l. 11   come [and see] *into* the apartment
*   l. 12   human face *as my guest*
            l. 17   not very well [lit] *lighted*
*   l. 20   the justest proportions [of architecture]
            l. 21   and *with the* most beautiful ornaments
*   l. 28   high bronze [candalabrums] *candalabra*
            l. 29   which appeared [under it] *underneath*
*   l. 31   many things of [a form I could not comprehend] *forms to
                       me unknown*
*   l. 36   from its dismal [appearance] *outside*
            l. 38   had sent me *t*hither
*   l. 40   contemplating [a scene which I could not comprehend]
                       this incomprehensible scene
*§   l. 41   and extending his arms [while he wept over them[2]]
*p. 8,   l. 7   placed his [bed] *mattrass*
            l. 8   the recess *were* adorned with rich inventions
            l. 25   is [of a texture] able to suspend
*   l. 30   meal [set before met] *he offered*
            l. 31   my earliest [infancy] *fancy* had ever enjoyed
*   l. 32   the last [evening-adventure] *evening's adventure*
*   l. 39   A [warm] shower of tears
            l. 41   [there was] *I perceived* the old man
*p. 9,   l. 4   asked me *in kind accents* if[3]
            l. 13   I loved truth *and liberty* before[4]

1 The Printer's Copy reads "and fine white woollen ... and clasped with gold."
2 In the Printer's Copy, "and" is deleted in pencil.
3 In the phrase "such immoderate grief" below, "immoderate" is underlined in the text
   and marked in the margin for deletion in pencil in the Printer's Copy.
4 In the Printer's Copy, "before" is altered in pencil to "above."

*p. 9,   l. 15   all that makes [life] *existence* desirable in the prime of life
*   l. 17   with *rational* society
*   l. 19   composed and [tranquil] *resigned*
*   l. 20   the voice of [an angel] *a parent*, [I] took some food
            l. 22   this [oblivious] abode
*   l. 23   I can scarcely entertain a doubt [(said he)]
            l. 24   the temper of the [tyrants] *tyrant*
            l. 32   a tender look at the [picture] *portrait of the female*
*   l. 39   [I came here] *here I came*5
            l. 41   this [sombrous] *sombre* dungeon
*p. 10,   l. 2   [by shewing me that they are a] *like a splendid but* useless
                     possession
*   l. 5   *Yourself* <italics added in 1810>
*   l. 7   becomes *doubly* a duty
*   l. 8   Perhaps ... [perhaps] *and possibly* I may
            l. 9   this [immensely] *vast* massy tower
*   l. 12   I hope *to learn* much
*   l. 14   *here* <italics added in 1810>
*   l. 21   at my first [coming here] *imprisonment*
            l. 26   its full [effects] *effect*
*   l. 27   when [this] *the* Nile
            l. 36   a participation of this [attribute] *benevolent office*
    p. 11, l. 5   my family [are] *is* noble
*   l. 9   [at] *before* twenty years of age6
            l. 31   we were both [again] arrested
*   l. 32   vigilance of the [state] *government*
            l. 36   of [my] despair ... with [my] *our* family
*   l. 37   keeping [my] *an* oath, to *obtaining* my liberty7
            l. 38   at length *my parents*
*   l. 38   weary of [my] *this* firmness
*   l. 39   [my freedom was given me] *set me free*8 on the condition
                     of [my] accepting [the] *a* knighthood
*p. 12,   l. 2   *and* I [went to] *embarked* for the island

5 In the Printer's Copy, "my virtues, for for my virtues I came here" is altered in pencil
   to "my virtues, for they brought me here."
6 In the Printer's Copy, "my proficiency" was altered to "the profiency," but the change
   was not incorporated in the 1810 text.
7 In the phrase just above, "alleviation of my despair ... compromise with my family"
   was altered in the Printer's Copy to "alleviation of despair ... compromise with our
   family," but the change was not incorporated in 1810.
8 The Printer's Copy reads "I was set free."

p. 12,   l. 2   the severest [services] *service*
*   l. 3   the warmth of [my] *an* enthusiastic passion
*   l. 4   by perishing in an honourable [service] *manner*, to extin-
                 guish my [life] *existence* and *my* love together
*   l. 9   my [affection] *attachment*
*   l. 13   my [own] *native* country
*   l. 14   [my] *a* dying father's embraces
*   l. 16   my mistress had taken her vows *of celibacy*
*   l. 19   quit for ever [my native] *the Venetian* soil
*   l. 19   I was *much* too warm
*   l. 20   and [in] the *idle* attempt had nearly [lost] *cost me*9
*   l. 23   and, having passed [so] much [of my life] *time* in the
                 [Levant] *Mediterranean*,
         l. 28   In this journey, *taking a circuitous route*, I saw
*   l. 35   this [accursed] *detestable* country
*p. 13, l. 1   I am obliged [to you for] *by* your services
*   l. 4   *with us, power is all*, and you must not hope
         l. 6   a merchant or *a* physician
*   l. 6   I might [the easier] have been
*   l. 8   it cannot be allowed [on any condition]
*   l. 8   my [guards] *officers* will take care
*   l. 13   deprived me of *my mental* faculties
*   l. 17   with [a] *some* prospect of success
         l. 21   Born [in] *to* an exalted station
*   l. 22   by [natural] pursuits *the most laudable*10
p. 14,   l. 3   subsiding thunder*s*
         l. 4   I came here in [my] *the* prime *of life*
*   l. 5   the delights that [its] *youth's* happiest state
*   l. 8   for which he *probably* was
         l. 9   excited [on] *in* my features
         l. 12   still more [and more] staggered
*   l. 13   [but] *yet* if you find nothing
*   l. 15   the state of mankind and the construction of [his] *our*
                 organs [renders] *render*11
*   l. 19   noon [approaches] *is fast approaching*
*   l. 20   the sun arrested [all] *the* travellers
         l. 21   the eyes *even* of the [very] crocodiles

9 The Printer's Copy reads "and, in the idle attempt, had nearly lost."
10 The Printer's Copy reads "by natural pursuits the most laudable."
11 The Printer's Copy reads "our organs renders."

*p. 14,   l. 22   *the* hippopotamos has descended to his cooling [reeds]
                    weeds

*   l. 25   awakened by *the notes of* the reed sparrow and the [cool]
                    mild breezes of the evening, [we will] then *let us* com-
                    mence

*   l. 28   was *agreeably* surprised

           l. 38   has [no] *not* such good water

*   l. 39   [and] *whilst* I, like Orpheus of old,

*   l. 41   and air may [enlighten] *enliven* you and make your water
                    more [agreable to the taste] *palatable*

 p. 15,   l. 2   an Indian [vina] *Mandolin*

*   l. 2   [went to] *ran through* my very soul

*   l. 3   bred in the [very] bosom

*§   l. 10   a [physician] *musician*

           l. 13   [from] *after* such a beginning

*   l. 16   Your eulogium *(he replied)* would

*   l. 17   at the beginning of our [acquaintance] *narrative*

*   l. 20   my *mode* of life

           l. 22   slightly [inducted] *instructed* in a few ornamental arts

*   l. 23   the [fruits] *fruit* of an illegitimate amour

*   l. 26   ladies [of] *belonging to* the Haram, of Greek extraction,[12]

*   l. 28   [entirely] in an instant *entirely*

           l. 30   who [held] *presided in* an office

*§   l. 32   [many exchangers] *money-changers*[13]

*   l. 33   had [also] an attachment

           l. 34   passions were [very] violent *in the extreme*

*   l. 35   to carry on [this] *an* illicit correspondence

*   l. 36   young men of the [court] *palace*

           l. 39   ingratiate himself [into] *in* my esteem

*p. 16,   l. 1   [and] after a very short [time] *period*[14]

*   l. 2   at the risk of life to [serve him] *promote his wishes*[15]

           l. 3   have been [suspected] *expected*

           l. 6   ease, *and* luxury [and ignorance]; *ignorant* of the world

*   l. 9   falling from a [height] *precipice*

           l. 11   a merchant *who dealt* in trinkets, *and* whose presents

12 The Printer's Copy is altered to read "ladies of Greek extraction belonging to the
    haram."

13 Corrected to "money exchangers" in the Errata (1798).

14 The Printer's Copy reads "and, after a very short period."

15 For "at the risk of life," the Printer's Copy reads in pencil "at the risk of my life."

*	l. 12	had been [first] employed
	l. 13	seduce me from my [duties] *duty*
*§	l. 14	received me with [pleasure] *cordiality*, but soon shewed an [alacrity] *anxiety*[16]
*	l. 16	the story of my [disgrace] *dismissal and its motive* to [buy] *barter commodities in exchange for* gold dust;[17] he wants [a servant] *an assistant*
*	l. 24	which [has] here *has*
*	l. 31	sailed [up] *through* the Delta
*	l. 32	My master was [also] a Jew, and *perhaps* [one of] the most [reserved] *tacitunre* <sic>[18]
	l. 36	many instances of *his* humanity
p. 17,	l. 1	[shot up into] *changed to* the most
*	l. 3	my *careless* loquacity
	l. 4	[by] *in* taking me out
*	l. 8	seemed to have *entirely* changed
*	l. 15	*be my son, and I will be a father to you* <italics added in 1810>
*	l. 17	so [favourable] *distinterested* an offer
*	l. 31	should we get [back] safely *back*
*	l. 32	and you alone shall *be my heir, while we* enjoy, in repose, in repose, the reward of my [continued] *long-procrastin-ated* labours[19]
*	l. 38	accommodation we could wish *for*
	l. 39	in the Abyssinian [domains] *dominions*
*p. 18,	l. 4	We *then* prepared to return, but the [good] *hospitable* Africans
	l. 5	with whom [we] *he* had dealt honourably
*	l. 7	in [feasts] *jollity* and dances
*	l. 9	with the rapidity of [men] *those who are* exhilarated
	l. 11	in comparison [of] *to*
*	l. 14	habit and *the love of* wealth
*	l. 19	They inhabit *peaceably* an island
*	l. 21	if one may judge from [all] accounts of them
*	l. 27	without war, [yet] *and* happy
	l. 32	who is there [that] can hinder us

16 "alacrity" is changed to "anxiety" also in the Errata (1798).
17 The Printer's Copy reads "to barter for gold dust."
18 The Printer's Copy reads "and one of the most taciturne."
19 The Printer's Copy omits "while we."

p. 18,　　l. 36　　an old African, [a Caafra²⁰] *a native of Caffraria*, whom he
　　　　　　　　　　[had] called on
p. 19,　　l. 10　　the old [negro] *Caffre*
*　　　　　l. 11　　with the [ancient] weapons of his nation
*　　　　　l. 12　　[a] *an* European
*　　　　　l. 17　　brackish [springs] *waters*
*　　　　　l. 18　　hordes *occasionally* alarmed us
*　　　　　l. 20　　and *at last* even I began
*　　　　　l. 22　　I could see he *deeply* repented [of]²¹
*　　　　　l. 25　　surpassed our [imagination] *expectation*
　　　　　　l. 29　　a [rising] *mountainous* country
*　　　　　l. 29　　came to the [borders] *swampy margin* of a mighty river²²
*　　　　　l. 30　　necessary [for us] to pursue
*　　　　　l. 32　　and [then we should] *afterwards to* ascend
*　　　　　l. 36　　[where] *there*, before the dry season
p. 20,　　l. 4　　notwithstanding [all] our united care ... [sunk] *sank* at last
*　　　　　l. 7　　where we [were] *designed* to repose
　　　　　　l. 8　　no efforts [of mine] could
*　　　　　l. 9　　we formed *for him* a verdant hut [for him]
*　　　　　l. 12　　Here we [reposed] *rested* some days, [and] *while*
　　　　　　l. 17　　to the [old] worn-out
*　　　　　l. 18　　you perhaps [may] *will*
*　　　　　l. 32　　[he] embraced us both
　　　　　　l. 34　　in [all] our dealings
*　　　　　l. 36　　where, [he reports, that] during the short stay [which was]
　　　　　　　　　　permitted him
　　　　　　l. 40　　bury me [on] *in*
*p. 21,　　l. 3　　affectionate looks *and tender embraces*
*　　　　　l. 5　　to pass *here, the season* of the summer rains [on this spot]
*　　　　　l. 6　　preserving his honoured [remains] *ashes* from the inroads
　　　　　　　　　　of *wild* animals
　　　　　　l. 7　　and *by* the advice
*　　　　　l. 9　　the closing of the [rains] *wet season*
*　　　　　l. 14　　to let out the [smoke] *vapour*
　　　　　　l. 16　　[our] *the* smoke in the [rainy season] *winter*²³

20　The common alteration of "Caafra" or "Caffree" to "Caffre" is not recorded hereafter.
21　The Printer's Copy reads "he deeply repented of."
22　The Printer's Copy reads "we came."
23　In the Printer's Copy "rainy season" is deleted, but nothing is substituted for it. Perhaps
　　it should be "the summer," for below on p. 22 he speaks of "the rainy months of
　　summer."

*p. 21,   l. 24   the ceremonies of [my] religion
*   l. 39   and equality *among them is as* [almost] *nearly* general[24]
*   l. 41   that [among] *in* the words [that] he pronounced[25]
*p. 22,   l. 12   never [make] *succeed in making* me
           l. 14   in pursuit of [the] antelopes
*   l. 16   a spacious *refreshing* cave
*   l. 17   surprised to find, [a rock] on [whose] *the* surface *of a rock*,
                    [was engraven] the *sculptured* figure of a man
*   l. 19   youth, [with] *of* a most beautiful countenance
*   l. 21   grove, *overhung with climbers*[26]
*   l. 23   *while* the waves
           l. 24   [in the form of] *forming* a circular bay
*   l. 24   [and washes] *after washing* over
           l. 26   rock; [and his] *its* action
           l. 27   was, [as] I thought very majestic; [which] *and* was aided
                    in a great measure
*   l. 28   to make [the youthful figure] *him*
*   l. 29   and to [make] *add* another figure of the same *noble* char-
                    acter
           l. 36   any *other* motive of [other] curiosity
   p. 23, l. 2   and [which] when dressed
*   l. 3   *wild* vines also grew [wild] here
           l. 5   to [whet] *sharpen* my impatient ardour
           l. 10   plant, which [had] *put forth* monthly shoots
*   l. 11   day [arrived] *happily dawned*
           l. 12   camels *having* quite recovered [in] their flesh
*   l. 13   I [shed some tears] *dropped the tear*
           l. 15   three dogs, [neither] *not one* of which
           l. 16   half my [property] *gold*
*   l. 17   [and] *for*, once
           l. 18   when a valuable [sack] *packet*
*   l. 18   he [smiling] *smiled*, and by signs, expressed[27]
           l. 19   leave that mischievous sand [there] *where it was*
*   l. 32   mixed with *affecting and* confused imagery
           l. 34   [of] *on* a sudden

24 The Printer's Copy reads "and equality nearly general."
25 The Printer's Copy reads "that among the words he pronounced."
26 The Printer's Copy reads "climbers," 1810 "clibers."
27 The Printer's Copy reads "smiling, He by signs, expressed."

*p. 23,   l. 38   with a *soft* [suffocated] *suffocating*[38] voice to be calm: [as]
                    and we should never *never* more be parted*!*

           l. 41   day [was emerging from the] *had began* to dawn

  p. 24,   l. 8   at the same time [that] they

           l. 9   *and* reminded me of [his] *the* courage *of him*

*   l. 10   companion of my [confinement] *miseries*

*   l. 11   I *presently* rejoined [him presently after] *my friend*[29]

*   l. 13   after [the] *his* usual attentive enquiries

           l. 14   he *thus* continued

           l. 15   my son [(said he)]

           l. 20   are *slightly* brackish

*p. 8,   l. 25   the [Caffre] *negro* colony

           l. 28   wells [of] *and* shelter

           l. 30   we [however] found

*   l. 32   our property *remained* in the most perfect security

           l. 33   [a] rather *a* timid and gentle race

           l. 34   their women, *even* to me

           l. 38   but *we* carefully [concealing] *concealed* from their enquiries

*   l. 39   *had they suspected such to be our intention,* they would never
                    have permitted us to take to the desert [had they sus-
                    pected such to be our intention]

*   l. 41   [so great a] *such a perfect* horror[30] ... that [had they] *if they
                    had* thought

  p. 25,   l. 11   [these] *those* burning sands

*   l. 13   very [unquiet] *little* repose

*   l. 15   next [lonely] day's *lonely* journey

           l. 15   near [to] the margin of the lake

*   l. 19   *at sun-rise,* I beheld, to my inexpressable satisfaction [at
                    sun-rise]

*   l. 21   to which all my wishes [tended] *extended themselves*

*   l. 23   saw, on the sands, *distinct* traces

           l. 26   [for] *to* a considerable distance

*   l. 27   with large *juncs and* reeds

*   l. 28   multitudes of ostriches *and bustards*

*   l. 29   seeing a [large] drove of [them] *these*[31]

28 The Printer's Copy reads "suffocated."
29 The Printer's Copy reads "presently I rejoined him."
30 The Printer's Copy reads "so perfect a horror."
31 The Printer's Copy reads "a drove of them."

*p. 25, l. 30 we took [some] fresh eggs

       l. 31 all [of] which *circumstances* were

* l. 34 uncommon*ly* good spirits, I was *even* gay

* l. 35 was *suddenly* awakened

* l. 36 and *on opening my eyes* saw

*p. 26, l. 2 *al*though early accustomed

* l. 3 [but] *and,* for my own part,

       l. 8 [an adust] *a burning* vapour

* l. 10 impeded by [it] *its pressure*

* l. 15 the [sands] *thirsty lands*[32]

       l. 19 scudding away *entirely*

       l. 23 my eyes [I then thought] had ever beheld

* l. 36 *thou art* Love! <"Love" italicised in 1798>

   p. 27, l. 2 their [soft] *gay* plumage

       l. 4 the island *so long the object* of my desires

* l. 7 to my great *alarm and* astonishment

       l. 22 the [camels'] *camel's* splashing steps

       l. 40 usually accompanied [it] *this wind*

   p. 28 l. 4 to hear [that they were] *it was* ... [they had] *it was inhabited by* none

       l. 13 [coming] *come* to collect

       l. 20 [jewels and gold] *gold and jewels*

* l. 22 [yet] still I could not

       l. 25 pride [then] *at that time* kept me ignorant

* l. 36 over [my] *the* mind[33]

* l. 37 [even] *nay* concupiscence

* l. 40 some of their *women of the* most accomplished [women] *forms*

       l. 41 little also did *I know myself* <italics added in 1810>

   p. 29, l. 2 might have been soon *entirely* corrupted

* l. 3 must be *made* of the grossest material if their example do*es* not

       l. 9 *and* kissed it fervently

* l. 20 warm springs [in it], whose waters encrease the milk of [the] cows

* l. 21 explaining, [as well as he could] *with difficulty,* all those particulars, a flock of birds *of the parrot kind* flying by

       l. 25 committed [a] murder

32 The Printer's Copy reads "the thirsty sands"; "lands" appears to be a misprint.
33 The Printer's Copy reads "over mind."

*p. 29,   l. 27   hide [them] *it* in a bush along with [it] *them*
*   l. 30   nearly [naked] *as adorned by nature*[34]
          l. 31   They ran up to [him] *my guide*
*   l. 36   we should be [siezed] *arrested*
          l. 38   sufficient *to have enabled them* to lift me
*   l. 41   rudely laid together *on two uprights, the ends being rocks*
*p. 30,   l. 9   an aged man [with a full beard, and] *whose beard was full,*
                  folded up in a woollen garment as white as snow,
                  [whose] *the broad* edges *of which* were
          l. 12   a crutch ha..dle [to] *on* the top of it
*   l. 19   and *looking at one of the youths*, to my unutterable astonish-
                  ment [looking at one of the youths]
*   l. 21   I perfectly understood him, [he] asked where they had
                  encountered [us] *the intruders*
*   l. 26   [they kill] *killing* the birds
*   l. 27   *they are* come [here] *hither*
*   l. 34   the good [Energy] *Being*
*   l. 36   instruments of [destruction] *death*
*p. 31,   l. 11   [and] *then,* falling
          l. 31   the love of virtue [alone]
          l. 38   [all] *the whole* of which
  p. 32, l. 2   send you [all] *both* together
*   l. 3   is to *guard the coast and* examine
*   l. 5   any *worldly* gain from us
          l. 8   [while he remains among us,] in order to induce him to
                  conduct himself with modesty and decorum *while he*
                  remains among us
*   l. 21   Who [is] Alla *is*[35]
*   l. 29   we *all* retired
*   l. 31   *Lycas*, at this period, [Lycas]
*   l. 32   the outer *prison* door [of our prison]; the [grating] *clanking*
*   l. 34   the fall of a *heavy* draw-bridge
*   l. 38   his *singular* narration
*p. 33,   l. 7   he *usually* retired
*   l. 8   his *declining* voice, [I could easily] *it was easy to* judge
*   l. 14   without money [and] *or* friends
*   l. 16   [and] *for* besides [its] being strong[36]

---

34 The Printer's Copy reads "as by nature adorned."
35 In the Printer's Copy, "is" is deleted but no corresponding addition is made.
36 The Printer's Copy reads "as" rather than "for."

p. 32,   l. 23   one [continuous] *continued* prison
*   l. 28   flattering [prospects] *dreams* of escape
          l. 36   opposite *to* the opening
          l. 38   seemed to be *of* tufts of wool
*   l. 39   between [each] *every* mattress
*p. 34,   l. 1   over [each] *the* pillow
*   l. 2   at the foot of [each mattress] *all the mattresses*
*   l. 4   ornamented above [the mattrasses] with pannels in the
                   centre of [each of] which
          l. 12   some creeping [flowery] *flowering* plant
*   l. 13   vases [each of which contained] *containing each* a single
                   flower
          l. 17   groves of *healthy and* graceful trees
          l. 18   by [all] the male part of the family
*   l. 23   like *pale* gold; and others, under a [kind of] *rural* shed,
                   preparing [their] food
          l. 30   running in the portico [with the velocity of antelopes] to
                   dry themselves[37]
*   l. 36   the like materials, but [red] *rose-coloured*
*   l. 37   these *with smiles* they [set] *placed*
*   l. 39   in [a] general chorus
*p. 35,   l. 5   three *platted* girdles
*   l. 12   and, [though small boned] they were in general what the
                   French call[38]
*   l. 13   their *whole* deportment
          l. 14   said something [archly] *arch*
*   l. 14   passed in with the super-trays, *to create harmless mirth*
*   l. 30   accompanied with [the] girls
*   l. 35   if I could *but* keep time
*   l. 36   this [wench] *lass* (said one of them)
*   l. 41   took off all my attention [to] *from* my own part, but made
                   me *quite* ashamed of my [European] awkwardness
p. 36,   l. 3   take his share, *which he did*
*   l. 9   took me *by the hand*
          l. 11   to distinguish [that] *the couch*
*   l. 13   to see our camels *feeding*

---

37 The Printer's Copy moved the phrase "with the velocity of antelopes" to after "to dry
themselves" rather than deleting it. Below, "at the close of which" was altered to "at
whose close" in the Printer's Copy but not in 1810.
38 The Printer's Copy has "what the French would call."

*p. 36, l. 14 seated on a soft [bed of litter] *pile of fodder*, in the recess of the cave, *forgetful of decorum*, throwing my arms around her

* l. 16 to take [the greatest] *improper* liberties; but [what] *how keen* were my feelings

* l. 21 to [avoid] *have avoided* the interview

* l. 30 consolation they [are likely to] *ultimately* afford

* l. 32 the girl has mistaken *you*

* l. 41 except that of [banishing me back again] banish*ment*

*p. 37, l. 10 you are one of our [stray] children, I will, if you [will] condescend

* l. 23 it became [under this roof] doubly my duty

* l. 30 only *to be* miserable

* l. 34 an invisible and generous [power] *agency*

* l. 36 to follow temperately their natural instincts, *and the dictates of conscience*

*p. 38, l. 16 a virgin [that] *who* was unattached

   l. 23 the fibres of the butterfly's wing [is] *are* not of bone, yet [it resists] *they resist*

* l. 33 want of *human* sense

   l. 41 took my hand, [placed] *and placing* the palm

*p. 39, l. 16 composed in *tranquil* sleep

* l. 17 having placed me on a [mattress] *couch*

   l. 22 whose cries much [resembled] *resemble* the parroquet

* l. 26 sounding *mellow*-pipes

* l. 35 around [the body] his chest, or threw it *carelessly* in folds [carelessly] over the shoulder[39]

   l. 40 [every night] *generally* as a coverlet

   l. 41 a [grave] *long* cloak

 p. 40, l. 3 any idea of [misusing it, so as to throw an odium on one part more than another] *using it otherwise than as conveniency dictates*

* l. 4 like the [ancient] statues *of the ancients*

   l. 5 [and would have spurned at the unnatural depravity that affixed ideas of shame to the most necessary, wonderful, and noble organs of the human superstructure[40]] *and in their active and athletic images, a Phidias would have found an endless number of the finest models of the human structure*

39 The Printer's Copy reads "over his shoulder."
40 The Printer's copy reads "human structure."

*p. 40,   l. 15   like a bird *on the wing*
           l. 17   among the *surrounding* crowd
           l. 25   a small company *of men*, and some women
*   l. 26   [on] *upon* the yellow mattresses
*p. 41,   l. 3   she is *very* gay and very lively
           l. 4   has *as* yet formed
           l. 15   forego all *the* thoughts
*   l. 22   [consider] *respect* even a tree as your fellow creature
*   l. 32   all our customs and *all our* laws
*   l. 36   to live [solitarily] *solitary*
*   l. 40   the destruction of union and *political* equality
*p. 42,   l. 24   ['No, (said I), we send them out into the world to get their
                    living, just as we dispose of our superfluous cattle] *I
                    replied* – no we send them out into the world to get their
                    living – Just *so (he said)* we dispose of our superfluous
                    cattle
           l. 27   [consuming] *as we consume* much milk
*p. 43,   l. 9   there [was] *were* no absolute [rule] *rules* of architecture
           l. 12   accessible [by] *to* every inhabitant
           l. 13   Doors [indeed] were solemnly prohibited
*   l. 15   most of them were [made] *constructed*
*   l. 17   nearer to the *fine* works of the Japanese
*   l. 22   (he [said] *observed*,) it must arise[41] from their being [good]
                    competent judges
*   l. 25   the only rules [we acknowledge] in art *we acknowledge*
*   l. 40   [For] Neither age nor sex were exempted from
           l. 40   the necessity of *washing or* bathing twice a day;
           l. 41   [and] which habit
*p. 44,   l. 1   to [which] *this* practice
*   l. 10   with [gay] *agreeable* songs, sung by a party of *girls and* boys
*   l. 18   till *near* the hour of supper when the females went to
                    prepare it, [supped themselves apart,] and returned to
                    [their husbands] *the men* to dance
           l. 21   [went] *retired* to separate dormitories, and never met again,
                    in private, till the next day [after dinner] *at the same time*
*   l. 23   the generality [went to] *reposed in* sleep

---

41 The Printer's Copy seems to read "rise." In the grammatically difficult sentence; "No
house was permitted to be built but in a situation that could be served with water in
abundance, yet whose situation was such that no water could lie near its foundations",
the copy in the Australian National University Library is altered uniquely (and I believe
wrongly), apparently by George Cumberland, to read "any water."

*p. 44,	l. 24	For at [that] *the* hour *of noon*
	l. 25	all kinds of noise [was] *were*
*	l. 28	too young to [want] *require* any; for *here* all marriageable people [here] are married
*	l. 37	what were [there] *their* marriage ceremonies?
*	l. 40	and [the Energy] *affection* instructs them
*	l. 41	I perceived, *with regret*, that they [had] *seemed to have* no forms of marriage, but that, with them cohabitation [was] *constituted* matrimony; *and*
*p. 45,	l. 5	to adopt *most* of the manners
*	l. 6	before the [head] chief *magistrate*
	l. 15	the melody of *the* birds
	l. 16	[but] others in small parties
*	l. 18	we were [all] suddenly alarmed
*	l. 24	were all [bathed in tears] *violently agitated*
	l. 36	in a mass of [ruins] *ruin*
*p. 46,	l. 1	by [our] *this* acquisition
	l. 13	a countenance [and beard] impressed
*	l. 14	marks of [gravity and] sense *and gravity.*
	l. 31	and *having* been seconded stoutly
*	l. 39	[open to] *embracing* the side of the hill
*p. 47,	l. 12	and [who] many of [them] *whom* have
	l. 16	the shrubs afford them [also] shade
*	l. 18	to recline [on] *upon* during
*	l. 36	[as well as] *and* at the cool indifference
*p. 48,	l. 1	deprive me of [it] *my merchandize*
*	l. 2	I should be [deprived] *plundered*
*	l. 5	if I chose to leave [it] *the yellow dirt* among them
	l. 7	the most unjust and imprudent [imaginations] *suspicions*
*	l. 10	by the [old] *afflicted* Caffre
*	l. 17	the latter *gravely* addressed me [gravely]
*	l. 20	[for], *as* for myself
*	l. 21	from [your] *those* hasty conclusions
*	l. 27	unknown to us [all]
*	l. 28	there are [no] *few* men among us capable of such an un-provoked atrocity
p. 49,	l. 1	Tears *now* poured from my [head] *eyes*
*	l. 4	Base people [only] shed tears
	l. 6	when they are deprived of [animal] *sensual* enjoyments
*	l. 10	we are become wiser men from [it] *experience.*
*	l. 20	*Chilo* <sic> [soon] relieved me
*	l. 29	surprised to see in [our] *the* rear

*p. 50,	l. 29	the number ten, *or any number*
	l. 35	an explanation of our method*s*
*	l. 36	but [he,] never suspecting ... *he* did not enter
*p. 51,	l. 38	to be shrinking into a [dwarf] *pigmy*
p. 52,	l. 4	antelopes fed around *us* as calmly
*	l. 14	a continual [bestower] *bestowing* of the blessings
*	l. 24	It [was long, and] had a string
footnote		*An Indian song perhaps.*
*p. 52,	l. 34	of music I then knew [nothing] *little*
*p. 53,	l. 5	I now returned to the building [(where I found my companions),]
*p. 54,	l. 4	buildings were [there] to be found
	l. 29	spring pouring into a *white* marble shell
	l. 36	the meanders of a [silvery] *silver* stream
*p. 55,	l. 1	[in a word], *while* the whole expanse
*	l. 3	but [what was] *I can scarcely* describe my surprise, [I can scarcely describe,] when
p. 56,	l. 8	the entrance *itself* was a noble arch
	l. 9	whose roof was [at equilateral angles] *parallel* with the earth
*	l. 11	on which [some] *the* magistrates
*	l. 13	and *the* ebony rods
	l. 17	after [a] *an agreeable* conference
*	l. 24	and, in the [centre] *front*,
	l. 24	instead of any other ornament*s*
*	l. 28	nearly without [ornament] *embellishments*
*	l. 30	The pavement ... was of [purple granite] *porphyry*,
*	l. 32	an avenue was [constructed] *conducted*
*	l. 36	a [large] *magnificent* tank
*p. 57,	l. 5	Putting his right [arm]-*hand* on my shoulder, he placed the other [hand] over my eyes
*	l. 9	the girl may [also] have deep designs
*	l. 21	the [salons] *saloons* of the Asiatic princes
	l. 22	more simple in [its] *the* general effect
*	l. 31	support an immense [roof] *covering*
	l. 38	[the whole of] which composed one entire side
	l. 41	shady, [capacious] *spacious*, refreshed with fountains
*p. 58,	l. 1	[of] the symmetry of whose architecture, [which] you can only judge of from[42]

42 The Printer's Copy reads "only judge from."

*p. 58,	l. 8	although nearly unornamented – *and wholly depending on geometrical correctness, and nicely balanced proportions*, inspire the [soil] *soul* with dignified and virtuous pride
*	l. 12	created by human industry, *with fitness and simplicity*
*	l. 15	these [noble] *lofty* halls
*	l. 30	had been [the] *my almost* sole relief [of] *during* this long solitary confinement.
*	l. 35	hastily unbarring the [doors] *pondrous valves*
*p. 59,	l. 19	we distinctly heard the *direst* lamentations
*	l. 21	the [keeper] *jailor* drew back
	l. 33	blown backwards and forwards by the [winds] *wind*
*	l. 37	Fortunately [however] for the poor man
*	l. 40	*while* we returned to our confinement
*p. 60,	l. 1	the proof we had [had] *acquired* that imprudence may augment even the miseries of capitivity *for life.*
	l. 10	we invited him to partake of [a] *some* sherbet[43]
*	l. 26	it is *undoubtedly* lawful [undoubtedly]
*	l. 35	[This] *The* speech *of Lycas* excited in me
*	l. 39	with much complacency *thus* resumed the narration
*	l. 42	the ruling men of [the] *that* country
*p. 61,	l. 2	finished in a manner [that] *more splendid than* I had [never] *ever* before witnessed
*	l. 19	for [their] *that* temporary loss
*	l. 25	brought nearly to perfection
*	l. 26	gently agitated by *regular* tides
*	l. 35	the law allowed none to be *positively* poor
*	l. 38	and was, [when] *if* proved, punished
*	l. 40	His title ... consisted in his having children born to him *by his wife.*
p. 62,	l. 9	from some [such] motive
*	l. 12	like soft music to my *attentive* ears
*	l. 18	went straight to view [the] *this original* city
*	l. 34	when I [was] arrived at the top, [he] told me
*	l. 35	You should *still* ascend [now]![44]
*	l. 40	the steps of *our* reason
p. 63,	l. 9	If our soul be immortal, [she] *it* will be so; if [she should] *if be* not, [she] *it* will be where [she] *it* ought to be. During

---

43 Below, "guitar" in 1798 and 1810 is changed, properly, to "vina" in the Printer's Copy.
44 The Printer's Copy reads "You should still ascend now!"

[her] *its* mortal period *connections,*[45] [she] *it* will be employed, probably, as [she] *it* is with us, in guiding matter, as far as [her] *its* powers extend.

p. 63,   l. 13   by the help of *the* mind

l. 16   by *leading* simple and innocent lives

l. 18   by the help of [that] *the* experience

*   l. 28   no guilt [rested] *dwelt* within it

l. 31   [the name of] *Mica* <*sic*> was on my lips, but I suppressed [the name] *its utterance*

l. 33   that sublime proportion, which [one rather feels than sees] *is rather felt than seen*

l. 35   approaching the [semicircular] theatre

l. 41   the more aged *in one* much like this I now wear, the younger *were* without either turbans or robes

p. 64,   l. 6   related [my] *the* manner of *my* coming

l. 9   the singularity of my [possessing] *being acquainted with* much of the language, and our [mutual] desire

l. 13   as he had before used *in ascending,* [joined] *and joining* us

*   l. 25   *Oh!* [what] *unutterable* happiness! the lovely and compassionate *Mica* <*sic*>, with *dishevelled* locks [dishevelled]

l. 27   some time [under] *in* the strong delerium

l. 29   I would have arisen [to] *in order* to throw myself

l. 34   relieving [the] *my* over-heated brain, *at last* gave me utterance

*   l. 42   during all which time, *a seraphic fire,* a healing balm

*p. 65,   l. 12   my deep *festering* wounds

*   l. 14   that [my] *the* fever

l. 14   [from] *after* this interview

l. 23   The [first] *chief* motive for the ballot

l. 25   my being [a conductor] *an importer* of merchandize

l. 27   seemed [carried away] *captivated* by the irresistible attraction

l. 31   you [possessed the attachment] *were in possession of the affections* of a female citizen

l. 34   permit [your] *you a* limited residence

l. 36   conform to the manners of the [islands] *island*

l. 38   or [preparing] *in the preparation of* rewards to be diaposed of

*p. 66,   l. 1   a *small* single ear-ring

45 The Printer's Copy alters "period" to "connections."

*p. 66,   l. 5   the date of the year, [on the days of assuming them,] being
                   engraven on each *on the day of assuming them*, which con-
                   stituted, in every family, a species of festival *annually
                   observed*

*   l. 21   *in all cases* <italics added in 1810>

*   l. 22   obedience [in a child], to the will of [his] parents

*   l. 27   object of my [early] choice

*   l. 36   and is so [sure to take] *certain of taking* place

           l. 38   [or dissuasives] *nor disuasion* to prevent it

  p. 67,   l. 2   while your mutual [attachments last] *attachment lasts*

           l. 14   My account [seemed] *appeared* to astonish him

           l. 18   as he was [to reconcile] *at* my approbation

*   l. 19   of such [abominable] *ridiculous* errors

*   l. 26   explicit laws of [procreation] *propagation*

           l. 28   the finer feelings

           l. 35   a thought so profligate [that it] sickens my very soul

           l. 38   can reconcile them to such [legal prostitution] *habits*

*p. 68,   l. 10   faithlessness, *often* follows such ill-contrived connections

           l. 15   threw a bright light [through] *over* the former prejudices

           l. 20   no other security [for] *of* her fidelity

           l. 23   which relates to this [delicious] *delightful* union

*   l. 25   we [never] *rarely* punish infidelity

           l. 28   we esteem *female* chastity

           l. 33   polygamy, as you call the having [two wives] *more than one
                   wife*

           l. 34   which [might] *may* make such an arrangement

*   l. 35   *in some cases* prudent

*p. 69,   l. 1   neither are they [treated with contempt and scorn] *spurned*
                   by their own family

           l. 2   women, *the disease of* whose minds is equally [pitiable] *to
                   be pitied*

*   l. 5   And [then it happens that] *hence* these errors[46]

           l. 6   for [experiencing] the repeated [neglects] *neglect* of their
                   lovers

           l. 8   family asylum which is always *in mercy* open to them

           l. 9   and beauty [decaying] *decayed*

           l. 13   the best guardian of [their] *her* rising relations

           l. 13   As to those who [should] *could* be capable

           l. 16   the person who [considered] *should consider* it

46 The Printer's Copy reads "And thence that these."

*p. 69,   l. 17   an access of a frenzy fever, *or a stroke of the palsy*
*   l. 18   very humane, and *even* according to my ideas
           l. 23   in what manner [are they] *is the offending party* punished
*   l. 27   inconstancy[, if carried to excess,] was followed with the
                    loss of [the men's] *our* esteem
*   l. 36   We know [as well as you], that
           l. 37   the disorders [of the] *occasioned by* passions
*   l. 39   physical causes, *and* whose prescriptions
*   l. 41   to prescribe a *sexual* connection [with the other sex,] as a
                    remedy
*p. 70,   l. 4   parents have saved their children's lives or senses, by [tem-
                    porary connections, the fruit of which, at worst, has
                    been an augmentation of the family; but which has]
                    means that have[47] often terminated
*   l. 6   effected by the same [operation] *regimen*
*   l. 7   occur but *very* seldom
*   l. 14   we can conceive no [personal] distinctions
*   l. 17   there are men so *meanly* foolish
*   l. 19   the madness of [really] *actually* receiving the homage
*   l. 32   seduction ... when proved to have been [more than once]
                    the practice of any offender
           l. 34   labour for life [is the lot of all], accompanied with whole-
                    some instruction, *is the lot of all*
*p. 71,   l. 14   saying *also* a thousand extravagant things
           l. 20   The [darkest] *dark* grove, the [sweetest] *sweet* melody
*   l. 37   I kissed her *ivory* feet
*   l. 40   she postponed [the consummation] *my happiness* till the
                    moon rose
p. 72,   l. 8   they had [all of them] the generosity
*   l. 10   making me a [happy] father
           l. 22   castle, [of] *in* the kingdom
           l. 26   had [nothing to do with any reward] *no reward in view*
*p. 73,   l. 9   implements of agriculture *clean and* carefully preserved
*   l. 17   contemplation of the eternal [Energies] *powers*
           l. 18   they deign, in [their] complacency, to survey the [orderly]
                    scale of their vast universe
*   l. 19   our conversation *naturally* turned [naturally]
           l. 28   useful instruments and [conveniences] *conveniencies*

47 The Printer's Copy omits "means that."

*p. 73,   l. 34   suggest to him[48] with energetic solemnity[49] the real ne-
                      cessity of practising *truth* <italics added in 1810> [and
                      sincerity]

            l. 39   must be inculcated [betimes] *early*

*p. 74,   l. 5   the leading feature of all [instruction] *education*

            l. 15   After a short pause, [which no one interrupted, for the
                      silver tone of his instruction vibrated, in a grateful ca-
                      dence, on our ears,] he *then* continued –

            l. 18   agriculture in all its [ramifications] *branches*

            l. 22   the most valuable part of [what] *that which* nature

*   l. 33   after [passing] *crossing* a great water ... losing many of his
                      people in [crossing] *passing* large spaces of sand

            l. 39   nothing was wanting [towards the sustenance] *for the sup-
                      port* of life

            l. 41   For [speaking] *having spoken* with manly freedom

p. 75,   l. 2   he might establish his [unprejudiced] system

*   l. 3   it could *only* flourish, free from interruption, [only] in a
                      perfect solitude.

            l. 6   that colossal [youthful] *juvenile* figure

*   l. 9   he meant to represent *Love* <italics added in 1810> the
                      universal cause of all *happiness*

*   l. 11   it was [meant] *designed* for himself

*   l. 14   we *weak mortals* have never been able

*   l. 16   is that *Power* which always

*   l. 27   which made *them* all

*   l. 28   When [however] he discovered

            l. 40   a climate so [friendly] *genial* to man

            l. 40   *where* the sweet cane

p. 76,   l. 19   whatever part of mankind [have] *has*

            l. 28   It is my idea, that [men first took up arms] *the use of arms
                      first became general from men's taking them up* to defend

            l. 37   [whose] *the* chief inducements *to which* are power ....

p. 77,   l. 3   many remain [from] *through* false shame

            l. 8   set at stake thoughtlessly [that] *blessings* which

---

48 The following MS passage at the bottom of the page in the Printer's Copy is marked
   in duplicate (both erroneous) for insertion in mid-sentence after "suggest to him" and
   after "energetic solemnity": "Gratitude to that omnipotent being to whom they are
   indebted for every earthly enjoyment should also in a more special manner be incul-
   cated." It was not printed in 1810.

49 The Printer's Copy reads "also with energetic solemnity."

p. 77,   l. 10   An art that [militates] not only *militates* against

        l. 12   affords scarcely any means

*   l. 13   or *for* retirement in old age

        l. 19   from the gratification of the lowest vanity, *that of* personal appearance decked with the gaudy badges of dependence: *from* the meanest applause

        l. 25   who ridiculously [enough] styles himself

*   l. 30   have no [snares] *baits to* allure me

        l. 35   the fowler, the [warrior or] robber

p. 78,   l. 3   the hunter's family declines

        l. 10   indeed, [farming] *agriculture* is by far the simplest

        l. 16   For, [here excepted] *except in this island*,

        l. 17   I have found [it] *that state*

*   l. 34   the unsophisticated [embraces] *society* of her

        l. 34   [whom, of all her sex,] *whose bosom* I had selected, *of all her sex*, as the [pillow of] *repository of all* my virtuous thoughts

        l. 37   seated in the very [bosom] *lap* of contentment

        l. 38   I [followed] *cultivated*, for mere amusement, the polished arts

        l. 40   who [knew nothing of] *were unacquainted with* commerce

p. 79,   l. 4   more land than was necessary for his [existence] *subsistence*

*   l. 8   by disinterestedly [contributing] *dedicating* the whole of my property

*   l. 10   procuring, from their neighbours, [of what I possessed] *the richer metals*

*   l. 14   when gold was *greatly* wanted, to invite some [foreign merchants] *foreigner* to procure it

*   l. 20   they knew little or nothing of Europe [with certainty] *or Asia*

*   l. 21   rendered [pearls] *jewels* of scarce any use

*   l. 26   at the end of [my] two years of probation

*   l. 28   proceeded immediately to *the city of* Sophis

        l. 32   the dear pledges of our [affections] *affection*

*   l. 34   we exchanged two garlands of [everlasting flowers] *amaranthus buds*

*p. 80, l. 16   they had [no] *neither matter nor* taste for tragedies

        l. 21   [the subject of] which happening at this season

*   l. 23   I shall, *for your amusement*, as briefly as possible [relate] *describe*[50]

50 "relate" is not altered in the Printer's Copy.

*p. 80,	l. 25	*and* [it] commenced *at the western end of the great square*, with the dawn of the day, [at the western end of the great square]
	l. 29	[This] *The* plain shrine
	ll. 34,37	bas [relievos] *reliefs*
*	l. 40	The attitude of the figure [was] *is* formal
*	l. 41	The wings [which] extended [were] *are* of silver; the body of gold, with exception of the hair and nails, which [were of silver] *are enamelled*, as well as the little figure in the shrine of the bosom. The figure [stood] erect, and the soles of the feet [rested] *resting* on a circlet of silver. The back ground of the whole [was] *is* a kind of [black enamel] *dark sardonix a*nd on [the back] *it*
*p. 81,	l. 16	no temple, [priest,] or idol, being permitted
*	l. 28	a gay parterre was formed, [which] *that*, as a ring, kept off the crowd
*	l. 30	[but] *and* between the cavity
*p. 82,	l. 1	the firmest, [fullest,] and most finely proportioned bosoms
	l. 9	since [this] *the* festival had long become
*	l. 14	the entrance of the [town-house] *magistrates'* portico
*	l. 37	he thought, *it* would be folly
*	l. 39	He saw, that *existence* for a limited period [being alone] was lent him
	l. 41	he found man's *true* interests
*p. 83,	l. 3	the dark superstitions *and idolatries* of the times
*	l. 4	calling themselves priests of *the* Gods
*	l. 7	the [right] system of universal benevolence
	l. 8	have attained *to* that peace
*	l. 17	whose sentiment [which was a solemn adoption of this advice,] will ever ... be rooted in my [heart's core] *heart*
*	l. 34	retirement had *completely* reclaimed from such evil practices as were prejudicial to the [peace] *peaceful order* of society
*	l. 41	these members to [society] *the community*
*p. 84,	l. 2	receiving with [triumph] *modesty* the reward of praise from [all the city] *the citizens*
*	l. 22	benches of *sun-dried* clay, covered [when used] with soft moss; – the stage was confined by [two] beautiful groups of trees
*	l. 26	composed of three immensely large [triangular frames] *hollow prisms, perpendicularly erected*, turning each on a centre[-post], the inside of which served for the [per-

               formers'] apartment *of the mechanicians*, and which, by the simple operation of being [turned] *moved* on the fixed point, afforded an almost endless variety of buildings, illustrative of the drama, [and dressing-rooms for the actors]

*p. 85,   l. 1   none being *either* remarkably poor, or [remarkably] rich, [unless] *although*

*   l. 3   an indisputable distinction, *and evidently obtained respect*

        l. 7   The artist had painted her[, quite naked,]

*   l. 11   but to [me] *my then weak judgment* it seemed

*   l. 13   every fleshy protuberance being so warm [and rosy]

*   l. 14   You wonder ... at the artist's having given so much carnation; [yet you own you are pleased]

*   l. 27   you will not be very far from her [skirts] *footsteps*

*p. 86,   l. 2   as far as related to diet, bathing, [&c.] *and animal indulgences*

*   l. 7   all sorts of exercise, [but] *and* chiefly abstinence

*   l. 11   *was merely a tube, with a continuity of surface* <italics added in 1810>

*   l. 15   by injecting it [that of] *we*[51] *neutralize acridities in* the viscera

*   l. 16   they applied the caustic [or cautery]

*   l. 20   Pregnant women [never] entertained [any] *no* idea of danger

*   l. 25   and *the word* silence was inscribed over every sick *person's* chamber[52]

*   l. 31   administer to the [ease] *cure* of others

*   l. 33   *water cleansed from infectious taint by destroying virus*[53]

*   l. 38   to prevent temptation to amass *wealth*

*   l. 39   *the law* disposed <italics added in 1810>

*   l. 39   [but] with a careful attention

   p. 87,   l. 3   the reward of *up*right wishes

*   l. 3   generated [it is true] by disgust

        l. 5   [torn] *hurled* at once from the summit

*   l. 8   I had indeed been *deeply* wretched

51 The Printer's Copy omits "we."

52 At the foot of this page in the Printer's Copy is a faint manuscript sentence in pencil not clearly attached to any pasage of text which reads: "The injudicious application of cold & wind is highly dangerous"; it was not printed in 1810.

53 "by destroying virus" was altered and the whole phrase italicized in 1810.

*p. 87,   l. 14   *adieu then,* and may the recital

*   l. 18   [and we parted;] for both our souls were full of deep reflection, *and we parted*

*   l. 22   emotions raised by intruding remembrance*s*

*   l. 23   [A variety of recollections kept me nearly sleepless all that night, with which the elements seemed to concur], *I was kept awake, through the night, by a variety of disquieting recollections, and the elements seemed to sympathize with my perturbed state*

*   l. 25   that which *now* arose

*   l. 27   part of one of the [walls] *bastions* rent away

*   l. 28   the atmosphere was still gloomy and obscured, *nor had the yelling winds subsided*

*   l. 31   the danger of the *sunken* rock

*   l. 36   effectually [suppressed] *drowned* our voices

*   l. 36   the vessel was suddenly *struck on the rock, and was* wrecked before our eyes; [and] the screams of the women [heard through a peal] *which we heard at intervals between the peals* of thunder *were* now followed by a [sudden] *gloomy* silence, more dreadful, if possible, than their [out-]cries

          l. 41   the [sulphureous] *transitory* glare *of lightning* exhibited

*p. 88,   l. 7   my companion always [pay] *paid*

*   l. 7   particular [attention] *veneration*

*   l. 11   returned to [their] *the* dripping reeds

          l. 12   the sands [assumed] *wore* a purer tint from [humidity] *the effects of the rain which had fallen*; and our [bodies] *frames*

          l. 15   Lycas, *viewing* in my impatient looks [recollecing his promise] *a demand for the performance of his promise*, began

          l. 17   [If] *That* the catastrophe

          l. 22   *But to proceed*, I departed

          l. 25   arrived [at the first station from] *within one station of* my house

          l. 27   and *indeed* nearly all our connections

          l. 33   my impatience [encreased] *redoubled*

*   l. 34   and [arrived] *felt alarmed at arriving* alone, [alas!][54]

*   l. 37   *had* already fancied her[55]

          l. 38   [warm] *clasped* in my [nervous] arms; [that I felt] *already did I feel* her breath *glowing*

---

54 The Printer's Copy reads "was alarmed to arrive alone."
55 The Printer's Copy reads "already had fancied her."

*p. 88,   l. 39   the essential sweetness of her pure [body] *person*
*p. 89,   l. 1   our tears of pleasure *inter*mingled
           l. 5   like a [bandage] *cloud* over my heart
           l. 7   [and,] unwilling to give entrance
*   l. 22   *Is she dead?* <italics added in 1810>
*   l. 27   *and* each [man] weeping bitterly
*p. 90,   l. 2   the root is *still* left to renew the stock
*   l. 15   and that *in consequence of that incumbrance* they all perished
*   l. 22   the arbour, which, *sweet spirit!* ... she had been constructing
           l. 26   my grave also had [happily] *haply* swelled the sod
*   l. 35   the pains of remembrance, *for she still lives in my veins*
*p. 91,   l. 9   teaching every where [the love of our fellow] *humanity and love to all* creatures
*   l. 15   Liberty, *justice*, and even humanity
*   l. 16   that coarse *and crooked* policy
*   l. 27   this [darling] *daring* virtue would never have possessed me
*   l. 28   extinguished the [light] *lamp* of my life
*p. 92,   l. 1   setting up some fantastical [deity] *leader* of their own contrivance
*   l. 2   asylum on the lake of Zambre, *where I trust I may succeed in engrafting the noble fruits of revelation on their wholesome wild stock of natural faith, thereby adding all that is wanting to make them the best and the happiest nation on earth* (first *however* depositing this manuscript in the hands of some European trader). *And* may the lessen have its proper effect, if happily, it should ever come [there] *forth*

Appendix II

Description of the Manuscript of Part 2

Binding Bound in three-quarter Brown leather, gilt, over Brown mar-
bled boards, with "THE / CAPTIVE / – / VOL. 2." on the spine, the whole
in a style of c. 1835 – the paper watermarked 1834 is conjugate with the
endpapers.

Contents Titlepage (f. 6^v), "Preface" (f. 7^{r-v}), text (ff. 9^v–371^v, mostly on
odd-numbered leaves); *blank* on ff. 1–6^r, 8^r, 12, and thereafter on al-
ternate (even-numbered) leaves on ff. 14–370: ff. 372–77 are also blank;
377 leaves in all.

Numbers Numbered 1–89 in old Brown ink in the top middle of every
fourth recto (every second text-leaf) on ff. 9–363, with a few exceptions
– two numbered leaves are inserted between f. 9 and f. 15, two more
leaves (numbered "*71") are inserted between f. 291 (numbered 71) and
f. 297 (72), and one leaf is omitted between f. 361 and f. 363; "12" ap-
pears on f. 55^v rather than f. 55^r; f. 207 has the normal ink number
"50" and also in pencil "200". On f. 8^v is a "Note / The paging of the
manuscript is not to be attended to as they were numbered by sheets of
paper, as a guide to the binder –".

Watermarks

G YEELES / 1834
(half the leaves
without watermark)

on ff. 1–8, 373–77, and even-
numbered ff. 10–360, 364–70

G YEELES / 1830

(1830 on separate
leaves)

on odd-numbered leaves ff. 9, 13–
41, 47–9, 119–65

HALL

on f. 11

Crowned crest
(half on each leaf

on odd-numbered ff. 43–5, 51–
117

DEWDNEY & TREMLETT / 1831
(half the leaves
without watermark)

on odd-numbered ff. 167–363
plus f. 362

J BUNE / 1831
(half the leaves
with watermark

on ff. 365, 367, 369, 371

The G YEELES / 1834, DEWNEY & TREMLETT / 1831, and J BUNE / 1831
watermarks are in wove paper without chain lines, while the G YEELES /
1830 and HALL watermarks are in laid paper with chain lines.

Gathering Pattern   Each of the two-leaf (one-sheet) numbered gatherings
of text on 1830–31 papers has a leaf of G YEELES / 1834 paper pasted
to the inner margin of the recto of the second text leaf. (These inserted
leaves are on folios which are multiples of four – ff. 8, 12, 16 ... 364,
368, 372.) Every second text-gathering (bearing odd sheet-numbers) is
inserted in a folded sheet of G YEELES / 1834 paper. (These blank
wrapper-sheets comprise folios which are odd-numbers multiplied by
two – ff. 18 and 22, 26 and 30, 34 and 38, ... 282 and 286.) After the
insertion of f. 291, the wrapper-leaves are not conjugate.

The text then consisted of alternate gatherings of three leaves ($2
blank) and five leaves ($1, 3, 5 blank). Each pair of gatherings was then
joined, making an eight leaf group, with the even-numbered folios blank,
and these eight-leaf groups were sewn in (after ff. 2, 10, 19, after every
eighth leaf on ff. 19–283, 297–376), with blank leaves at the beginning
and end, ff. 1–5, 372–7. (Ff. 5–7 are conjugate with the front endpapers,
and ff. 373–5 with the back endpapers.)

Transcription The manuscript was written, presumably transcribed
from a rougher draft, in a clear, smooth hand, with only a few alterations

– most pages have only one or two – on paper watermarked 1830. The MS was then interleaved with paper watermarked 1834 and 1831, and a few corrections were made, sometimes on the blank pages facing the passage to be altered. The fictitious names (e.g., Stefanus, Foozo) and some of the real ones (Aronzo) are frequently (some of them always) added in a different ink in blank spaces left in the text for them. At p. 269, the ink, the pen, and perhaps the hand become different. The last step with the MS was numbering the leaves for the binder.

Index